The Haunting of Avis Lovelock

Also by MK Hardy

The Needfire

The Haunting of Avis Lovelock

mk hardy

SOLARIS

First published in Great Britain in 2026 by Solaris,
an imprint of Profile Books Ltd
29 Cloth Fair
London
EC1A 7JQ

www.profilebooks.com

1 3 5 7 9 10 8 6 4 2

Printed and bound in Great Britain by
CPI Group (UK) Ltd, Croydon, CR0 4YY

A CIP catalogue record for this book is available from the British Library.

Our product safety representative in the EU is
BGC Sustainability & Compliance,
7 avenue du Général Leclerc, Paris, 75014, France
baldwinglobalconsulting.com

ISBN: 978 1 83786 696 0
eISBN: 978 1 83786 699 1

MIX
Paper | Supporting responsible forestry
FSC® C013604

Prologue

Aloysius Hood turned the pocket watch over in his hands, then closed his fingers around it. They were lean and pale, with a dusting of dark hairs Avis found curiously repulsive. Across the knuckles of his left hand, arcane symbols were etched in ink; she recognised one as John Dee's *Monas Hieroglyphica* and schooled her lips into a serious pout lest she somehow betray her derision.

She glanced around the table at the flickering faces of the other sitters. There were six today, in addition to Avis and Hood, bringing the total to eight. Hood was a traditionalist, insisting upon "a precise balance of masculine and feminine energy", and indeed it was on this basis that Avis had been able to insinuate herself as an extra body—the manager at the Egyptian had got wind of it somehow and secured her a spot in an uncharacteristic fit of helpfulness.

Sitting between the medium and Avis herself was the host of their afternoon activity, one Sir Reginald St Simon, in whose gloomy London townhouse they presently sat. He was a gaunt man with a hooked mouth who looked as though he viewed dissatisfaction as a hobby rather than a thing to be avoided, an impression borne out by his wife's pinpoint pupils. She was directly across the table from Avis, and kept looking at her with a benignly curious expression. Avis had a feeling that she had a sharp mind, dulled by the laudanum she used to tolerate a husband who would hire a psychic medium but would not pay for enough staff to keep their London residence properly cleaned and maintained. She must have been quite isolated if she had not been able to find friends of her own to balance out the female half of the company. Anger stabbed at Avis's stomach. She would enjoy dismantling this man's purchase.

Hood's eyes rolled back in his head 'til only a flickering crescent of iris remained, the rest just bloodshot sclera. Avis rolled her own eyes heavenward and folded her arms; time for a fishing expedition, apparently.

"Yes, this item is very charged, the spirits are very active. It means a great deal to you, this watch." The medium's voice was breathy, pitched so that the guests around the table had to lean in to catch his words. All the better, for the position would give them a restricted view of his hands and feet, obscured as they were by the dark table covering.

His target, a soberly dressed man with a stiff, dark moustache, gave a short nod. "It does."

"It is not new—it belonged to someone very dear to you."

At this the man sucked in a breath and Avis resisted a groan. From what she had glimpsed of the watch before it disappeared into the medium's tattooed grasp, it was a dull gold covered in worn engravings. Obviously it wasn't new; even a child could have gleaned as much.

"A father figure of sorts…"

"Yes, my uncle! He was very close to my family, after my father passed."

"Ah, yes, of course, an uncle. He's close to us now. His spirit is still very strong. It has been mere weeks since his passing?"

The moustache quivered. "That's right! Just last month."

"I can feel him trying to reach out to you, to speak to you…"

The mark leaned forward eagerly, as if physical proximity would make any difference at all. "I'm here," he said beseechingly.

"Your uncle wants you to know… that he's sorry. So very sorry."

The man shook his head. Avis was surprised to see his eyes bright with unshed tears. She hadn't pegged him for a crier, but then, he had come along tonight, hadn't he? Anyone who voluntarily put themselves in the hands of Spiritualists was in need of something—even if she personally thought that something was a firm shake and perhaps a slap.

"He has nothing to apologise for. Nothing at all."

"Still, there is unfinished business." It was a crude, calculated gamble—again, the man had come for some reason, even if he didn't quite know it yet himself. Avis watched the medium watch his target, and when the man frowned, shifting in his seat, the performer immediately continued. "For leaving you, and your family, as your father did before him."

"I… He was old. It was his time."

"Yes, yes, but still, you did not get to bid him farewell. But you can do so now. He's here. He's listening."

The man was shaking his head now; Hood was losing him, and Avis fought a satisfied little smile. "I was at his side when he passed."

Suddenly there was a sharp report, like someone had struck a cane against a door-frame. The man jumped, and now it was the medium's turn to shake his head, his features shaped into a rueful expression. "The spirits insist! He says there is still something left unsaid… something he wished he could have told you. Something about your sister…"

"I—"

"No, your brother. Yes, that's it. A warning he needs to pass on."

Damn, he had him. The mustachioed man leaned in, a fish willingly gaping for the hook. Their host was drinking this in with interest. A gossip, then. Avis had been wondering what was in this for St Simon—she had not identified any particular unfinished business on his part—and it seemed to be a simple enjoyment of seeing others exposed, their linens hung out in public view, clean and dirty alike. What an unpleasant little man.

Avis unfolded her arms, slipping her hands into the pockets of her skirt. She felt the room's shadows darken, and quietly braced herself. The outline of a figure flickered in her vision, standing on the other side of the table, but did not come into focus. Patience.

"What about my brother?"

"Your suspicions about him. They are correct," the medium intoned.

They are not.

"He has betrayed you."

He has not.

Patience was here now, and insistent, her dark gaze boring into Avis's from across the room. Avis set her mouth, kept her attention on the matter at hand. She had become quite practised at ignoring this particular distraction.

The grieving man took several short breaths one after the other, each an attempt to find words to speak, but Hood reached with a clammy hand to grab his as the table began to shake between them.

"*Hear me*," the medium croaked. "*Listen to your Uncle H…*" He broke off with a hacking, guttural cough. "*Your Uncle Hhhhh…*" He appeared to be struggling to speak.

Only initials on the watch, then. It mattered not, for the mark was in deep and happy to help at this point.

"*Henry!*" the man cried, tears rolling down his cheeks, clutching at the medium's hand. "Uncle Henry, please!"

Avis had seen enough. "Oh for— Stop, stop this immediately. And turn the lights on!"

The medium's hacking choked to silence; all that was left were the man's sobs, though they faded as well in the awkward seconds that followed. Avis waited and, when no one obeyed her order, strode to the wall and began to twist the knobs to bring the lamps back to full brightness. The illumination revealed the full extent of their surroundings: a large room panelled in dark wood, heavy curtains hung over the windows obscuring Belgravia's streets. The gathered guests were spaced around the table like pearls on a necklace, their hands linked in accordance with the medium's instructions.

"What is the meaning of this?"

Sir Reginald St Simon had a long face that was growing redder by the second, and a calf's lick that refused to bow to his no doubt mighty will. Avis offered him her best impression of a charming smile as she returned to the assembled group.

"I'm afraid you are playing host to a charlatan, sir, and I for one simply could not let it go on a moment longer."

"A charlatan? How dare you!" This from Hood, who dropped the pocket watch to the table with a dull clunk. He didn't rise, however, and Avis knew she'd won.

"While I could list all the ways in which your 'communications' from the spirits were nothing more than guesswork helped along by a willing victim, I think this should prove more than sufficient to demonstrate my claims." She dropped to her knees, drawing gasps from the society gentlemen and ladies, and delved beneath the cloth that dripped over the table and down to the floor.

"He insisted on entering the room alone, didn't he?" she asked, tipping her head to catch St Simon's eye. "Alone and in good time, ahead of the arrival of the guests."

"Er... yes. Said he needed to attune himself to the... resonances of the room." St Simon was desperately trying not to be distracted by the flash of ankle she'd exposed as she tussled with the tablecloth.

"Of course he did. Whereas in actuality, he was preparing his little tricks."

"Excuse me!" Hood cried as her fingers found his shoe. "Unhand me! This is unacceptable, I must insist—"

"Oh shush, I'm nearly finished. Just… here!" Avis rocked back onto her heels, pulling a long silver wire from beneath the table. "Correctly attached, it can help its owner do all sorts of tricks—agitating the table, for one, and causing strange noises. Quite a helpful little thing, but a spirit it's not."

From there matters unravelled much as Avis would have predicted, after all, it was quite hard to surprise her. The mustachioed man punched the medium, and would probably have beaten him to a pulp had he not been pulled away and subdued. The medium blustered and argued and went through various stages of attempted denial, then an admission of guilt—but *only* to the wire, not to his contact with the departed—and then simply thinly veiled blackmail, implying that he knew a great deal about the St Simon family that might prove embarrassing to all should any of the events of the evening escape that room.

Strangely, nobody was ever *glad* when Avis exposed these spirit mediums for the fakes they were. She couldn't understand it personally: surely it was better to be in possession of the facts, even if said facts were embarrassing in the moment? But no. Those fortunate souls she disabused of their beliefs were only ever angry with her, or at best merely annoyed. They never said thank you.

Only one person spoke to her again that whole night. As she emerged, still buttoning her coat, from the dim townhouse and into the cool, still air of an early spring evening, a tall, passingly handsome man who could have been aged anywhere from thirty-five to a well-preserved fifty, caught up with her.

"That was quite the show," he said. "Not necessarily the one folks expected, I think." He hadn't spoken at all during the séance, so this was her first encounter with his distinctive drawl.

An American. Lord spare her. "Well. Thank you. I think." She trotted down the building's front stairs, but he fell into step beside her.

"I'm very sorry, Miss Lovelock—I know you by reputation,

but I didn't introduce myself," he said, rounding neatly on her as they reached the pavement. "My name is Carlton Brooksbank, and I have a proposition for you."

Avis took his proffered hand but laughed at his words. "Oh, I shan't be needing any of those, Mr Brooksbank."

An easy, white-toothed grin. "You misunderstand me. I'm impressed with your skills, but don't you think they're wasted here in England?"

That, at least, was true enough. "Without wanting to seem ungrateful, sir, please make your point, for I think I hear a hackney approaching."

"Come to America! I have a number of contacts in New York and Massachusetts who would be delighted to make your acquaintance, and I don't mind saying I'd very much enjoy introducing you to them. I think you could really shake things up."

This was new. Avis frowned. "As flattered as I am, I don't think that will be possible." She wasn't about to admit it, but the sad fact was that the earnings of a theatre performer with the hobby of irritating every credulous aristo in the country didn't exactly stretch to transatlantic jaunts.

"Without wanting to sound indelicate, Miss Lovelock, I'd like to make it possible. There's a passenger liner, *Excambion*, leaving from Portsmouth on Tuesday. I've got a first-class ticket with your name on it, if you'll take it."

It wasn't often that Avis was rendered speechless. Fortunately, it was only ever a temporary affliction. "I can't possibly accept such kindness from a stranger," she said.

"Then don't be a stranger. Let me take you to dinner. I've a booking at the Savoy."

"Mr Brooksbank, whatever you're expecting here, I must warn you—"

The man held up his hands in surrender. "No expectations, I promise. Except that you'll make for interesting company, and perhaps hear me out."

Well. It had been some time since she'd dined at the Savoy.

* * *

"NOW, MR BROOKSBANK. I think it's best we get right to it so that I might enjoy my steak. What's the catch?"

Brooksbank lifted his neat, dark eyebrows. He was well dressed and well manicured, and had an easy sophistication to him that spoke to a relatively affluent background. Avis was no expert in the American vernacular but to the best of her knowledge he sounded as though he was from the Northeast. Not Boston, though. Upstate New York, New Hampshire, or perhaps the one in the middle—Vermont? "You assume there is a catch."

"You and I both know there's no such thing as a free lunch, as your countrymen would say. Come on now, out with it."

Brooksbank sighed. "I was operating under strict instructions to broach my further request only once you were on board."

"Well, I don't know why you thought that would work."

"Yes, in hindsight I'm realising that was wishful thinking." Brooksbank lifted his wine to his lips; he held his glass like one would a tumbler and looked at it as he set it back down for fear it might imbalance on its long stem. Not usually a wine drinker—did he think one had to here, to move in polite society?

"This is *Excambion*'s swansong," he said at length. "Her final voyage. As part of the Hamburg Line, at any rate. She's been sold. Or, well, nearly."

"Congratulations?"

"The buyers are… superstitious."

"They definitely shouldn't buy a boat then. Who are they?"

"I don't know. I don't!" Brooksbank protested when Avis lifted her eyebrows. Again that gesture of surrender. "I'm just an agent from the owner's investors; I've never so much as spoken to the buyer. All I know is that almost a dozen men resigned from *Excambion*'s crew in Cherbourg, and several more in Portsmouth. When I left for London yesterday, they were still scrambling to replace them."

Avis had a sinking feeling—pun intended. "Why?" she asked, although she already knew the answer.

"They say *Excambion* is haunted."

The bark she let out was as far away as one could get from "ladylike" and still use the same alphabet. "Mr Brooksbank. Please. Remember to whom you're speaking. You may as well tell me the hull is constructed of Swiss cheese—in fact, I'd more readily believe that, knowing next to nothing about naval engineering as I do."

"I'm not saying I believe it myself," Brooksbank replied, though there was a waver to his voice that told Avis he didn't quite *not* believe it, either. "Only that the buyers are concerned with the rumours and want them laid to rest before the sale is completed."

"So I'm to, what, certify this tug is completely spectre-free so that a bunch of investors can get richer, is that it?"

"Ideally, yes."

"Well, that's simple enough. I can do that for you now. Your boat isn't haunted."

"Technically it's a ship."

"Regardless. Still." Their food had arrived. Avis took a moment to saw a corner off the thick wedge of meat seeping juice onto the pristine white plate. "I suppose I have no fixed plans." After all, what was stopping her? There was nothing keeping her in England. Not any more.

One

"Miss Lovelock? Avis Lovelock?" The porter who greeted her was red-faced, no doubt just having run down his fiftieth flight of stairs in order to meet her at the embarkment point. Luckily for him, Avis travelled light; there was only a small monitor trunk sitting beside her on the dock.

"That's me," she said, and he needed no more prompting to heft her trunk easily and nod up the gangplank.

"I'm told I'm to give you a tour through the main living areas," he told her, his somewhat shrill voice echoed by the cries of the gulls overhead. "If you'll follow me."

Avis strode after him, pausing midway to cast a final backwards glance at dry land. The harbour was a hive of activity; first, second, and third class alike buzzing with anticipation—and nerves—ahead of boarding SS *Excambion*. And no wonder—it was an enormous ship, its painted metal sides looming over the pier like an encroaching tidal wave. And here she was, walking up the gangplank towards the shadowed gap in its side, ready to be swallowed alive.

The ship might want to reconsider. A meal as sour and tough as you might give it indigestion.

Avis ignored the voice, refusing to search the gangplank for a dark, hovering figure out of place and out of time. Stalwartly she marched onward, following the porter through the hatch and stepping foot on board *Excambion* with her head held high.

Inside the ship was no less lively, though the noise and activity were dampened by the thick carpet underfoot. Avis followed the porter up a flight of stairs, then another, and lost count of the twists and turns they took around bulkheads covered with polished wood and past panes of carefully wrought stained glass inset in the doors. She was puffing by the time they emerged into a foyer of sorts, its ceiling soaring far higher above them than the constraints of a ship should've allowed.

"Is this what all first classes look like?" she said, her voice echoing off the domed skylight above. Black lines traced their way to the centre like spokes on a wheel, and the elaborate designs sandwiched between them were picked out in gold. "Like Sedding himself was sick all over them?"

The porter chuckled, slowing his steps a little to allow her to catch up. "I've heard some of the new White Star Line are even grander, if you can believe it."

"I've no reason to think you a liar, so I suppose I have to." Avis took in her companion with an up-and-down glance, automatically noting and cataloguing the little details that loomed large to her critical eye.

His uniform was clean and neat, as would be expected from a first-class porter at the start of a voyage, save for a smear of white paint on one of the cuffs of his jacket. No doubt there were small touch-ups and repairs happening even now, and he'd happened to brush too close on one of his many trips through the corridors. Avis would have to be wary lest her own skirts became mottled.

His chin was smooth and close-shaven, but his moustache, while well-groomed, was just slightly shorter on the left than the right. This was commonplace in men who rarely visited the barber, relying on their own hand to keep their facial hair trimmed. She knew *Excambion* contained both first and second-class barber shops, but it seemed the crew had to make do on their own.

He wore no jewellery save for a pair of cufflinks; at a closer look they did not bear the *Hamburg* insignia that she had noticed on other crew but instead sported a pair of proud horse heads wreathed with a golden horseshoe. A racing fanatic, then. She wondered if the habit left him with money to spend, or if he was one of the unlucky types always scrambling to pay his debts. If so, she supposed work aboard a steamship might provide a welcome escape from hungry creditors.

And look. Tucked in his breast pocket—not a handkerchief but a note. "To Thomas, my love." It seems it's not just creditors he's left behind. Perhaps he's running from her as well.

Avis rolled her shoulders and shook her head, though of course it did nothing to dislodge the voice in her ears or shake the tightness in her chest.

Running away only worked when your problems weren't yoked to your soul.

In hopes of distraction, she focused on her surroundings as Thomas whisked her from the grand foyer into the rooms beyond, each more opulent than the next. Sensing her deep and abiding curiosity, he described the function of each room. The main dining saloon was trimmed with polished walnut and coated in white enamel, giving it a stark character that reminded Avis of a hospital ward. It boasted the largest footprint of any room on the vessel, presumably to underline the grandiosity of the first-class experience, and the portholes were covered by faux windows, erasing any evidence that they were aboard a ship at all, save for the swaying beneath their feet.

"It doesn't make a great deal of sense, does it? Surely people who've bought tickets for a transatlantic journey know very well they're on a ship. Why go to all that trouble to cover it up?"

Thomas Surname Unknown shrugged; she got the feeling she might've voiced a pondering he'd had himself. His voice when he spoke, however, was studiously neutral. "Some folk don't like the idea of being out on the open sea. It can be disorienting, being surrounded by all that water."

Avis snorted. After the close press of the buildings and streets of London, the idea of an unbroken expanse of ocean was an intriguing change of pace, not frightening. But then, very few things worried her. She'd hardly be able to do what she did if she was easily scared.

"Out those doors is the garden verandah. It sits on both sides of the A deck and is fully enclosed from the elements."

Peering through the windows, Avis could make out a riot of greenery and wicker. "Heaven forfend the ladies get their hair mussed," she murmured, leaning closer until her nose was all but pressed against the glass. There was bronze trim everywhere, and chequerboard floors that recalled Parisian cafés (or so she assumed).

"The smoking section is here on the port side," Thomas said, gesturing, "and the non-smoking is on the starboard. In case that's of interest."

"I don't smoke. Ghastly habit," Avis told him. "But I've no objection to those who do. We all have our vices, eh?" Her eyes flicked down to his cufflinks and she watched him stiffen, his smile growing fixed. She hadn't meant it as a rebuke, but men were so touchy about their little foibles.

"Mm. The verandah is only one of the gathering spaces available to guests; we also have the reception room, the lounge, the reading room, and the men's smoking room towards the aft," he said, beginning to walk once more. They left the saloon and descended another set of stairs to the living quarters, which looked like nothing so much as the corridors of a fancy hotel. "And promenades for all classes, though they're not always used. If you're keen to stretch your legs, you might also make use of the gymnasium or the swimming pool or the squash courts."

"Hang on," Avis said, raising a hand. "There's a swimming pool. On the ship."

Thomas nodded. He had sped up his steps as they walked.

Keen to offload her, or just eager to set her trunk down? It wasn't all that heavy, though she had included a stack of pulp magazines that might have added to its heft. "Some guests enjoy the opportunity to maintain their exercise routines on the crossing."

"Well, now I've heard everything."

Any further thoughts on the absurdity of a swimming pool in the middle of the Atlantic were forestalled as she caught sight of a familiar lanky figure: Carlton Brooksbank, her sponsor. He was loitering near one of the stairwells, presumably one which led to the lower decks, and as she watched a dark-haired officer in a natty uniform emerged from below and leaned in to speak to him, their heads close. It was impossible to catch what was being said but it was clear from the way they canted towards each other that they were not strangers, and that their discussion was intended to be a private one.

Avis liked nothing more than inserting herself where she wasn't invited, and she peeled off from Thomas's tour to aim herself at the murmuring pair. "Ahoy there, Brooksbank!"

They sprang apart as if singed, the officer nearly stumbling backwards down the stairs. Brooksbank put a hand out to grasp his forearm, though as soon as the officer had stabilised the hand was removed and shoved into a pocket. "Miss Lovelock," Brooksbank said smoothly, as if she hadn't just interrupted what had apparently been a clandestine conversation. He turned towards her, smile wide and apparently genuine. "You're aboard."

"Very well observed. They should put you in the lookout tower, we'd be safe as houses."

"Navigation aboard the ship is actually a much more complex operation than just watching from the crow's nest," the officer said. He was a nervous-looking chap with high cheekbones and low-set eyebrows, giving him the countenance of a man always squinting towards the horizon. Brooksbank favoured him with a knowing look. Avis's suspicions sharpened.

They could just be friends, you know. That's a thing people have.
Well, most people.

"I'm sure once Miss Lovelock has gotten her bearings she'll want to hear all about it, but for now, we shall let you return to your duties, Third Officer Baynes."

Avis watched as the officer hesitated, turning towards the stairs before shaking his head and reorienting himself in the direction from which Avis and Thomas had just come. "I'll just… this way, I think," he said, his voice quivering. "Welcome aboard, miss, and goodbye." His gait was a nervous, ungainly thing, like a hoop bent out of shape and wobbling a strange orbit.

"What a strange man," she remarked, once he was—probably—out of earshot. "If that's who's in charge of the ship, perhaps I should be worried."

"The crew are impeccable," Brooksbank assured her. "Nothing at all to fret about. You're on your way to your cabin, I take it?"

"Yes, and my expectations are quite high, I must say. Thriving gardens, haute cuisine dining, swimming pools… Perhaps I won't disembark at New York but commit myself to eternally crossing back and forth across the Atlantic in the finest of fashions."

He chuckled, and gave a gesture to Thomas that he should go ahead with the trunk to Avis's room. He had an easy charm to him, and even the elevated status that allowed him to dismiss crew members with a wave sat well on him, rather than rankling Avis's sensibilities.

"Somehow I have the feeling you won't be able to resist the big city. Nor it you. But certainly, while we're here, you should take advantage of everything available to you."

"You make it sound like I'm to be a lady of leisure." Avis tsked. "But I have important work ahead of me, Mr Brooksbank, and I shall not be distracted from it. Except by free champagne. And perhaps a Turkish massage or two."

"Quite. And I have no doubt that you will perform your duties admirably," he said. "But first, let's get you settled in. Your berth is this way."

Two

The room glittered in the lamplight; gilt reliefs on the ceiling glistened like stalactites. All around them mirrors lined the walls, creating the illusion of endless velvet-covered chairs and footstools lounging into infinity. SS *Excambion* was a first-class steamship, and no expense had been spared in her outfitting, not least in the first cabin lounge. Passengers had begun filtering through in the hour before dinner, many of them dressed in fabrics and jewels to rival the furnishings. It was gaudier than the busiest music hall, though none of the occupants would have been happy with the comparison. Avis had come for the free drinks and the people-watching. So far she'd seen three adulterers, four philanderers, and someone she was certain had somehow made their way in from third class furtively enjoying the luxury on offer.

She felt a strong kinship with the latter; she didn't really belong here either.

A stately older woman in evening gloves suddenly made a beeline across the room towards the nook where Avis sat, the light of recognition in her grey eyes. "I've *just* realised where I know you from—I saw you reading minds at the Egyptian!"

Avis, who had been trying to avoid the woman's eyeline from the moment she had entered the saloon already in full-throated conversation with her husband about the "simply marvellous" decor, rearranged her face into a polite grimace as she turned to face her fate.

"You're mistaken," she said, slipping into her usual well-worn spiel. "I don't read minds. Everything I observe is just as visible to you as it is to me."

"Nonsense, simply nonsense. There's no way that it was anything other than the spirits themselves imparting their wisdom!" Her opponent—for already this had the feel of a debate, or the overture to a full-fledged battle—was resplendent in a plum-coloured dinner dress draped in lace and flounces. Avis was a drab portrait in contrast, in her dark bodice and skirts. "You were quite good, one of the best I've seen. Really, there's no need for this modesty."

Avis glanced about for an ally, but though all eyes in the saloon were fixed on her, they had the hungry look of marks and believers. This would not be pretty. "It isn't modesty. You can learn a great deal about someone just from observing them for a few short moments."

The woman's gaze sharpened. "To what end?"

"Well, for one, if one wanted to convince them that ghosts and spirits truly do exist." Avis tried for an "all in good fun" grin that she feared must look like a smirk. People never responded well to her friendly grins. She narrowed her eyes in a momentary appraisal. "I'll show you," she said.

It was less than three hours after boarding this sardine tin at Portsmouth and Avis Lovelock was already breaking the promise she had made to herself. The urge to perform was simply too strong. A shiver ran down her spine: half anticipation, half dread.

She gestured to the necklace around the woman's neck. It was surprisingly plain for her otherwise well-put-together ensemble, which meant it was most likely of sentimental value, and therefore a prime artefact to glean from. "Might I borrow that locket for a moment? I promise I won't make it disappear."

"My goodness! Jeremy, would you, please?" the woman said, turning her back to her husband to unfasten the necklace post-haste. The husband—Jeremy—appeared a biddable, unassuming sort, and Avis was happy for his sake; a woman of such Valkyrian bearing would have been badly matched with a man interested in gainsaying her on any matter.

Avis pursed her lips, turning the woman's locket back and forth. It was silver, though not pure, its tint betraying its age and country of origin along with the design sensibilities. French. Twenty, perhaps thirty years old. Pretty, well made, but mass-produced, not worth selling onward, and certainly not at the sorts of auction houses this well-to-do woman would frequent. So, bought new, single owner, given to her in her teens by the look of her. Sets of initials, one beneath the other on the back.

S.M.

C.M.

The monogrammed pocket square of the man hovering around his spouse like a fruit fly around a ripe plum read *J.F.* That would do for now.

"From your sister. Bought in France and gifted..."—a pause for effect, and to gauge the emotion in her subject's eyes, the specific flavour of nostalgia at play—"... on her return."

"Heavens, that's right—every word!" The woman's eyes gleamed, and a wave of murmurs swept around the room. "I simply refuse to believe you can tell all that through simple observation."

"I assure you, there is nothing mystical at play here. After all, why would there be? Your sister is alive and well, is she not?"

"Why, yes, she is alive," the woman said in a satisfied tone, as though Avis knowing this was yet more evidence in her favour. "But the spirits, they know everything. They're watching, always."

A wisp of fabric quivered in Avis's periphery, there and yet not there. She ignored it. "Again, madam, there are no spirits. Only observation and deduction. I am the one who is watching. I, and your sister..."

A cold breath on her ear. A clench in her stomach.

"… Clarissa. Isn't that right, Clarissa?" Avis raised her voice to address the assembled company, her tone breezy and self-satisfied.

A gasp from off to the side, and Avis turned to smile at said sister, a woman who could scarcely look more solid if she had been cast in bronze. She'd seen them come in together and noted the resemblance immediately. Cousin had been as likely as sister, but the fact that they were travelling together and the presence of the locket had given her enough to go on to make the guess.

Clarissa laughed. "Remarkable!" she exclaimed. "How, then, if not the spirit realm?"

Avis smiled and tipped her head to the side. "You two could scarcely look more alike if you were twins," she said. "You see?" She turned back to return the locket. "Simple observation, and a bit of luck."

Clarissa's sister accepted the locket, her lips pressed together in grudging acceptance. "Perhaps this time. But I've seen things no simple observations could explain," she insisted, and Avis was suddenly so very tired, too tired to argue. It was the same refrain every time, the same refusal to accept the mundanity of the world around them. "The spirits *are* real."

EVENTUALLY CLARISSA AND her sister—Sarah—were persuaded to carry on to the dining room, with Sarah's husband in tow, and Avis slumped down onto one of the chairs beneath the curtained porthole. They were far less comfortable than their plush appearance promised, and she harrumphed, drawing a footstool closer to prop one foot on. She ignored the daggered looks of the passing first-class passengers who clearly disapproved of her vulgar comportment.

Even with the turn of the century approaching and a war between Spain and America brewing, some things never changed. The rich were still credulous, more willing to believe in make-believe than in common sense. She could not help but think back to the séance that had led her here: the spirit medium's protestations, the embarrassed anger of their host, and the teary-eyed pleas of the mark, who—despite it all, even despite his anger—insisted that "Uncle Henry" was there, and if he could only have another minute to speak with him…

It was the same every time. No matter how compelling the evidence, no matter how far-fetched the claims, there were always people so desperate to believe that they would ignore the truth right in front of their eyes.

Tricks, that's all it was. Sometimes nothing more than clever sleight of hand, sometimes inviting the mark to do the work themselves, filling in the gaps left by a trailing sentence, an expectant pause. When in doubt, guess the popular names of the day and chances were you would light upon the correct moniker thanks to nothing more than pure probability.

Clarissa is hardly a popular name.

And one did develop a knack for these things, over time. Practice. A honed intuition.

Avis. Listen to me.

Avis rocked forward, boots thumping against the polished wooden floor. She'd learned all this when she was nothing more than a slip of a girl; why was it so difficult for grown men and women to grasp? Why did delusion trump logic, hope trump fact?

You know why.

Her concentration broke, tugged by the sting of that needling voice, and as she refocused away from the middle distance, Patience resolved, a dark stain in her peripheral vision. Her goad, her burden, her constant companion. Her sister, dead these thirteen years and yet never far from Avis's side.

As always, Patience's presence brought a sweep of cold across Avis's skin. The warmth of first class turned clammy and close. Familiar too was the twist in her stomach, the sudden fracture in her monumental self-confidence. The longer she tried to ignore her sister's ghost, the more it plagued her, and so it was that she looked straight at her, refusing to quail under Patience's dark gaze. The two stood, locked in a stalemate, until Avis raised her chin and blinked the spectre away. It was time for dinner, and with any luck the champagne would be free-flowing. She intended to skim every drop of cream she could from the saucer over the next six days, and if doing so helped her forget her steady descent into insanity, well, so much the better.

Three

THE DINING ROOM was filled with the sound of gently clinking glass, so much so that stepping inside felt like sticking one's head into a chandelier. Avis was steered towards a half-empty table in the middle of the room, where a familiar face lit up at her arrival.

"Miss Lovelock, glad you made it." Brooksbank rose, looking every inch the gentleman in a well-brushed tuxedo jacket. He pulled out the empty chair beside him and Avis took the cue, sliding into the seat with minimal fuss. He smiled as he took his own seat once more. "So nice to sit down to dinner with you again."

"And you—I'm wondering what you'll offer me this time. An island in the Caribbean? Actually, best not, perhaps, given the current situation with Spain. I don't have the funds to put down a rebellion."

"Do you start every conversation with a provocation?"

"Whenever I possibly can, yes."

Brooksbank beckoned a waiter over with a wave of his hand. "I've heard you already caused quite the stir in the lounge. Didn't take you long."

"It was not by choice, I assure you. It seems my face is difficult to forget."

"Now that I can believe."

Avis readied herself to bite back, but the statement ended there, with no further insinuations to fend off. It was just as well; she knew she was hardly a beauty, with a narrow, suspicious face and a beakish nose, though this hardly seemed to matter to some men, who still tried to act as if she should be grateful for their attentions. It would appear that Brooksbank had taken her initial rebuttals in the spirit in which they were intended, however, and indeed he swiftly moved the conversation onward.

"What do you think of the ship now that she's properly at sea? Rather grand, isn't she?"

"Quite. It's good to know that should her steam engines break down we'll be able to reach New York by sail power alone," Avis said, indicating the pristine span of tablecloth before them, and the dozens of identical tables lining the room.

Brooksbank chuckled with what looked to be genuine amusement. "Indeed. Though I'm assured there's no danger of that happening. Something about redundant boilers and all that malarkey."

"Oh, boilers and malarkey, very reassuring." Despite her better judgement Avis liked this American, and she liked him even more when the waiter arrived and filled a coupe glass with champagne for her. The crystal sparkled as she lifted it, and those sparkles rushed through her as she drank until she felt lighter, gayer. "I suppose there's some backup jiggery-pokery if things get truly dire."

"Y'know, they didn't cover that on the tour, but I bet so."

"Oh, you've had a tour of the inner workings of the ship? I wish I'd known those were on the cards so I could bask in gratitude at having avoided it—I can't abide naval architecture."

Brooksbank cocked his head. "What a specific dislike."

"Mm, formulated just this very moment at the thought of climbing up and down all those stairs. Cheers." She hefted her champagne, the crystal cool against her palm.

"Well, you're missing out," said Brooksbank, clinking his glass to Avis's. "It was riveting."

"I'm sure the rivets were only the half of it."

Though Avis could've passed the evening quite happily trading quips with Brooksbank, their table was soon filled with a selection of other passengers joining them for the evening meal. There was Mr and Mrs Thomas Armitage, who had been on the ship since Hamburg and were thoroughly inured to the grandeur of it all; Dr Samson Usher, a grizzled man who barked with laughter when Brooksbank introduced Avis and her "profession"; and another young woman, a Miss Lily Douglas-Gordon, who tittered nervously each time she was spoken to. Her companion, an aunt or second cousin of some description, was currently ill in their shared cabin, granting Miss Douglas-Gordon a taste of freedom that was going entirely unappreciated.

The dining room was fairly full up at this point, awash in a din of small talk and cutlery that drowned out even the ever-present hum of the ship's engines. Suddenly the noise dampened, then dropped to silence, and Avis twisted round in her seat to see what had caused this sudden hush.

The two newcomers had entered side by side, and it was obvious even from here that they were not just brother and sister but twins. They each had the same tall, willowy frame, the same fine-boned features, the same colourless cheeks and ice-cold eyes. The woman's hair was mostly concealed beneath a bonnet and veil, but the few tendrils that escaped were the same flaxen waves that framed her brother's smooth face. They were both dressed in black from head to toe.

"The Duquesne twins!" Mrs Armitage exclaimed at the same time that Dr Usher grunted, "What the devil?" Avis stayed quiet, watching as the two cut-paper silhouettes drifted to a table with two empty chairs remaining. Clearly, they were expected.

As they sat, the dining room erupted into a salvo of conversation. "It's *the* Duquesnes!" Mrs Armitage said again, and this time it was the retiring Miss Douglas-Gordon who took the bait.

"Wh-who *are* they?"

"They're frauds, all dressed up in crepe paper and Catholic frippery," Avis drawled. All eyes turned to her.

"They're Spiritualists," Mrs Armitage corrected, and her husband gave a resounding "Hmph" through his nose, presumably in support of his wife's statement.

"Exactly as I said." Avis smiled and lifted her glass for a sip.

"Are you implying that the many good people of my acquaintance have willingly sat for frauds?" Mrs Armitage asked. Her cheeks flared pink, bordering on crimson, a fetching shade against the white and gold of the dining room.

"I can't speak to their willingness," Avis said, shrugging, "but if they attended supposed séances with the aim of speaking with the dead, and believed they had by the end, then yes, they sat for frauds. You call them good people; I call them gullible."

Mr Armitage flinched, courtesy of his wife's sharp elbow in his side. "Now see here, that's quite enough. These are society mavens we're talking about, not weak-minded dupes."

Avis had quite a lot to say about society mavens, actually, but before she could launch into it, Brooksbank cleared his throat, stopping the conversation cold. "I believe we're due a toast," he said, lifting his glass, and like well-trained children they all followed suit before the diversion fully registered. "To the SS *Excambion*, her captain and crew, and to her safe passage to New York. May it be swift and smooth."

The table echoed his sentiments and clinked their glasses, and the act seemed to release the tension that had been building like a thundercloud. Avis would have been more than happy to strike the conversation up again, but Brooksbank caught her eye and gave a subtle shake of his head. He couldn't have her thrown overboard, she was relatively sure, but she relented all the same. If she wanted his promised introductions in New York, she'd do best to stay on his good side. There'd be time to drive her point home later, no doubt.

As the table talk slid back towards discussion of European sojourns and winter holidays, Avis's attention drifted, and her gaze went with it. It passed over clusters of tuxedoed gentlemen and lace-swathed ladies before landing on the table where the new arrivals now sat, ensconced among the finely dressed passengers like cuckoos among the songbirds. Gideon and Rachel Duquesne: twins from America, so-called Spiritualists, and two of the most successful swindlers Europe had seen in some time. She'd never been able to inveigle her way into a showing as they had spent the last several years touring the Continent. Avis was puzzling over a niggling feeling when the sister—Rachel—seemed to sense she was being observed. The young woman looked up from staring at a fixed point on the table and unerringly turned her head until she was looking straight back at Avis. Despite the veil she wore, Rachel's eyes skewered straight through her, an icy arrow that left her cold and pinned to her seat.

Oh dear. You'll need to watch out for this one.

Avis refused to break eye contact, instead lifting her champagne saucer in a subtle toast before draining the entire glass. Duquesne blinked, only looking away when one of the many-feathered women beside her placed one hand on her wrist, gesticulating with the other to the rest of the table. Avis smiled triumphantly and turned back to her compatriots, who were deep in discussion about—what else?—the twins.

"… uncle *died*. So tragic!" Mrs Armitage pronounced. So *that* was what was off; by all accounts the uncle was ever-present, chaperoning the twins everywhere and ensuring they were adequately compensated for their "generous" service.

"Hardly a tragedy, if they can speak with him at will," Avis observed.

Some might even claim to grow closer in death.

She ignored the observation and gestured a waiter over. "More fizz, so we can drink to long life and good health, if you please."

"How can you be so glib?" Mrs Armitage said. "They're clearly deep in mourning."

"And yet they're supping on champagne and caviar, just as we are." This pronouncement drew a belly laugh from Dr Usher, who had matched and then exceeded Avis's consumption of the free-flowing champagne on offer.

Any further rejoinder from Mrs Armitage was forestalled by the arrival of the soup, and as Avis was keen not to be barred from first class on her first night, she allowed the subject to change without further comment.

An excruciating millennium of irrelevant small talk later, the meal finished, and the diners rose to move onward, whether to one of the saloons or ballrooms, onto deck to take the air, or simply to repair to their cabins.

Avis dropped her napkin on the table and turned for the door. Brooksbank appeared by her side. He had a nervous skip to his step, like a toddler with a full bladder.

"I suppose I must commend your bravery, putting yourself within swinging distance," Avis breezed.

Brooksbank made a noise that probably denoted an attempt to convey amusement but sounded more like he had a bit of gristle stuck in his throat. "Was escape ever an option?" he asked.

"What do you think?" Avis stopped short of the door, moving out of the general thoroughfare and slipping her hands into the pockets of her dress. "All right, well, you're here. Talk. I take it the presence of Europe's most celebrated liars is not a coincidence."

Beneath his moustache, the man's mouth went through a series of closed-lipped contortions. "The Duquesnes were in need of transport. It's a mutually beneficial arrangement."

The gears within Avis's mind began to whirr as the pieces clicked into place. "The dead uncle. Yes, I see. And I suppose they're here for the same reason I am."

"It was felt that there should be... balance... to the investigation."

Avis pouted in thought. "When did you recruit them? The Duquesnes have never toured Britain, only the Continent. They must have embarked at Hamburg."

"Cherbourg, actually. They were touring France with their, ah, patron."

Glancing back in the direction of their table, careful not

to stare for too long, Avis saw now that the twins were not the only people in funereal black in their little retinue. A handsome woman perhaps ten years her senior was also in mourning, and hanging on to Gideon's every word. "Good grief, they found a widow," she muttered.

"Madame Charlotte Berthault, of Giverny," Brooksbank confirmed. "I'm told her husband was in business before his untimely passing."

"Now she's caught up in business of a different type." Avis's keen eyes roamed over the group. Berthault was richly dressed, bedecked with rings, her pale cheeks flushed with wine and something more. Gideon was speaking, still, and illustrating his point with flourishes of his long fingers. The other twin sat silently beside him, her shoulders hunched.

She looked, for all intents and purposes, like a frail and insubstantial waif. But there was something about her—the set of her spine, the tilt of her head—which spoke to Avis of a far more vital presence. And then there was that piercing blue-green gaze, the memory of which pricked gooseflesh all along her arms.

Avis gave her head a shake to clear it and returned to the matter at hand. "That doesn't answer my question, though. You weren't in Cherbourg and London at the same time."

"I was not. I've yet to speak to the twins in person. I was planning to find a moment tonight."

Avis's eyebrows winged upwards. "D'you mean to say they don't yet know why they're here?"

Brooksbank nodded in assent. "Right now, they know only that a silent benefactor who appreciates their talents wishes to help their uncle safely to his final resting place."

"I see. Funny, Berthault could certainly afford their passage. Perhaps they haven't finished buttering her up. Or they have other plans for her..."

Brooksbank made a face. "Not everybody has an ulterior motive, Miss Lovelock."

"Nonsense, of course they do." Avis turned towards

Brooksbank more fully, reaching to clasp his arm in both hands. He flinched, stealing nervous glances around them. "You mustn't tell them," she pronounced.

"Excuse me?"

"About the job. This haunting business. Don't tell them about it."

Brooksbank frowned. "That doesn't seem entirely fair…"

"I disagree strenuously. Consider: if they know there's a supposed haunting, they will pull whatever tricks they can to prove it authentic for their own ends. But if your boat is genuinely haunted, and if *they* are genuinely gifted in the Spiritualist arts, well, then they will sense these ghosts for themselves without prompting, will they not?"

"I… suppose, but—"

"Then it's settled. The Duquesnes remain in the dark."

Brooksbank slumped. "Very well," he said, scooping a fresh glass of champagne from a passing tray. "Have it your way. For now."

"I always do."

Before long Brooksbank excused himself to chat up some industrialist holding court at one of the central tables, and Avis left him to it. She was about to steal a bottle of champagne and make for her room when the opportunity for an even more amusing diversion presented itself. The black-clad trio stood and began drifting through the dining room like motes of soot, gently steering towards first one table, then another. At each one they paused, bowing their heads and allowing the diners to exclaim and gush over them. It was a practised move, Avis could tell, and indeed with each table they passed they gathered up one or two fawning passengers. She was unsurprised to see Mrs Armitage add herself to their party, and disappointed to see the sisters do the same, though Clarissa at least seemed keener to chat than to simper in silence. By the time they made it to the exit, near which Avis loitered, they had a good-sized flock around them: a cloud of perfumed idiots.

"Excuse me." Avis schooled her voice to a breathy pitch.

"You're not… the Duquesne twins, are you? It seems so hard to believe and yet when I saw you walk in…"

The group halted as Gideon turned to face her. His austere, high-cheeked features contrasted with the generous curve of his lips; no wonder the women behind him were fanning themselves. Said lips bowed into a smile and he inclined his head. "We are." His voice was warm and mellow, sunlight across oil. It was the first time Avis had heard either twin speak and she was immediately fascinated with his accent, a rich, caramelised tone at once kindred with French and entirely different. "Are you a follower of our work?"

"Oh, yes," she said, and it amused her that there was no lie within the words she uttered. "Quite avid, actually. You're not…"

"Conducting a séance? We are indeed." He liked to fill the empty pauses, as she'd expected. He gestured to the gaggle of hangers-on behind him. "Please, join us. Witness the peace that we can bring to those of troubled mind."

Those who had been at the dinner table with her earlier looked surprised as she folded herself into the group, but Avis merely smiled and touched a finger to her lips. What better way to get a handle on her newest opponents than at the table, incognito? Except it seemed she was not *entirely* accepted as a member of the flock by at least one shepherd; as they departed the dining room for their destination, Rachel Duquesne looked back over her shoulder, face now shrouded by her veil. Avis couldn't make out her expression but felt that same pricking sensation the other woman's gaze had raised before. Behind her she could hear the susurration of Patience's skirts, the wet rasp of her hem on the carpet.

She knows you. Not yet by name, perhaps. But somehow, that woman knows what you're up to.

Four

THE SMALLER OF the two ladies' saloons was situated towards the stern of the ship and thus was an interesting shape, tapering towards one end. This added to the theatre, in fact, for with the lamps turned low the odd angles of the walls cast curious shadows about the room. The drapes were all drawn, of course, and screens erected around a large table at the centre, the other furniture pushed back out of the way.

Avis immediately added this to her stack of questions—who had been roped into shifting all this furniture? Surely the captain wouldn't approve of his staff being put to such frivolous use, especially during the dinner service.

"Please," Gideon said in his honeyed voice. "S'il vous plait, if you will give us a moment. We must take time to attune to the spirits."

Avis suppressed her derision, just barely. Normally the mediums that said this used it as an excuse to secrete themselves away in the room alone to set up their tricks. The fact that the twins were allowing them in the room was interesting, but perhaps it was just unavoidable. It wasn't as if the crowd could retire to the room next door (she was pretty sure it was some sort of baggage compartment).

The group milled about the cabin, murmuring to one another. It was very obvious they were collectively caught between nerves and excitement, though some hid it better than others. Mrs Armitage and Sarah F were positively vibrating, heads close together as they muttered feverishly about what was set to occur. Meanwhile Clarissa, a woman after her own heart, made a beeline for the drinks trolley in the corner to fix herself a sherry. Charlotte Berthault stood apart from the rest, turned away slightly. Her head was bowed, eyes closed, and she was drawing and exhaling long, deep breaths. Whatever the other women might be expecting from the coming performance, Berthault was taking it entirely seriously.

Meanwhile the twins orbited the table, "attuning" themselves. To Avis's surprise Rachel sat down first, at the point furthest away from the screens' entrance. She placed her hands flat on the table, her pale face blank and composed. Gideon continued to circle, turning down the lamps, reaching out to straighten the black fabric draped across the table and pluck imaginary pieces of lint from its surface. Avis knew all sorts of shenanigans could take place underneath that cloth and wondered what had been hidden there—a board for them to rap their feet upon? Fake shoes to mislead those sitting on either side? She considered spoiling the fun before it had even begun, but held back. Better to let them truly implicate themselves before pulling the curtain back entirely.

At last Gideon was content that the scene was set, straightening the single precarious candle that sat in the middle of the table, having doused every other source of light. Avis had seen no other candles on board the ship and could not imagine that they were generally allowed—special dispensation must have been granted for this specific purpose. Gideon gestured to the waiting audience. "Please, if you'll join us."

Spirit mediums varied greatly in what they required for a séance to take place. Some insisted that there must be twelve seated around the table. Some went further, insisting that those twelve must comprise six men and six women exactly, citing a need for balance. The twins presumably required no specific number, particularly not since at least one of them had agreed so readily to Avis's inclusion. She was mildly surprised that Clarissa was not prevented from bringing her drink with her to the table. Tempted though she was, she did not fetch one herself—she had no wish to see it upended and good liquor wasted by some ghostly stunt. When she attempted to take the seat beside Rachel, however, the medium raised a hand to stop her.

"Forgive me," she said. "While you are welcome to join us, the energies of the room are sensitive." She looked up, piercing Avis with those ice-chip eyes. Her voice was lower than Avis had expected, and rougher, as if part of her cloistered breakfast routine involved the smoking of several cigars. She had the same curved lips as her brother but on her they sat oddly, perhaps due to the frown that adorned them. "I must ask you to sit further around."

Avis held back a snort. Very well. If she could not sit directly beside one of the twins, she would do the next best thing: sit directly opposite where she could observe them both without the obstacle of other figures in her line of sight.

Charlotte took the seat Avis had made a bid for, and Gideon sat on Rachel's other side; they made a sombre tableau, their black raiments melting into the shadows cast by the screens. The others quickly pulled up their own chairs—Sarah and Clarissa on Avis's left, and Mrs Armitage to her right. The room felt charged; not for the first time, Avis marvelled at what mere suggestion and anticipation could do.

"We are grateful to you all for joining us tonight," Gideon intoned, the words feeling well-worn as they tumbled over his lips. "We gather to call the spirits to us and, if they abide, invite them to speak, to share their knowledge of the Other Side." His voice was smooth and inviting; Avis grudgingly admitted he was not half bad at the performance. "Please, your presence and energy is important to our work, but we cannot have any interruptions. Do not speak unless invited. Follow every instruction you are given. Respect the spirits and honour the dead. Do this, and you shall be safe." A frisson ran through the group. Avis frowned, but stayed silent. Tonight, at least, she meant to get the lay of the land.

Gideon bade them link their hands. Mrs Armitage's fingers

trembled as Avis clasped them, from fear or anticipation, she was unsure. Clarissa, on her other side, had a warm, dry grip—comfortable, confident. If Avis was the sort to have friends, she would have been glad to name this amiable, sensible woman among them.

Gideon fell silent then, and an expectant air descended over them. Avis looked from twin to twin, cataloguing their every breath, every blink. Gideon looked almost pleased, his cupid's bow lips slightly curved in an expression that made Avis want to throw Clarissa's drink in his face. Rachel, by comparison, looked completely unaware of the attention being paid to her. Her eyes were half-lidded, gaze fixed on the flickering flame of the candle. From Avis's vantage point across the table—and on the other side of said candle—it gave her face an eerie mien, pinpricks of light dancing across her pupils.

Suddenly, at some unseen signal—probably just a nudge under the table—Gideon cleared his throat. Mrs Armitage jumped and then gave a nervous giggle.

"We call upon the spirits here with us tonight. Come to us. Speak to us. Make yourself known."

Avis was used to the silence that followed this, the deathly calm where all you could hear was those around you breathing. This time it was different, of course; the low, ever-present grumbling of the ship's engines crept into the foreground of hearing, the sloshing of the ocean against the hull, the fresh hiss of the wind.

The ship gave a tiny lurch, and Rachel took this as her cue.

"Je suis là. Mais je me sens faible." Her voice was even rougher now, deeper, and despite herself Avis leaned in until her breastbone was pressed to the table edge. Damn that she had never learned more than a smattering of French.

"Henri!" Despite the instruction to be silent, Charlotte could not seem to help the name that burst from her lips. She tightened her grip on Rachel's hand, turning to face her like a flower to the sun.

"Mon trésor," Rachel sighed. "Où sommes-nous?"

"We are on a ship, Henri." Gideon spoke in English—did the late Monsieur Berthault speak it as well, Avis wondered? "You have come very far to find us. To find Charlotte."

Rachel continued to speak in that low, gravelly French, and Gideon began to translate for their audience a few seconds behind, both for Rachel and for Charlotte.

"*My love,*" "Henri" said. "*Why are you so far from the earth of our home?*"

"*Our friends must take their uncle to America to bury him. I've come with them. I did not want to be without you.*"

Charlotte's voice cracked, and Rachel turned in towards her, her hand still clasping Gideon's but her attention otherwise entirely focused on the widow. "*The Veil is strange here,*" she intoned. "*It ebbs and flows like waves on the shore. I may not be able to stay long.*"

Mrs Armitage gasped. Charlotte had lifted Rachel's hand to press it against her cheek.

"Henri," she murmured, and leaned closer, voice dropping to an urgent whisper as she spoke directly into Rachel's ear. If Gideon could hear what was being said, he chose not to translate it. Avis's stomach gave a curious twist at the spectacle, the sudden feeling of intruding on a private moment between lovers. She strained to catch any scrap of the words passing between them, but beyond one reference to "Gideon" she could not make out a single word of their breathy exchanges, Rachel's replies as quick and quiet as Charlotte's. Their foreheads pressed together, their eyes fluttered closed, and for a moment Avis thought they might—

The candle snuffed out suddenly, plunging them into darkness and drawing a gasp from the assembly.

"Il est parti!" came the cry from the widow Berthault, and around the table came noises of sympathy and sadness. Avis groped around until she found the box of matches that had been left near the candle and struck one into flame. It flared, throwing distorted shadows over the faces of the women and men around the table. The light glinted off the tracks of tears that ran down Charlotte's cheeks, and she turned away as Avis relit the candle, pressing a handkerchief to her eyes. Mrs Armitage was bending to comfort her, all reassuring chatter and fluttering hands. Clarissa and Sarah sat still clasping hands, their eyes wide.

Rachel did not offer comfort, nor did she respond to her brother's entreaties as he tried to regain control over the gathering. Instead, she stared through the flame straight at Avis, her cheeks high with colour. She was not smiling, but there was a flare to her nostrils and a tip to her chin that said plenty.

I'll be watching you.

AVIS DEPARTED THE ladies' lounge without saying any goodbyes, and without any intention of returning to her berth. Instead she strode along the corridors, following a hint of cool breeze until she emerged through a door onto the upper decks. Despite the merrily twinkling lights and glinting railings, she felt a moment of disorientation, as if she had stepped out onto the peak of a mountain and was balanced now on the precipice. The night beyond the ship was dark and vast, stretching out around them like so much nothingness. Avis was drawn to it, her steps taking her towards the stern of the ship onto a completely deserted deck. Loungers and collapsed parasols littered the polished boards, waiting to spring into action come the sun, but Avis couldn't shake the sensation that she was surrounded by the carcasses of better times gone by.

Morbid thoughts for the start of such a grand adventure.

"As if you'd know any better. Everything is death with you."

Avis turned, finding Patience a dim blot against the darkness. The figure grew more opaque the longer she looked, until her sister was there, as solid as the railing behind her. Her face was alien yet familiar, in many ways a mirror of Avis's own, though slightly plumper and kinder, with a more generous curve of lip. It was pure fancy, of course; she had no idea how her sister would have looked at this age. She turned away again, facing out over the black ocean.

You must forgive the dead for their preoccupation. That the living share it is the real tragedy.

It was true enough. Death consumed them all. Even this ship could be viewed as a panacea against the certainty of mortality: a bright, shining beacon in the midst of the flat, empty sea. To fall into the water would be a death sentence, and yet hundreds willingly stepped aboard, flouting the ocean's inhospitable conditions with banquets and state rooms and gilt chandeliers. Did none of them feel it, the magnetic pull of the sea's expanse? Were they insensible to its emptiness, or was that what drove their laughter, their overindulgences? No wonder the twins had agreed to the journey; this grand cathedral of a ship was as suitable a chamber for their morbid performances as any crypt.

Careful, Avis.

She found she was leaning over the railing, fingers clenched around the iron until her knuckles popped and protested. Directly below, the sea was not calm, but churning and foamy like the scurf of acid in a wine-sick stomach. She breathed in, straightened her arms, stepped back. Her gaze stayed on the water. "Keep your caution. I'm fine."

Patience was silent. After a moment Avis wheeled away from the railing and headed back towards the safety of the cabins. Only a fool would stay out in the night, in the dark, all alone. And Avis was never knowingly a fool.

Five

WAKING AT SEA was much the same as waking on land, save for the enormously loud whistle that dragged Avis from a sound and sozzled slumber to reluctant consciousness. The first-class cabin she had been gifted was far more sumptuous than her usual digs, and despite the ringing in her ears she was tempted to burrow back under the blankets and doze the morning away. Only the lure of *Excambion*'s so-called haunting could pull her from her bed, and the anticipatory triumph of unmasking yet another set of Spiritualist frauds. She rolled out of bed and shuffled over to her washbasin, where she splashed her face with tepid water and ran her damp hands through unruly waves of hair. She and Patience both had the sort of hair that was a mother's woe: thick and curling, but only ever against the fashionable set.

There was a chill in the room, despite the many soft furnishings bolstered against the walls and windows. A finger dripped down her spine. Avis turned away from the bowl before the water could settle back to a mirror finish that might reveal more than her own face staring back at her.

A vessel of this size didn't sway much for the most part. If she stood entirely still a moment she could feel its gentle rock, but striding along the narrow corridor towards the dining saloon for breakfast she could barely discern it. And of course it mattered little if she could, for she fully intended to spend a significant portion of the trip at least mildly inebriated. She arrived at the door to the saloon at almost precisely the same moment as the inimitable Clarissa M, who beamed to see her again. She had a little dog with a terrible face tucked into the crook of her arm, who she introduced as Bouillabaisse—"Bou Bou" for short. Avis despised it on sight, and the feeling appeared to be quite mutual.

"Miss Lovelock, how wonderful to see you. Won't you join me? I've always wanted to dine with a celebrity." The dog curled its lip at her, and she accepted the invitation to spite it.

Avis allowed herself to be swept along to a table, where Clarissa promptly ordered a hearty spread from the neatly clad waiter. Avis ordered the same, though her usual morning meal was a strong cup of tea and dry toast. Her performances paid decently enough, but between her agent's cut, the cost of maintaining her tiny garret flat, and the inevitable flush of coins from her pocket any time she entered a pub, there wasn't much left over for poached eggs and hollandaise sauce.

"I'm sorry to disappoint you," Avis said when the waiter departed, "but I'm hardly a celebrity. I highly doubt you'll be thrilling dinner parties recounting our repast."

"Nonsense." Her companion tapped the table with one satin finger. "I've paid money to see you perform, that's celebrity enough in my book."

"And are you of a similar mind to your dear sister—that I am in fact in contact with the beyond regardless of my protestations to the contrary? Or are you of a more practical persuasion?"

"Oh, I don't spend my time thinking about morbid things like that. Perhaps you are, perhaps you're not—in the end, does it really make a difference?"

"To me, very much," Avis replied. "But it's refreshing to make the acquaintance of one for whom such philosophical matters are *not* a persistent preoccupation, I suppose."

Clarissa tipped her head to one side. Her auburn hair was slightly threaded with grey, but her face was unlined and her eyes bright and perceptive. "It sounds like you've been spending time with the wrong people."

"Oh, most assuredly. I cavort with all sorts." She shot Clarissa a winning smile. "But I'm happy to make an exception just this once and court better company. Oh, that looks like us."

They tucked into their meals, exchanging polite chat in between nibbles—or generous bites, in Avis's case. Clarissa was more than happy to expound upon the plans she and her sister had for their trip to the States. Avis had to admit she made it sound rather exciting; beyond writing to a handful of venues on the East Coast she hadn't really made any arrangements for her time abroad. Then again, Brooksbank had promised to "introduce her around", whatever that meant.

"... of course, some of that may change if the Duquesne twins are to take to the stage."

Avis's other ponderings came to a sudden halt at this, and she froze, egg dripping from her fork. "The stage? The twins have never done stage performances, only private séances."

"Mm, quite," Clarissa said, eyes still on her plate as she cut her own muffins into neat little pieces. "That's what would make it an unmissable event—well, as far as Sarah's concerned anyway. I just go along with her, it's easier." She laughed. "But yes, Sarah got chatting to Madame Berthault's seatmate at dinner the other night and *she* said that *Charlotte* said that *Rachel* said that they are considering a residency in New York."

"They are, are they?" Avis narrowed her eyes. "Interesting."

She sat back, her breakfast forgotten with the heady distraction of a new puzzle to unpick. Why this sudden change in approach? They had come from America originally, having caused quite a stir in their small town when their ability to converse with the deceased first "manifested". From there it was churches and wealthy patrons, until one day they had packed up and headed for the Continent. Rather than making the most of this new stage and performing widely, they had restricted themselves to private showings only. The better to avoid scrutiny and exposure, Avis thought darkly.

But now that was changing. Were they bolder now? More assured of their tricks and misdirections? Did they assume Americans would be easier to fool than the worldly, discerning European crowds? Or was it something simpler, something baser?

"It must be the money," she declared, drawing the tines of her fork through the yolky morass on her plate.

"Hmm?"

"Hm? Oh!" She speared a final shred of egg-soaked bread into her mouth, pushed her plate away, and stood. Bou Bou gave a yap of perturbation at the sudden movement. "Never mind," she said through her mouthful of breakfast. "Much obliged to you for the company but I must be off."

Clarissa raised her eyebrows, more in amusement than irritation perhaps. "Another mission? It is possible for one's mind to be *too* active, you know, Miss Lovelock."

"Nonsense." Avis grinned. Was there spinach between her teeth? She half hoped there was; that would be ghastly. "If ever you see me at leisure, just put me in a box and bury me. Adieu."

AVIS HAD BEEN told on multiple occasions that she was a formidable figure. Normally she assumed this was just a thinly veiled way of deriding the volume at which she spoke, but watching the sauntering hoi polloi scatter before her as she strode down the corridors, she considered that they might have had a point. Still, it suited her not to have to weave and dodge, and she certainly didn't think she could stomach any small talk getting in the way of her current objective: namely, to corner Carlton Brooksbank and make him tell her everything about everyone on this bloody boat.

It was a large vessel, but had only so many places to socialise, and so it was not long before she found Brooksbank up on the top deck, clad top to toe in cream linens and deeply engrossed in a game of shuffleboard with a diminutive walnut of a man who looked like he had probably seen the start of the century and was damned if he wouldn't see it out at the other end. Brooksbank was letting the old man win; the old man knew it and didn't care.

"Gainfully employed, I see."

Brooksbank lit up as Avis approached, provoking a cackle from his wizened companion. "This'll be the remarkable Miss Lovelock," he divined, and Brooksbank rushed to introduce them.

"Miss Lovelock, please allow me to introduce you to Mr Harlan Sheridan King. Mr King is one of the owners of *Excambion*, and several other ships beside."

Mr King favoured Avis with a pipe-brown grin and pumped her hand up and down like it was a fireside bellows. "A pleasure," he said. "A delight. Miss Lovelock, I can't thank you enough for agreeing to come on this trip. We're really very obliged."

"Yes, as you should be. Seeing how grand everything is makes me realise my fee should be at least twice as high—you can clearly afford it." Twice zero was still zero, but she doubted he knew of her generous offer to work for free.

The old man barked a laugh, clearly unoffended by her candour. "You'll have only seen the residential areas. The truly impressive views are all in engineering. As a matter of fact... She really ought to see it, oughtn't she, Carrie?"

"Oh, most certainly. Miss Lovelock is absolutely fascinated by naval architecture, she was telling me earlier."

"Well, that settles it! A tour it is."

The last thing Avis wanted to do was climb more stairs and look at more pipes, but if she was going to investigate the hauntings then she was going to have to get familiar with the workings of the ship. And besides, it would give her a chance to observe King and divine his angle; there was more to this story than Brooksbank was telling her, she was sure. "How generous, *Carrie*," she muttered, shooting a glance at her liaison, who looked infuriatingly amused.

"It's the least I can do after you agreed to help with our

little problem." King abandoned his shuffleboard cue against a pillar, re-arming himself with a silver-topped cane which he used to beckon her towards the stairs. "Come, this way! We'll start in the bowels."

Brooksbank fell into step with Avis as Mr Harlan Sheridan King puffed on ahead like a particularly determined tugboat. Now that they were side by side, Brooksbank's grin had faded. Perhaps he sensed that this was not to be a light-hearted jaunt through the corridors of the ship.

"'Our little problem', eh?" she said. "He clearly doesn't think this is anything to be concerned about."

"Mr King takes a more… top-level approach to the goings-on aboard the ship."

"Meaning he doesn't deign to speak to the people who've reported these sightings."

"Something like that."

"Interesting," Avis said as they approached another stairwell, this one leading down to second class. "He goes down every set of steps backwards as if they're ladders. Even the normal stairs. Should I be doing that? Am I committing a faux pas every time I set foot on a staircase facing forwards?"

Brooksbank shrugged, managing to make the gesture look somehow graceful. "Sorry to disappoint, but there's no specific etiquette as far as I'm aware."

"Hm. And so it's *not* King who called for me to be brought on board?"

"Not directly, but he was all for it when I suggested it after the buyers got cold feet."

"I'm sure." Avis frowned. "I'm going to try it," she said.

"I'm sorry? Oh…" Brooksbank's brow unfurrowed as Avis grabbed the banister before them and turned to face him. "The stairs. I see."

They descended into a narrow utility corridor near the aft, all unadorned metal and bare walls and unwaxed floors. "This way!" King was calling, already halfway off towards the next set of stairs.

"Good Lord, he's indefatigable."

"He's very… spirited," Brooksbank muttered.

"I wouldn't worry," Avis said. "He's very deaf, only pretends to hear half of what you're saying even when he's lip-reading. So, these superstitious buyers—who are they?"

"I told you, I don't know," Brooksbank protested when Avis stopped and turned to stare at him. He held up his hands in a gesture of surrender, just as he had on that first night they met. She didn't fully believe him—though he perhaps wasn't certain, he had an inkling, she was sure of it—but for now she let it slide.

"And the investors want the sale completed as a matter of urgency?" He nodded, and Avis released a sigh that was possibly disproportionate to her irritation. Why the rush to sell the ship? Why *now*? Before she could say anything more, the shiny pate of Mr Harlan Sheridan King appeared around the corner, his expression expectant.

"Well? This wasn't just an excuse for the two of you to canoodle in my corridors, was it?"

"Certainly not," Brooksbank said, his protestation colliding with Avis's. "Well, you've caught us now." Brooksbank shot her a bewildered look, but King just cackled again and gestured them onward. She waited until they had fallen into step behind him to continue her interrogation.

"Have you had the police aboard?"

"The police? What for? There's been no crime, as far as I'm aware."

Avis frowned, disappointed by his lack of imagination. "Fraud is a crime."

"You think the sailors, who would rather quit their jobs than stay aboard, were committing fraud?"

"I think it's very likely *someone* is. I just need to figure out who. Perhaps it's them."

"Who?" Brooksbank asked, though it was clear from his resigned expression he already knew the workings of her lockjaw mind.

"The twins!" she said, with an irritated flap of her hands. "What better way to make a name for themselves than introducing the world to a haunted ship? It's certainly never been done before to my knowledge. You must almost give them credit for the creativity."

"I'm afraid there are a few problems with your theory. As I said last night, they boarded in Cherbourg, at my invitation—long after the hauntings had started."

"So-called hauntings. And they could have had an accomplice—someone who set things up ahead of their arrival."

"You really think they'd go to all that trouble?"

"My dear Brooksbank, you have no idea how elaborate these schemes can become."

"Mm. Then how come they've made no claim of the haunting themselves?"

This stymied her for a moment—it was odd that they weren't whipping the passengers into a frenzy and presenting themselves as the only solution—but then it came to her. "They're waiting for the crossing. A captive audience, as it were. Just you wait. Now that we're properly underway they'll suddenly pick up messages from the spirits, and they'll probably demand money for the act of 'calming' them."

"I suppose time will tell," Brooksbank said, his expression distinctly dubious.

Their surroundings were getting warmer and louder. Avis's attention was drawn from Brooksbank and his consternation back to King, who gestured at them to follow him through a wide, robust doorway.

It was the engine room, obviously, and it was extremely noisy. Everything was metal and grease, with pistons and pumps moving steadily up and down, or back and forth, without end. Everywhere she looked there were brass-ringed dials full of numbers and pipes—so many pipes. There were a handful of men monitoring the equipment, though fewer crew than they'd seen elsewhere. King stumped to the middle of the room and then turned, grinning widely at her. "Quite a marvel, isn't she?"

Avis grinned in return, and turned back to Brooksbank, raising her voice to be heard over the engine noise. "So they're here on your invitation, and their passage *isn't* being bankrolled by the French widow."

Brooksbank blinked. "You're obsessed," he said.

"I'm focused. There's a difference."

"Yes, yes, two furnaces per boiler, hand-stoked. Would you like to see them?" King shouted.

"If she's not paying their way, why is she here?" Avis asked.

"Surely! This way!"

Brooksbank shot Avis a warning stare before smiling and nodding at the oblivious King, ushering Avis to walk in front of him along the metal walkway, reaching to steady her elbow as an excuse to lean close in behind her to speak in her ear. "How the devil would I know? I suppose she's genuinely attached to them."

Avis frowned. "There must be a longer-term strategy here."

"I can't hear you."

She turned and shouted, "What's the long game?"

"Yes, all single-ended Scotch boilers!" King replied.

She caught the roll of Brooksbank's eyes before turning back to pick her way across the walkway. He pitched his voice to be heard over the racket. "You'll be shocked to know I didn't perform probing interrogations on any of them before they were invited aboard. Their intentions are known only to themselves."

"All right now, come on, keep up!"

Avis grimaced and followed after King, who moved with surprising alacrity, given the cane. Thankfully they emerged from the engine room into another, quieter section, most of which was taken up by two large, hammered-metal tanks.

"Fresh water," he told her with a sage nod. "Five hundred tonnes! Quite the irony, isn't it, that we should be surrounded on all sides and yet still need to carry our own with us?"

"Fascinating, really." Avis waited until he had started off again to speak to Brooksbank, now beside her. "So, to sum up: the only reports of any strangeness have come from the crew and the passengers in third class. The Duquesnes have made no claims as of yet and if—*if*—they aren't the cause of all this madness, then they have no idea it even exists."

"Unless they've found out on their own. Or the spirits—"

"Don't even say it," Avis said, holding up a hand. "Any esteem I hold for you will not withstand the blow you would strike should you finish that utterance."

Brooksbank shook his head, though she could tell by the dimpling in his cheek he was repressing a smile. "I certainly haven't told them a thing, as requested."

"Well, that's something. I do so like having the upper hand," she said, triumphant. "I suppose I should thank you for that at least."

"You can thank me by giving the ship a clean bill of health and waiting until we've disembarked to pursue whatever strange vendetta you have against the Duquesnes. Surely you can wait a few more days before ripping down the curtain."

"I'll consider it," Avis lied. "On one condition."

"Which is?"

"Tell me their cabin numbers."

"Absolutely not."

Avis cast her eyes to the ceiling. "Is there much more to this tour? I have investigations to be getting on with."

He sighed. "Go on, I'll make your excuses for you."

"Thank you, Carrie," Avis replied in a sing-song voice. "Tell the old man I think his bilges are simply divine."

"You don't know what bilges are, do you?"

"And with any luck, I never shall."

Six

Avis's current irritation was that she hadn't thought to interview the men who had departed at Portsmouth; she'd been confident that it would prove an easy feat to pin down the source of the "spirit activity" and unravel whatever mechanisms were behind it without consultation. What she hadn't counted on was the sheer size of the ship. Or how terrible her sense of direction was without the familiar landmarks and signposts of London to guide her.

Attempts to retrace her steps had been immediately abandoned; everything looked the same this far into the bowels of the ship. Left and right were equally plausible choices and so she threw her fate to the wind and began to meander randomly, trying to stay out of the way of the crew bustling here and there. The ones that took note of her presence issued challenges, but the application of Brooksbank's name was a panacea that smoothed the way considerably. The man seemed to know everyone.

With each interruption she asked after the departed crew, and whether anybody remaining had seen the so-called spirits on board the ship. Eventually she was pointed in the direction of the "Glory Hole", which she inferred to be the name for the quarters where the engineering crew lived and slept.

Apparently a greaser by the name of Mills had been one of a gang of men who'd encountered "something strange" a few days previous, and would be willing to talk, for a price.

The lowest decks of the ship smelled unlike anything Avis had ever encountered before: a mixture of hot metal, sweet oil, mildew, and the pong of sweat from dozens of men—for it was mostly men this far down, with only a few stewardesses to be seen. This part of the ship was, if anything, even more labyrinthine; each room she peered into was a maze of bunks stacked on top of and beside one another until there was barely enough room to turn around. Avis was used to close quarters, but she couldn't imagine living quite so intimately with a dozen other people, not to mention their associated smells and sounds.

A few more questions, a few more rooms, and at last she found Mills, who was hunched over a bowl of something brown in the staff canteen. He scowled at her to begin with but brightened up when he heard she was there for his recollections of the haunting.

"It was the eeriest thing. We was in the engine room, first thing in the morning. She was sluggish and we was trying to find the cause. All of a sudden Bowman shouts, and we all turn and look and there's these… shadows, floating around the ceiling." Mills waved his hands above his head in an enthusiastic—if not entirely descriptive—manner, spoon still gripped between his fingers. A glob of brown threatened flight. "People's shadows, like. But not ours, couldn't have been anything like that."

"You're sure about that." Avis raised her eyebrows; if she'd come all this way for some shadow-play on the ceiling… well, she'd hardly be cross since she'd had a free cruise out of it.

"Shadows is the wrong word. It was like smoke or something, all gathered up in the shape of people."

"And the smoke… people. They weren't doing anything? Not trying to communicate in any way?" The "spirits" were always desperate to communicate, in Avis's experience. How else would they convince their targets to fork over their life's savings to the sainted medium who spoke for them? If this was a hoax there had to be *some* angle the hoaxer was working, though right now that angle was as clear as mud.

He shook his head. "Nah. It was almost like they was sleeping or something."

"Is that it?" The man frowned, and Avis rose a hand. "Forgive me. What I mean to say is, as eerie as that sounds, I can't see any man leaving a paying job because he saw some strange figures." She narrowed her eyes. "There has to be more to it."

Mills glanced about them, his mouth flattening to a line. The mess was busy, but no one seemed to be listening in to their entente. "We all agreed not to say," he muttered eventually.

"Spit it out, man, this is important."

"It was…" He made a face, glanced around again. "It was just… frightening. Something about it made you feel like you couldn't breathe, like the air was bearing down on you. Robbie—he left in Portsmouth—he, um…" He leaned closer, lowered his voice. "He wet himself."

Avis congratulated herself on keeping a straight face; contrary to claims from those who knew her best, she was the very soul of discretion and decorum. "I see. That must have been a frightening sight indeed."

Mills nodded solemnly, settling back on his bench. "After that him and Walt wouldn't go back into the engine room, even after the foreman docked their wages. Can't do much greasing if you won't go in the engine room."

Whatever "greasing" entailed was immaterial to her questioning, though she couldn't deny she was curious. "And they departed at Portsmouth?"

"Not much reason to stick around, wouldn't you say?"

"No, indeed. Thank you, Mr Mills. This has been most enlightening."

He nodded, then extended his spoonless hand across the table. "The papers usually pay their sources, don't they?"

"I'm not a… Oh, bugger it, fine."

Figuring it was easier to shove a few coins in his palm than explain the entirety of her mission, Avis soon left the mess, her pocketbook lighter by half and her questions more than doubled. The engine room was a maze of machinery and scaffolds, not to mention constantly occupied by half a dozen crew. Anyone looking to set up a trick would have little opportunity to do so unobserved, and it was hardly a steady, controlled environment. Whoever was behind this was skilled, she admitted grudgingly. Did the Duquesnes possess the knowledge and resources to pull off a deception like this, especially prior to boarding? It was looking less and less likely, unless they were in league with yet more Spiritualist fiends. She imagined the ship crawling with such pests; she shuddered, half in delicious anticipation.

More confident of her route this time, Avis left the crew's quarters and made her way back in the direction of the central engineering deck where she was relatively certain she'd find the stairwell back to the various passenger levels. With each step the walls closed around her, half comforting, half claustrophobic. Beyond the ever-present thrum of the engines there sounded the occasional shout of one crewman to another, the groan of metal shifting under stress. She imagined she could hear the beat of the waves against the ship's skin but it was only that, imagination, for she was nestled deep in the belly of an enormous beast, surrounded on every side by growling, churning metal.

As she neared the central corridor her steps slowed, a cold tide sweeping through her. Something pricked her attention, like the flicker of candlelight across a thread anchored to a medium's sleeve, drawing her eye to one of a half-dozen doors set along this section of the passage. There was absolutely nothing notable about it, save for the urge she felt to approach it; had King mentioned it in his tour, perhaps, and the half-heard remembrance drew her there? Never one to ignore her instincts, Avis indulged them now, glancing quickly over her shoulder before depressing the lever and slipping inside.

The room was dim, lit only by the light in the corridor filtering through the porthole window. The temperature dropped yet further, and it took Avis a moment to realise this was no foreboding chill; the room was physically cold. Vaguely she *did* remember King's monologue as he had swept past this area—something about a series of brine refrigeration conduits that fed upward to the storerooms on the passenger decks. It seemed despite their best efforts at insulation there was a certain amount of residual cold. She hooked her hands in the fabric of her sleeves, arms crossed over her middle. It did nothing to warm her.

The room was empty save for a low shape against the wall; if this was a storage room, it was extremely under-utilised. Avis stepped closer, squinting to try and make out the details of the oddly shaped thing—trunk or crate, she couldn't quite tell.

Can't you? It's a coffin.

Normally she knew to expect Patience's presence by the advent of goose pimples across her arms and neck, but the chill of the room had brought them out as soon as she'd stepped inside. She didn't flinch, just, but gripped herself tighter all the same. The shape resolved into a shadowed box, exactly the length and width of a body. Avis's stomach clenched.

"Of course it is. A room kept cold by the running of conduits nearby—the perfect place to keep a body on a transatlantic crossing. This must be the Duquesnes' dearly departed uncle… Weymon, Leland…"

Waylan.

"Yes, I'm aware. What an odd name." She knew the Duquesne twins were from a Southern state—Louisiana or Georgia, perhaps. They'd been orphaned young and taken under the wing of Uncle Waylan, who'd quickly put them to work, touting their "gift". People ate up the story: precocious children, tragically bereaved, that magical twin connection. All the pieces fit perfectly. They'd spent a few years in America touring society homes before striking out for the Continent, clearly looking for richer targets and more lucrative opportunities. They'd never performed publicly, however, and Waylan Duquesne had done an extremely thorough job ensuring only the vaguest rumours escaped from their sittings, leaving them shrouded in mystery and ever more sought-after.

And now he's dead, and they're returning home. What will they do without his guidance, I wonder?

"Nothing, if I have my way." With any luck they'd arrive into New York having been thoroughly debunked and unmasked as the charlatans they were.

Stripping them of their livelihood in the moment of their deepest grief. Ah, Avis, you always were a tender heart.

Patience loomed out of the darkness and Avis shrank away, telling herself it was only the bitter cold and the unexpected coffin that had her trembling. "They have no care for the grieving; why should I?"

An eye for an eye, is it? Certainly you seem to be stumbling around blind. You have no idea what this haunting is about, the Duquesnes have the rich biddies wrapped around their fingers, and time is ticking down. Seems more likely our arrival in New York will herald your humiliation, not theirs.

She would not let that happen. Her own triumph would be sweet, but sweeter still would be ridding the world of the Duquesnes and their parasitic ruse.

Seven

Brooksbank had taken the liberty of seating himself with the party, along with several choice characters including the sisters Sarah and Clarissa (whose surnames she now knew to be Fenwick and Melbourne respectively), the Armitages, and Dr Usher, who practically elbowed Brooksbank out of the way to pull back her chair for her to sit.

"Can't tell you how delighted I am by my table this evening," he said as he settled down beside her (Brooksbank had clearly decided that seating her *next* to the twins would be a step too far). "Just the fresh blood we need," he added, leaning to mutter in her ear. He was an alcoholic: his nose was ruddy and his breath already reeked of whiskey, a hip flask weighing down his jacket on his off side (the right—he was also left-handed). She had noticed a pronounced limp on their first meeting, which judging from his bearing he had probably received in battle. Perhaps drinking was how he dealt with the pain, whether from his gammy leg or the memories that came with it.

The Duquesnes were the last to arrive—along with Madame Berthault, of course—the trio sweeping in ladies first, Gideon stalking in the rear. Berthault was magnificent, now that Avis had a proper look: taller than the already tall twins and positively Rubenesque, her lace-adorned mourning gown accentuating her generous figure. The contrast with her companions made the spindly twins appear all the more insubstantial, wraiths floating in her wake. It was comic, and she snorted in amusement. Just like the previous night, Rachel's eyes snapped straight to hers.

In spite of herself, Avis's breath hitched. It was an effective trick—even more so today for the medium's veil was lifted away from her face this evening, no barrier but the air between them as their gazes locked.

Introductions were being made but Avis only nodded vaguely along, her whole attention focused on Rachel Duquesne as she drifted into her waiting seat, held by Brooksbank. Everything about the woman was delicate—the lace pointing on her collar, the circumference of her ivory wrists—but there was something in the way she moved that set Avis's mind at odds with itself, not unlike the feeling she got when looking straight at Patience. It was as if she was seeing double, the figures overlaid atop each other: one pale and gauzy and indistinct, the other solid and near vibrating with energy.

Then she blinked, and the figures melted together until it was just one slim woman sheathed in black, who gave Avis a final hard stare before turning away. The sound of conversation rushed in like waves on the shore.

"… can't believe this is your first time crossing to America!"

"Oh, but with the Continent so close there's never been any need," Mrs Armitage was saying. "No offence intended, of course," she rushed to say, smiling ingratiatingly at the twins. "I'm sure there's a great deal to do there. It's just, you know, so *far*."

"No offence has been taken," came the reply from Gideon. "My sister and I have spent our fair share of time on the Continent ourselves and can speak to its charms firsthand."

"Are England and America so different in any case?" Charlotte Berthault interjected now, and Avis grinned in anticipation as the Armitages visibly bristled.

Rachel leaned slightly in toward Berthault, who sat between the twins, and murmured in French. Avis didn't catch all of it, but she did hear the end—"les Écossais". Quite.

Brooksbank cleared his throat. "I had the good fortune to visit Glasgow during this trip," he directed to Mrs Armitage. "It actually reminded me a lot of New York—smaller, but every bit as beautiful. I'm sure you'll love it there."

Avis's eyes darted back and forth as the exchange took place, filing every gesture, every reaction away, adding it to her mental casebook for each of the diners. Mrs Armitage was quick to take umbrage to anything and everything. Berthault was singularly unflappable, unbothered by the offence she had caused in a manner that struck her as peculiarly French, and yet the way in which she had simply listened and nodded at Rachel's correction spoke to something more, a measure of dispassion, detachment from the moment at hand. Still grieving, then. Brooksbank was a peacekeeper of the highest order, and a talented one at that. She would have to shake him off if she was to have *any* fun.

And as for Rachel Duquesne… she was too clever by half. When Avis glanced back in her direction, Duquesne was once again watching her. Her face was impassive, but her eyes sparked with interest. Avis had been caught mid-analysis.

Well. Good. Let her watch. Avis would unravel her lies all the same.

"What about you, Miss Lovelock? Have you ever ventured Stateside before?"

Avis glanced over at Mrs Fenwick, giving a short, sharp shake of her head. "Never had the pleasure. I'm afraid that, popular though my act may be, my music hall wages don't stretch to steamships, even if I were to descend a few floors to where all the unfortunates who can't afford windows are penned."

"And yet you are here now," Madame Berthault observed. There was no censure in her voice, but Avis could see some of her tablemates shift uncomfortably at the implied question.

“Indeed.” Avis grinned and reached for her champagne. “Your powers of observation are unmatched, madame. What shall you treat us to next, a recitation of tonight’s menu?”

“A little respect, if you please.” For a moment Avis thought it was Gideon speaking again, but no, the rebuke came from Rachel, seated on the widow’s other side. “She is in mourning. Your rudeness has no place here.”

Avis opened her mouth to observe that bereavement did not render a woman incapable of defending herself, but Brooksbank cleared his throat loudly before she got the chance.

“Oh, don’t mind Miss Lovelock,” he said, “she’s just hungry. Ah, and here comes our first course—not before time, eh, Avis?” He smiled across at her without a scrap of reprimand or warning behind his eyes and somehow that was *more* irritating. Yes, Avis would definitely have to get Carlton Brooksbank out of the way if she was going to dismantle this charade, no doubt about it. The man was a damned saint.

Food was a welcome arrival, not least because for once Avis didn’t feel the desire to hold forth and captivate her audience. Most of them would be easily impressed, of course, by her observations and witticisms, but every time Rachel’s gaze fell on her she felt a shiver of *something* run down her back. It was like being seated across the table from a cobra, and an ill-tempered one at that.

The meal was elaborate, heavy on cream sauces and meats. Larded fillets of hare, saddle of mutton, cauliflower and French beans, calf’s head, and stuffed young chickens were all brought to their table, and the room was full of murmured exclamations and the *tink* of cutlery on china. Avis couldn’t help paying at least as much attention to her companions’ plates as her own, and so it was that she quickly noted how little both Gideon and Rachel appeared to consume of the indulgent meal. It struck her as strange; surely if they had spent the last however long in France, they would be used to sweetmeats and cream? But they were both of them intent on cutting their food into smaller and smaller pieces and pushing them around the plate instead of actually eating.

Berthault remarked on it too. Though she pretended not to notice, her eyes kept straying to Gideon's plate as he ate, with a twist of well-worn concern to her full lips. This apparent lack of appetite was usual, then, and their current patron did not like it.

Eventually the mains were cleared away, and starched waiters brought the final course: toasted Bakewell tarts with fruit sauce, creamy Charlotte Russe cakes, and dishes of delicate orange-flavoured ice cream. As expected, the twins shook their heads at everything but the frozen dessert.

Avis dug into her tart with gusto, though she kept a weather eye on the Duquesnes, learning their mannerisms, their ticks.

"Now, I've been meaning to ask the captain but perhaps one of you will know: this course won't be taking us anywhere near the hostilities, will it?" Mrs Armitage asked, her fork poised above her plate. "With all the sabre-rattling the Spanish and Americans are doing, I fear no one in those waters will be safe." Rachel Duquesne paused in her cursory investigation of her ice cream; she did not lift her head, but it was clear from her stillness that she was listening closely.

"We'll be quite a bit further north than all that," Brooksbank replied. "Much closer to Canada than the Caribbean, so I hope you've all brought your overcoats."

"Oh, I expect we shall just stay below deck while we're in the far north, won't we, Clarissa?" Mrs Fenwick had cheerfully declared she would try one of each dessert, and Avis had warmed to her considerably as a result.

Her sister nodded, pausing between bites of her own cake. "Plenty to keep us entertained indoors, I'm sure. Speaking of which, when will you be gracing us with a performance, Miss Lovelock? I'd so love to see one before we part ways."

"Was yesterday's impromptu stunt not quite enough?" Avis asked. "It was even personalised."

"Perhaps Miss Lovelock's shows cannot be mounted without

preparation." Rachel had already "finished" her ice cream—the nearly full portion was pushed aside. The medium's implication was clear, and Avis schooled her features into impassivity.

"I assure you," she said, "I need nothing more to practise my art than my own two eyes and a clear mind. But I have not been employed to perform."

"Why, then? By your own admission you have not the means to be sitting here. Presumably your presence is meant to serve *some* purpose."

"Miss Lovelock is my guest," Brooksbank piped up then. "I thought New York deserved to see her."

"New York. Mm." Rachel's shapely lips lifted into a mirthless smile. "Yes, I'd say New York and Miss Avis Lovelock deserve one another, indeed." The insult was clear.

"*Now* who's being rude?" Avis said, and her tone was all the tighter for the flush she could feel creeping up her cheeks. "Are you in mourning too? Excuse me, but your behaviour is most unusual for someone in the depths of grief."

Now that's a question indeed.

Avis flinched as Patience's voice sounded in her ear; a miniscule reaction, but she could feel Rachel's scrutiny fasten on her like a leech to a vein. "I would have expected the spirits to tell you about such matters," Avis ground out. "That is, if they truly existed. So I suppose it's no surprise you're in the dark."

Rachel wore a rather handsome stick pin through her lapel, whorls of gold wrapped around a large emerald. She reached up to touch it meditatively. "Darkness is my burden to bear, Miss Lovelock. What's yours?"

Avis smiled thinly. For this, at least, she had an answer. "That of illumination," she said simply. "Even when it causes pain."

Into the silence that followed, Dr Usher injected a lubricated harrumph. "Well, now," he said. "This has been most entertaining. Who's joining me for a brandy and a cigar, hm? Brooksbank? Armitage? Fenwick?"

Sarah's husband was so shocked that anybody had even remembered he was at the table that he gave a start.

Brandy sounded very welcome right about now, but Avis knew that brazening her way into the gentlemen's lounge so early in the trip risked earning her an ostracisation that her behaviour had thus far skirted. "Quite right," she said briskly, dropping her napkin on her sauce-strewn plate. "Let's away with us to the ladies' saloon, shall we?" At the very least there would be sherry.

"Oh, but there is to be another séance," said Mrs Armitage.

"Delightful." Avis was unsurprised; they had a willing, captive audience. Only idiots would pass up the opportunity to milk them for all they were worth. She smiled widely. "Let's all do that, then."

Gideon bristled. "I don't think—" But Rachel reached past Berthault to rest a hand over her brother's.

"It's all right, Gideon," she said. "Why shouldn't Miss Lovelock join us? Her presence did not disrupt the spirits last night, after all. As long as you don't mind, Charlotte?"

The widow, nonplussed, tipped her head in bemused assent. Gideon still did not look happy, but clearly he had been overruled. With a few final swigs of their drinks, the group peeled away from the table, and Avis followed, swallowing down a satisfied smile.

Eight

THE SALOON WAS set up much as before—the screens, the table, the candle at its centre. Avis swept her eyes over the scene, looking for the obvious tells of tampering, but could not see anything apparent. The twins were already seated, though in a different arrangement to the night before: Rachel was in her previous spot and now Gideon sat across from her, where Avis had been.

She smirked at this; clearly they were planning something, then. And she was ready for them.

"Please, be seated," Gideon said, turning as the group filed in. The widow Berthault sat next to Rachel, of course, and Mrs Armitage next to her. Clarissa and Sarah had excused themselves from the evening's proceedings and were replaced by several guests gathered during the Spiritualists' procession through the ship. It was altogether more crowded than the previous evening, which made Avis's job trickier. The best magicians and mediums were masters of misdirection, and with so many people to play off of, there would be plenty of that tonight. That said, the extra bodies milling to be seated did have one advantage: when Avis slipped into a chair on the other side of Rachel Duquesne tonight, the rest of the seats were already taken, and to move her Rachel would have had to make a proper fuss.

Tonight there was a bell added to the accoutrements on the table. The candle was already lit, the lamps already out. Avis squinted at the bell, trying to discern in the darkness whether it had a string attached.

Again, it was Gideon who did the opening spiel, reminding them not to speak, inviting them to link hands. Duquesne's hand was cool and dry in hers, her fingers lean but her grip firm.

Avis felt a frisson of anticipation; this was the part she liked best. All the potential stretched out in front of her, with the satisfaction of a solution close at hand.

Rachel's fingers tightened around hers, and suddenly it was hard to keep her attention on the table, the guests, and everything else.

"Ma chère?" came the opening gambit. "Are you there?"

Berthault shifted eagerly, turning towards the medium. "Bien sûr, I am here. Speak to me, Henri."

Rachel opened her mouth to speak, but before the words could come she doubled over, coughing. Berthault gasped.

"Be still," Gideon said. "Lend her your strength. For the spirit to reach us, to breach this plane, it must draw upon my sister's essence."

Rachel began to twist back and forth, the chair beneath her creaking with the strain as her whole body warped and contorted. The warm weight of Rachel's leg shifted to press against the length of Avis's, from thigh to ankle, resting there like a counterweight as her upper body leaned in the opposite direction, and with a low groan she buried her face in the crook of Berthault's neck.

The Frenchwoman gasped. Rachel's grip shifted, turning Avis's hand palm up and weaving their fingers together, trapping her hand against the table. She was trembling. Gideon gave a strangled cry, tipping his head back, the whites of his eyes gleaming in the candlelight. He too, was gripping the hands to either side of him, lifting them off the surface of the table, writhing and shaking as though caught in a fit.

Avis could hear Rachel murmuring, but couldn't make out a word, either in French or English. What she *did* notice was the table begin to shift, rocking back and forth.

"Oh, for *heaven's* sake—" she began, but Mrs Armitage hushed her.

"*The spirits!*" she hissed, and before Avis could speak further the table lifted clean off the floor, rising and banging back down repeatedly.

There was a collective gasp from the assembly, but not merely—she realised a second later—at the rather violently levitating table: beside her, Berthault and Rachel had locked lips in a deep, passionate kiss. The table continued to buck beneath their linked hands, Avis's own still pinned to its surface beneath Rachel's iron grip. The little bell in the centre overturned with a shrill tinkle, adding its voice to the clattering of the table as it rolled back and forth.

Berthault gave a strangled moan, and broke contact with Mrs Armitage to grope desperately for Rachel, cupping her face, and the table dropped immediately to the floor with a deafening thump. Gideon slumped forward, suddenly limp, and Rachel released Avis's hand to reach for the widow, extricating herself gently from their embrace. "Charlotte, please…"

"Henri! Reviens à moi. *S'il te plaît!*" Rachel patted the Frenchwoman's cheek, murmuring quietly as Berthault began to weep. Avis had to look away; sham though the séance might have been, Berthault's reaction was all too real.

Slowly Gideon "came round", giving a groan and pressing back from the table. "Are you all unharmed?" he asked, and received a flurry of responses.

"I've never seen anything like it!"

"Good Lord, why are you asking about us, man? Are *you* all right?"

"That was quite taxing," Gideon admitted, his pale face drained of all blood. He looked like a waxwork come to life, a marble statue who had gained the power of speech. "But all will be well, with some rest…"

That was enough to rouse Avis's ire; the whole performance had been a farce, of course, and while pulling back the curtain on "Henri" was not what she was here for, she'd happily do it *gratis* just to put these charlatans properly in their place. She was about to stand and begin her oration when something stopped her: a flicker passing across Rachel's face, like she'd heard something discordant from another room. The other woman's eyes slid from hers, darting first over her shoulder, then searching the room almost frantically. Avis felt a prickle of apprehension at how quickly Rachel's expression had shifted, how hunted she suddenly looked. If it was a performance—which of course it was—it was a very good one.

"I think that's certainly enough for tonight," Gideon was saying as he came to stand at his sister's side, all assumed authority and well-practised charm. "We should retire now. Connecting with the spirits is no easy work."

Rachel didn't seem to hear him, her attention entirely elsewhere. Gideon frowned and reached out to place a hand on her shoulder, causing her to startle at the touch. Her eyes flicked up to his face. "There's something here," she said, hoarse voice rasping over the words. "Gideon, I can feel—"

"You're tired," he said loudly, and Avis could tell by the rigidity with which they both held themselves he had tightened his grip on Rachel's shoulder. Avis frowned; was this not the perfect opportunity to announce to their hangers-on they had sensed another presence? To spin them into a froth that would spill over to the rest of the ship in no time at all? "You need to rest, dear sister."

"If I could have but a moment…" But Rachel clearly knew her protests were useless, and she trailed off into silence. Avis watched, frowning, as Gideon ushered her from the room, his firm grip brooking no resistance. Once they were properly departed, she was on her feet immediately, bending to delve beneath the black cloth that draped the table. There were no wires, no strings, but then, she hadn't expected there to be—the movements were far too violent for that. They had clearly just jostled the table with their feet, letting the high emotion of the performance amplify what everyone had felt. And yet, as Avis pulled herself to her own feet she felt the solidity of the table and frowned. Most tables used for séances were small and relatively light, but this one was heavy, as befitted the furnishings aboard a ship.

Grasping the edge in both hands, she pushed against it. It did not shift.

Frowning, she braced herself and lifted again, managing to hoist it slightly and skid it across the rug a mere few centimetres. It thumped back down definitively, and Avis frowned. If that was all she was able to do with her two hands… how had the waifish Duquesne twins managed to lift it clean from the floor without either of theirs? It didn't add up.

None of it did.

Nine

"You should *see* the elaborate setups I've uncovered. Trapdoors and pulleys and puppets and props—most of them so obvious once you shine a light on them, whether figuratively or literally—but people get carried along because they *want* to believe, you see, and so..." Avis broke off her well-worn tirade with a disgusted sigh and threw herself bodily into one of the club chairs scattered about the smoking room. Only Brooksbank and Usher had remained by the time she arrived in the ostensibly gentlemen-only space, and neither had either the inclination or the courage to eject her.

"But this..." She shook her head, reaching for the freshly poured brandy in Brooksbank's hand. It was his brandy. He relinquished it without a word and went to fetch another. "The candle trick was simple enough—there are any number of ways of doing that. And the rest... was pure theatre. The tension. The performance. The *story*..." Avis cast a despairing look up at her drinking companions. "They're clearly well-practised at this, and they have a pet widow to boot. How do I debunk when there's nothing *to* debunk?"

Brooksbank shrugged. "Maybe you don't?"

Avis met his gaze with a scowl. "Very funny."

"What would happen if you were to challenge them? It's

their word against yours, yes?" Usher looked clearer-eyed than Brooksbank at this late hour, and almost animated by the puzzle Avis had put before them.

She knew Brooksbank would have her drop the matter, but somehow it was all the more important to discredit the Duquesnes, preferably before they could insert themselves in the so-called ship haunting. "I suppose. Except that they have the fact everybody wants to believe them on their side."

"Mm, but you have the truth on yours. In the absence of anything truly unexplainable happening at these sittings, might you not put on the pressure for them to be more… demonstrative?"

"Oh, hm. Goad them into attempting something I *can* disprove." Avis tocked her tongue in thought. "Perhaps. That woman is made of iron, but the brother… He might waver, if he felt threatened. It's worth a shot."

"Why not leave them be?" Brooksbank tried again, his tone as tired as the rest of him. He had returned his fresh brandy to the trolley, untouched. "They're not hurting anybody even if they are lying."

"Spiritualist frauds are parasites who prey on the lost and the grieving," Avis hissed, suddenly incensed. "And if you're going to make excuses for them then this working relationship will be very short indeed."

"That's not what I…" The tall man sighed. "I'm bone-tired. I'm going to bed. Don't get caught in here."

Usher watched him leave, then rose and went to top up his glass with the contents of the abandoned one on the trolley. "Interesting character, that. You onto a promise there?"

"Hm?" Avis blinked. "Oh *God*, no."

"Does he know that?"

"Yes. I think so. No, I'm certain. He's too comfortable by half."

"Not all the time. I'm sure you of all people noticed the little flinch he gave at dinner when he was asked about the fighting down in Cuba."

Avis frowned. She hadn't. Her attention was elsewhere.

"Shut up. Sorry, not you, I—"

Usher chuckled, waving away the apology. "Oh, not to worry. I've had worse for less. It's none of my concern what a man and woman get up to on a transatlantic cruise. As you were."

She thought about protesting again, but repeated insistence that something didn't exist often strengthened belief further. Instead she just smiled and took a sip of her brandy before redirecting the conversation. "So you think this business in the Caribbean is something we ought to be worried about, then?"

"I think people with power will go to great lengths to keep that power," he observed with a shrug. "The Spanish have enjoyed playing king with their colonies for centuries. So no, I can't see them happily handing over the reins without a fight. And the Americans, well, they can sense weakness; this seems like as good an excuse as any to roll out the troops." His voice was loose and whiskey-tinged, but there was a tension to it and his shoulders that no amount of shrugging would shake off.

"You know your military strategy, I see. Is that because you served yourself?"

"I did," he said, inclining his head. "A long time past. I've been in private practice for nigh on twenty years."

He was trying to redirect as well. An interesting tactic, though not one Avis was likely to fall for. "Mm. And were you a doctor in the Army as well?"

"Doctor's a generous word for it—half the time you're a butcher, sawing off limbs, swimming in blood." He recounted it matter-of-factly, but she could tell there was a simmering discomfort beneath that she couldn't help but poke.

"So, private practice for twenty years, that would mean you saw the Civil War?" she hazarded, having made a quick calculation using the sprinkling of silver in his sideburns as a guide.

"Nothing civil about it. I saw brother marching against

brother, bayonets through eye sockets, all over a question that shouldn't even need to be asked. Sorry, sorry," Usher said, making a face. "This isn't really the sort of conversation a young lady like yourself should be subjected to."

"There aren't many 'young ladies' much like myself," Avis quipped. Was he truly concerned about propriety, or did he have a deeper-seated objection to rehashing his past? Either way, she would let it lie—for now. "It's fine, I'm not the squeamish sort."

He seemed to relax a little, quaffing half his brandy in one swig. "I suppose you wouldn't be in your line of work. Morbid stuff, that."

"Oh, because of all the death and so-called spirits? It's not real. Well, the death is. The rest of it…" She waved a dismissive hand.

Usher gave a quiet huff: amusement, not disbelief. "So I've heard. Must've been some shock seeing those twins show up. 'I met a seer, Passing the hues and objects of the world,'" he quoted, clearly enjoying the chance to show off. Avis could understand that. "'The fields of art and learning, pleasure, sense, To glean eidólons.'"

"Hm. *Leaves of Grass*," she said, sipping her brandy. "Not bad. And hopefully not as much of a shock as *me* showing up for them."

Usher grinned approvingly. "I have no doubt they'll rue the day they stepped foot on board."

"If I do my job right, certainly."

Usher was right: she needed to stop the Duquesnes from running this show, from setting the rules of engagement. Perhaps there were no physical strings hidden under cuffs or tied around bells, but there were strings all the same, of a different sort—of trust, affection, emotion. One way or another she would get hold of them, and she would tug them 'til they broke.

* * *

THE GOOD DOCTOR made a cursory insistence on escorting Avis back to her room, but she waved him off and he was happy to let her go her own way. She so appreciated manners when they didn't come hand in hand with a strict adherence to the rules.

The ship was quiet at this time of night; Avis didn't see anyone as she navigated her way from the smoking lounge save for one solitary crewman, who gave her a short nod but otherwise let her be. What a strange life it must be, serving on board a ship. Unmoored from dry land, marooned among an ever-changing sea of faces. And while the passengers could hole up in their cabins come a squall, the staff had no such refuge. It must be a hard life, and lonely.

You're one to speak. Did you even have anyone to inform of your departure?

Avis disregarded the question; Patience only meant to needle her, and she was too distracted to rise to the bait.

She had committed a vague map of the ship's layout to memory, though in truth most of her navigation thus far had been following Brooksbank around. The carpet was the same pattern as the lounges and dining area, a busy mishmash of shapes and rich colours that shifted and warped beneath her feet the longer she looked at it. How much had she drunk? There had been the champagne at dinner, a fortifying sherry after the séance, and then a brandy or two in the lounge… or was it three? At any rate, she was a seasoned enough drinker that it shouldn't have affected her ability to find her cabin, but as she turned down yet another wood-clad, bronze-edged corridor she had to admit she was perhaps a little turned around.

She knew her cabin was towards the back—the aft—of the ship, but which way was the aft? She had emerged from the lounge, which was around the midline, and turned right—and yet now she felt the room numbers were going the wrong way. She reached out to put a hand against the wall to steady herself; was it the brandy or was the ship rocking harder now, the floor dipping and rising like a restless mount? She felt her stomach start to pitch as well and steeled herself against the sensation.

"Bloody boat," she grunted, pushing away from the wall and setting off once again. She reached a crossroads and turned determinedly, stalking down the hallway and watching as the gold plaques on the doors counted down. That was correct, wasn't it? She was relatively sure that was correct.

She had been walking for a minute or two before she realised that the rocking had calmed. Each step grew easier, as if she was heading downhill, gravity itself aiding her return. Was the ship listing? Someone would have noticed if the ship was listing, surely. There would be alarms, or crew rushing about, or something.

It was strange, but she was cocooned in the warmth of the brandy and the tangle of a good puzzle, and it wasn't until the water was pooling about her ankles that she thought to worry. She wasn't sure when it had seeped in, but here it was, ice-cold and rising to her calves as she continued to slosh forward down the corridor. The lamps flickered, as if they too felt the encroachment of the unwelcome sea. The room numbers were familiar now, which was reassuring, but she was concerned that the water had reached her knees, soaking into her skirts and making it difficult to move at pace.

And where was everyone? Why was there no shouting?

Avis reached her room at last and fumbled with the latch. Her fingers were clumsy and cold. At last the door opened and she waded in. A figure lay on her bed, sodden, stiff. Despite herself she cursed aloud and recoiled against the wall, hard enough to knock the back of her head. For a moment lights spun about her, a halo buzzing from the lamp by the bed. When she blinked it away, the figure was gone, collapsed into a pile of clothes hastily thrown from her carryall.

She looked down. There was no rising water lapping at her

thighs. Her skirts were dry, if tangled. The carpet was mosaic bright, plush and unsodden.

She let out a brittle laugh. “Only nerves,” she muttered, and waited for Patience’s mocking reply.

It never came.

Ten

"The *moment* they emerge from their coffins today I want to know about it, Carrie. I'm relying on you here."

The garden verandah was lovely. A promenade that stretched along one side of the dining hall, it was fully enclosed from the elements and filled with the greenery that gave it its name. Deckchairs and seats lined the polished wooden walkway, and Avis stood before one now, hands pasted on her hips.

She cleared her throat.

The figure in the deckchair did not move. Avis kicked it—the chair, not the figure, though it was a close-run thing. Brooksbank's hat fell off his face and he started awake with a strangled cry, his bloodshot eyes flying open.

"What? Who? What?" Recognition registered in his expression as he focused on Avis, and he slumped back with a melodramatic groan. "Why do you torment me?"

"Did you make it back to your cabin last night or did you sleep here?"

Brooksbank pushed into a sitting position, movements stiff and jerky like a shadow puppet's. "I woke at dawn sick as a dog and couldn't get back to sleep. Came up here for some fresh air." He wiped his hand across his face. "Usher is the devil."

"He's an alcoholic."

"Mm. And your excuse?"

"I'm a joyless spinster," she said. "Up, move. I know something you can drink."

"It's raw eggs, isn't it?"

"It's raw eggs."

Though the waiters *would* have been convinced to bring a brimming mug of raw egg, Avis's powers of persuasion were stymied by Brooksbank's charms. He argued her down to an omelette, with a strong cup of coffee and a flaky pastry, and she found she didn't feel like countermanding him, what with his wan smile and peaky complexion. She was growing soft.

"So when you woke this morning, was it because of the ship?"

He looked up from his coffee, which he held in both hands like a lifeline. "I'm sorry?"

"We hit some choppy waters, no? Felt like we listed very heavily at one point."

Brooksbank was nonplussed, shaking his head. "Not that I noticed. Perhaps I was unconscious at that point." He narrowed his eyes. "When was this? I can ask the first mate to check with the night watch."

"No," Avis said immediately. "Don't, it's fine." Suddenly she did not want to know how much of the previous night's experience had been real or imagined.

"If you're sure…"

"Yes, yes, it's fine. Now. Onto the real business of the day. The twins didn't mention the haunting last night. It was all 'Henri this' and 'Henri that'. They're playing the widow hard."

"Perhaps they've got nothing to do with it," Brooksbank said, and he looked grateful that he was out of kicking distance. "It was a pretty far-fetched theory to start with."

"Nonsense. If you'd seen some of the things these people get up to… I've discovered hidden doors to let in accomplices from another room, doctored tables, fake limbs… And there was the story of a Spiritualist in Hackney who took to stuffing their helpers up the chimney, just so they could listen in and send 'messages' to the willing dupes in the room."

"While I don't disbelieve you, it does seem like in this particular case you may be on the wrong trail. They can't benefit from the haunting if they don't reveal it, can they?"

Avis's frown deepened, and she shook her head until her hair came loose from its hastily scraped bun. "They were ramping up to it. At the end, Rachel started to put on the act—looking about the room, getting herself into a fluster." With a bit of distance and time it was much easier to view it dispassionately. Of course Rachel had been playing at her so-called discomfort; she was a talented fake who had duped hundreds. That Avis had been thrown by it was mildly embarrassing, but she oughtn't feel bad about a temporary wobble.

"And then?" Brooksbank interrupted her thoughts, expression expectant. She cursed him under her breath.

"Then nothing. Gideon forestalled any announcement and put an end to the séance then and there. Perhaps he was waiting for a bigger audience," she said, but even as she tried to imbue the theory with weight she knew it was flimsy at best.

"Hmm."

"Don't 'hmm' me. Just because I don't have the answer yet doesn't mean there isn't a very reasonable explanation for this nonsense. There always is." There had to be.

"I don't share your conviction, but I envy your confidence."

"At any rate, the cure is the same. They have power because people believe in what they do." She'd woken up early, plagued by the question of how to respond to this new kind of threat, the kind that could not be exposed by a bit of bright light and a pair of scissors. "If I can't debunk them through my usual channels then I'll just have to change my tactics. I need to do a show."

"I thought you didn't want to perform on the ship," he said, looking bemused. "You specifically said—"

"Forget what I said. New challenges require new strategies. If I can make it clear what they're doing, *how* they're doing it, then people will turn against them. Even if they do claim the haunting, no one will believe them."

Are you sure that's why? Or are you just jealous of the attention they're getting?

Patience was suddenly there behind Brooksbank's chair, her dark eyes gleaming at Avis from over his shoulder. Avis dropped her gaze to her plate, feeling clammy sweat spring up on her neck, her cheeks.

"… happy to arrange it," Brooksbank was saying, completely unaware of her sudden affliction. "If you think it will help."

"Do you have any better ideas?" she snapped, and he frowned, looking like a kicked puppy.

At least he's finally seeing your true colours. As will the rest of them when you stand up in front of them and claim that spirits aren't real. Avis Lovelock, liar and hypocrite.

She squeezed her eyes closed, sucking in a deep breath through her nostrils and nearly gagging at the smell of fat and eggs. "Apologies," she said as she opened them, mustering a smile. "I don't know if it will help, but it's the best I can do just now. I'll keep investigating, of course, but I need to nip this in the bud, before it causes *more* trouble. The last thing we need is the Duquesnes spreading rumours and causing panic, wouldn't you say?"

"Right now the only person spreading rumours aboard the ship is seated at this table," he pointed out, with a bit of his previous spirit.

Avis wagged a finger at him. "Just you wait. As soon as they find it suits their purposes they'll be circulating stories faster than the *Evening Mail*. Unless I can expose them for the frauds they are, they'll have the hoi polloi in an absolute state."

"Panic's rarely good for anyone, especially when you're confined to a ship," Brooksbank agreed.

Avis kept her eyes on him even as Patience faded, there one moment, gone the next. "Quite right. A little rational thinking will be just the thing, just you wait and see."

Her companion nodded, though he seemed less sure than he had a moment before. It seemed even Carlton Brooksbank's faith was finite.

"Oh, you, hello!" Determined to salvage things, Avis snagged the sleeve of a passing waiter and offered her most winning smile. With Patience's disappearance came a manic sort of energy bubbling through her, desperate for escape. "Two raw eggs, if you will. Out of the shell. In a mug. With Worcestershire sauce. For the gentleman here."

"At least if you kill me the Duquesnes will be here to listen to my laments," Brooksbank groaned.

"Mm. Oh, actually I've always wanted to do this with my friends but I don't have any: we must come up with a special codeword you'll say if you *do* die and come back to speak to me from the beyond. What would you like to use? How about 'portmanteau'? Or 'flabbergasted'?"

Her companion reached up to rub a hand across his face, his single-word reply muffled and desperate. "Mercy."

"No, far too easy to guess. It might even come up in a phony's usual patter. No, I think it should be more unusual, like… 'martingale'. Yes, that's perfect. Are we agreed?"

The waiter arrived back at their table, setting down a pristine white mug in which floated two bulbous yellow yolks tinged with brown. Brooksbank glanced at it, visibly paled, and covered his face again. "The codeword is 'vomitorium'."

THIS WAS DAY two at sea (the evening they embarked did not count). Following today they could safely expect another four days' travel, all being well. Four days in which she had to both expose and discredit the Duquesne twins *and* get to the bottom of the shadows in the engine room and other phenomena. The show would help with the first objective, while the second would be served by nothing other than a keen eye and a thirst for the truth.

She could not help but notice that her tour, such as it was, had taken them through the nicest areas of the first-class accommodation and then straight down into the bowels of the ship where the machinery lived. It was clear what Mr King cared most about: his fancy floating hotel and the gears and engines that made it go. For all that it was impressive, it also wasn't the whole story—and right now Avis needed every last page.

The primary witnesses of these spectres or what have you had been crew, but Brooksbank had also mentioned that some passengers had reported odd sights on the crossing from the Continent. Many of them would have departed at Portsmouth, but some would be bound for America and the hope of a fresh start. Perhaps there would be a thread to follow in third class, one that led in a more plausible direction than the engine room. Thus decided, she wove her way not back upstairs but down, in search of the third-class accommodation.

Unsurprisingly, the surrounds were decidedly less glamorous down here. It was still a well-made, well-appointed ship, but the gilt and shiny wood that adorned every surface of first class was gone, replaced with painted metal walls and bare wooden floors. She traversed a row of tightly packed cabins; a peek through a narrow door that hung open revealed a small but clean and well-appointed interior with two tiered berths. Nobody who passed her gave her a second look—though Avis had packed her finest clothes for the trip, by day she favoured simple cuts and sturdy fabrics that nevertheless fit better here than they did upstairs.

Before long she found exactly what she had been looking for: the third-class lounge, which was nestled between a room marked *WINCHES, CPSTNS & GEAR* and one of several dining saloons. The low-ceilinged room was far less ornate than the first-class lounges, with practical upholstered booths lining the walls instead of the overstuffed chairs and low tables above decks. There were portholes for natural light, at least, but they were small and let in only a meagre amount of sun, casting the room into a sort of not-quite-day, not-quite-night shadow.

Most of the passengers here were out on the promenade but the lounge was far from empty. She noted the card game in the corner booth that looked as if it had been running since the voyage began. Another booth had been taken over by a young man with several sheets of paper spread out before him; he was carefully penning what looked to be a letter on one, his brows furrowed as he traced out the words. All about the room were the signs that this space was a lively one of an evening—dark and glistening rings from cups and jugs, floor scuffed from dancers, the lingering scent of spilled beer impregnated in the upholstery. At the far end of the room stood a peeling upright piano, sheet music littered across its top, which also sported a battered violin and a small concertina.

For a moment she had a heart-squeezing moment of regret; she could have been billeted here, in third class, and likely would have found herself quite happy indeed. But she was too ambitious—and fond of her comforts—to turn down a first-class berth, and it was just as well, as she needed to keep a close and wary eye on the Duquesnes.

Besides, she was here now, and there was nothing she liked more than having the best of both worlds.

"Any room at the table?"

The card players looked up, to a one somewhat bemused by this new arrival at their table. Avis grinned, withdrawing a hand from her pocket to flash a few notes their way.

"Go on then," said a sandy-haired man who was gripping his cards as if they might escape his grasp at any moment. "Take a seat."

His name was Jim, and he was losing badly, but keeping up a brave face. With him was a young woman called Lydia for whom he carried an unrequited torch, and a man they had met only the previous day, who said his name was George—which was a lie, though Avis was not entirely sure why. George was better at cards than either Jim or Lydia, but not as good as Avis. She had to be quite careful not to win too readily, particularly given she could probably spare the funds at least a little better than any of her new companions.

The chat was sparse as they played out their hands, but slowly—from remarks here and there –Avis began to build a picture. Lydia, who was American, was headed home after an extended stay in London. Jim, who had never been out of London, was following her home. This was a terrible plan, but Lydia was letting it happen because she enjoyed his company and liked to feel wanted. It was easy to see why he liked her: she was smart and pretty, with a mane of copper hair and an infectious brand of cheerful confidence, but she wasn't remotely ready to find a nice boy and settle down. Avis predicted she would desert him almost as soon as they set foot on dry land, for all she would feel bad about it. Jim would he heartbroken, but he'd recover, and be stronger for it.

George claimed it would be his first visit to America also. This was another lie. He was trying to clean the pair out at poker, and might have succeeded was Avis not now in play. The first thing she did was convince them to switch to brag, a game which played far more to her talents, with its increased need for bluffing and its unshuffled deck. Soon enough she had the measure of both the deck and her fellow players, and had funnelled funds back from George towards poor doomed Jim, keeping herself more or less evens. If he couldn't get the girl, he could at least win at cards.

She tried a few tentative forays, asking if they'd seen or heard anything odd, but none admitted to it. This was perhaps unsurprising; Lydia and Jim had only been aboard for as long as she had, and George looked as if he'd rather have a tooth extracted than speak more than three words at a time. Before too long a gaggle of children invaded the room, filling it with an ear-splitting din that quickly put paid to any further rounds. George excused himself, and Lydia and Jim began to confer, clearly planning their escape as well.

Avis scanned the assembly and soon spotted a nexus of activity around a jolly-looking woman perhaps ten or so years her senior. She had the distinct air of a den mother about her and, sure enough, the various children in the room moved broadly within her orbit, whether or not they bore any resemblance to her or one another.

"May I borrow these?" Avis directed at Jim and Lydia, scooping their forgotten cards up into a pile. At their bemused nods, she left them to one another's company and made her way to her new target.

"Well now," she said to the various youngsters milling around, "who wants to see a magic trick?"

Avis's morning was for the most part turned over to card tricks for the children—sleight of hand, a spot of cold reading, nothing elaborate. They ate it up, and after a couple of curious looks from the aforementioned den mother she introduced herself. The woman's name was Frieda, and she had been on board since Hamburg with her husband and four of the some dozen children running about in the saloon. Her English was excellent, and she hoped this would stand her in good stead in making a new life in New York. Her mechanic husband was absent, having signed up as crew in Portsmouth following the mass resignation of so many of the original staff. She had barely seen hide nor hair of him since—a fact that appeared to bother her not in the slightest—and she was in good spirits, perhaps due to the alleviation of their financial situation that would have come with one of their number becoming paid crew rather than a paying passenger. This was as good a lead-in as any to some careful queries about the departure of the old crew members, and the state of mind of those who were left, though Frieda didn't know much.

"They keep mostly to themselves," she said. "Friedrich comes back sometimes to sleep in our cabin and he is other times with the crew." She smiled. "I don't mind, he snores. He says they are… abergläubisch, eh, strange beliefs, rules to follow?"

"Superstitious?"

"Ja, yes, like all sailors. Friedrich isn't a sailor; he does the work, he eats, he sleeps. This talk of strange figures and disappearing water, he ignores it."

Avis frowned. "Disappearing water?"

Frieda shrugged. "He says some of the men see the floods everywhere, even where it isn't. The water is there, and then—*phft!*—it's gone." Frieda waved her hand. "He does the work. No time for stories."

The memory of last night's trek to her cabin washed over her unbidden: sodden socks and skirts, the bite of briny water as it climbed her calves. A body crumpled on her bed, rimed with sand. But then she was well used to seeing things that did not, could not, exist. Her mind was nearly as adept at telling stories at night when the shadows were long as it was at dismissing them later in the cold light of day.

Avis was a sceptic like Friedrich, but that didn't mean she dismissed stories outright. After all, humans had been telling stories since the first fire was lit, and every day the broadsheets carried tale after tale to hungry readers. The facts might not be true—might be hallucinated, or inflated with each telling, or concocted as a clever ruse to draw attention away from reality—but stories always held a grain of truth, a reason for existing. She'd be a fool to think there wasn't *something* going on aboard *Excambion*, even if the stories of flooded rooms and floating bodies were impossible.

"Well," she said briskly to Frieda, "sounds like your Friedrich is eminently more sensible than half the sardines on this tin can." The German woman screwed up her face at the colloquialism, but Avis was already on her feet, slapping her palms against her thighs with gusto. "Let's go see what the little fishies say."

Eleven

FRIEDA AND FRIEDRICH might've had no time for stories, but right now they were all Avis had. She tried to shake other rumours loose from the folk in the lounge but her presence was still too new, too foreign. She'd have to return, build up goodwill, if she was going to get them to open up to her.

As she made her way back towards the thoroughfare that would take her up to first class, her attention was drawn once more down a particular passage. It was nothing so esoteric as a feeling that pricked her interest this time, but rather the echo of panicked shouts. And, Avis being Avis, she immediately gave in to her curiosity and followed them.

This part of the ship was a strange mélange of passengers and crew, storerooms and bunkrooms lined up side by side like neat kernels on a cob. A cluster of men disgorged themselves from one of said rooms as Avis approached and made for the stairs, carrying a stretcher between them. The man being carried was moaning in pain, though the sound was nearly drowned out by his companions, who were all arguing at full volume about the quickest way to bring him to the medical quarters. Avis noted a familiar scarecrow figure among them, uniformed and quiet while the others squabbled.

"Third Officer Baynes!"

The man spun on his heel, and Avis gave him a jaunty wave. "Miss… Lovelace?"

"Lock."

His eyes widened. He nodded. "Miss Locklace, what can I help you with?"

"Mm, don't worry about it. What's all this?"

"There was an accident," he said, Adam's apple bobbing nervously as he gulped past the words. Not a lie, but not wholly the truth either. "A crewman was injured."

Avis peered over his shoulder; the man was bleeding copiously from a gash on his head, and one leg was lying at a peculiar angle. Every time the stretcher shifted he groaned in pain, and it was shifting quite a lot. "That seems to be something of an understatement. What happened?"

Avis watched him suppress his instinct to resist, which one might argue would be fair enough given it was not remotely her business nor her concern. "Some crates were not properly secured. They fell."

"Oh, well, I assume that must be something that happens on ships all the time…" she mused, albeit with a note of query to her tone.

"Er, yes. Not generally on still days like today, but it does happen," Baynes owned.

"No, no, I told you, we hit something!" The man in the stretcher spoke through gritted teeth, his face a picture of agony, but there was a dogged glint in his eyes. "There was an impact on the hull, beneath the waterline. The whole ship was rocked by it. You must have felt it!"

"Nonsense, man," Baynes barked. "Nobody felt anything. You're delirious. Delirious and clumsy." He turned back to Avis. "I'm sorry ma'am. We didn't mean to disturb your…"—the officer frowned as though it was only occurring to him just now to be confused at Avis's presence here, this liminal space between classes—"… walk."

Avis cocked her head. "He doesn't seem delirious."

"Then perhaps he's drunk," Baynes said, a touch too quickly

and too sharply. A flicker of uncertainty in his expression indicated that he knew he had misstepped, but though Avis remarked upon it, it was hardly her place to chastise him. It was she, after all, who was out of place—whether in first class, in third, or here.

The man clearly wasn't drunk either, but before Avis could argue further Baynes was ushering the crewmen off along the corridor, presumably to the sick-bay.

An impact, one significant enough to topple storage chests, but felt by only one man. If he was of sound mind, what, then, could explain it?

Avis gave a little shudder, and a little harrumph that echoed down the empty corridor. No. She was not here to chase mysteries. She was here to lay them to rest.

This investigation was proving far more complex and time-consuming than she'd budgeted for. She'd hoped to debunk early on and then spend the rest of her time enjoying the first-class amenities before her triumphant arrival in New York. As it stood, she was just about able to squeeze in lunch in the dining room before continuing her work. She had not seen any familiar faces when she arrived—or rather, none that she wanted to sit with—and so she had found an empty table and placed her order in solitude before turning her attention to the notebook in which she had scribbled her observations on the "case" so far. When the food arrived, she'd only picked at it, diverted by the tangle of stories and motives before her.

"Is this seat taken?" The voice was familiar, and only slightly sozzled.

Avis smiled down at the pages. "Afternoon, Usher."

"Please, Samson."

"Under no circumstances." Avis heard the creak of the chair opposite as he sat. She closed her notebook and straightened in her seat. "I insist on propriety at all times."

He chuckled, flagging a waiter with a raise of his hand. "I've seen your propriety in action. Inviting yourself to the men's smoking lounge is likely only the tip of the iceberg, I'd wager."

"It's a ridiculous division. Why should I curtail where I go and who I speak to just because of a sign on a door?"

"You won't catch any argument from me," he said. The waiter arrived and Usher turned his gaze to the menu, allowing Avis to cast her attention further afield. A trio of black-clad figures crossed the far end of the room—Berthault and her two carrion crows. They exited into the verandah, chased by Avis's scowl. If it wasn't for her half-finished meal, she'd be minded to hunt them down right then and there. When she looked back to Usher he was watching her with a surprisingly keen stare, his head canted to one side.

"Brooksbank asked a fair question, you know. Why involve yourself in any of this?"

Avis shrugged. "I don't like liars." She frowned at the flicker in her periphery.

You're one to talk.

"Oh, we're all liars in one way or another. But truly, it sounds as though this pair mostly fleece those with more money than sense. Is it honestly worth your time to worry about how some rich European wastes their fortune?"

Another waiter arrived to pour Usher some coffee, which he immediately spiked from his hip flask. Avis watched the simple, practised movement as the little leather-wrapped flask emerged from and returned to his inside pocket.

"Well now, that's a question for the ages, isn't it?" she said, lifting her fork to tap it idly on her plate. "Do we measure the severity of a crime based only on the harm caused to its victim? Or are some acts—dishonesty, fraud—simply wrong?"

"Perhaps we should get our new friends to summon up Bentham and Kant and see if we can't hammer it out one evening, hm?"

Avis gave a bark of a laugh. "In any event, we cannot know the true reach of these lies, or the harm caused either to the victims in question or to their family and friends."

"What if they truly believe they're doing the right thing?" Usher's expression was keen; Avis wondered how often he allowed himself to truly engage with the world around him. In larger groups he seemed content to act the sot, but it seemed his curiosity and sharp mind could not be fully subdued. "Surely intentions should matter. If they say they're trying to help…"

"Once a liar, always a liar. They may claim good intentions but at the end of the day it always comes back to the same things: greed, self-aggrandisement, power."

Usher's food arrived, and he picked up his knife and fork, his movements methodical. "Every time?"

"Even if it wasn't that—which it is—should it matter?" Avis leaned forward, gesturing at him with her fork. "If someone should, I don't know, accidentally remove your bicycle from its station and pedal away with it thinking it's their own, have they not committed a theft?"

"I suppose either way you're left without a bicycle," Usher said, moustache twitching.

"Quite. Intentions matter when it comes to forgiving a faux pas, *not* theft and fraud."

"You know, I can spot someone with a grudge at twenty paces," he drawled then, between bites of his Chicken à la Maryland. "Yours was visible at fifty. What's behind all this bad blood, anyway?"

Surprisingly her first instinct wasn't to deflect or barb; unlike Brooksbank, she didn't get the feeling he was winding up to chide her. She gave a casual shrug, delaying her answer as she speared and nibbled potted shrimps from the tines of her fork. "I've seen the harm they can do first hand."

"Ah. Family?"

Flashes of her mother's face, pale and tear-streaked. Patience's ghostly visage.

She nodded, not trusting herself to speak. He nodded too, and didn't press further, merely slicing his chicken into neat pieces with practised flicks of his knife. Once a surgeon, always a surgeon, it seemed. Avis was relieved at the silence and took up her own cutlery in earnest, smearing bits of beetroot pink and bloody across the plate.

It was only as they were both finishing their meals that Usher spoke again. “You know, solo crusades don’t usually go very well. If you need help with any of this…”

Knowing his predilection for the classics, Avis offered, “No man is an island, eh?”

The bell rang out for the second sitting of lunch, and Usher chuckled. “For whom the bell tolls,” he said, with a nod of acknowledgement.

“I feel like I’m back in boarding school.” With a sigh, Avis jammed a last half-slice of bread into her mouth and pushed to her feet. “D’you play shuffleboard?”

“No.”

“Excellent, then I shall be in with a chance.”

It was perhaps unsporting to challenge a man twenty years her senior with an obvious war injury to a shuffleboard match, but that didn’t stop the sweet flush of victory Avis felt when she won. It was a fine distraction from the surprising weight of their earlier conversation, and just what she needed. She tried to entice Usher into another game, but he begged off, informing her he was just going to “read in his cabin” until dinner, which she took to mean that he’d be snoring in a whiskey-soaked fug for the rest of the afternoon. That was all well and good for retired doctors, but for Avis it was time to get back to work.

It was as she was storing the cue-sticks back in their sockets that her next steps became clear. The little party of mourners emerged from the verandah onto the deck, and Avis stepped back behind a bulkhead, peeking past it to watch their progress. As pale as they were in the warm-lit evening saloons, the Duquesne twins looked positively translucent in the sunshine, bleached of colour. They trooped back below decks, and Avis followed at a safe distance; if she knew where their cabins were, she could track their movements that much more effectively, hopefully presenting her with an opportunity to catch the widow alone.

They were a queer bunch. Charlotte with her impenetrable French mien, barely reacting to anything, even as a fellow passenger nearly collided with her coming round a corner. And the twins, limpeting nearly as closely to her as they did to one another. Gideon was solicitous, always murmuring to her, guiding her with a light hand to the elbow. Rachel was silent, her gaze caught between her brother and the widow. Avis couldn't tell who she was watching more closely.

It was clear Madame Berthault had money; her clothes and her bearing were enough to attest to that. It was equally clear the Duquesnes had designs on that money—but how did they intend to bilk her out of it? The tried and tested means was for the dearly departed to convince the living that the kind, generous medium deserved some recompense for their efforts. She'd even heard of a phony going so far as to get the deeds to their victim's house signed over to them, though thankfully that had a happy ending. Nothing in "Henri's" speech had seemed to point in that direction, though of course Avis's French was piss-poor at the best of times.

The trio fractured upon reaching the living quarters. Rachel leaned in to murmur to her brother, who nodded and then guided Madame Berthault to the right—or starboard, as Brooksbank had reminded her that morning. Rachel waited a moment then, just standing stock still in the middle of the corridor, such that when she began to move once more Avis had no choice but to follow her instead of her brother and their patron, having lost track of them entirely. A few seconds later she realised this was no coincidence when she turned a corner and found herself face-to-face with a waiting Rachel Duquesne.

She considered walking briskly onward and brazening it out, but given the narrow hallways she would have had to barge past Duquesne to do so. Instead she lifted her eyebrows in greeting and doffed a non-existent hat. "Bonjour."

"You are following us." It was an accusation, not a question.

"That's quite the sense of self-importance you have there. Perhaps I'm lost, or doing a lavatory audit, or simply trying to get some exercise," Avis said with her sunniest smile.

"You're lying. Do you know how I know? You have a tell," Rachel said. Her voice was less gravelly than the night before, but still incongruous with her appearance.

"Do I?"

"Yes. You open your mouth and speak."

Avis laughed, loudly, ignoring the waft of cold air that breezed across her neck. "If I had a shilling for every Spiritualist who accused me of lying, I'd be a rich woman. And yet they're the ones with doctored slates and papier-mâché limbs."

Duquesnes's nostrils flared. "You're not as clever as you think you are. And if you don't leave me and my brother alone, you'll regret putting your nose where it doesn't belong."

Accusation to threat in just a few seconds. Avis's smile widened. She had them worried.

"I have an exceedingly high opinion of myself, it's true," she said, "so it's very possible that I am not as clever as *I* think I am. Fortunately..." She dared to step closer. Rachel Duquesne smelled like sandalwood and cloves. Avis's skin prickled. She lowered her voice. "I need only be cleverer than you." She paused. "Or your brother. Which is easier still, I suspect, hm?"

She saw Duquesne's jaw tighten, could practically *hear* her teeth grind together. *There it is.*

Careful, Avis.

Rachel blinked, her brow furrowing briefly before she smoothed her features back to impassivity. "Careful, Miss Lovelock. You are playing with things you know nothing about. Money. Love. The bonds of family. They can be messy. And dangerous."

"Oh, I know all about the bonds of family, believe me. And nobody in my position in life could be accused of being ignorant to financial matters. Love, I'll grant you: that is a complication I have been fortunate enough to avoid. With that said… I think I shall take my chances." Avis stepped back and slipped her hands into the pockets of her skirts. "Thank you for your time and cooperation, Miss Duquesne. This has been most illuminating."

Duquesne muttered something in French, too quietly and too quickly for Avis's unschooled ear to catch. With a final hard look she pushed past, all but shoving Avis against the wall with the force of her passage. Avis leaned back against the dark wood panelling and drew a few restorative lungfuls of rather stale, stuffy air. She would have to ascertain the Duquesne–Berthault cabin situation later. It was almost time for dinner.

Twelve

Entering the first-class dining room was like stepping past a curtain—a theatre curtain in this case, with bright lights and an expectant audience turning their gaze to Avis as she swept in. She knew how to entertain, how to keep them eating out of the palm of her hand, but for once the prospect felt tiresome rather than exciting.

Losing your edge so soon?

She steadfastly ignored her sister's voice, flashing a grin at the nearest table of diners and looking around for a pair of familiar faces.

"Ah, there you are! Haven't missed starters, have I?"

The twins did not seem pleased to see her. Gideon looked somewhat queasy as she slid into a chair at their table, while Rachel was merely incensed. Madame Berthault was impassive as always, and the rest of the table were unfamiliar to Avis, though easily read. Across the room she could see Brooksbank goggle-eyed at her impudence, and she gave him a little wave of her fingers before turning back to the denizens of her table. "Love these centrepieces, don't you? Fresh flowers aboard a ship, what a silly luxury."

"Who is this?" one of the strangers asked, a woman whose strawberry-blonde hair was swept up in a drooping pompadour like a deflated pastry. In her mind's eye Avis compared it with Lydia's wild copper waves and found it decidedly wanting.

"Avis Lovelock, entertainer and medium-buster," she said, not trusting either of the twins to introduce her properly. The woman sniffed; clearly this was less impressive than she had been expecting.

"Miss Lovelock, I don't believe that is your spot," Gideon said then. "Perhaps you'd be more comfortable at another table."

"I'm quite comfortable right here, thank you." She began to pile her side plate with oysters, each shell making a satisfying *clink* as she stacked it. The briny scent turned her stomach, but she ignored the sensation. The conversation resumed around her, though it was muted now, everyone eyeing the newest arrival. Well, good.

Avis was not the only late arrival to dinner: as the soup bowls were being cleared away and the mains carried in, a man entered, all but staggering his way over to the nearest table. It was impossible to hear what he was saying all the way across the room, but fortunately Avis's skills extended to lip-reading, though she was out of practice. Squinting, she leaned back in her seat, watching as he sat down heavily and reached up to scrub a hand across his face.

He says he's seen something. Strange figures on the boat deck.

"I know, I know," Avis muttered.

They were prone, lying there as if felled by lightning. But when he went to investigate...

"There was nothing there."

Belatedly Avis realised that her surveillance—and mumbling—had drawn the attention of several others at the table, chief among them Rachel Duquesne. The medium was staring at the newcomer with a frown, and Avis knew if news of this so-called sighting spread she'd never hear the end of it. She had to think fast.

"I must say I'm looking forward to this evening's sitting," she said, turning back to the table. "I heard you were planning a more elaborate demonstration of your channelling skills following last night's rather underwhelming performance."

That certainly did it. Rachel's gaze whipped round as Gideon shifted in his seat. He rested his fork on the edge of his plate, the flakes of sauce-drenched salmon forgotten. "It might have been underwhelming to you, Miss Lovelock, but what matters to *us* is that Madame Berthault has been comforted by the presence of her dear husband."

"So you're not going to do anything more than a bit of play-acting?" she enquired. "I see. Interesting. Good to know. Makes my job all the easier."

"You have no job," Rachel stated baldly. "Only a self-imposed crusade."

Gideon frowned, reaching over to place a stilling hand on his sister's arm. She tolerated it—just. "I am curious about your hatred for our work. In all my years I've never met someone so opposed to communing with the spirits. Tell me, when did this begin?" He tilted his head to one side, his expression curious, open.

"You might just as easily ask when I first began to have rational thoughts, for the answer would be the same," Avis said.

"Oh..." A slow shake of the head. "I doubt that. That scepticism is perhaps innate to you, given your particular character. But the *hostility*... No, I think that came later. I think that is in response to something. I wonder what."

Avis felt rage bubbling up within her and arranged her face into a broad smile. In her lap, safely hidden beneath the tablecloth, she clenched her hands into fists.

"And I wonder when you began to commune with these spirits—or pretend to, at any rate."

"You are free to believe what you please, Miss Lovelock," Duquesne murmured. "But my earliest memory is that of waking in the night to see our parents standing at the foot of our bed. They were fully dressed for travel, their lips forming words and yet not a sound emerging. My sister was already awake, her fingers a vice around mine." He paused for dramatic effect and Avis stifled a derisive snort. This was a well-worn story, she was sure. She awaited the punchline, and sure enough, "The next morning we learned that their carriage had overturned on the road home, throwing them with such force that they died immediately."

"Many people dream of the death of their loved ones," Avis said. "Plenty experience such coincidences and do not build a career as fraudsters off the back of it."

"It was not a dream," Rachel said, interjecting for the first time. Her voice was hoarse and hot. "And it was not coincidence. If you cannot respect the losses that led us here then you are not welcome at our table—to dine *or* to observe."

"Believe me when I say that I have every respect, and every sympathy, for those who have lost those closest to them," Avis said. "Indeed, it is that depth of feeling that drives my desire to verify the existence or otherwise of life after death, to know whether the spirits are reaching back from beyond to speak to the living. Nothing would please me more than to find a spirit medium who was not a fraud. So I must ask: if you and your brother are truly able to channel the spirits, what have you to fear from my presence? Moreover, don't you *want* the opportunity to prove to me that they exist, and turn a detractor into your strongest and most enthusiastic proponent?"

She watched Rachel's nostrils flare as she considered the challenge. Avis knew she'd accept it—the Duquesnes were too proud and too sure of themselves to do the smart thing and withdraw.

"Miss Lovelock—" Gideon began, but now it was Rachel's turn to manage him, slipping her hand from beneath his and raising it in a stilling gesture.

"We would never turn down a person in need," she said, the gentle tone of her voice at odds with the lift of her chin, the set of her shoulders, her steely eyes. "And it sounds as if you are in very great need. Of course we will offer you the solace you seek."

After a dinner during which the twins once again ate almost nothing under Madame Berthault's concerned gaze, they repaired to ready themselves for the sitting. Avis delighted in this: the previous night they had been happy to have observers during their "attunement" but this time nobody was to come into the room until they were summoned. They were planning some theatrics, and Avis couldn't wait. Even better, it meant that for the very first time she could speak to their patron without Gideon at her elbow.

"How have you been finding the food on the voyage so far?" she opened. "It's been very rich, wouldn't you agree?"

Madame Berthault gave a desultory shrug. "It is acceptable. Of course when they are trying to show class, they imitate la cuisine française."

"Mais bien sûr. Although in spite of this, your companions seem disinclined to partake. Have you noticed?"

"It has always been the way." She sighed. "The poor darlings. They do not eat, they barely sleep, they are always cold… The price of their link to the other world. It is very tragic."

"How long have you been acquainted?"

"It has been… perhaps four months? Since they came to Giverny."

"And their dear uncle was still alive at that time?"

Berthault's lovely face, which had been relatively impassive since Avis had met her, now folded into a moue of distaste. "Yes, he was with them when they arrived. I do not believe they went anywhere without his accompaniment."

Avis lifted her eyebrows. Interesting. "You didn't like the older Mr Duquesne."

"I did not say that."

"But am I wrong?" Avis pursed her lips. "What was he like?"

Berthault sighed and took a sip of her wine. "He was very… autoritaire. He was always there, telling them what to do, what to wear, where to go. They had no freedom under his surveillance."

"And now they are free? Or does he continue to instruct them from beyond the grave?" Avis couldn't help the little dig, and Berthault gave her a disappointed look that very nearly made her feel guilty.

"They are bringing him back to America, to bury on their soil, as he requested." She didn't specify whether this request had come before or after his death. Avis wondered if she knew. "But while I do not think he is instructing them now, the legacy of a man such as that will reach very far."

"Is that why you've stayed by their side?" Berthault seemed to be about to answer, but Avis went on. "My apologies, that is to say, I know that it must be a salve for you to be able to continue to speak with your husband. But is that all? I get the sense that perhaps you have also come to care for the twins themselves?" This was a risk; showing her hand like this could cause the widow to shut down altogether. But Avis wasn't sure when she'd next get her alone, and her reaction should be informative even if she refused to be drawn on the topic.

Madame Berthault took another sip of wine, and Avis wasn't sure whether it was a delaying tactic or just her innate Frenchness. Possibly both. "It is difficult not to," she said eventually, fixing Avis with an even gaze. "I know you think me a fool, mademoiselle. But the fact is, they have provided me with comfort when there was little to be had. And still they do so, even in their own grief. Perhaps if you did not approach them with your sword already drawn you would see the good they can do for those that need it."

"It is not only about good or harm, madame. It is about right and wrong. About lies and the truth."

The Frenchwoman gave a tut. "How British of you, to be so uncomfortable with… how do I say… ambiguïté?"

Avis shot her a thin smile. “Ambiguity.”

“Ah! Bien. Yes. Some things in this world sit on the edge of our understanding, Mademoiselle Lovelock. It is not merely a question of truth or lies. It is also a question of heart, of faith. The twins bring Henri back to me. That is my truth.”

“You don’t care if they’re lying to you? About the Veil? About him speaking through them?”

“I hear him when she speaks.” How could she be so damned calm about it? “That is what I care about.”

“Through the mouth of a woman half his age?”

A tiny smile tugged at the corners of Berthault’s full lips. “Does that trouble you more? That he speaks through a woman? How—”

“British of me? Yes, I’m sure. And no—”

No?

“No. What troubles me is lies. I appreciate your candour, Madame Berthault. I hope you won’t take it personally that I continue to seek the truth, even if you are content with your own version.”

“Mais non. Le cœur a ses raisons que la raison ne connaît pas. You must do as you must. And now you must go,” she said, as Gideon appeared outside the door to beckon the waiting witnesses into the lounge.

Avis rose, frowning when the other woman did not follow her. “You’re not coming?”

“I do not wish to interfere. It is possible that if I am there, Henri may try to break through and speak.” Berthault placed a hand on her breast, her fingers curled just so, a cage for the fluttering bird of her heart. “This is your sitting. I wish you well, mademoiselle. May you find what you need.”

Thirteen

IN HER YEARS of debunking, no medium had ever read for Avis. They often claimed her energy was unsuitable for the process and tried to have her removed from the room altogether. She'd been turfed out on a Regent's Park side street on more than one occasion. Not only were they afraid of her keen eye and quick wit, but Spiritualists relied on a combination of preparation and on-the-spot analysis to ply their trade, and she was an empty book for both—a most imperfect customer.

Upon being invited to a storied house, the first thing any successful medium would do was visit the local graveyard and meander through, notebook in hand. There they'd find a cornucopia of names and dates from which to draw inspiration, for it was likely that the current heads of the family would be overjoyed by a visit from one of their dearly departed relatives. It was simple enough to get the details right when they were laid out in granite in neat, orderly rows.

Avis, of course, had left her dead far behind. No medium was going to find those buried secrets, certainly not stuck aboard a ship in the middle of the Atlantic.

There was, of course, always the option of using mentalism to divine details about the living and thus impress, as Avis did at each and every one of her shows. Clothing, jewellery, manner of speech and body language could all supply a wealth of information about the unsuspecting target, but Avis was far from unsuspecting. Her clothing was for the most part nondescript, her adornments unremarkable. She had banished the most obvious traces of her Leeds accent and while she was sure the way she moved and acted betrayed something of her character, it was certainly not enough to give any hint at her background. The frauds saw all this and knew it was pointless to attempt a reading; they would only come up empty.

So why, with all these assurances in place, did she still feel a twist of nerves as she sat down at the table that evening next to Rachel Duquesne?

"You really needn't trouble yourself with this," she said in a conversational tone. The friendliness was barely skin deep, a thin veneer over her distaste, and Duquesne would know it. Avis didn't care. "Far be it from me to protect swindlers from embarrassment under normal circumstances, but the champagne is free upstairs, so can we at least make it quick?"

"The spirits cannot be rushed," came the predictable response, "nor can healing." Avis scoffed loudly at this, drawing hostile looks from the others settling at the table. Who had invited Mrs Armitage, of all people?

Avis studied the set-up before them, leaning forward to sweep her hands beneath the cloth that dripped over their knees. She could not feel anything beneath the edge of the table or along the floor, but that didn't mean there weren't tricks afoot. As before, it was Gideon who shushed them to silence, and Gideon who spoke first.

"As we travel through this world we cannot help but to draw the spirits to us—those we've lost, who cannot find solace in the afterlife without imparting their final messages. Do not be scared," he intoned, his expression beatific, "for it is a kindness that we do here at the table, to allow the spirits to reach out to us and communicate, for it gives both the living and the dead a chance to put old ills to rest." Avis felt her lip curl, but was distracted from a response as Rachel's slim, strong fingers suddenly grasped hers. "Please, take one another's hands and lighten your hearts. Believe, and the spirits will speak."

"Did you tell Berthault to stay away?" Avis murmured, head tipped so that her words would reach Rachel's ear only. "Worried that she might spot your tricks when they're employed on a new subject? Or are you afraid she'll be jealous? If it helps at all, I don't have a dead husband to play-act."

"No, I should think you don't," was Rachel's rejoinder. Avis did not like her tone. There was something knowing in it. Avis did not like anybody other than her knowing things.

An anticipatory silence built around the table, each linked hand a conduit for the nervous energy of the sitters. Rachel's grip was as cool and steady as her gaze. Avis felt a cold finger run down her spine. *Oh no. No, no, no.*

Around the table the shadows seemed to shift, just a trick of the flickering candle, but Avis couldn't help but search the gloom for Patience's pale face. Whatever inscrutability she claimed, a turn right now would surely give the Duquesnes something to grasp—nothing real, of course, but evidence of weakness that Avis couldn't afford to reveal. She decided to go on the offensive.

"Looks like the spirits are shy tonight," she said, and huffed a laugh she didn't feel. "Can't say I know how that feels."

This seemed to be the opening Rachel had been waiting for. She turned towards Avis, still grasping her hand firmly. "The spirits are here," she said in that low, hoarse voice. "They're drawn here, by us. By you, and the pain you carry."

"Come now, you can do better than that," Avis said. "Everybody has pain."

"It's an old pain, an old wound, not new. No, this is not fresh hurt—it festers." Rachel's pupils were large in the candlelight, and Avis felt dizzy, as if she might tip into them and drown. "The spirits don't cause pain, they are not malicious. But they cannot help but sense it, attuned to the aether as they are."

Avis curled her lips into a mirthless smile, turning a little more towards Rachel and shaking her head. "Obvious," she goaded. "Novice work." She tried to ignore the dark pressing at her back, the cold. She would not let Patience unsettle her, not here, not now.

"I sense one of them now, closer than the others. They want to reach you. Why won't you let them speak?"

As if Avis had *any* control over Patience's endless intrusions. She felt cold breath on the back of her neck and swallowed heavily. "I thought that was your job."

"Yes, someone close—not a distant relative, but someone you shared a life with." The rest of the participants, Gideon… they had all faded into the background by now. It was just Avis and Rachel, two sets of eyes locked in challenge, two hands gripping tight enough to drive the blood from their fingers. "And now they're gone, and the gap they've left is like a crack in the world. One you try to fill with rationality and logic… but it's too hungry for reason. All it wants is your pain."

Avis forced her smile wider. "You have nothing," she said.

Rachel's thumb stroked across the back of Avis's, just once. "No," she said. "That's you. Or so you'd like to think."

"This is what they do, you see," Avis said, raising her voice now to welcome the other attendees back into the conversation. She tore her gaze away from Rachel's, using her chin to gesture between the twins while her hands remained linked and trapped. "These people. These liars and cheats. Careful guesswork and safe assumptions, dressed up to feel personal. They can be very clever, at reading your face, your movements, at getting you to lead them along a path. Clever. But false."

"Give us a name," someone said, she wasn't sure who. "Tell us who is with us now." She could hear the longing in their voice, the desire for validation, for proof. It helped stoke her anger, a welcome bloom of heat rising through her.

Rachel shook her head. Avis knew she wouldn't attempt it; she had nothing to go on, not even an initial. Then she spoke. "You must have patience."

Avis was extremely well schooled in controlling her

expression, and it did not fail her now. But her hand did, spasming, her grip tightening just briefly around Rachel's fingers.

Duquesne did not miss it. She could not possibly understand what it meant, of course. Would have no clue that she had stumbled across a truth, of sorts. But she knew she had said something significant, something that had unseated Avis, and her eyes flickered with cool triumph. She would remember this, store it away, take it out and turn it over in her mind later. Avis had given her something.

Cursing her lapse, Avis fought the urge to draw her hand back. "I wonder," she said, dropping her voice again, though anyone keen of ear would no doubt still be able to hear her in the hush of the room, "will Charlotte have a private sitting after this? Or are those Gideon's purview?"

Now it was Rachel's turn to flinch, and though Avis had struck a point she felt very little satisfaction at the victory. She felt cold and raw, and not nearly drunk enough to ignore the way the medium seemed to shrink in on herself just a little, and how that made her feel like she'd overstepped the line. This was it. This was how she'd unpick them. But when the time came to turn the screw, she found she didn't have the stomach for it.

She felt the shadows gather and grow heavy and the chill creep in, no longer held at bay by the flickering candle on the table. Patience would make her appearance soon, and Avis could not endure being probed by those sea-blue eyes while her sister's ghost hissed poison in her ear. She tugged her hand from Rachel's grasp and shoved her chair back, the rug rucking beneath its legs. "This farce has been amusing, but I've seen enough. I hope you can now see what is patently obvious to me: these two have no more access to the spirit world than I do the crown jewels. Less, for at least those exist, and the spirits most certainly do not."

Ignoring the stares and protests of the other sitters, she stalked from the room, head held high. Despite her triumphant demeanour, she could not pretend this was anything other than what it was: a strategic and hasty retreat.

Avis took the long way back to her cabin.

It wasn't because she was lost this time—no, she'd explored the ship enough that her bearings were beginning to align—but she was restless and dreading the still and quiet of her rooms. She had never been very good at being alone with her thoughts. Leaving the warmth and light of first class behind, she wound her way to the outer corridors of the ship, climbing the stairs until she emerged onto the promenade.

On this level it was almost pleasant, lit by lamps and screened by bulwarks which kept the worst of the wind out. The deck chairs and small tables had been tidied away so that the deck stretched out unblemished, a polished collar that ran around the entire bow of the ship. As Avis paced along the boards she encountered a few other passengers, all of them cocooned in warm coats and huddled shoulder to shoulder in their own private universes. Which was fine, really. She didn't need company when she had movement.

Her strides ate up the deck. As she neared the bow of the ship the bulwarks fell away, revealing the lower promenades and, beyond them, the great expanse of the sea. The moon was fuller tonight, casting a cold light over the waves as they broke before the ship. A northerly wind rose up to greet her, running icy fingers over her scalp and down her back. She was only wearing the same plain woollen dress she'd worn to dinner, and though it was warm, it wasn't a patch on a good coat.

Rather than stop and let the wind work its way further beneath her collar, she kept moving. One hand trailed the railing, and she chanced a look down to the second-class deck and the boat deck beneath it. That was where the man from dinner had claimed to see bodies, lying prone "as if struck by lightning". How would he have even known?

Still, she could understand where the claim had come from. Staring down at the drop, it was easy to mistake the bunches of rope and chains for figures on the deck. She stopped and peered more closely, narrowing her eyes like she was reading the small print on a particularly nasty contract.

Why, in the watery light of the moon it was even possible to see a leg crooked just there, a hand lying outstretched towards the railing. The bodies did not move, did not breathe. The looseness of the limbs, the puffiness of the face, the flesh—it was suddenly, sickeningly familiar.

They were not dead of a lightning strike. They were dead of drowning.

As the wind rose again, Avis was surrounded by the scent of brine and felt cold, clammy flesh under her hands. She jerked away from the railing, scrubbing her palms against her legs.

"No, it's not real. It's simply suggestion. You know this, you *know* this," she hissed, but still the body lay there, skirts tangled about its knees, eyes blank as they stared up at the silver shard moon. *Her* eyes, or nearabout, in *her* face, though plumper, kinder. Younger.

The sob that tore itself from her throat was an embarrassment, but Avis didn't stick around to see if anyone had heard her. She fled to the safety of her cabin and for once, the solitude was a welcome respite from the world at large.

Fourteen

THE AVERAGE PUNTER told you a great deal about themselves long before they sat down in the audience. Back at the Egyptian, it was Avis's usual habit to do a walkthrough of the audience as they found their seats, getting the measure of them, picking out a few likely marks. Though it might seem a risky venture at first blush, to gather information so openly, she could count on the fingers of one hand those who had noticed her over the course of scores of shows. In general, they were far too busy with their own affairs to take notice of a solitary woman of unassuming appearance milling among them, picking up stray names and observations.

Mediums would, where possible, know in advance at least some of the people they would be sharing a table with. How much prior information they would be able to collect varied greatly of course and they tended to have operational practices that played into their preferences—some were blatant about it, demanding to know precisely whose "energies" they would be sharing the table with; others fancied themselves more able to roll with the punches, picking things up as they went. For Avis, there was both risk and reward in the larger audience: far less control over the situation, more people to win over, but more opportunities also.

Today was different. Avis had been aboard *Excambion* for three days now, and though she had not been deliberately gathering trivia and compiling mental dossiers on her fellow passengers, it had become second nature to do so. Rarely had she shared a room with such a large collection of marks. The trick would be narrowing it down.

The audience had assembled in a rather casual fashion in the main saloon, some seated around tables, some standing around the edges. There was no particular stage, but Avis enjoyed this—it added an extra air of spontaneity and excitement to be able to move freely among her willing victims.

She did not wait for an official introduction, instead launching into her usual spiel, raising and widening her voice to command the room into silence. It was now her turn to spin a tale, and to unweave the mystique with which the Duquesnes had tried to shroud the ship.

"Welcome, all, to an afternoon of mystery and insights. My name is Avis Lovelock. Those of you unlucky enough to have made my acquaintance will already be aware that I know far more about you than you do about me—perhaps even more than you know about yourself. For those of you who have not yet had the dubious pleasure, I will say only this: what you are about to see and hear may appear to test the limits of rationality. It may seem that I have done the impossible, that I have discerned information that I simply could not have gained by any earthly means. But I assure you, there are no spirits at work here—unless some of you are already on the whiskey, and who wouldn't forgive you? We are after all at sea."

There was a mixed reaction to this: a smattering of laughter mixed with a cooler, more sniffy response. A few of the denizens of first class had viewed Avis with a certain amount of disdain since they'd set sail, clearly labouring under the belief she was riff-raff, whether because they had been made aware of her identity or just through observation of her plain dresses and uncompromising demeanour. Unfortunately for them, Avis now held them captive and could take the opportunity to exact a little revenge.

She began with one of her favourite little warm-up gags. Closing her eyes, she ran the audience through their paces.

"There are no hidden strings here," she reminded them. "Everything I do, I do in plain sight. Now, were I on stage at the Egyptian, I might demand that an assistant tie a blindfold around my head, but here I think you can all see that my eyes are quite closed. Regardless, I still wager that together we can find someone—a very special someone—through the process of elimination. Now, it would be easy enough for me to pick someone and guide things with a subtle touch, but that would be all too predictable. With that in mind, I'd like to ask every man whose name begins with J to raise a hand. Careful, now, John, no need to jostle your poor wife! Actually, you can put your hand down—and the rest of you Johns. Let's have just the… Hm, actually, why don't you decide? Somebody choose a J name, call it out."

There had been occasions when a name other than "James" had been chosen after John had been ruled out… but they were rare. The audience before her now complied perfectly, and she had to suppress a grin. Avis then began to narrow the field further, eliminating features, some based on broad demographics and the law of averages, and some more specifically targeted to rule out particular people. Sideburns, silk ties, and those who worked in banking all dropped their hands; she could hear the rustle of wool and the mutter of the crowd as her pool narrowed. It was a calculated risk. Any number of the criteria she chose might accidentally rule out the wrong person, but she accounted for that, putting some hands back up a couple of questions from the end.

When the moment came for the final question, the one that ruled out all but a single James, Avis, eyes still shut, turned dramatically to face squarely in just one direction. There was a tiny titter from off to one side of course—someone who couldn't help laughing at her impending embarrassment.

"And now..." Avis raised a finger, opening her eyes and pointing at the same time, even getting a few gasps for her trouble as she pivoted at the last moment to one side to turn her attention correctly to the final James, whom she had picked out at the very beginning and guided the audience towards choosing.

"I appreciate that it's rude to point, sir, but I hope you'll forgive me, seeing as we now know one another so well. Now, I know what you're thinking," she added, turning to look directly at another audience member: a well-dressed young man with all the telltale markers of an academic background. He blinked, his expression halfway between disbelief and disdain. "You—yes, you, sir—are thinking that I might have fooled others, but you see right through me. While everybody gasped at my intuition, you observed that in fact this was a cheap trick where the Jameses did all the work. I didn't truly know anything at all. Am I wrong? Of course not, I'm never wrong." And after all, nobody was going to correct her when she was calling them clever. He preened like a rooster. "You know it was nothing but a ruse, and anyone here could learn to do the same with a little practice. Why don't you join me? We'll see if we can't shed some light on how that's done..."

The young man stepped up to join her. Avis didn't know his name or much about him at all, but that didn't worry her. Normally Patience would be here by now, her cold shadow sweeping across the stage, sending prickles down her spine, but even without her help Avis knew how this went.

"Thank you and welcome, sir," she said, extending her hand. He shook it without thinking, and before he could pull away she tightened her grip, trapping him mid-pump. "You have a firm grip, but I detect no calluses on your palms. This, along with the fine cut of your jacket and the fact that I've seen you supping on caviar in the dining room is a sure sign that you're no manual labourer. Am I correct?" He laughingly agreed, and she pressed on. "There are a hundred small details that people carry with them that, once you know what to look for, will give insight into their day-to-day lives. Completely obvious, and yet when you state them without showing your working it can look quite amazing. For example, what if I should tell you that I know for a fact that immediately before this you were in the billiards room, enjoying a game?"

"Why… yes, I was." She could hear the murmurs of the audience, and grinned, lifting his arm and indicating his sleeve with her free hand.

"Blue chalk on your cuff. A good half of any cold reader's job comes down to observation, pure and simple. The clothes people wear, the disarray of a lock of hair or the uneven snag of a fingernail: all of these can tell you something about the person sporting them. Of course, we are all individuals, as unique as the stars in the sky. And yet, as with the stars, observe them long enough and certain patterns begin to fall into place. Cultivate your sense of observation and you too can hold a dinner party captive with your insights." There was a polite titter of laughter and Avis released her mark's hand, immediately pivoting on her heel to stalk across the floor.

"The other half of the job is equally teachable, though perhaps harder to practise without a ready supply of volunteers. You, sir," she said, turning to face the young man once more. "I sense you have someone in your life, a figure that you respect and admire. A mentor of sorts, who has taught you a great deal. Am I correct?"

"Why, yes," he said, looking impressed despite himself.

"And you have not told him—for it is a him—how much you admire him, for fear of being rejected in your esteem."

"Oh no, I have expressed my admiration quite openly."

She cursed internally; if Patience had been there, she would not have made a misstep. She moved swiftly onward. "Ah, then, you worry he may not be in your life for much longer, that you may lose him before you are ready to let him go."

The young man—she was thinking of him as a Percy, though there was no logic behind it, just a general assumption that all rich young men were named after men much more impressive than them—nodded effusively. Oh, she had him now.

Avis continued, flush with the heady triumph that came with performing. "What you may not know is that this admiration goes both ways. He is as grateful to you as you are to him. In fact, he wishes he could tell you this. You should seek him out upon your return so that he might share his praise."

"Truly?" Percy breathed, well and truly hooked now.

"Oh, how should I know?" Avis waved a hand dismissively, watching the young man wilt right in front of her eyes. Her next words were for the audience at large. "Do you see what I did there? Let me outline it for you. Firstly, I took what I could divine from my mark's general carriage: his fine clothes, soft hands, and clear disdain for my general person, and extrapolated that he had likely attended university, at the very least. From there I made an educated guess that he would have among his acquaintances someone he considered to be a mentor, as most people gain either through their time in study, or once they begin employment. It's a vague enough term that it might apply to any number of relationships, allowing the mark to substitute whatever is most appropriate without requiring me to be more specific—and risk getting it wrong. And next, you will notice that indeed I did get it wrong in my supposition that he hadn't shared his admiration. This is more common than you will likely realise, because the trick is to move swiftly past it, without giving the mistake time to take root. Instead I suggested another likely scenario: that, given the age of my friend here, somebody that he counts as a mentor might be of advanced years and thus likely to join the great majority." She noted a few queasy expressions in the crowd. Well, good.

"And lastly, I appealed to his vanity, suggesting that his mentor admires him as much as he is admired. This is doubtless one of the best tricks of the trade, for who doesn't like to be flattered? It is easy to believe a charlatan telling you what you want to hear."

"But that's cruel," Percy protested, now red-faced and shaking a little with ire.

"I agree," Avis said quickly, pleased that he had played his part so well. "It *is* cruel, and yet Spiritualist frauds rely upon this and other tricks to ply their trade on the desperate and the grieving, for who among us does not long for reassurance and closure?" She let her gaze drift over the audience, her expression beatific. This would only reach a few people, those with the intelligence and good grace to realise the truth of the matter, but perhaps that would be enough to tip the scales.

Any further gloating stuttered to a halt as her eyes fell upon a slim, dark figure: Rachel Duquesne. She had apparently managed to sneak in during the reading undetected. She now stood at the back of the room like a fold in the curtains and was flanked at her elbow not by her brother, but another shadowy presence: Patience. The two women stood nearly shoulder to shoulder, both of a height, both staring straight at her. Avis gaped at the sight ungracefully, and it was only the shifting attention of the audience that drew her back to herself.

"Of course," she said, voice shaking, a pale shade of her usual confident patter, "you're all prepared for that now. You know their tricks, how they might try to draw you into their confidences, convince you they speak for the spirits of the dead." The crowd was restless, sensing her unease. She was losing them, losing her opportunity to turn the tables. "You'll know better than to fall for empty promises and pretty lies..." She faltered. She did not want to satisfy Rachel by looking her way too often, but in her periphery Rachel and her sister seemed to merge together, one overlaid on the other, like the optical illusion where you could create a sausage between your touching fingertips.

She had become distracted again, and the audience was beginning to fidget. Damn it all.

She gave her head a little shake. "That will be all, Percy."

The young man gasped, and so did the audience, a little belatedly. Too late, she realised why.

"I... I never told you my name was Percy," her mark stammered.

And nor did I.

"Well," Avis blustered, raising her voice in an attempt to recapture control. "I knew it wasn't John."

This got a laugh. The crowd was back on the hook. Avis did not—could not—look at Rachel. She turned back to the audience.

"You'll forgive me if I don't reveal *all* my secrets," she said. "But rest assured, I did not ask his dead ancestors."

After the struggle of her show, Avis couldn't bear the glitter and disdain of first class. She excused herself as the first dinner seating filtered out of the lounge and made her way down the stairs.

"You look like you lost a shilling and found sixpence." Lydia was in good spirits as Avis entered the third-class saloon, surrounded by a gaggle of other young women now, with Jim nowhere to be seen at present. The ale had clearly been flowing, the room thick with smoke and chatter, and a curly-haired lad was on the piano, punching out a jaunty American tune that sounded like teeth in a barrel. All but the oldest children were now gone, although judging by the screaming and laughter Avis had heard as she passed the bunkrooms en route to the saloon they were far from asleep.

"I see you picked up some turns of phrase while you were here," Avis observed, grabbing a nearby mug that looked more or less clean and filling it with beer before perching on a stool at the end of the booth.

"I was in London nearly two years."

"So why're you headed home?"

Lydia shrugged and grinned. "Time for a change."

"Here, you're the one that was doing card tricks before, ain't ya?" one of the other girls at the table said. "Show us one?"

Avis smiled but shook her head. She was far too distracted for sleight of hand at this point. "How about I read your mind instead?"

After one read, and then another, a crowd began to coalesce, eager for any sort of entertainment. They were a much more receptive audience for her act than the first-class passengers had been, gathering round to hear her patter and insights. Following a detailed rundown of one young woman's profession, hobbies, and a potted history of her recent personal life, somebody asked the question.

"You one of them psychic mediums then?" The man had a flat cap and a bristly moustache. Judging by the flush across his cheeks and nose, he'd been helping himself to the ale for some time.

"No such thing," Avis said. "I am just very good at seeing what's actually in front of me." There was a somewhat disappointed murmur.

"Shame that, we could do with one of them down here."

"Or a priest."

Avis lifted her eyebrows. "Oh?"

Bristly moustache nudged the tow-headed lad beside him. "Tell her what you saw, go on."

The young man looked somewhat reluctant now that he was put on the spot in front of a crowd, but at Avis's nod of encouragement he shuffled forward.

"I saw… people," he said. "Floating in mid-air like they were dangling there. There one minute, gone the next."

Again the floating people. Two different witnesses having the same hallucination was unlikely, which lent credit to the theory that there was *something* physically occurring on *Excambion*. Still, she had to question, had to needle. "You weren't a touch seasick and delirious?" Avis suggested. "Or, dare I say it, drunk?"

A smattering of laughter, but the lad shook his head with such determination that it shut them right up. "I know what I saw," he insisted. "I wasn't sick, and I wasn't drunk, and I've never seen anything like it before. I've never felt such cold in all my life."

He was deadly sincere, and in spite of herself Avis felt a shiver creep up her spine.

"Nonsense. I have worked in the bowels of this ship for weeks and I have seen nichts—nothing." A lanky Teutonic man brought the atmosphere back into the room with a dismissive snort, pint in hand. At some point the children down the hall had stopped caterwauling and Frieda had slipped into the room, and she sat next to him in the booth now, one plump, fond hand on his arm. This must be Friedrich, then. "This ship is haunted by nothing more than imaginations too big for the heads they sit in."

"Imagination is a powerful force," Avis agreed, twisting on her stool to face him. "Did you know that during the dancing plague of 1518 hundreds of people were swept up in the shared mania because they believed they were cursed by St Vitus to dance until they died?"

"Dancing until you drop over dead? That does not sound like imagination to me," Frieda said, sucking her teeth. "It sounds like illness."

"And so it might have been, but that did not stop people from attributing the event to a curse, or even to demonic influences. These things have a tendency to escalate, particularly in times of trouble—or in a confined space such as this."

Friedrich nodded. He had an open, weathered face that Avis found herself liking immensely. "Then perhaps the people on this ship are ill and imagining impossible things. You are not a doctor, are you?"

"I'm afraid not. Just extraordinarily clever and observant."

The man seemed to take her at her word on this rather than balking at her ego. "Then I'm sure you'll find a way to… to, er, im Keim ersticken. To kill in the seed."

Avis smiled at the translation but did not correct it with its English equivalent: nip it in the bud. "I appreciate the vote of confidence."

She wished she could share it. With one man already seriously injured and babbling about phantom collisions, and another seeing bodies in the moonlight, rumours would only escalate until she had extinguished them entirely. But in the face of such exciting gossip, and with the strangely magnetic Duquesnes stoking speculation around the unknown, how was reason to will out?

Fifteen

"THE PROBLEM I have, you see…" Avis brandished her fork before spearing the sausage on her plate. Fat erupted from the wound, rivulets seeping across the surface down to the plate beneath. "The problem is that it's rather difficult to prove a negative. Let's say I tell you in all certainty that in my expert opinion, this ship is categorically not haunted. So what? As much as I'd love to be taken at my word, I never am. I mean, for heaven's sake, I tell people I can't read their minds 'til I'm blue in the face and half of them *still* don't believe me. My act rather relies on it." She pushed some potato onto her fork along with the sausage. "This is just how belief works, how superstition works. I don't see how I'm to persuade your buyer of anything if they want to believe different and are prepared to take the word of some plausible sailor or wide-eyed tourist over mine."

Brooksbank frowned into his coffee. He looked less worse for wear than the previous morning, though not by much. At least this morning his cheeks were shaven and his shirt fresh. "All right, I take your point. So what do we do about it?"

"Haven't the foggiest," Avis said. "Oh, I could investigate the ship's records and whatnot but again, all I'd ever be doing is failing to find anything. I need to be able to prove something positive. Which, unless your haunting had actual culprits behind it, I'm not going to be able to…"

She trailed off as the man who'd appeared looking frightened two nights ago entered the dining saloon. He still looked… well, haunted. A flash of swollen, blue-tinted flesh flickered in her mind's eye. She frowned and shook her head. There was a way through this; there had to be. *Can't prove a negative.* It was like the Duquesnes and their boring séance—no tricks, no stunts, nothing to disprove. Until… "I can't disprove a haunting that has no evidence against it…" She looked back at Brooksbank, a triumphant smirk dimpling her cheeks. "But I can prove that one has deliberately *fabricated* evidence."

Brooksbank rubbed his hand across his face in a familiar gesture of fatigued bemusement. "I'm sorry, what?"

"You need to tell the Duquesnes about the haunting."

He frowned. "You *specifically* said not to. You were pleased that they didn't know."

"I made a mistake. I need them told, and I need them actively investigating it. Enlist them explicitly. Offer to pay them if you have to."

"I don't—"

"Don't you see?" This was punctuated with a stab from her fork that sent a few flecks of meat and potato flying across the table to land in front of Brooksbank. Clearly he did not see. "If they're investigating, they'll feel the need to mount some form of performance. To put on a show. I might not be able to debunk the *haunting*…"

Realisation dawned on him with a mildly horrified grimace. "But you can debunk *them*."

"And, in turn, discredit anything they have to say about said alleged haunting, and that's about as near as you'll get to a clean bill of health. Which is what you want. You get to sell your boat."

Brooksbank raked his fingers through the silver-shot hair at his temples. "And you get your disgraced spirit mediums."

"Which is what I want. All rather neat, isn't it?"

"I mislike this."

"And?"

The American sighed. "And I'll speak to them after breakfast."

"I'll come."

"I'd really rather you didn't."

"HAVE YOU BEEN in third class?"

Brooksbank looked sideways at her, stepping past an older couple huddled next to the railing in the garden verandah. "Now, or ever?"

"Obviously now. I don't need your life story, for God's sake."

"We've only been at sea for three days."

Avis sighed. "I'm aware of the passage of time. Is that a no, then?"

"I've not had the chance, no."

"Hm."

"Hm, what?"

"Hm? Oh, nothing, just 'hm'."

"You're in a peculiarly bad mood today," Brooksbank said. "Something eating at you?"

"Don't be ridiculous."

Avis made a point of berating Brooksbank mercilessly as they continued along the verandah, to underline her high spirits. He broadly ignored her. As they traversed the main promenade, however, he stopped short. "King," he said. Sure enough, the old man could be seen busy scamming some other poor bastard at shuffleboard, just across the deck. "I'd better tell him."

"Fine, I'll meet you there. Where am I headed?"

"Thirty-eight, thirty-nine, f— Damn it, don't go talking to them without me, all right? You want this done, let me do it. I'll only be a minute."

But Avis was already headed for the stairs downward to the maze of first-class staterooms on the main deck.

She was looking forward to this. Imagine the looks on their faces when she presented them with this opportunity: a whole ship, haunted, and they the sainted mediums who could prove it to a grateful board of directors. They would salivate over the possibilities, she was sure of it, just as she was salivating over the chance of catching them in their fakery once and for all.

The staterooms were arrayed in groups of four, each pair facing another pair with a stretch of carpet between them. Without the room numbers, Avis could've wandered for some time, peeking her head around innumerable corners. As it was, she approached the junction confidently, slowing only when she heard the telltale hiss of someone trying to conduct a dressing-down entirely in whispers. Skidding to a stop, she pressed her back to the wall, inching closer until she could make out the words in near perfect clarity.

"There's nothing to be gained from this rushing and pushing." Gideon's voice, its rich honey now wound tight. "Do you want to ruin what we've built?"

"It's not me that's ruining it." Rachel, of course. "Mr Brooksbank has connections. He said he can set up a show at the Grand as soon as we arrive. But we only have three days—*three days*, Gideon—to make our decision."

"There's no decision to be made. We don't need tawdry performances to pay our way. We have Charlotte. And Uncle's money, when it comes."

Rachel grunted, and Avis could picture her grimace perfectly. "You and I both know Uncle's money will be a pittance. He wasn't saving what he took from us, he was spending it. On himself."

"You don't know that."

"Regardless, I will not be beholden to that man any longer. As for Charlotte—"

"She is nearly ready to agree," Gideon said. "Just another nudge from Henri, and she will be ours."

"She will be yours, you mean." Was it Avis's imagination, or did Rachel sound envious?

"You know you will be welcome in our home. She will likely insist on it. Even once we're married, she'll not be ready to say goodbye to Henri, and I have no intention of stopping your communion."

Avis blinked. Gideon intended to *marry* the widow? It made a certain mad sense; she was surely very wealthy, and devoted to the Duquesnes. Securing her hand would be a lucrative windfall indeed. They wouldn't need to run their scam any more, except the ongoing and reprehensible hoax that Berthault's husband was encouraging this… this farce. Avis nearly rounded the corner and started shouting right then and there, but she was halted in her tracks by Rachel's next words.

"Perhaps you would be happy with this arrangement, with being a kept man, with lying to a good woman. But I would not. I *cannot* go along with this. It is time for us to make our own way in the world, see what we can make of it without lashing ourselves to another."

It was a strange thing, to hear one of these swindlers just admit out loud that they were lying. Some of them, Avis knew, came to believe that they really were channelling the dead, and even once their tricks were exposed would maintain that they only used them to add a touch of theatre to an otherwise authentic communion with the hereafter. Others, once unmasked, would go silent, offering nothing but the occasional expletive in Avis's direction once their deception had been proven.

But never had she heard one medium talking openly to another about their fraudulent act, as simple as you please. Part of her ached to just rush in crowing, to point and shout, *I caught you! I caught you!*

But that wouldn't resolve anything. She couldn't prove a thing, and it would be her word against theirs. No, she had better stick to the plan: have them conduct their investigation, and then she would have them.

"There you are." Avis jumped as a hand landed on her shoulder. As soon as she recovered, she twisted around to shush Brooksbank as quietly as she could.

"Can't you see I'm investigating?"

He glanced between her and the cabins, realisation dawning all too quickly. "You can't be serious. *This* is how you investigate?"

"You really have a lot to learn about how the world works, Carrie."

"Oh for—Come on, enough lurking. Let's go." His hand moved to her elbow, giving her a tug before he stepped around her and entered the gap between cabins. Peering around him, Avis could see one of the cabin doors was ajar by a few inches, though Brooksbank ignored that fact in favour of rapping on the door-frame. "Mr Duquesne? Are you in?"

There was a pause before the door swung open, revealing both twins, as Avis had known it would. Gideon nodded to Brooksbank politely before his gaze slid to Avis. "Mr Brooksbank. Miss Lovelock. To what do I owe the pleasure?" If he had any suspicion that she had been lurking around the corner, he didn't betray it. Rachel was silent, her lips pressed together in obvious displeasure, though it was probably just at the interruption.

"There's something that I've neglected to tell you that I feel it's my duty to rectify," Brooksbank said, pulling his shoulders back as if this was some noble task he was about to undertake. "Something about the ship and your invitation on this voyage."

"It's haunted." Avis sidled up until they were shoulder to shoulder in the short corridor. "Not really, of course, since that would be utter bunk, but there are rumours. Stories. Hearsay."

"Erm, yes. As Miss Lovelock says, the ship is rumoured to host spirits—not all of them friendly." Avis frowned. She hadn't heard *that* detail before. "You and Miss Lovelock were invited aboard to certify—or disprove—their existence."

"Ah, of course," Gideon said, nodding. "We have felt strange energies ever since we came aboard. This explains a great deal."

Avis raised an eyebrow. "Funny that none of them showed up in your séances thus far, isn't it?"

"The spirits are fickle, and often reluctant to connect with strangers."

"And yet they've been showing themselves to random folk all over the ship." Their looks of surprise were all too satisfying. "I can't think why they wouldn't want to talk to you… Unless, of course, they're not real."

"The dreams." Rachel reached for her brother's arm, drawing him back to look at her. "It must be. They've been reaching out, trying to forge a connection."

"Of *course*," Avis said, unable to help a chortle at this newest claim. "Of course they're reaching out to you in dreams, just like they can only manifest in the darkest rooms. So shy and reticent, these spirits."

"The Veil is difficult to pierce for many. Of course they struggle." Rachel glared at her, and it was all the more delicious that Avis knew she was lying through her teeth, *knew* this was an act—one she would dismantle piece by piece.

"If there are spirits—" Brooksbank began.

"Which there are not," Avis supplied.

"If there *are* spirits aboard *Excambion*, we will need some form of proof. I'm afraid that dreams and intuition won't cut it. The owners, for reasons upon which I cannot elaborate, are very keen to have this matter settled decisively, one way or another."

Avis watched Rachel Duquesne's elegant features pinch slightly, and she pictured that sharp mind working at a rate of knots, calculating the impact the outcome of this current "job" might have on her future opportunities under Brooksbank's wing.

"Of course," she said eventually, inclining her head to one side as if this was a perfectly reasonable arrangement to be making. "We shall get you your proof, Mr Brooksbank. Have no doubt." Beside her, Gideon nodded.

"And by 'we', of course, we mean the three of us," Avis said, stepping forward with a cheery grin. "Naturally I will have to be present for any supernatural event you might want to cite in your evidence. For verification purposes."

"Mm, the spirits are very sensitive to negative energy. Miss

Lovelock's presence may well disrupt the very phenomena we are trying to capture." Rachel spoke to Brooksbank alone, clearly having decided that ignoring her was the best approach.

But Brooksbank already knew the part he was here to play. "I'm afraid Miss Lovelock is correct," he said. "However, I have counselled her that merely scoffing will not be sufficient proof of charade. While we will require some sign of paranormal phenomena from yourselves that cannot be explained away by other means, Miss Lovelock will have to provide concrete proof verifying any falsehood."

"'Mere scoffing', Carrie? I'm mortally offended."

He sighed; she was going to have to take it easy on him if she didn't want to lose one of her main sources of information on this damned boat. "Please, Miss Lovelock, can we all just agree to work together in a professional manner? We only have a few days to get to the bottom of this. There's no time to waste."

"Indeed, Mr Brooksbank," Gideon said smoothly. "We are happy to help. If you will excuse us, my sister and I will begin our preparations. This evening, we will attempt to contact these spirits and learn what draws them to this vessel."

Avis did not speak, and neither did Rachel, each regarding the other in silence. The medium held herself coiled, ready to spring into action as soon as the interlopers had gone, eager not to waste a moment of time in her quest to prove herself. Because it would be Rachel behind whatever would come next—Gideon was the honeyed voice, the pleasant smile, but Rachel was the brains. Of that, Avis was sure.

Sixteen

Both parties needed time to prepare—the Duquesnes their tricks, and Avis her wits and senses. This was set to be the biggest, most public debunking she had ever performed. She wanted it done *well*.

There were a few items that any good debunker always carried, of course. A knife, for severing threads and working between wooden slats. A candle, for sudden illumination. A mirror, for seeing things meant to go unseen. All of these, along with a box of matches, Avis laid out neatly on her dresser after a lunch with Usher, during which she tried her hardest not to betray her nervous excitement. Later, when the Duquesnes gathered their audience in their location of choice, she would come fully armed. For now, following them around the ship as they "attuned" themselves, she would bring only her sharp eyes and healthy scepticism.

Brooksbank had arranged for them to meet in the main first-class saloon, which on this slightly blustery day was bustling with well-dressed passengers. The little group certainly drew some interested looks as they coalesced—enough gossip had spread about both the twins and Avis at this point that the sight of them entering the room together was enough to pique some curiosity. Madame Berthault was with them, but as they prepared to depart Brooksbank suggested that she instead allow him to chaperone her for the afternoon and leave the Duquesnes and Avis to "do their work". Apparently not overly enamoured with the idea of traipsing around the ship climbing stairs and exploring crannies after the inevitably bickering trio, Berthault had readily agreed, and left the Duquesnes and Avis in the capable hands of Third Officer Baynes, there to ensure their access wherever they needed—and that they did not get lost.

Baynes was eager to chaperone, and Avis couldn't tell if he was a secret Spiritualist at heart or had heard of her reputation on the music hall circuit. After a few minutes, however, it became clear that he was mostly a fan of the ship, like King, and enjoyed the chance to show it off, even to three with very little nautical knowledge or interest. He was also desperate for a cigarette; she wondered how long he would hold out before lighting up.

"You say that there have been sightings all across the ship?" Gideon asked as they made their way down the stairs that led to the first-class cabins.

Baynes bobbed his head like a pigeon. "Yes, in some of the passenger areas, out on deck, even down in the engine rooms. Both crew and passengers have seen them all over."

"Curious. The spirits are usually drawn to where the Veil is weakest, congregating there in the hopes of reaching through."

"I don't know what to tell you, sir. That's just the reports I've had."

"No need to apologise, Mr Baynes," Avis said. "People are suggestible. They hear about a supposed haunting and soon you've got spirits popping up in every nook and cranny. It's just human nature."

"Or perhaps," Rachel said, "this ship has seen its share of tragedies and losses. Do you know its history, Mr Baynes?"

He perked up. "I do, ma'am. She was built in Govan, in Scotland, and launched on 2nd February 1890. She's belonged to the Hamburg Line her whole life, er, so far, making the transatlantic run from Hamburg to New York, variously via Portsmouth, Southampton, and Cherbourg. Her fastest time…"

Avis couldn't help but smile as the crewman went on, at some length, about the history of the ship. This was not the level or type of detail Rachel had been looking for, and watching the medium school her expression into one of polite interest was a delicate pleasure all of its own.

As it turned out, *Excambion* had experienced some misfortunes: it had run into a pier when docking not long after its maiden voyage, necessitating rather involved repairs. Additionally, it had suffered from some sort of fault with the water pipes to the boiler, for which it had also needed to be docked and repaired.

"Do boats regularly encounter so many… setbacks?" Avis enquired. "It seems after a certain point one would be better off just scrapping the lot and starting from scratch."

"Oh, no. It costs far too much to build a ship to just write it off the moment a problem is uncovered," Baynes said with a shake of his head. "No, they'll almost always opt to undertake repairs. Properly, of course."

"Well, I should hope so!"

"In point of fact, just last year, after a minor incident where she ran aground, her bridge was almost entirely refitted with brand-new instruments using the latest technologies."

Rachel was frowning. "There's been nothing more severe? Nothing that would have caused deaths aboard?"

"Not as far as I'm aware," Baynes said. "Just the usual scrapes and dings."

"That is… odd. Normally spirits congregate at sites of meaningful significance," the medium said. "Graves, the homes of loved ones, wherever they might be able to reach those who would listen."

Avis rolled her eyes. "Gratified to know we're agreed on the point that this does not appear to be a haunting, for all we haven't reached the conclusion from a remotely similar direction. Shall we call it a day, then?"

"You are welcome to do so," Rachel told her, offering a poisonously sweet smile. "My brother and I will carry on. Please, Mr Baynes, if you would."

Feeling increasingly like a duckling following along, Avis allowed sheer spite to propel her after the twins as they glided through corridors and cabins and compartments, pausing here to touch an object, lingering there in a "thin spot". She kept her eye-rolling and scoffing to what she felt was a minimum, though she still drew the occasional glare from Gideon.

Rachel, on the other hand, didn't seem to mind at all. Indeed, in contrast to her previous suggestion that Avis take her leave, Rachel was now amused, even pleased, to have Avis along with them on their travels. She would glance across at her often, and it was unusual for Avis to look Rachel's way and not find Rachel staring right back, either at her or sometimes, curiously, just over her shoulder, eyes slightly narrowed.

It was a smart move—just unsettling enough that it made it more difficult to observe the twins' activities. It also made it more difficult to get the measure of Rachel herself, for Avis had to steal glances as and when she could at unexpected moments, catching a fine-boned profile here, eyes shuttered in a pensive affect there. The most expressive part of her face was her lips, the set of which spoke volumes about her current mood and state of mind.

For the most part their performance was quite staid—a lot of looking, touching, standing with eyes closed and expressions serene. Only one moment stood out from the general fare, and that was when they were exploring the labyrinth of cabins towards the aft of the ship, near where Avis herself was berthed—not that they knew that. Up ahead of her, Rachel Duquesne stumbled suddenly and reached to steady herself against the wall. That much was not so strange; everybody was prone to the occasional moment of instability as they exercised their sea legs. Even here below decks, the heaving of the ship could take one by surprise.

No, the strange thing was that when Gideon went to help

steady her, hand to her elbow, asking, "Are you all right? What happened? Was it a spirit?" and Rachel said, "No, no, it was nothing, I just lost my footing for a moment..."

... she was lying.

IT WAS A strange crop of onlookers and participants who joined the Duquesnes for their sitting that evening—before rather than after dinner, for a change. They'd chosen a small lounge in second class, which had to be closed off for the purpose. This was, of course, to avoid spreading panic, but the sight of the Duquesnes, accompanied by a small collection of first-class passengers and crew, trouping into the room all the other passengers had been turfed out of for the evening, would be enough to spread gossip by itself. Another clever move.

They had initially tried to persuade Brooksbank that the sitting should be in the garden verandah, with an audience of whomever wanted to assemble, but this thought had been quickly quashed, much to Avis's relief; if the whole of first class became fully convinced that the ship was haunted, she could disprove it 'til the cows came home (and then disprove it to the cows for good measure), and it wouldn't make a scrap of difference. The ship would be haunted forevermore.

Instead, Brooksbank had agreed that they could share the information with a small selection of their existing coterie of followers, in strictest confidence. Even those he had vetted. Tonight, only Usher, Clarissa, and Madame Berthault were in attendance—clearly Brooksbank had the measure of Sarah Fenwick and the Armitages and knew that if they were involved the whole ship would be talking about it by the end of the first sitting of their evening meal.

What preparations there were had been hastily made. There was a table, and a candle, but the rest of the lounge was still intact, so that the remaining chairs and tables were scattered about as if prepared to host any ghostly spirits that might join them for tea.

The crew milled fitfully. There were a handful only, a mix of seamen and other staff, still variously uniformed. Brooksbank had told Avis they'd been selected to attend to "preserve the integrity" of the event and report back truthfully to their superiors. It was clear that some wanted to be there more than others. Baynes—the only one she immediately recognised—hovered with an expression of intense concentration as he tried not to appear nervous. Another crewman was genuinely annoyed to have been enlisted for this duty, every twitch of his face betraying his intense derision for the whole situation. A couple of serving staff, clearly friends, were bored and eager to get the affair over and done with.

As Avis drifted nearer the centre of the room, her keen ears picked up some bits and pieces of the murmured conversation currently going on between Rachel Duquesne and Charlotte Berthault.

"If I could just speak to him..."

"Charlotte, I promise, later I'll try, but we have to do this. Wouldn't you prefer we were in private anyway?"

Charlotte gave a low, wry chuckle, reaching to place a gloved hand briefly on Rachel's arm, and Avis felt heat spring to her cheeks. She turned abruptly towards the ever-present drinks trolley.

It wasn't the fact that both were women—she had been on the music hall circuit far too long to bat an eyelid at that, or its inverse—but the naked intimacy that they shared was unexpected, especially among the other buttoned-up first-class passengers. There was something about that low laugh, too, that needled at her. That was not the laugh of a woman soberly awaiting the chance to speak to her dead husband. It spoke of anticipation of other encounters, and a knowledge that the person she was speaking to shared that anticipation.

The twins bring Henri back to me. That is my truth.

Avis had taken that to mean the memory of him, but what if, in her characteristically French way, Berthault had meant something else? The feeling of being wanted, cherished.

Companionship, comfort… Perhaps even passion? Such things were entirely alien to Avis, of course. With her sister—or at least, the figment of her—at risk of being conjured up by her ill mind at any moment, Avis had never entertained the thought of finding a companion of any stripe, even a platonic one.

Rachel was wearing the stick pin again. She wore it most of the time, Avis had noticed. It sparked in the candlelight as if daring her to speak.

"The spirits are here with us tonight," Rachel announced suddenly, and Avis jumped, splashing sherry over the rim of her glass. She grimaced and wiped at her hand with her sleeve, knowing it would be damp and sticky and not much caring. "We should begin."

They had no sooner gathered around the table, however, than they were interrupted. The double doors at the end of the room banged open and a red-faced crewman rushed in, headed straight for Baynes. Every eye was fixed upon him as he whispered into the third officer's ear. Baynes paled, eyes darting about the room, lost for who to look at, for what to do. Along the corridor came a clatter of dress shoes on polished floorboards, and Brooksbank appeared on the crewman's tail. He knew exactly where to look: directly at Avis.

"Someone has been hurt." Rachel's words echoed Avis's thoughts. Brooksbank didn't speak, eyes still fixed on hers, as though he could not give voice to what needed to be said and was trying to project the information directly into her mind.

"No," Avis said. "Someone has died."

Seventeen

GIVEN HALF A chance, the whole party would have trooped down to gawk, but in the end only Avis and the twins were permitted given their ongoing investigation. The doctor had already been and gone; he'd confirmed the death, though a more thorough examination would have to come in the morning.

They had put Friedrich in a cold room.

Avis stood in the doorway, frozen to the spot. It was dim inside, lit only with a single lamp, and she was thrown immediately back to the encounter with Uncle Waylan's coffin: the dark murk of the room, the chill. Friedrich's body was not boxed away but laid out in the middle of the room and covered in a canvas sheet that nevertheless did nothing to obscure the truth of what lay beneath it. She could make out the cuff of his trousers, the peak of his shoes. It was mundane and horrendous, and it made her feel sick.

What's the matter with you? You've seen a dead body before.

She had—she *had*—but it wasn't the body that was throwing her, it was the anguished wails that echoed down the corridor. Frieda had been told, probably at the same time as they'd been fetched, and she had not taken it well. Avis couldn't make out the words, not being a speaker of German, but she didn't need to understand the language to grasp the sentiment.

It was the sound of a heart breaking, and it was all too familiar.

"I don't think this is proper. This isn't something ladies should have to see," Third Officer Baynes was saying from his station in the middle of the room, and thankfully Brooksbank was there to smooth things over because Avis wasn't sure she could summon any quips just now.

"It'll be brief, but believe me, both ladies are more than equipped. Just… one moment, please."

Reluctantly the officer nodded, stepping aside to allow access to the canvas-covered mound behind him. Rachel was the first to approach. Garbed in black and slender as a scythe, she looked like Death itself as she knelt down and reached to lift the sheet.

"Wait," Avis said suddenly, and was instantly struck with embarrassment as Rachel looked up at her.

"You don't have to be here." Rachel spoke quietly, without rancour, but it was enough to shake Avis from her fug. She would not allow the Duquesnes to best her, not here, not now.

Avis cleared her throat loudly and stepped forward, wiping her face of emotion. "Go on."

She concentrated on the sound of the water against the hull of the ship, the dry rasp of canvas as Rachel pulled it aside. Anything other than Frieda's cries.

Friedrich's body was no shock, really; it looked much like he had in life. Unlike in life, however, there were no tells, no cues for her to read beyond the obvious. He was wearing homely, rough-spun clothes marked here and there with grease. His hands too were smudged with grease, his nails blunt and his palms calloused. His kind face was now slack in death, and there were no obvious injuries or signs of struggle. The only oddity was the damp patch beneath the body—not blood but water, slowly seeping from his clothes into the floorboards.

"You said he was found in the engine room?" she asked, turning back to Baynes. "Not on deck?"

"Engine room, aye. Just lying on the gantry, like he'd collapsed." He made a gesture with one hand, digits spreading wide then falling, a rose wilting and shedding its bloom.

"But he's wet."

"I don't know how to explain it. His clothes were wet when we found him." His eyes widened. "Miss Duquesne, please—"

Avis frowned and pivoted just in time to watch Rachel lean in and press a finger to the dead man's cuff, then raise it to her lips. "I can taste brine," she said thoughtfully. "It's from the sea."

"I-I…"

"It's possible he encountered a spirit," Gideon said then, too confidently. "Perhaps it took him by surprise."

Rachel nodded, her expression measured. "If he had a weak heart, that would be enough."

Baynes paled. "You think a spirit did this?"

Brooksbank reached out to put a steadying hand on Baynes's elbow. "I think that's probably quite enough of this. I'd say we could all do with a nice, fortifying brandy, eh?"

Rachel was persuaded to come away from the body, though she placed its hands on its chest and re-covered it with the sheet first. Avis fell into step behind the twins, and she was so distracted by her thoughts that she almost didn't notice them peel away from Baynes and Brooksbank, allowing the two men to carry on towards the stairs to first class while they turned into the third-class saloon. After only a moment's hesitation, she followed the twins.

The atmosphere was a far cry from her last visit. Frieda sat in the booth rocking and giving small sobs, surrounded by a half-dozen other women whose expressions ranged from sympathy to discomfort. It was busy; many third-class passengers had crowded in to share in her grief, and though there was beer being passed around, it was a sober affair.

Are you sure you should be here?

Avis wasn't sure at all. The grief settled on her like a shroud and her every instinct was to back away, to turn and run. To her surprise Rachel and Gideon split up—he approached a small knot of solemn-looking children, and she made her way to the booth where Frieda sat. Avis watched as Rachel pulled over a chair, sinking into it with an ease and a cant to her limbs that made her look like an entirely different person. It was easy to forget the Duquesnes' humble beginnings when they were swanning around first class like upper-crust remoras, but here in the saloon it was all too apparent.

There was too much hubbub in the room to make out what Rachel was saying, so Avis merely observed, watching as she reached across the table to take Frieda's hands in her own without pretence or awkwardness. The German woman's face was puffed and red, suffused with gratitude, and it wasn't clear if she recognised the medium or if she was just glad of any comfort at all. Rachel's thumbs stroked the back of Frieda's hands, smooth and strong, and for a moment the table fell silent except for Frieda's snuffling sobs.

This should have left space for Avis's anger to come roaring in. Normally just the thought of a Spiritualist humbug preying on the fresh and tender grief of the bereaved was enough to stoke her ire, but she watched, and waited, and felt nothing.

Maybe it was the slump of Frieda's shoulders as she relaxed into the touch, the lessening of tension that allowed the other women around her to breathe, shift, move closer.

Maybe it was the way her face brightened, just a bit, at a question from Rachel, and the animated response she gave, even as tears tracked down her cheeks.

But mostly it was the bone-deep conviction, as Avis stood watching Rachel Duquesne sit at that table and draw the poor woman back to herself, that she was truly seeing her for the first time.

After a long moment she turned away, gaze landing on Gideon, who had gathered the children to him and was speaking to them in a low, soothing voice. His hands were spread before him, pale spiders poking from his sleeves, but the children didn't look scared. *How* were they so capable, so calm? How did they know how to tend this newly opened wound? Avis had been here before, and her every attempt had only made things worse. She felt sick with envy and something else besides, a longing that her heart didn't know how to name.

You could talk to them, you know.

Patience stood behind her, a dark shadow in the periphery of the corridor. Avis's skin prickled with cold. "Go away," she muttered.

It's not a weakness to want solace. It's human. You are human, aren't you?

As if she'd heard the question, Rachel looked up, her gaze connecting with Avis's across the busy room. Each time it happened it felt less like a trick.

Unable to bear the weight of her regard, Avis spun on her heel and fled from the room.

Running away again?

"Shut *up*," Avis said, ducking her head and forging onward. She couldn't outrun Patience, but she could ignore her. And drink until she fell quiet.

She was moving at such a clip, with her eyes focused firmly on the floor, that it was inevitable she should plough straight into someone. Luckily for her it was Brooksbank, who absorbed the impact with a winded "oof". "I was just coming to find you," he said upon recovery. "Where did you all disappear off to?"

"The saloon," Avis said with a weak gesture back the way she'd come from. "The fakers are still there, comforting the masses. I'm sure they'd love your attention." She began to pull away, but Brooksbank stopped her, shifting to block her path as he peered down at her in a trepidatious fashion.

“Is everything all right? I’m sorry about the body. You seemed quite gung-ho to see it.”

“I’m more than capable of seeing a corpse without fainting, I’m hardly a shrinking violet,” Avis retorted, more sharply than she’d intended. To his credit Brooksbank didn’t bristle; if anything, his expression grew more concerned, which in turn irritated her further. “Out of my way, I’m for the drinks cart.”

He moved aside, quite annoyingly falling into step behind her instead of finding anything wiser to do. She ignored him, walking in silence until she reached the smoking room two decks above in the hopes that he would take the hint. He didn’t.

“Make it a generous one,” she instructed him, and then went to slump in a chair by one of the overly filigreed partitions. It was quiet tonight, the brocade sofas and overstuffed armchairs empty of puffed-up men and their cigars. She was struck again by how *solid* everything was. How much must all this wood and glass and gilt weigh? How could the ship possibly stay afloat under such a burden?

“You know this is a men’s room,” he said as he moved to do her bidding. It wasn’t a question.

“I don’t see any men in here right now.” As if on cue, a pair of older gentlemen did walk through the door at just that moment. She fixed them with a baleful stare, and they turned around and left. Avis glanced at the clock. Dinner was still in its first sitting; it would be some time before anybody else repaired here.

Brooksbank approached with a glass of amber liquid held before him like a peace offering, and grudgingly she gestured him into the chair opposite. He had his own glass (less full) and steadied it carefully as he sat down, long limbs splaying out like a sigh. “To Friedrich,” he said, saluting her.

“To Friedrich,” Avis agreed distractedly. “And Frieda.” She barked out a laugh. “They were Frieda and Friedrich, my

God…" She swallowed a large gulp of her drink to tamp down the sudden lump in her throat and gasped at the unfamiliar burn. "That's not brandy."

"Rye whiskey," said Brooksbank, grinning. "You'll settle into it."

"I suppose I'd better," she said, stretching her legs out in front of her and crossing them at the ankle. Brooksbank obviously noticed the decidedly unladylike pose but chose to say nothing about it.

Instead, he decided to continue his irritating ways. "I didn't realise you were close to the deceased. When you said you'd been down in third class, I thought you meant as a passing fancy. I'm sorry."

"No, I wasn't." Avis frowned. "I'm not *close* to anyone. Either in this case specifically or in general terms. I spoke with them only briefly. But make no mistake," she added, "this…" She gestured around them. "This is the passing fancy. And fancy it is, indeed. I belong far more to third class than first."

It wasn't entirely true. With a father in the cotton trade, while he lived, she had been brought up in relative comfort, in a nice, terraced house in a medium-sized town of no consequence, with her own bedroom and even an indoor privy. He had even saved enough to send both his daughters away to school—a gift for which they were not at all thankful at the time. It wasn't until his death had rendered the family's funds a rather more finite resource that the Lovelocks had experienced true financial hardship, and by then Avis was well into her teens. And Patience…

"Another thing I think you'll appreciate about America," Brooksbank said. "Class distinctions are so much more flexible there. No one cares if you were born in a shack, as long as you've got talent and gumption. And you, Miss Lovelock, have more than enough of both of those." He was clearly trying to cheer her up. It would have been endearing if she hadn't been so thoroughly committed to her terrible mood.

"I don't believe it for a second. People never miss an

opportunity to judge or lord over one another. The Americans might do it differently, but you'll be no exception; I guarantee it."

He shrugged, truly unbothered about her prophecy. But then, what did he have to fear from judgement? Whatever hardships Carlton Brooksbank had faced, he'd clearly come out of them perfectly fine. "It's a land of opportunity, for better and for worse. Still, I think you'll do just fine there. Better than fine, if you can give Hamburg what they need to complete their sale."

"The Duquesnes' heads on plates. Now *that* I'll drink to," Avis said, lifting her glass and then taking another, slightly more moderate draught. It was smoother now, and a little sweet. "I don't like it," she declared anyway, on basic principle.

He roused then, setting his own glass aside. "You'll enjoy it more on a full stomach. You haven't had anything to eat. We should really head to the dining lounge, I'll get them to squeeze us in."

"Mm. No. Not interested."

"Miss Lovelock, please—"

"No. Thank you."

He sighed and pushed to his feet, and for a moment Avis thought he might drag her bodily from the chair. Thankfully he crossed the room instead, flagging down a crew member from the corridor and muttering instructions sotto voce. She clicked her tongue and took another sip.

"Not that whiskey on an empty stomach wouldn't be enough to give anybody a headache," he said upon returning and settling back into his chair, "but there's clearly more to your mood than that. Care to share your woes?"

"Not especially." When Brooksbank sat forward and raised his eyebrows expectantly, she attempted a different diversion. "He was soaked with salt water," she said. "He wasn't above deck. It makes no sense."

"So you believe there *is* an element of the paranormal here?"

"No! I mean, only insofar as it's not normal," Avis said,

swilling the liquid in her glass around. "I'm sure there's a logical explanation for it. It's just yet to be found." She closed her eyes, her brows drawing together. The moment seemed balanced on a knife edge: disclosure or deflection? "My sister drowned," she said after a moment, puncturing the silence. "When I was sixteen. I suppose that's distracting."

"Oh, Miss Lovelock, I had no idea. I'm sorry."

Obviously he had no idea—she'd never told him. She'd never told *anyone*, not anyone that knew her in this new life. She'd run so far to get away from her sister's death, her mother's grief.

"What was her name?"

Avis gave a dry chuckle. "Patience. What d'you think of that, eh?" She could feel a little of the North creeping into her words as she spoke, vowels long abandoned in favour of the anonymous intonations of Proper English.

"It's a lovely name." He was so damned nice, so *sincere*, it made her want to grind her teeth to dust. "What was she like?"

"She was my fourteen-year-old sister, what d'you think she was like? She was awful."

"That's fair. Still, to lose a sibling… I'm sorry. I can see why you were so shaken, now."

Avis slouched back in her seat, waved a hand. "It was a long time ago."

"Time doesn't always seem to act rationally when it comes to matters of loss and heartache." Brooksbank's smile turned melancholy, and she knew she should take the obvious conversational opening and ask about his own "loss and heartache", but she simply couldn't. She'd be no good at giving him comfort, anyway. Really, he ought to seek out the Duquesnes to have his heart salved.

"Well, it's rude. At least my mother had the good grace to go to pieces with haste. Within the year she was in the madhouse, and I was free to make my own way in the world."

"Oh, Miss Lovelock—"

"Enough. I didn't tell you to milk your pity," she said sharply, "only so that there was a… an explanation for my reaction earlier today. I am still more than capable of carrying out this investigation, and I'll thank you not to speak a word of this to King or anyone else."

"Of course," Brooksbank said, and his expression told her that should she want to speak further, he would be a receptive vessel. All Avis could offer was silence, and it was hardly companionable, but he still sat with her, both sipping their whiskey in contemplation until a waiter arrived at the door of the lounge, two covered trays in hand.

"Ah, here we are," Brooksbank said, waving him in, but Avis stood abruptly, making a slightly uneven path over to the drinks cart.

"I'll take it in my room."

Brooksbank's expression flickered from disappointment in his gesture being rejected to disappointment in *her*, and who could blame him? He probably thought they were forming a friendship, opening their hearts to one another, sharing their innermost confidences. He hadn't yet realised that Avis didn't *do* that, didn't make friends, or share secrets, or show weakness.

She couldn't, because if she did, eventually they would find out the truth.

Patience's death was her fault.

She had killed her sister.

BROOKSBANK HAD ORDERED her the prime rib. Between that and the half-full snifter of brandy she had taken from the smoking lounge, Avis had never had so rich a meal before her. She sat at the dresser in her cabin with the plate and glass in front of her and willed herself to pick up the cutlery and devour it, but just the thought of eating made her stomach turn. The meat sat on the plate, leaking pinkish juices that stained the mash surrounding it, and she couldn't help but think of Friedrich Müller, his jacket and trousers slowly staining the floorboards.

A dark shape in the mirror. Patience resolved, her hands folded before her. The hem of her dress dripped onto the carpet.

"I should have known you'd come to gloat," Avis muttered, pushing the plate back until it clinked against the mirror. She grabbed her glass and took a mouthful, wincing as she swallowed. "Well then. Have at it."

Aren't you going to eat?

Patience drifted closer, her face pale and painted in shadows—her eyes, her cheeks, the curve of her forehead. Avis felt a nauseous twist in the pit of her stomach.

"I'm not in the mood. Seeing a dead body will do that."

You're lucky, you know. That your hunger goes away. That you can sate it.

Avis frowned, staring at her sister in the mirror. For all that Patience was a figment, a concoction of her guilt-ridden mind, she could *feel* her presence at her back, the cold that radiated off her. She was never glad to see her, but sometimes she provided a twisted sense of reassurance, a morbid certainty in a world that went by in a blur of gin-soaked inconstancy. But then there were nights like these, where Patience wasn't her sister but something darker, a shade of the sardonic, lively girl Avis had known. Something hungry.

She couldn't turn around, couldn't let Patience see the way her hand trembled as it reached for her brandy. She overcompensated, as she always did, chuckling and swilling the amber in her glass. "Would that you would go away and leave me in peace. Didn't you hear the Duquesnes? Spirits are supposed to find it hard to travel over water. Perhaps you should have stayed at home."

Wherever you are, I am. You'll have to go a lot further if you want to get rid of me.

The smell of meat rose up, wet and suffocating. The shadow behind her shifted, drew closer. Any moment now she would feel Patience's hand on her shoulder, the cold seeping into her like spilled ink over a blank page. Bile and brandy on her tongue.

She considered the knife that lay alongside the plate. Its edge was serrated, teeth ready to rip and tear. What would it do to a spectre that had followed her across the ocean, to a memory that would not let her rest?

Her fingers closed around the handle; she shut her eyes and gathered her nerve. When she opened them again, the only face she saw in the mirror was her own.

Eighteen

When Avis woke, the stiffness that suffused her limbs was not only due to the lingering unease from the previous night's tragedy: the air in her stateroom was frigid. It condensed in front of her with every exhalation, and it took a moment for her to steel herself to push back the bedcovers. Though the radiator was hot to the touch (she immediately hung her stockings along it to warm them) it was no match for the arctic temperatures, or the frost encroaching across the inside of her little porthole window—albeit rather sluggishly, constantly beaten back by the thin film of salt that encrusted so many surfaces on board, even occasionally inside.

Donning a thick woollen skirt and a knitted bicycle sweater beneath her coat, Avis was forced by her stomach to venture forth. People were similarly bundled up in the dining saloon, the men in overcoats and top hats, the women layered in shawls and capes. Nearly every table was furnished with presently unused muffs made from the fur of just about every animal under the sun, it seemed, as if they had each brought a small, well-behaved pet to breakfast with them. Avis wondered if Bou Bou was being put to alternate use in this new frigid climate.

The Duquesnes (she hated that she now scanned every room for them upon entry) were nowhere to be seen, as was usual at this time, but Brooksbank was already at breakfast. Though she was keen for an update on any overnight developments in the investigation of Friedrich's death, she was reluctant to speak to him after her confidences of the previous night. She opted to eat a quick, cold breakfast of a scone and conserve before forging out onto the deck in search of a useful member of the crew.

The cold hit her in a wave as she emerged onto the promenade. The sky was a white sheet, and wind whistled through every nook and cranny, the rigging groaning and cackling like conversing trees in an old pine forest.

There were plenty of crew up here, but they did not look at all minded to field questions from passengers. They were flitting this way and that with the slightly bouncy stride of people who would rather be running. Every face was a picture of tamped-down panic. She stood a while observing their comings and goings, trying to get a sense for where they were coming from, going to, what they might be doing while they were there. Judging by various sheets of tarpaulin, strapping, and similar, she eventually ascertained that they must be engaging in some form of weatherproofing effort—and in a hurry. Something had gone wrong.

She grabbed the arm of a passing boy, moving to block his path before he could shake her off. "Baynes?"

The boy blinked. Then, too confused and in too much of a hurry to argue, he said, "Bridge."

Avis wasn't at all sure she'd be able to gain entry to the bridge, but she certainly intended to try. Though she wasn't entirely sure in which direction she was meant to go, a few moments carefully observing the flow of staff and crew began to show a pattern. When next a higher-ranking crewman passed, she fell into step beside him. "I don't know that you'll know this," she said, "but I've been employed by the Hamburg Line to investigate goings-on on this ship." It was *almost* true. "Perhaps you've heard about me?"

The man, a tall fellow who'd been dragged out of bed without a shave or breakfast, shook his head.

"Well, you can ask Brooksbank or King about it, but for now all I require is to speak to Baynes, who I believe may be on the bridge at this moment?"

Her explanation hadn't convinced him, but throwing names around like confetti was clearly the trick. He nodded and gestured for her to follow him, and she pulled her knitted sleeves down over her freezing hands and set off with him.

The bridge was impressive, as no doubt it was meant to be: redolent with polished wood and brass, full of instruments that were no doubt state of the art and very expensive. They were also at that moment being subjected to a tirade of abuse from a white-haired man in a rumpled, braid-trimmed jacket.

"… shit-cogged worthless piece of— Hold on, who's this? Lady on the bridge!"

He and the other ragged-looking officers straightened up, and it was all Avis could do to keep a straight face. "At ease, gentlemen. I'm no lady, and it looks like you've got better things to do than make yourselves proper for me. Avis Lovelock, spirit debunker and temporary icicle. What's with the freeze?"

The man—Avis assumed he was the captain, for he had the fanciest jacket, and though he wasn't wearing a hat, looked like he ought to be—grimaced. "We've, ah, taken a small detour northward, into colder waters. But don't worry, madam, the crew will ensure all cabins and staterooms are as cosy as possible very shortly."

"I see. I…" Avis almost moved on to her original purpose for being here, but in the moment she found that she needed to know more. "I'm sorry, are you in the habit of losing track of where you are?" The captain began to splutter in consternation and she lifted a hand for clarification. "My apologies, sir. That is to say, I assume that your navigators are skilled professionals, and I'm wondering whether you've been able to ascertain why and how this happened."

"The navigators are skilled, yes, but only as skilled as their instruments will allow. Something's gone wrong with this antique bloody course compass," he harrumphed, gesturing to one of the inset instruments that frankly looked like all the other inset instruments. Behind him, Baynes shifted and cleared his throat. The captain's frown deepened. "I assure you, it's rare but certainly not unheard of, and no cause for alarm. All will be right soon enough."

The captain was maintaining his composure with no small amount of self-control, and Avis was impressed, because he was lying. Whatever malfunction they had discovered, he—as of yet—had no idea how to resolve it and was deeply worried about it. Still, it wasn't why she was here. "In truth, I came for an update on the unfortunate Herr Müller. Was the doctor able to find out any more about his death?"

If anything, the captain's expression grew stormier. "The doctor has been temporarily relieved. We will have to wait until we reach New York for an autopsy to be carried out."

"I'm sorry, 'temporarily relieved'? Can I ask why?"

"Because he's gone mad. Which is a shame, because I have no doubt our passengers are going to start complaining of frostbite any moment now."

Avis frowned. "Mad? Mad, how? Could I perhaps speak to him?"

"She really ought to," Baynes said then, and the captain gave a gust of a sigh.

"By all means, ask him to tea if you want. At least *you* won't be swayed by his preposterous claims."

Avis was used to working alone, for the most part. She didn't like sharing the spotlight on stage, but as it turned out, investigations benefitted from more than one pair of eyes, and possibly even more than one brain with which to suss things out. She'd run into Usher on her way through one of the lounges and hadn't thought twice about inviting him along. She barely knew who she was any more. "Thank you for joining me."

The corridors below decks grew quite narrow in places. There were broad concourses and hallways and foyers between the various first and second-class saloons, but once one was into the accommodation and utility areas, they were often barely double file. Thankfully there was a broader hallway leading to the sick-bay, presumably to account for the transportation of casualties, and here she and Usher could walk—or, in his case, limp—two abreast.

"Anything to help the remarkable Miss Lovelock," Usher replied, with a smile to pretend he was joking.

"Too kind. I'm surprised they didn't immediately attempt to draft you in, to be honest. Isn't that usually the way in a situation such as this?"

"Possibly, but I'm listed as 'Captain' rather than 'Doctor' in the manifest. Mind you, there must be other doctors on board. I would bet they've been too distracted by this navigational business."

The doctor, she had been informed, was still in the sick-bay, refusing to leave his tiny office. The crew had simply hung a sign on the door declaring it off limits and left him to it. Avis pushed the door open and peered inside; in the tiny cabin at the other end of the bay she could see a figure moving back and forth. She knocked on the door through which she had just entered.

"Doctor, er, Klein? It's Avis Lovelock. We met briefly last night?"

The doctor was a bald man with a fringe of dark hair ringing his scalp, which had been subject to repeated and excessive disturbance of late. His glasses were smudged, and she could see a bloodstain on his collar—not a patient's, thankfully, but a remnant of a shaving injury from shaking hands. "Yes, I remember you. The debunker," he said. "I suppose you're here to tell me how stupid I've been. Well, you can say what you like. It won't change what I saw."

"I'm not here to berate you, sir. I just want to hear your side. What's happened?"

He shook his head and began to pace again, which was quite a feat given the size of the office and the fact that she and

Usher now occupied a good portion of it. "I was investigating Herr Müller's death, as is protocol. I was expecting a clear-cut case—weak heart, or something of that ilk—but I intended to be thorough. As it turns out, the cause of death was very clear-cut indeed, but it was not his heart that killed him, no."

Avis waited expectantly; silence was as effective as a prompt, sometimes more.

"It's a wild claim, I know. I would hardly believe it myself if I hadn't been the one to uncover it. And yet there it was, undeniable as the break of day."

She raised her eyebrows and tipped her head encouragingly.

"I've got it all written up, of course, but the captain simply doesn't believe me. He says I must have a screw loose to have put forward such a wild theory. But that's just it—it's no theory! It's scientific fact."

"*What* is?" she asked, finally breaking.

"Why, it is my professional opinion that Herr Müller died by asphyxiation. More to the point, his lungs were suffused with water. Cause of death: suffocation by way of drowning."

THE DOCTOR WOULDN'T be drawn further, except to say that there was no sign of the kind of physical battering the man would likely have taken had he fallen overboard—added to that, of course, the fact that somebody would have had to both retrieve him and carry him several levels below decks afterwards. At Avis's urging, Usher promised to ask if he too might examine the body and give a second opinion, but when they brought this request to the first mate he forbade it out of hand. There were protocols to be followed, he contended, and besides, the body was now in lock-up and the crew were far too busy dealing with the impacts of their navigational mishap to accommodate what he most certainly viewed as the whims of a pair of entitled, time-wasting passengers.

"Did the doctor seem mad to you?" Avis asked as they strolled in the general direction of the main saloon.

Usher pursed his lips, making his gingery moustache fan out in every direction. "'Much Madness is divinest Sense - To a discerning Eye - Much Sense - the starkest Madness.' He appeared distressed," he said. "Not insane."

"Mm. I thought the same."

"Still, the conclusion is pretty outlandish. No way that fellow could have drowned without several people being in on it. And then there's the question of *why* someone'd even bother." He pulled out his flask, taking a deep swig and then offering it to Avis. "Did Müller have enemies on the ship? A reason to want him dead?"

Avis shook her head, both to the question and to the proffered flask. "He was a third-class passenger with his family before he signed on as crew. Well-loved or hardly known, and a competent mechanic by all accounts."

"Well then. I've got nothing. I hate to say it, but this spirits claim is looking more and more plausible by the minute."

"Don't, Usher, I'm relying on you to be my fellow rational thinker here. There has to be a logical explanation." Avis sighed, jamming her hands into the pockets of her skirt.

Usher glanced sideways at her, and she recognised that look: he was sussing her out, trying to judge whether she would be receptive to what he had to say next. "Dear God, don't tell me you believe in this dross," she said with a sigh. "You're a man of science."

"'Believe' is a strong word. But I can tell you that the more we learn about science, the more we realise there are some things we might never understand." He looked away, focusing on the ground as they walked, his back-and-forth gait more pronounced than ever. "You know my history with the Army. The things I saw beggared belief—the cruelty, the disregard for human life."

"Yes, yes, I know, war is hell. But the explanation for all that is very clear: people are terrible shits. Nothing supernatural about it."

He ignored her and continued, "And when we won, what did we do? Did we learn our lesson? Did we hell. Went right back at it with the Indians, except this time we weren't doing the right thing." Usher shook his head, stopping their march to peer wistfully out of the nearest porthole. The sea was a frosty grey, gunmetal under a bleached-bone sky. "I don't know why I stayed—I suppose I thought I wasn't complicit. After all, I was just doctoring, not parading out there on the front lines. But every soldier I patched up went back out there and picked up a rifle and butchered those poor men and women. My hand was on the stock as much as theirs."

Avis reined in her tongue, knowing that he'd get to the point soon enough and any hectoring from her would only distract. She'd never seen him like this, morose and contemplative, and wondered whether she needed to seek out a new partner in crime. Sadly, the list of possible replacements was short, nearly non-existent.

"Anyhow, we were out at Camp Robinson at the end of the campaign, and the scouts come in, said they'd found a camp of Cheyenne up the river. Mackenzie packs us all out and we push on until we reach Camp McKinney, and a snowstorm hits and we have to hunker down and wait it out."

"Sounds a bit familiar," Avis said then. The cold had started to seep in as soon as they'd stopped moving, and she fancied she could see the puff of her breath before her.

Usher shot her a distant smile, his attention clearly elsewhere in memory. "It was the worst I'd ever seen it. Howling winds, a complete white-out. We surgeons were kept busy. Half the men were in danger of frostbite or worse; we'd been on the move for so long and our equipment was so worn. At the time I thought it was just hallucinations, caused by exhaustion and a guilty conscience."

"You thought *what* was hallucinations?"

"I saw things out in the snow. Figures moving around when no one could've actually been out there. Indians, I thought, though they didn't have their big buffalo robes or blankets. Warriors, women, even little children, all trudging through the snow like they were being driven onward. Some of them fell and didn't get back up again." He blinked, and she realised he was in danger of crying. The idea made her supremely uncomfortable. Americans were almost as bad as Europeans when it came to embarrassing outward displays of emotion. Luckily he drew in a breath, gathering himself together. "It wasn't real, couldn't have been. But I know what I saw."

"No doubt you were exhausted," Avis said, attempting gentleness. "There's no shame in that, in seeing things because your body was under stress."

"I'm not ashamed of that, though I've got plenty else to feel remorse about. Like I said, for the longest time I did think it was just that. But now, after hearing about what people are seeing on this ship, what Klein thinks happened to Müller… Maybe I'm wrong. Maybe there *was* something out there."

"Hmm." Avis scrunched her fingers in her pockets, attempting to force warmth and feeling back into them. Something didn't sit right about Usher's story, but she was too cold and distracted to pinpoint it. "Well, at any rate, there's still time to get to the bottom of all this. Brooksbank said this redirection will add a few more days onto our journey. If I didn't know better, I'd say the Duquesnes did it themselves to earn more time to convince folk of their ridiculous claims. Speaking of, I wonder where the string-bean degenerates have got to," she mused at length. "Though now that I think about it, I rarely see them before noon anyway. You?"

"Can't say that I have."

Avis chewed her lower lip, which was even more chapped than usual by the cold, and tender from her absentminded worrying at it. "Well. Perhaps I shall set up camp near their staterooms—it's more important than ever that I track their movements, I suspect."

Usher gave her a half-hearted nod, his hand straying to the pocket of his jacket where he kept his flask. She could tell the memories stirred up by his story would not be sitting quietly, and she urged him to at least seek out company in the saloon while she continued her expedition.

Nineteen

First class was perhaps spared the worst of the chill. The thick carpets and stodgy wood protected it from the cold seeping in from the deck, and it was above the waterline, beneath which freezing ocean waves slapped at the walls. Still, she hoped to hook onto the Duquesnes soon enough; perpetual motion was the only way to keep warm, absent a roaring fire to curl up next to.

Her time lurking and eavesdropping had served her well. There were actually quite a few little nooks one could tuck into to watch the comings and goings of the passengers, if one didn't mind occasionally getting a funny look from someone turning into their room (Avis was immune to funny looks). She spent some time amusing herself by counting the layers of clothing coating the passers-by, but thankfully did not have to play at that game for too long. Her quarry emerged from their rooms in a carefully coordinated display, though that was where their synchronicity ended. Gideon and Charlotte turned left from the corridor, clearly aiming for the stairwell up to the dining hall, while Rachel turned to the right. The brother shot a disapproving look in that direction, which the sister duly ignored.

Avis was briefly torn. She was fascinated by the dynamic between Charlotte and Gideon, however, if Rachel was bound for somewhere else alone, it seemed far more likely that it was she who would be furthering any preparations to perpetuate their deceptions. At first, she was minded to tail Rachel all the way to her intended destination, but she quickly disregarded this idea. As always, the direct route was far more fun.

"Off somewhere interesting?" she asked as she trotted to catch up, falling into step beside Rachel as they hit a broader stretch of corridor.

Rachel didn't start or flinch—disappointing. She kept up the same steady pace, not even sparing a look to the side at her new-found companion. "I'm going back to third class. This isn't part of the investigation. Your presence is not required."

"Well then, I suppose I shall have to accompany you out of the goodness of my heart."

"I am doubtful any such substance exists. You simply have nothing better to do."

Avis swooned melodramatically, clutching her hands to her heart. "You wound me! But very well, I shan't stay where I'm not wanted." She slowed her pace, let Duquesne pull ahead. "I suppose you won't want to hear what I learned from the ship's doctor, either."

Rachel's steps faltered. Hah! She had her. "What did you hear?"

Avis grinned triumphantly. "Tell you after lunch."

Duquesne huffed, speeding up once again, and Avis sniggered as she followed.

The lounge was less full than their last visit, but the mood was about as sombre. Rachel made her way to the group at the booth and enquired after Frieda; apparently she had emerged from her berth for tea and toast that morning but was now back inside, presumably with her gaggle of children. The medium nodded thoughtfully, and Avis expected her to make a beeline for the cabin, but instead she drifted over to the piano and lifted the battered fiddle from its place on top.

Avis slipped into a booth populated with a handful of at least passingly familiar faces and watched Rachel quietly plucking its strings and tweaking its rather creaky pegs to tune it for a minute or two, tightening the bow, bouncing it a few times on the back of her hand. The fiddle had no shoulder pad, and so she removed her scarf and rolled it up, resting the makeshift pad on her shoulder before lifting the fiddle to her chin and beginning to play.

It wasn't a song Avis recognised, which was somewhat surprising. Between her boarding school education and her time in the music halls, she'd heard her share of tunes, so she expected Rachel to play something she knew—a well-known hymn or ballad, perhaps, something for the crowds. But the unfamiliar notes gave way to an unfamiliar melody, and it became clear very quickly that Rachel wasn't playing for anybody but herself. Her entire being said so—from the way she closed her eyes tight, pale lashes pressed to her cheeks, to the ease and sway of her body as she followed the song through the rise and fall of its cadence. It was in a minor key, of course, and it fitted the mood of the room as if she had tapped into the invisible, unheard waves of emotion and increased their volume.

Directly behind her, gazing across at Avis, stood Patience, as solid as Avis had ever seen her. She watched her sister reach out a hand towards Rachel's pale, wavy locks. She did not touch her—she couldn't, after all—but all the same Avis watched Rachel sway in towards Patience's hand like a cat inclining its head for a scratch, and in spite of herself, Avis gasped.

The music stopped abruptly, and Rachel's eyes flew open, immediately fixed on Avis's. In the silence that followed, nobody clapped, but there was the scraping, shuffling sound of the lanky dark-haired pianist unfolding himself from his booth and sidling up to the piano. He looked at Rachel in question, and she nodded her assent, rising from where she sat on the piano stool and moving to stand by the instrument, at the ready. The boy struck up a tune that sounded familiar without being one Avis could specifically place—an American traditional song, she'd guess—and Rachel soon picked it up and began to play along. Patience was gone.

Folk filtered in, drawn by the music. Avis noted that Not-George was now wearing the overalls of a crewman; perhaps he had stepped in to fill the role vacated by Friedrich. That was interesting. He did not strike Avis as the type to be interested in working for his passage, even if it benefitted him financially. Soon enough, Frieda herself shuffled through the door. She looked the worse for wear, her eyes reddened and swollen, but she summoned up a ghost of a smile when she saw Avis and approached the booth. "Fraulein Lovelock. If I had a cabin in first class, you wouldn't find me down here, especially now."

"It's warmer in here," Avis said. "And the company is better. I'm so sorry, Frieda."

The woman's smile faltered, and she let out a heavy sigh. "Vielen Dank. It feels like I am still asleep, like ein Albtraum. I wish I could wake from it."

"How are the children?" The youngsters were beginning to filter in now that Frieda was here—still a huge multi-family gaggle, but decidedly less boisterous than the last time she had seen them.

"They are children. You know. They understand a bit but not everything. It will come."

There was a tug at Avis's cuff. "Can you do tricks again?"

Avis smiled. "You go find me some cards and I'll see what I can do." Her eyes kept being drawn to where Rachel stood, swaying in place as she coaxed a ballad out of the rather weary instrument in her hands. Her expression was relaxed—at least, more relaxed than Avis had ever seen it—and like this, unbound from the strictures of her mediumship and the pinch-mouthed disapproval she directed specifically in Avis's direction, she was almost lovely.

Lovely, is she?

Avis sucked in a breath and Frieda looked over at her in concern, necessitating a quick shake of her head and wave of her hand. "Just gas," she said, and then, "Want a drink?"

A proper wake would've had hard liquor, but third class only had beer, so beer was what they drank. A drink became a hearty lunch of beef stew and potatoes, and as the warm food suffused Avis's insides she began to feel human again. Rachel had stayed also, slipping into the booth with Avis and Frieda and the children, though as usual she pushed her food around her plate rather than actually consuming it.

Frieda was having none of it. "You need to eat something, look at you. You are like the Spargel, there is nothing there. More potatoes, they will stick to you. Keep you warm."

Avis watched with fascination the myriad expressions twitching across Rachel's face. She could see disgust in the curve of her lip, annoyance in the lift of her eyebrow, but beneath all that, most surprising of all—*hunger*. Rachel Duquesne was starving, but all she did was use her knife to cut one of Frieda's potatoes into smaller and smaller pieces, until she finally speared one (now the size of a sixpence) and reluctantly lifted it to her mouth.

She wants so much, and will allow herself to have so little. Feels familiar, perhaps?

Avis wanted to say something suddenly, but tamped down the urge. Instead, she retreated to her usual position: that of the needle. Conscious that the last thing Frieda needed on this day was to bear witness to hostility, she waited for their tablemates to finish their food and leave them alone, Frieda moving to a table that looked to be Friedrich's crewmates, and the children to God-knew-where, before making a preparatory stab.

"Your dear brother must be wondering where you are," she said. "Should we expect him to join us in due course?"

Rachel frowned at her food. "He has other pursuits on his mind at present," she said. Her tone betrayed her pique at this state of affairs. Disagreement. Discord. Perfect.

"I suppose he must be much distracted seeing to Madame

Berthault's spiritual needs." Avis barely emphasised the word "needs"—just the tiniest extra weight—but Rachel caught it nevertheless, glancing up sharply.

"Charlotte Berthault is an intelligent, single-minded woman who knows precisely what she wants," she said. Her voice was quiet, and yet even in the busy saloon Avis heard every word in that gravelly alto that had at first sounded so out-of-step with Rachel's delicate appearance. "If you are the expert reader of faces and bodies that you claim to be, you know this already. And yet you continue to pursue this defence of her honour—a service she most certainly did not request. One begins to wonder why."

Avis shot her a serene smile. "I'm concerned only with the truth."

"Another lie. Perhaps you want the truth, or some version of it—your neatly packaged variety that accounts only for things you can see and touch. But regardless, it is *far* from your only concern."

"Oh?" Inwardly, Avis bristled. She kept her smile firmly in place. "Do tell. What am I so concerned about that I won't admit to?"

Rachel took the opportunity to lay down her fork so that she could turn in her seat, facing Avis more fully across the corner of the table. She narrowed her eyes. "Control would be the obvious choice. That's definitely a part of it. Power, certainly. That, I can understand—and I sympathise. You and I, our routes to power of any kind are so limited, we must grasp it where we can." She cocked her head to the side, eyes flitting about Avis's face as though every curve, every mark, every line told her something new. "The satisfaction of solving a puzzle—of course, you make no mystery of that, and why should you? But it gets just a tiny bit less thrilling every time, doesn't it?"

Avis flinched, and Rachel's mouth twitched towards the hint of a smile. Her lips were chapped from the cold and salt, though not as badly as Avis's. Perhaps she did not worry them ragged the way Avis did. They were just slightly asymmetrical, hooked downward a shade more at one side than the other. This was all entirely usual and ordinary and yet suddenly it was all Avis could look at. They sounded out another word, now, and Avis heard it a split second after.

"Catharsis." The tip of Rachel's tongue protruded between her teeth on the peak of the stressed syllable. It was not a whisper and yet somehow felt like one anyway; Avis felt the word as a breath on her ear. Her pulse skittered. "A sad way to seek release. There are better outlets, in my humble opinion."

"I didn't ask for your opinion." Avis couldn't help the retort.

"Forgive me, but you did. Just one last ingredient, I think."

Good. She wanted this to be over. How and when had her intentions, *her* motivations, become the topic of conversation? "And that is?"

Rachel seemed closer. Had she shifted nearer, or was it just an illusion because they were now alone in their booth? Her eyes, never quite either blue or green, darkened as she spoke, and this time her teeth caught her dry lower lip, biting down in emphasis.

"Revenge."

Twenty

It felt as though the ship was at a pitch, but perhaps she had drunk too much beer and eaten too little food. She barely recalled her escape from the saloon—she didn't *think* she had run headlong from the room, though she had sorely wanted to. She came to a halt as soon as she found herself alone, having turned down a poky utility corridor that housed a somewhat haphazard pile of bulky life jackets and a single narrow door marked with the mysterious legend *ACCESS*.

Here, she braced against the wall and sucked in long, deep lungfuls of air as she willed her heart to stop hammering.

It would not. It was as if she had run a mile, though Avis never ran if she could help it, and certainly not at distance. Besides, a mile wouldn't take her far enough from her problems—from this damned ship, its non-existent ghosts, and the hollow-cheeked woman intent on tormenting her.

There was a familiar scuff of noise behind her and she swung around, fully intent on laying every curse she could on Patience's head for intruding *now* of all times. But it wasn't her sister's ghost blocking the corridor. Rather, it was the very real figure of Rachel Duquesne, who glanced around herself curiously. "You left before you could tell me your news."

"My news? What news? Oh..." Avis scowled. "The ship's

doctor says that Friedrich Müller drowned."

Rachel didn't immediately challenge this assertion, her crooked mouth turning further downward in thought. After a moment she shook her head. "It makes no sense."

"Well, no, he was several decks down and there was no sign he'd been moved."

Rachel's eyes narrowed. "Which is compelling evidence that whatever happened here is supernatural."

"If such a thing was possible, which we both know is not the case."

"You have no better explanation," Rachel said with a dismissive wave of her hand, "or you would have offered it up by now. So you must concede my point."

"I'll concede that I have yet to alight upon an explanation other than the doctor being incorrect. That's my running theory. And since they won't let us have access for a second opinion, we can neither confirm nor deny it." Avis sighed, turning to lean back against the wall, which immediately began to radiate cold through her clothes. "Rendering it more the illusion of progress than anything concrete."

"It's progress nonetheless. We know there's something strange going on, that Herr Müller's death wasn't simply a natural passing. And it narrows down the possibilities—that either someone filled his lungs with water and left him to be found, or that the spirits somehow crossed into our plane fully enough to leave physical manifestation of their presence behind. Both of which give us further things to investigate. Your pessimism is unfounded."

Avis gave a growl of frustration. "Or he didn't drown at all and the doctor is wrong. Or delusional. Plenty of *that* going around. Did you know that there's a school of thought that the visions people saw at Salem were caused by ergot poisoning from contaminated grain? Perhaps we should be looking at the food supplies."

"Feel free," the medium said, turning on her heel. "I'm going to the engine room."

It took Avis a moment to parse this. "The engine room? Why?"

Rachel's voice floated over her shoulder, a rough caress. "Because that's where the body was found. And if we are to get to the bottom of this, that's where we need to start."

It made sense—indeed, any investigator would do the same. So why was it so irritating when Rachel Duquesne did it? Perhaps it was because when they arrived at said engine room, her "investigations" would no doubt comprise "attuning" and "communing" and nothing at all in the way of looking for evidence. Avis was minded to leave her to it, but her feet carried her along after the medium anyway.

Rachel was a brisk walker, and she did not offer small talk. Avis amused herself by imagining what it would look like if she did; would they discuss the price of black lace, maybe, or which widows in first class looked most dupable? She ignored the small part of her that thought they might discuss music, and perhaps Rachel would share the name of the piece she had played that morning, the melody of which was still winding itself around Avis's brain.

The engine room was not locked—it was a place you either belonged and knew how to get into, or did not and did not. Rachel, however, not unlike Avis, was clearly the sort of person who remembered a route having trodden it once. The heat that hit them as they pushed open the heavy metal door was all the more extreme today, when the rest of the ship was so cold.

"They said he was found on the gantry," Rachel said, her voice joining with the thrumming of the machines until Avis could not tell the two apart. "We should begin there."

Avis frowned, then nodded. It was as sensible an option as any. At the least, perhaps if he had a bucket of seawater tossed over him post-mortem there might be evidence of that encrusted on the metal walkway.

They didn't know exactly *where* on the gantry he'd fallen, of course, and drawing attention to themselves by asking questions was as likely to get them kicked out as helped. So they merely climbed the steps and made their slow progress, Rachel with one hand outstretched, Avis with a smirk fixed firmly on her lips. It was useful that the woman was still playing at this pretence; it helped her remember how absurd the Duquesnes were.

They'd traversed about half of the walkway when Avis felt a trickle of cold run down her neck. She glanced around, convinced that a leak had sprung from somewhere, but of course there was nothing. *Excambion* was a sturdy ship. Still, she couldn't shake the feeling, and the warmth of the room slowly eroded with each step until she was shivering and reaching to probe the collar of her shirt with questing fingers.

Ahead of her Rachel paused, then turned. She caught Avis's motion and tipped her head to the side like a bird. "Something the matter?"

"Yes," Avis said, huffing out the word and expecting her breath to condense in front of her. "You're wasting our time."

"Mm." Duquesne turned away again, fingers skimming over the railing. She didn't move on, however, merely rocking back and forth where she stood, in time with the great, deep *lub lub lub* of the engines.

"Can we skip the theatrics, please?" Avis said, moving to push past her. To her surprise, Rachel gasped, reaching to halt her with a firm, almost painful grip on her upper arms.

"Can't you feel that?"

In that moment, Avis could feel a great deal. The chill that was seeping into her bones. The bite of Rachel's fingers on the soft flesh of her arms. The heat of Rachel's eyes on her, searching, seeking.

"I don't know what you mean," she said. It was true enough. "That" could be anything and everything. "Miss Duquesne, there's just us two here. I know that you don't speak to the dead. You needn't keep up the charade."

She watched the muscles in Rachel's jaw work, her lips going pale as she pressed them together in... frustration? Anger? After a moment she released Avis forcefully and turned, tendrils of blonde hair snaking down her back in silent admonition. Avis felt the cold rush in like a dam bursting, and she reached to steady herself on the gantry railing.

"Fine," Avis said. "What is it you feel?"

"It happened here. I can feel... the cold. The water. Only a trickle, but..."

A shudder rippled down Avis's spine. "This is nonsense," she murmured.

Rachel turned back to her, and her dark brows drew together like curtains across a stage. "Your lips. They're blue." Her voice was strangely distant, echoing as though they were in a tunnel. Above it was a high-pitched drone, a thousand insects whirring at once in a thousand different sharps and flats.

Catch.

"What?"

I wasn't talking to you.

Rachel pitched closer suddenly, and then everything went black.

SHE WAS WARM now, at least. As the blessed oblivion of unconsciousness gave way to the reality of a thumping headache, Avis became aware that she was swaddled like a baby in multiple layers of blankets. With some reluctance, she cracked her eyes open to resolve a vague, brown room, empty save for the dark cloud of Patience's presence at the foot of the bed.

You're not alone.

"You moan in your sleep." That wasn't Patience's voice.

"Christ in heaven…"

"I have to assume you don't believe in *that* either."

Avis groaned. As Rachel swam into focus, she realised that the room was not in fact brown, merely poorly lit and unadorned, a single lamp turned low painting warm streaks across those porcelain cheeks. The berth in which she lay was a narrow bunk, with another not far above her head. The mattress was significantly harder than the one in her stateroom, although Avis had slept on worse.

"Now. Are you still going to insist you didn't feel anything in there?" Rachel shifted, leaning over to tend to something on the small table between them—a teapot, of all things. "Because that would be very tedious."

Avis pushed up, then slumped back as another wave of pain rattled her head. "It signifies little either way. Suggestion is a powerful thing, and nobody is immune. We cannot always trust our senses. Mine, least of all."

"You think you did that to yourself? You truly are an egotist of the highest order."

Avis began to laugh, but it morphed into a cough. "I possibly am, but it's not ego that makes me mistrust my own senses."

Rachel wrapped her long fingers around the handle of the teapot, lifting it to pour one, two cups of steaming tea. "Even as you rely on them above everything else? Always watching everyone, noticing things they don't even notice themselves. Listening to conversations you've not been invited into."

Avis shrugged. "I contain multitudes."

The tea arrived at her bedside, the cup hovering by her hand until she roused enough to take it. "What is it, then? Why this self-doubt?"

"That's not your concern." Avis took a sip of tea. It was too hot. "How did I get here?"

"You danced, just like you're dancing around my questions." Rachel wrapped her fingers around her cup and blew across its surface. "It's a spare cabin. The crossing isn't fully booked."

This did not answer Avis's question, but fair was fair, she supposed.

"What time is it?"

"Time for pre-dinner drinks, upstairs." Rachel raised her cup in a mock toast.

"I suppose the after-dinner theatre will once again be courtesy of the Duquesnes? What will it be tonight? Drowned sailors or dead husbands?"

The cup lowered. Rachel's expression hardened. At the end of the bed, Patience's figure wavered.

"This refrain grows tired," Rachel declared. She stood, suddenly all angles and judgement again. "You may disbelieve what we do, the solace we bring, but our communion with the spirits serves an important purpose. It is not just play-acting and theatre."

"*There are no spirits, damn you!*" Avis put her cup down, sloshing tea out onto the nightstand, and pushed upright, this time with more success. She had only fainted, after all, probably disorientated by the sudden heat from the engine room. She wasn't some delicate lady swooning after a dramatic event. She fought the cocoon of blankets around her like a fly struggling in a spider's web, eventually freeing her shoulders and swinging her legs off the berth. As she rose, she hit her head on the upper bunk and cursed loudly, stumbling to her feet. Hands gripped her upper arms, and her senses filled with the scent of sandalwood and spices as Rachel rose to meet her, to steady her. In every way but the strictly physical, it had the opposite effect.

"I know you do not speak to them, and you know it too," Avis spat. "If you're going to maintain this tired charade, I must once again request that the least you could do is drop the pretence when there's nobody in the room but me."

As it had before, Rachel's gaze drifted over Avis's shoulder, her eyes defocusing, fingers tightening. The room felt too close and the bunks loomed around them. Then she returned to herself, blinking as if she had just woken from a fitful sleep.

"At least one of those things is untrue," she murmured. "Dare I call it a lie? But no matter. I am needed elsewhere, and clearly you have no need of my help." She dropped her hands, stepping back until she was all but pressed against the door. "Be well, Miss Lovelock."

Only once the door had clicked shut did Avis sink into the chair Rachel had vacated, burying her face in her hands. Heat stung the back of her eyes, and her arms and legs trembled, though this cabin was not at present particularly cold. This situation was slipping through her fingers, no matter where she tried to find purchase. The Duquesnes, Müller's death, the ship itself: every mystery before her was an unfamiliar shape, every puzzle missing pieces.

There was nothing to be gained from wallowing here feeling sorry for herself, Avis knew. Rachel was right about one thing: there was *something* amiss on *Excambion*, and the only way she would find it was by refusing to be blocked or gainsaid. But in that moment, sitting in a chair warmed by another, heartsore and weary and confused, tears came, and wallow she did.

Twenty-One

The lounges were stuffed with people ahead of the first dinner sitting, all of them keen to gather together and generate as much heat as possible. Normally Avis would have been in her element, moving between groups like a swan angling for bread crusts, but all the glittering jewellery and high-pitched laughter seemed calculated to exacerbate her headache. She gripped her champagne glass tightly and girded herself as she made her way into the throng.

Unsurprisingly, many of the conversations revolved around the erroneously diverted course their ship had taken and, more importantly, when it might be rectified. There was talk of filing complaints with the captain, of demanding to be compensated for their discomfort—a dozen self-involved whinges that Avis had little interest in. She sidestepped the moaners and continued onwards, steering herself towards a knot of familiar faces, including Usher, who nodded to her as she arrived.

"Well, I've never heard of this happening before, have you?" Mrs Armitage asked, sniffing. "Just losing track of where the ship is and going in totally the wrong direction."

"Actually, ships go off course all the time," Avis volunteered helpfully. "It's quite terrifying, really. The oceans are *extremely* large and it's quite easy for a ship to just... disappear. The number that set off from one shore or another and never turn up where they're supposed to should really make us all reconsider whether this is a valid means of travel altogether."

"An extremely helpful observation while we are currently *on* a ship," Mr Armitage said. He patted his wife's arm, though Avis could tell it was only to forestall hysterics, not out of genuine worry for her well-being.

"I still think it must have something to do with this war that's heating up," Mrs Armitage went on as though nobody else had spoken. "We must surely have diverted to avoid danger at sea."

"Well, if that's the case, I'm glad the captain is doing what he must to keep us safe," Clarissa said, pulling her wrap more closely about her. It shifted, and Avis realised the dog was tucked up inside, just the tip of its ears visible. "Though I can't say I agree with that whole conflict—surely the Spanish should be allowed to do what they want with Cuba. It's their territory, after all."

"Just because a country's responsible for a people doesn't mean they always have their best interests at heart," Usher said then, uncharacteristically outspoken on the matter. Avis thought of the way he'd reddened when he'd described the U.S. Army's encroachment into Indian territory. "Why should historical ownership mean anything for the future precedent?"

"Well, it's just that they understand it all," Sarah said. "I'm not saying the Americans are *wrong*, you understand, but to charge into another country's business uninvited seems rather rude."

"The English obsession with politeness is ridiculous," Usher replied with an irritated twitch of his moustache. "Rude or not, standing up for freedom is the right thing to do."

"Especially after that ship was blown up," another man said. Avis didn't recognise him, but he had a rather jaunty pair of spectacles perched on the end of his nose that looked minded to tumble off at an errant sniff.

"Well, yes, they could hardly let that go," Sarah allowed, nodding.

"Over two hundred and fifty dead," Usher said, that note of outrage returning to his voice. "Almost a hundred more injured. It was a travesty."

"And this is what I'm saying: ships, very unsafe," Avis interjected, hoping to keep things from getting too weighty—and boring. "All that water just waiting to rush in. Whose idea was it to put these tin cans in the middle of the ocean?"

This prompted a chuckle from the assembly with various degrees of nervousness, and soon enough the bell rang for dinner. Avis ensured that she went with Clarissa and Sarah—as a pair they talked a great deal but seldom required a response, and chattering company without the requirement to muster up conversation for her own part was precisely what Avis craved at that moment, disinclined either to socialise or to be alone with her thoughts. Unfortunately, it was not to be, for as she followed the two ladies (and one husband) toward an available table, a lanky presence fell into step by her side.

"Where were you all day?" Brooksbank asked. "I looked for you after breakfast."

Avis sniffed. "I thought you'd be pleased to have me out of your sight for a few hours," she said. "I've been rather monopolising your time."

"Since when did you care about that?" Brooksbank chuckled. "Anyway, I've begun to worry more when I *don't* know where you are. Means you're probably up to something. So?"

"Mm? Oh! I was up to something. Several somethings. Say, did you know the doctor's been relieved?"

Brooksbank's expression sobered and he nodded. "I heard. Raving about an impossible drowning?"

"And the captain won't let anyone else examine the body now, so we can't verify otherwise. Though it has to be nonsense, of course."

"He, er…" Brooksbank hesitated under Avis's glare but steeled himself and continued. "He *was* soaking wet," he ventured.

"Lots of things can make a man soaking wet that aren't

dying of drowning on a metal gantry in the hottest, driest room on the ship."

Brooksbank had no riposte to this, and as they took their seats at the dinner table he lowered his voice. "I'm told tonight's sitting will be down in the bowels of the ship," he said. "They've chosen a storeroom of some kind, I think. *She* wanted the engine room but the captain forbade it. I assume you'll be there?"

"I don't think so."

Her companion's eyes widened. "What? I thought that was your…" He waved his hand. "You know, your *raisin detrah*," he mangled. "How are you going to debunk them if you aren't there to see them?"

Avis shook her head. "There'll be time enough for that," she said. "Let them do their play-acting; people are already getting bored of it. The best way to prove them wrong now is to prove what did happen. Müller's a dead end until we reach dry land now, apparently. So I need to investigate this navigation system situation."

Brooksbank raised his eyebrows. "You think it was more than a random error?"

"Not necessarily. But I *do* think that regardless of how it happened, we need to find the mundane answer so that it can't be attributed to some ghost that really wants to visit Greenland. These buyers—who did you say they were again?"

The man gave a start, and a hunted expression passed over his features. "I didn't," he said. "I told you, I don't know."

Avis narrowed her eyes. "But you have an idea."

With a grimace, Brooksbank rested his hands on the table as though he might stand and leave there and then. "Honestly, Miss Lovelock, if you keep at it I'll have to eat in my quarters and I really don't want to. Can't we talk about something else?"

"The weather?"

Brooksbank winced. "Something… other than that."

"Did you see Gideon and Madame Berthault at all today?"

"Actually I did," Brooksbank said, relaxing somewhat. Apparently Avis's tired obsession with the Duquesnes was a welcome return to form. "They had lunch together—alone—then disappeared off somewhere. No sister." His dark brows twitched with realisation. "But you knew that, because you didn't ask about her."

"Look at Carrie, using his powers of observation."

"You know you're very hurtful sometimes." But it was delivered without rancour; Brooksbank much preferred being abused to being asked questions he didn't want to answer.

Avis glanced across the room now to where the Duquesnes were seated, and was strangely disappointed to find that Rachel was not mysteriously staring straight back at her. Her eyes were instead fixed on her empty place setting while Gideon muttered in her ear. Curiously, he was seated between her and the widow—usually Berthault was in the middle—and Avis noted that his hand lay next to Charlotte's on the table, nearly but not quite touching. She watched Rachel frown and blink a few times, and begin to lift her head, and then Avis looked away quickly. On balance, Rachel was *probably* not about to look her way, but it wasn't worth the risk. She'd had quite enough of that penetrating gaze for one day.

Baynes stiffened when Avis approached, and not only because it was cold in the corridor leading to the bridge.

She grinned. "Just the man I was hoping to see."

"Miss Lovelock, I've been instructed to inform anybody who asks that the captain is very busy, but that we are correcting course and will very soon be back on our original bearings," he said, with an air of defeat that suggested he knew already that his platitudes would not work on her.

"Actually I have a question for you, not the captain," Avis said. "You told us the other day that *Excambion* had her bridge instruments fully refitted last year, did you not?"

"I… Yes."

"And that would presumably include navigational instruments, would it not? Including the course compass?"

"Er…"

"So why did the captain describe said compass this morning as an 'antique'?"

Baynes opened and shut his mouth several times without saying anything. Eventually, he pressed his eyes closed for a few seconds, as though hoping that when he opened them again, Avis and her question would be gone.

His shoulders slumped. "It was refitted," he said. "With the older instruments."

"Why waste expensive nearly new instruments on a buyer who will never know they were there, hm?" Avis stepped closer. Baynes tried to step further away and his back hit the wall.

"D'you think I might take a quick look at the new—that is to say, old—compass, Third Officer Baynes?"

"I-I-I don't think the capt—"

"Is he in there?"

"… No."

"Let me onto the damn bridge, Baynes."

IT WAS SUBTLE enough that anyone might have missed it—indeed, even Avis had when she was in the room earlier that day. You would have to be looking for it to spot the fresh wear on the screws around the base of the compass, the little flecks of metal shavings in the grooves.

"Now I'm no engineer, Baynes," Avis said, "but I know a little bit about magnets. They're very easy to disrupt with just a scrap of metal." She shot him a quick smile. "I've disrupted a few myself in my time." She ran her finger over the disturbed screws. "I'd suggest that you lift this out of its housing and take a look beneath."

She stepped back, folding her arms. There was a long moment in which Baynes, the navigator, and the furious-looking first mate stared at her in silence.

"Well? No offence meant but I haven't got all night and I'm supposed to be a guest on this ship. Go fetch a screwdriver!"

They sprang into action then, as if really all it took to command a ship's crew was an imperious attitude and the right tone of voice. A brass screwdriver was produced from one of the back rooms and applied to the pedestal, though the navigator grumbled throughout about "recalibrations" until Avis pointed out that was a task he would have to do regardless, and at least this had a chance of actually addressing the problem.

Between them they carefully lifted the compass, and Avis knelt on the deck and peered beneath it, brows furrowed. She wasn't sure exactly what she was looking for, and eventually raised a hand to run a finger around the inside of the mount. It was somewhat unpleasant, with a film of grease coating the interior, but eventually she straightened up, grinning.

"Aha! There we are..." She held up a thin strip of metal that she had fished out from the casing; it had been pressed into the housing like a playbill pasted to a subway wall. "I'd wager that's not supposed to be there."

The first mate took it from her, frowning. "That's solid steel—enough to throw off our readings well and good."

"But how did it get there?" Baynes mused.

"Clearly someone put it there."

"Well, yes. But who?"

Avis lifted her eyebrows. "Do I have to do everything around here?" Baynes began to splutter, and she waved a hand. "We don't even know if they're still on board. And it's not as though I've met all your crew."

"You think this was a member of *crew*?" the first mate said. "That's quite a serious accusation, Miss Lovelock." He was going a little red, and Avis narrowed her eyes.

"I think that at this stage we have no idea who it was. Or, for that matter, why they did it. Well, I say that..." She pursed her lips. "I do have at least one idea there. Baynes, do you know which godforsaken storage closet those accursed siblings have commandeered for their nonsense this evening? I think it's time I joined them."

There was a crew member at the door, of course, but Avis merely raised her chin and strode past him. His weak protest was cut off as she shut the door behind her.

She entered into near darkness; one thing valued by frauds the world over was a good cover for their crimes. It sounded as if the "communion", as it were, was nearly over. She could hear Gideon speaking, trying to coax a few last words from whatever "spirit" his sister was "channelling". She was surprised to see Brooksbank at the table; he had thus far avoided attending any of the séances, though she hadn't been able to discern whether it was out of professional discretion or a personal aversion. He shifted restlessly in his seat and *that* at least was easy to read—the wooden stools from third class that they'd put around the table were damned uncomfortable.

Everyone else at the table was crew, save for Berthault and Usher. Presumably the other first-class passengers had balked at the idea of descending into the depths below decks, even for a séance. Avis did not walk any further into the room. Instead, she crossed her arms and waited.

"Thank you. Thank you, spirits, for speaking. We know you are here, that you yearn to break through the Veil to reach us." Gideon rolled his head back, gazing up at the low ceiling of the room. "We will speak to you again, but please, wait for us. Do not approach the crew or passengers of this great ship without our help. They may not understand you—they may even fear you. Cleave to us, and we will aid you. You have my solemn promise."

With that, Rachel gave a shuddering sigh and slumped forward, forearms resting on the table, her face pale and drawn. Berthault looked concerned, but could not reach past Gideon to comfort her.

In the silence that followed, Avis began to clap slowly. "Are we done? I need to commune with our Spiritualists. And you, Brooksbank."

The crew were more than happy to beat a hasty retreat, looking various shades of either shaken or bored depending on how seriously they had taken the preceding performance. "Come on, I'll see you back upstairs," Usher suggested to Berthault, offering her his arm. "We can wait in the main saloon."

When the door clicked behind the last of them, Avis moved to turn up the storm lantern that burned low on the small, pitted table. Rachel lifted her eyes to Avis's as the light hit them, turning her pupils into pinpricks and rendering them an almost luminous amber, not a hint of blue in the warm glow. She looked exhausted, and Avis felt a sudden pang of guilt for what she was about to do. The light also revealed that the room was much bigger than it initially appeared, every wall stacked deep with empty pallets. The flickering light on the rows of horizontal planks was rather disconcerting, difficult to look at for too long without leaving streaks across one's vision.

"I found the cause of the navigation error," Avis said. "It was sabotage."

Brooksbank straightened. "You're sure of it?" he asked, and she had to keep from chiding him. Obviously Avis Lovelock never made a declaration unless she was sure of it.

"Uncovered it with trustworthy witnesses *and* physical proof," she replied, looking first at one twin, then the other. "The way you're supposed to when you're trying to substantiate something."

"What looks like sabotage to a sceptic may well prove to have more mysterious origins," Gideon said, but she could hear the uncertainty in his voice.

"I assure you, this was mundane in the extreme. Then, of course, we must ask why. But I think you know the answer to that one, don't you, Brooksbank." It wasn't a question. "We both know who the buyer is. I think it's time we said it out loud."

"It's Spain."

Rachel sounded almost ill, she was so hoarse. The shocked look on Gideon's face almost made up for his sister stepping on Avis's big reveal. Apparently she was not the only one who had picked up on the clues—the mystery around the buyers, Brooksbank's jittery reaction to any mention of the war, the timing of the sale. Added to that was the fact they had deliberately stripped out new, more sophisticated systems and replaced them with older models—the Hamburg Line would put their new instruments into a sleek new liner, and *Excambion* would be consigned to running freight for warships. Not that Rachel knew that part, and it slightly annoyed Avis that she'd put it together without this final piece of the puzzle.

Brooksbank's shoulders slumped. "I don't know for certain," he said.

"But you're sure enough to be jumpy about it. And damn it, man, *this* is why it matters! There'd be no particular reason to scupper a ship from a rival line. But it seems highly likely that the Americans have somehow got wind of this sale, and plan to ensure that *Excambion* isn't fit to be sold."

"So not just a saboteur, but an American government operative?" Gideon scoffed. "That's more far-fetched than ghosts."

"So you admit ghosts are far-fetched then?" was Avis's quick rejoinder.

Rachel was silent. At length, Brooksbank cleared his throat.

"There may be some truth to your theory, though unless we somehow uncover this saboteur we may never know for sure. And there's all the other occurrences that are harder to explain—while a saboteur may well kill someone to further the rumours of a haunting, faking a drowning in the bowels of the ship seems somewhat elaborate."

"I'm afraid I can't speak to that, except that many people feel compelled to put on a good show to convince others of the impossible," Avis said, looking straight at Rachel. Rachel did not look back at her.

"Hmm. Well, I'll see if I can't convince the captain to let Doctor Usher examine the body."

"But we reached the spirits tonight," Gideon said, his sweet voice twisted into a petulant whine. "You were there, Mr Brooksbank, you heard them. You wanted proof of the supernatural and you received it, loud and clear."

Avis opened her mouth to impugn this claim but was cut off.

"Enough." Rachel looked up then, reaching up to tuck a stray wisp of hair behind the delicate shell of her ear. "One does not negate the other. Miss Lovelock may be correct—that does not mean we are wrong. And I think we shall see proof of that before very long. I only hope it is benign, and that Herr Müller is the only fatality this voyage sees." She was serious, Avis realised. There was no play-acting, no pretence here.

Rachel's eyes met hers, and a realisation shot through her.

She wasn't just serious—she was *afraid*.

Twenty-Two

No firm decisions or plans were made that night. It was clear that no agreements would be reached by those assembled, with too many frayed nerves and weary hearts. The ship began to sway alarmingly as they climbed towards first class; Avis was relieved to see Brooksbank staggering too, for neither Gideon nor Rachel appeared much affected by the turbulence. It seemed they were headed for stormy waters.

"Captain says there'll be a rough night before we're back in safe waters," Brooksbank said as they paused by the stairwell to the upper first-class level. "Best stay in your bunk and batten down the hatches." He paused as the twins left them, then reached out to cup her elbow briefly. "I'm sorry that I wasn't more truthful with you from the start. I couldn't exactly report on what was—still is, really—just a suspicion. This whole business… it's damned strange, I won't lie. But I'm glad of your help, even if it is rather… unorthodox."

Avis chewed her lower lip and tasted blood. In the past twenty-four hours, she'd worried it raw. "We need to decide who we can trust, and fast," she said. "The Duquesnes won't say anything—it's against their interests. But beyond that, who we bring into our confidences… This sabotage is real. It's not shadows and hallucinations and play-acting. People could be in real danger."

She kept repeating the words to herself as she picked her way along the wall to her own stateroom. *This is real. This is real. This is real.* She clung to it like a raft in a storm. That little strip of metal around the base of the ship's compass in that moment represented her link to rationality, to facts, to irrefutable truth. What went before—the bizarre nature of Müller's death, the cold of the engine room—could now be ignored, discarded, in the face of this evidence.

But it doesn't explain it all away.

"Silence."

It doesn't explain what you saw. What you felt.
It doesn't explain why Rachel Duquesne is frightened.

Avis slammed the cabin door behind her and glared across the room at her sister.

"Enough," she said. "I don't want to hear it."

Oh, you cannot help but hear it. You have always heard it. You just don't want to listen.

THOUGH SHE DID not mind being buffeted about too much, Avis was never the heaviest sleeper, and it took her a long time to drift into a fitful drowse. When her eyes flew back open it felt as though she'd closed them for barely a moment, though the room had once more dropped in temperature and the wind now howled outside, waves beating against the hull as it cut through the water.

No, not that. Listen.

Avis sat up, closed her eyes, and tried to filter out the whistling wind, the rain battering the porthole.

"… lotte? Charlotte!"

If the name hadn't been familiar, she might not have plucked it from the wind, but once heard it could not be denied. Avis sat up, her head throbbing at the movement. She couldn't make out anything beyond the name and the desperation with which it was being shouted, but that was enough to propel her out of bed and her feet into boots before she stumbled for the door, grabbing her coat as she passed.

The corridor was bitterly cold as she ran towards the stairwell, and the railings chilled her hands and fingers as she climbed. Ahead of her she saw the swish of dark skirts, and the voice echoed down to her. "Charlotte? Where have you gone?"

Now she recognised the speaker—precisely who she would have assumed, of course. She picked up her pace and fell into step with Rachel as she strode across a broad foyer towards the double doors to the garden verandah. "Where did you see her last?"

In any other circumstance, she would've been gratified to see the other woman jump. "I didn't," Rachel said, her pale cheeks stained with colour. "We said goodnight and went to our cabins some hours ago. But I woke when the ship began to pitch and I went to check on her and her bed was empty, the door open." Briefly Avis felt a knot of yearning in her gut and summarily banished it. "She must have gone walking to try and settle her stomach, but I've been through the lounges and the corridors and she's not there."

"She's a big girl," Avis said, though she stepped forward to push one of the doors to the verandah open all the same. "Surely she can take care of herself?"

"Of course," Rachel said, a little sharply. "But…" She exhaled in exasperation. "Think what you want, but I feel in my gut that she's in danger."

"Feel in my gut" was an improvement on "the spirits told me", at least—Avis, of all people, could identify with an intuition that didn't have any immediately obvious explanation. Often your subconscious had spotted something that your thinking mind had not.

"I'll fetch a crewman," she said. "If she's out on deck we'll be glad of the help."

Rachel hesitated, then nodded. She did not say thank you, but her look lost some of its chill.

By the time Avis had located a crew member and they'd climbed back to the verandah, it was empty. But a loud banging signalled that another door had been opened: one that led out onto deck. It was a supremely poor idea to venture out into the storm, and yet it sounded as though Rachel had.

Avis approached the doorway, pulling her coat more tightly around her as the temperature plummeted further. The wind was whipping by outside, its voice an angry howl. She felt the spatter of rain on her face, like a battery of tiny needles on her cheeks and forehead, and had to squint as she peered out onto deck. Rain lashed down on the exterior walkways, and she could only see a few metres ahead before the world dissolved into a thick grey morass of wind and water. The ship pitched dangerously as it crested a wave and she grabbed the doorframe to keep from falling.

"Ma'am, I think we should go back inside!" the crewman shouted, hand hooked into the railing. "Your cabin is the safest place to be in inclement weather!"

"We can't just leave them out here!" Avis called back, clinging to the railing and dragging herself forward. "That stupid girl is about as substantial as a slip of gauze!" Then she saw them: two dark dots shifting back and forth on the deck up ahead.

Willing to own that they couldn't simply abandon two people in possible peril, the crewman began to fight through the wind towards the bow. Up ahead of them, a door burst open and two more figures emerged. One was crew, and the other, Avis resolved after a moment, was Gideon Duquesne. Apparently Rachel was not the only person minded to check on Charlotte Berthault in the middle of the night.

Avis was willing to wager they made a ridiculous sight—four individuals growing rapidly more bedraggled and battered as they laboured towards the bow and the silhouettes dancing there. She couldn't hear a thing for the wind, and the rain felt as if it must be hardening to sleet as it slapped at her face, her shoulders. Beneath their feet the ship bucked like a recalcitrant horse. During one such dramatic manoeuvre, Avis pitched forward and then fell heavily to her knees, the impact radiating up through her spine and teeth.

"Fucking... Frenchwomen," she muttered, hauling herself to her feet once more. The figures began to resolve as they neared: the taller, Charlotte, clinging to the railing at the bow of the ship, and Rachel forging towards her, hands out. Regardless of Berthault's intentions, it was not a safe place to be: the ship was being flung back and forth by the storm, and any one of its violent pitches could cause even the strongest soul to lose their footing or grip.

As Rachel grew closer, dread began to crystallise in Avis's gut, and she hugged the wall, trying to duck out of the wind to speed her pace. With the roar of the storm, Avis couldn't hear anything else, but she could tell from the shift of Rachel's shoulders that she was yelling at the top of her lungs as she tried to reach Charlotte, who barely even registered her presence, still clinging to the railing and looking out across the water. Avis watched Rachel reach the last point where she had something to hold on to; between her and Charlotte there was now only a slick expanse of open deck.

In spite of herself, and knowing that there wasn't the slightest chance that anybody would hear her, Avis cried out "*No!*" as Rachel released her last handhold and rushed forward.

She had timed it carefully: the pitch of the ship helped propel her against the wind towards Charlotte. She caught the widow just as she was poised to pitch over the side, and she immediately grabbed onto the railing for them both, sheltering Charlotte against her. Charlotte slumped. Had she hit her head, or fainted? Either way, Rachel looked now to be supporting most of her weight, and in that moment Avis saw something she could never have predicted, as Rachel's long, slender arms enfolded Charlotte and lifted her clean from the ground. Rachel crouched low as she turned, trying to minimise the destabilising effect of the wind now at her back, and began to take step after agonising step back towards safety.

Avis and the two crewmen worked to meet them midway; Gideon was a figure in her peripheral vision, hanging back in the safety of a sheltered bulkhead. The crew had likely trained for situations like this and reached the two women first, linking arms and clasping hands to help haul them away from the open expanse of deck. Avis was extraneous to the effort but would not concede her presence, waiting until they neared and then anchoring her own frozen-fingered grasp onto Rachel's skirts.

Gideon gestured for them to follow him back towards the door where he had emerged, as if it was some inspired idea to get inside out of the howling wind and rain. One by one they all but fell through the doorway, Rachel stumbling but refusing to loosen her grip around Berthault's waist until they were safely inside and the door had been closed—and latched—behind them.

"What on *earth* were you thinking?" Gideon demanded, wringing his hands with the dramatics of an amateur player. "You could have been swept overboard!"

Rachel helped Charlotte to one of the deckchairs that lay askew beneath the canopy, gently settling her down. The widow looked far worse for wear, her dark hair plastered to her face and her pupils blown wide with shock. "I… saw him," she murmured, only barely audible above the storm. "Henri. He was here. I saw him."

Gideon shot a confused look in Rachel's direction at this, but soon crouched down beside Charlotte, reaching to stroke her hair. "It's all right, mon trésor, I have you. I'm here." Quite deliberately shifting his body to block Rachel from involving herself, he reached for the Frenchwoman's hand. "Blankets!" he barked. "Hurry, she's frozen to the bone!"

The crewmen scurried off to obey his order, and he continued to fuss and cluck, rubbing Charlotte's hand between his palms as if this might do anything. Rachel stood behind him, her expression indecipherable even to Avis. Belatedly Avis realised she should be helping and approached, reaching a cautious hand out to touch her shoulder.

"Come on, let's get below."

"*No*," Rachel rasped, shaking her head until wet tendrils of hair slapped her cheeks. "I'm fine." The chatter of her teeth betrayed her insistence.

Avis stepped closer and lowered her voice to a very ordinary volume that would only be heard in close proximity, with the wind still the predominant sound in the verandah. "You can't help her by freezing to death. The crew will see them both safe. Come on."

Rachel didn't reply, didn't assent, but she also didn't resist as Avis drew her towards the foyer door. Her steps were stilted and clumsy, as if the cold had locked her joints, and Avis had to help manoeuvre her around the benches and potted plants and down the stairwell. Luckily, she knew where the twins' cabins were, and was able to half lead, half accompany Rachel to her berth.

The door was hanging wide open, clearly forgotten in Rachel's worry and panic, and once more Avis felt a tight tug in her chest. Had she ever inspired concern like that in anyone? If she went missing, would anybody search for her? And if she ventured out into a killing storm, would anybody follow?

You know better than to ask questions if you aren't ready to hear the answers.

The thought curdled immediately within her, and her next words came unbidden. "You see what these fantasies do? Even someone who seems to know the game, someone who seems to be indulging in this maudlin play-acting for the wish-fulfilment and nostalgia that it truly is, can have their mind warped and their perceptions twisted if you let them run on too long."

The words landed like a slap. Rachel reeled back, wet garments sending droplets spattering across the floor and walls. "That wasn't… She isn't insane," she said through clenched teeth. "If Charlotte said she saw something, she saw something."

"If Charlotte saw anything at all, it wasn't a ghost," Avis insisted. "Didn't you hear me before? There is a *saboteur* aboard *Excambion*. She might have got herself killed, and whoever she did see—likely a person, but even if it *had* been one of your ghosts—one thing we both know is that it was not her husband." As Rachel stepped back, Avis closed in, rounding on her. "That was *your* doing. That is an image *you* put in her mind." Avis pointed beyond Rachel to the porthole, through it to the roiling sea. "If that woman had gone overboard tonight, her blood would have been on *your* hands! You people, you think these are harmless imaginings, and maybe they are in the safety of your little sittings, but it doesn't stop there. It never stops. There is *always* more. It eats them up from the inside, every day, every moment until all that's left is a shell, just a yawning hole of grief and recrimination and— and *wanting*, for something they can never get back!"

"'You people'?" Rachel searched Avis's face with eyes red-rimmed from the cold and wind, making them look almost turquoise, pale as sea-worn glass. She nodded. "I see," she said. "You were badly hurt. I'm sorry."

"Don't you *dare* presume to analyse me," Avis spat. "You have the cheek to accuse *me* of ego, when you play with people's lives like this. You're vultures. Parasites." It was too much, too vicious, she knew, when Rachel herself was clearly shaken, but a cruel black bile filled her throat when she thought about the woman on the deck in mortal peril for the love of a dead man—when she remembered her last sight of her own mother, unwashed, unshod, unrecognisable in a featureless white room, cursing Avis's name and conversing only with beings nobody else could see. This was where it led, where it always led.

"It's not that simple," Rachel began, stepping closer, her eyes glazing over and sliding away from Avis's. "You're too blinded..."

"By facts? By rational thought?"

But Rachel wasn't listening. Though she had stopped walking, she continued to pitch forward, and Avis realised just in time to reach out her arms as the woman fell against her.

Idiot.

"You're frozen to the bone." Avis was an idiot: Rachel was soaked to the skin, and trembling uncontrollably. She pushed away from Avis and began to fumble at the buttons of her dress, but her fingers were stiff and clumsy, and it wasn't long before Avis reached to help. Rachel mounted only a token resistance before allowing her arms to fall limp by her sides, letting Avis unfasten her dress and peel it off before stepping behind her to loosen the strings of her corset.

"What were you doing fully dressed at two o'clock in the morning?" she muttered, more to herself than to Rachel.

"It was cold," the other woman replied nonetheless, her teeth chattering as if to underscore her words.

It was now that Avis saw what she had realised in some recess of her mind when Rachel had lifted Charlotte Berthault away from the railing as though she weighed nothing at all. As the corset fell away, leaving just a thin camisole, translucent in its soaked-through state, it was clear to see that in spite of her sylph-like figure, what mass Rachel Duquesne had was entirely muscle. Her back and shoulders were carved and solid, her arms corded like a dancer's. In spite of the urgency of the moment, the need to get Rachel out of everything wet and into a cocoon of blankets, Avis reached for her on reflex as if to confirm the evidence before her with a touch.

"It was you," she said. "Not some crewman. You carried me to that cabin in third class yourself." A further realisation dawned. "And that's how you lifted that table, you and

Gideon, together. You hide it beneath mourning dress and by starving yourselves. Nobody would ever expect you to be so strong, and so they disregard it. *I* disregarded it."

"Is this…?" Rachel's shoulders hunched. She was shivering in earnest now, and her words were beginning to slur. "Is this really the time?"

Help her, you fool. Yes, there's not a scrap of fat on her: that's why she's freezing to death in front of you.

Avis shook herself from her reverie, and by mutual, silent agreement they made quick work of the rest of Rachel's clothing without pause or propriety. Avis unfastened and shrugged off her own coat. Having been better wrapped up and outside for less time, the nightshirt she wore beneath was only damp around the edges, and so she just kicked her boots off and turned both the room's oil lamps up to a high flame before climbing beneath the blankets of Rachel's bed and drawing an increasingly sluggish Rachel under with her.

"You mustn't sleep," Avis said, rubbing roughly up and down her arm. "Not until you're warm again."

"Feel warm now."

"No, you're numb. Listen. *Listen.*" Avis pressed her eyes closed, groped for Rachel's naked body in the dark, pulled her close. She began to hum, a melody that had been stuck in her head for hours. "That song you played on the fiddle, tell me what it is."

"I'm tired, Lovelock."

"Tell me."

"Slave song. It's… 'Lay me…'. 'Lay this body…'"

"Sing it for me."

She could feel Rachel's breath growing slower and shallower, and Avis opened her eyes to see Rachel's flutter closed. She shook her.

"Rachel Duquesne, sing me the damned song," she ordered. Rachel's lips moved, but no sound came out. "*Rachel.*"

Suddenly, Rachel's body twitched. She opened her eyes. Or rather, her eyes opened. But the irises that stared back at Avis's in the lamplight weren't only that strange pale seaglass but flecked with a deep mahogany that mirrored her own. Her damp hair was at once flaxen and brown, her cheeks at once carved out and youthfully plump. She opened her mouth and began to sing, her usually roughened voice in that moment a smooth, low whisper, the undulating tune barely discernible, and yet Avis could hear it in her mind as clear as morning birdsong.

Oh graveyard

Oh graveyard

Oh graveyard

Oh graveyard

I'm walking through the graveyard

I'm walking through the graveyard

Lay this body down

Lay this body down

I know moonlight

I know moonlight

I know starlight

I know starlight

I'm walking through the starlight

I'm walking through the starlight

Lay this body down

Lay this body down

And my soul

And my soul

And your soul

And your soul

We'll meet there in the graveyard

We'll meet there in the graveyard

To lay this body down

To lay this body down

The woman in the bed with her fell silent and snaked an arm around her waist, and Avis drew her closer, feeling the heat begin to leech from her into Rachel's body. Getting there. She shut her eyes tightly as hot tears spilled out onto her cheeks.

"Again," she whispered. "Sing it again."

Twenty-Three

When Avis woke in the early morning she became aware of two things simultaneously: the stillness of the ship's passage and the solid form pressed against her side. The wind had died down overnight and no longer howled outside the porthole, and all she could hear was the steady breathing of Rachel beside her. For a moment she allowed herself the indulgence of lying there, of being so close to another person that she could feel the lift of their ribcage, feel their breath on her neck.

But only a moment.

She slipped out of the bed, mounding the blankets back over Rachel's sleeping form before retrieving her coat from the floor. It was still wet and cold, and she cursed herself for not at least hanging it over a chair.

Thankfully it was early enough that she didn't encounter a soul as she departed the cabin. She noticed that Charlotte's door was closed now, and wondered where the widow had ended up after her misadventure—and with whom.

As was always the way when one went to sleep listening to a song or poem, that accursed melody dogged her steps as she picked her way back to her own stateroom, and with it a lingering presence, the firm knowledge that were she to stop and turn, her sister would be standing at her back.

How much of the previous night would Rachel recall? She had been barely coherent as they had lain entwined, Avis coaxing, cajoling, and commanding her to stay awake long enough for her shivering to stop, for their bodies to match in heat. Would she remember Avis's tears? The press of salt-chapped lips to her pale forehead? Avis could barely piece it together now herself, the strange vision her heartsick mind had conjured as she willed Rachel back to consciousness, the moment where she looked into Rachel's eyes and saw them mingled with her sister's.

No matter. Whatever Duquesne thought she knew, Avis could simply dismiss as a hypothermic hallucination.

Her room was blissfully empty when she returned to it—no shivering twin in the bed, no dark-eyed sister haunting the mirror. She allowed herself a moment by the lamp to warm her fingers before attending to the necessities of the morning: hanging her coat near the hot pipes so that it would dry, wetting a cloth to wipe her face clean, donning her stays and petticoat and dress. She felt almost herself by the end of it, the storm and the song firmly behind her and only tantalising answers ahead.

It was too early even for the first breakfast service, but Avis managed to cajole a pastry and a hot cup of coffee out of a passing waiter using her brightest smile. After a moment's thought, she told him to bring the same down to Rachel's room, and immediately pushed aside any implications the gesture might have had. She didn't want Rachel *dead*, for Christ's sake. How would she humiliate her then?

Avis very much wanted to track down Brooksbank and speak about the next steps in her investigation, but instead she schooled herself to bide her time. After the discovery of the previous evening, several people would no doubt have been informed immediately—the captain, Mr King. One of the three men would come and find her soon enough, whether to solicit her further expertise or to relieve her of her duties. She had a strong suspicion they would at least *attempt* the latter, given the sensitivity of the situation, and she half welcomed it. What with last night's events on deck, and after, Avis was increasingly weary of the whole affair. Perhaps she had better put all of this aside and spend the rest of the trip doing as she'd originally intended: drinking copious quantities of complimentary champagne and beating old people at backgammon.

"Miss Lovelock? You're up early." Poor Third Officer Baynes looked as if he regretted opening his mouth; clearly he had been so surprised to see her as he crossed the foyer that his good sense had temporarily abandoned him.

"Mm, in before the rush," she replied, waving the pastry in his direction. "I noticed we're not getting thrown about like sandwiches in a picnic basket any more—I assume the storm has passed?"

"We're into clearer weather for now, thank God."

"For now? I don't know if I like the sound of that. Still, I'll take any reprieve on offer. Last night was enough dramatics to last me a good long while."

"Ah, yes, I'd heard about the events on deck. It's a miracle no one was washed overboard from the sounds of it." He wrung his hands like a squirrel who'd forgotten where they'd left their cache. "Madame Berthault and Miss Duquesne most of all."

"No such things as miracles, Baynes. But seeing as you've mentioned it, where *is* Berthault, d'you know? She looked like she might have hit her head out there. I hope you lot haven't abandoned her to concussion."

"Of course not! She's in the sick-bay. Doctor Usher is looking after her."

"Klein still *persona non grata*, then? Interesting. Well, thanks very much." She stood, scooping up her half-empty coffee cup. "I'll just go pay my respects, make sure Usher's not treating her like some wartime invalid."

"I, er… Miss Lovelock?" The look Avis turned on him caused him to flinch, but he nevertheless continued. "Your work last night… was very impressive," he said, giving a single nod for emphasis at the end.

Avis's heart twisted. "Much good it's done us so far, Baynes. But thank you."

WHEN SHE ARRIVED at the sick-bay, Gideon Duquesne was already there. He barely looked better than she felt, though it could have been his natural gauntness and pallor that gave him the air of a sleepwalker. When he saw her enter the medical bay, he interposed himself between her and the tiny sick-bay cabin, wavering slightly where he stood.

"She's resting," he said, "and doesn't need your particular brand of interrogation right now. Be on your way."

"Is that Mademoiselle Lovelock?" The voice was weaker than Berthault's usual rich tones but unmistakable nevertheless. "Let me speak to her."

Avis allowed for a poisonously polite smile at Gideon and sidled past him into the cabin.

Berthault was still bundled up in a berth. Someone had brought her a pastry, too, but had eschewed coffee in favour of water. Reclining on the berth across the room from her was Usher, bleary-eyed from a combination of lack of sleep and undesired sobriety.

"Madame," Avis said. "I'm glad to see you're all right."

"I am glad to be all right—thanks to you, and the brave crew, and the doctor," she said, nodding to Usher, who waved away her gratitude. "When I think about what could have happened, it makes me cold to my bones. Mon Dieu, we could have all died."

Noting the significant omission from Berthault's line-up of saviours, Avis sank into the chair by the bed. "Do you feel able to talk about what you saw?"

The widow hesitated, and Usher used the pause to put his hands on his knees and rock to his feet with a groan. "I'm just going to go check up on stocks. There'll probably be a rash of seasick biddies needing attention after the night we had."

Only once he had gone did Berthault speak, though she seemed reluctant even so. "I know what you will say, mademoiselle. That I am a silly woman who has convinced herself of things that cannot be true. And perhaps it is so. But it did not seem false last night. I would not have done those things for a dream or a mirage."

"I'm not here to nay-say you, Madame Berthault," Avis said. "I would just very much like to know precisely what you saw, in your own words."

"I saw Henri. At least… I thought I did. It was dark and I had been asleep—as much as I could have been, with the rocking of the boat. But I heard a noise, and when I opened my door to look outside, there was a man there, striding past. And he looked so like my Henri, I had to follow…" Berthault's eyes gleamed, and she pulled the blanket in her lap closer. "I could barely believe my eyes, but it was none of the trickery you have claimed to uncover. It could not have been anything but *him*, I swear it."

"You said he strode past—did you see his face?"

"I… No. And I know what you'll say, mademoiselle, that it could have been any man, but he was wearing his uniform. He was in the cavalry. Whatever similarities there might be in the dark, I have never seen any member of this crew wearing a sabre."

Avis frowned. This was a civilian vessel; even the captain didn't wear a sword. "And you followed this figure up on deck?"

"Oui. I do not know where he was going, but he had a purpose, and I knew I must follow or lose him forever. And I have already lost him once." She sighed, bone-deep and weary. "But when we reached the deck he melted away, and there were only lights on the water."

"Lights? What sort of lights?"

Charlotte shrugged. "Je ne sais pas. Lights, floating. Flickering."

"Charlotte?"

Both Avis and Charlotte looked up sharply as Rachel pushed past her brother and into the room. Avis stood and moved to give way to her, though Rachel didn't sit, instead crouching by the berth and reaching for Charlotte's hand with both of hers. Berthault favoured Rachel with a smile that was as sad as it was tender, and Avis sensed something begin to shift in the dynamic between them. Whatever had happened the previous night, whatever Berthault truly saw, it had changed things. Avis left them to their murmured conversation and made her way out to the doctor's office, where Usher was wrist-deep in one of the cabinets inset along the wall. He turned as Avis took a chair, and slumped back against the wall, elbow knocking the cabinet closed.

"Don't suppose you've succeeded in gaining access to Müller yet?" she asked.

Usher barked a tiny laugh. "Haven't left this sick-bay since I got here. Give it time, Miss Lovelock. I'm sure the captain will want debriefed on the situation in due course. I'll make the case."

"What d'you think of Charlotte's vision?"

Usher shrugged. "It was dark and windy, she was tired. Hard to say. She's lucid though, no flies on that one."

"In other words, you have no idea."

"I haven't a clue."

Avis let out an expansive sigh, slouching further into her chair. "The ergot theory has yet to be disproven," she muttered.

"I'm sorry?"

"Mm, nothing. Could it be something in the air? Some agent causing everyone to hallucinate these… sightings?"

Usher folded his arms across his chest, appearing to give her suggestion due consideration. "I don't think so. Carbon monoxide could be an issue on ships like these, but I haven't heard anyone complaining of headaches—besides the self-inflicted kind after too much brandy. The key to avoiding those—"

"Is to keep drinking, I know." Avis frowned. "There *has* to be a rational explanation: for this, for Müller, for the bodies on deck."

"Pardon my saying so, but what does it matter?" She looked up at him sharply, earning a shrug. "I just mean, what's it to you if these rumours stop the sale of the ship? It's not as if you're earning a commission. Why not just let it be?"

It was a fair question, at least on a superficial level. Unfortunately the very fact he had to ask it suggested he would not appreciate or understand the answer, would simply not quite fathom the need, the obsession that drove Avis to solve every puzzle, to expose every lie. "Call it a matter of professional pride."

"Bloody-mindedness then."

"Touché."

AVIS'S BLOODY-MINDEDNESS LED her next to Brooksbank, whose movements she was beginning to know better than she would've liked. At this time of morning, he would be doing the rounds in the lounges, and indeed she found him in the more forward of the two first-class lounges, carrying a magazine under one arm as he stood chewing the fat with two old biddies.

"Where's King?" Avis asked.

"And a good morning to you too, Miss Lovelock, though only just. Good heavens, you look awful, are you quite well?"

"That's really not the sort of thing one says to a lady, Carrie, particularly not one who's south of thirty and still unattached." Brooksbank's expression of concern didn't shift and Avis scoffed. "I had a late night," she said as the two old women gave up and puttered away like little knitted tugboats. "Did you hear about our little jaunt up on deck?"

"Vaguely. Something about a ghost on deck?"

"A dashing French husband–shaped ghost, no less."

"And that's why Madame Berthault is in sick-bay. All right, I'm up to speed." Brooksbank slipped his hands into his pockets and stood in a lopsided fashion. Avis had never before seen someone who could look like they were leaning against something even though there was nothing to lean against.

"Correct, and now I need to speak to King." Avis folded her arms.

Brooksbank heaved a weary sigh. "I'm going to see him now. You might as well tag along."

King was busy playing chess with himself, and as usual, he was winning. He was up on the garden verandah, hunched over one of the little wrought-metal tables around its perimeter. The verandah had escaped the previous night's drama almost entirely unscathed. A single pane of glass had presumably been smashed by something or other, or simply given way in the wind, for it was boarded over. Everything else was pristine.

King was less smiley than usual today.

"Give me good news, Brooksbank."

"Well, ahem, I have Miss Lovelock here with me..." He gestured expansively.

The old man turned his beady gaze on Avis. "Do *you* have something good to tell me?"

"I do, in fact. I take it you've already been told what I found last night."

"I have. Nasty business."

"With your permission, sir, or the captain's, I'd like to take a look at the crew manifests, and if possible the ship's log. I believe I might be able to at least narrow down our pool of suspects."

King raised his bushy eyebrows. "I suppose that can be arranged," he said.

"Additionally, I don't know if Brooksbank has mentioned this already, but it could be very constructive if Doctor Usher was able to re-examine the body of Friedrich Müller."

"Yes, Carrie mentioned that. It would be far simpler to leave it in the cold store until we make land."

"Simpler, perhaps. But can you really take the risk of Klein spreading his story to all and sundry without contradiction or correction? A second opinion could nip that in the bud."

"All right, all right, I'll speak to the captain and see to it." King shot Brooksbank a broad smile. "You'll need to keep this one on a short leash," he said. "She's too clever by half."

"There isn't… Absolutely, Mr King," Brooksbank said, always one for the path of least resistance. He promised to come find King again after seeing Avis safely situated in the records room, and then he and Avis left the old man to his chess game to find a crewman to help.

Avis recounted what Berthault had seen. As convinced as the Frenchwoman had seemed, when she relayed it now, it was all too easy to dismiss.

"People are, after all, extremely adept at seeing what they want to see. I use it in my act all the time. Who knows what she really saw? Particularly with her companions filling her head with nonsense."

Brooksbank sighed. "I wish you would show more compassion for Rachel Duquesne," he said. "Her brother obviously plans to marry the woman, and it wouldn't surprise me if he's also the primary beneficiary of his uncle's will. Rachel, by contrast, has only this—and even that may go if Gideon follows through on his plans to settle down. A single Duquesne twin may not command the same interest the pair does. She must be very worried for her future."

Avis tutted. "He'll not see her put onto the street."

"Perhaps not, but is that a life *you* would choose? Entirely reliant on a family member for the roof over your head, the food on your plate, the clothes on your back?"

Unbidden, Avis's mind cast back to the sick-bay that morning: Gideon's proprietary air, Rachel's struggle to be seen, to stay relevant to their little trio as Charlotte Berthault began to redraw the various lines and boundaries between them. All this when it was Rachel, not Gideon, who had scooped the widow up into her arms and carried her back from the precipice. Would she want to be in Rachel's shoes in that situation? Of course not. And the more she knew of the Duquesnes, the easier it was to see how they'd ended up as they had, more through circumstance and the manoeuvrings of others than any nefarious schemes of their own.

"It is not," she confessed. "But I also could not countenance the idea of making a living through lies. Oh, he looks busy," she diverted now, pointing at a crewman trotting towards an external door. "Let's make him busier."

Twenty-Four

EXCAMBION'S RECORDS ROOM was in an organised chaos. The purser had been most reluctant to give them access, and it was clear now why: he was embarrassed.

"I've been running to catch up since the crew changeovers in Portsmouth," he said. He was a small man with round, wire-rimmed spectacles. If Avis had been asked to draw a picture of a ship's purser, she would have drawn this man. "What with resignations and hirings, and even passengers becoming crew, and now with the added administration of Müller's, er… In any event, the piles are correctly sorted," he said quickly. "But… well, there are piles."

"Calm yourself, sir, I'm not an auditor," Avis said. "Just point me at the original manifest and crew rosters, and the resignation pile. I'll cross-check for myself." This was going to take longer than she'd intended, but perhaps that was for the best. Free time would only have been wasted thinking about the events of the past twenty-four hours, ever since she'd followed Rachel Duquesne down to third class.

I wish you would show more compassion for Rachel Duquesne.

You could, you know. She shows enough for you, tolerating your hostility and narrowmindedness. Fix your face, the purser thinks you hate him.

The cross-checking was slow and laborious. Avis was not enamoured of paperwork at the best of times, and this paperwork was unfamiliar and densely lettered. First there were the crew rosters, which were not a single list but several separate lists, depending on the roles in question. Then there were the individual notes of resignation she had to check against them, which came in various forms, some written by the crew member in question and some in a tight, slanted hand she was coming to recognise as the purser's.

Then there were the hirings. She was fairly sure that anybody who came on as crew at Portsmouth could be removed from suspicion; the rumour-mongering around the ship being haunted preceded that point. But a handful of men and women had been passengers and were now crew. They had to be added to the suspect list, albeit with a note against them.

Breaking only for a cold, hasty lunch, Avis compiled her list and then moved on to the various duty rotas and logbooks, including the captain's log itself, which had taken no small amount of cajoling to get and she was under strict instructions to return whenever she was not actively using it.

This was where she hoped to begin building a picture. Surely the navigational error had not been the only instance of sabotage? There must be spoiled supplies or a malfunctioning... gasket, or whatever it was that kept the ship running smoothly. To her frustration, nothing immediately leapt out at her beyond the absolute ubiquity of Third Officer Baynes, who was in about four places at once judging by his signature on this duty roster and that stocktake.

The day was proving to be an utter waste of time—at least for Avis. The purser, by contrast, was delighted that he now had a comprehensive list of all the resignations and new hires for his records.

Avis eschewed dinner and drinks in favour of poring over more of the ship's logs, and her head ached with the sheer amount of names and facts therein. They refused to form themselves into any sort of helpful pattern or clue, merely piling up like snow over a trail of footprints. She held out hope that a good night's sleep might help her make sense of the jumble, but a much-needed collapse into her bed was forestalled by the dark figure waiting by her cabin. It was not cold—at least, no colder than normal—and the shiver that slid through her was not borne of dread but something less welcome.

"Miss Lovelock." Rachel detached from the shadows, stepping in front of the door as if she could sense Avis's inclination to push past. "I need a moment of your time."

A dozen mean-spirited quips sprang to Avis's lips at once, but when she opened her mouth to speak—perhaps to enquire whether she wasn't late to commune with the spirits in the galley or a nearby broom closet—the words died on her lips. This was the woman who had fenced with her these past few days, certainly, who had taken pleasure in scoring points in their game and taken her knocks in return. But when Avis looked at her now, it was hard to shake the memory of her up on the deck risking her life for Charlotte Berthault, in her cabin shivering in a sodden dress, in her bed clinging to Avis for warmth. And then there was the scene earlier that day, where she had arrived to attend to Charlotte to find that Gideon had already staked his claim and clearly intended to freeze her out of whatever was going on between the three of them once and for all.

Avis was a woman of scant sympathies, prone to hard truths and "I told you so"s, but she wasn't a monster. Rachel Duquesne's past twenty-four hours on *Excambion* had been difficult to say the least. She could spare her some grace.

She inclined her head, pushing open the door to her stateroom and standing back to let Rachel step inside. "I've only sherry, I'm afraid," she said. "And only one glass."

Rachel lodged no protest, and once inside Avis helped herself to the first mouthful before setting the half-empty glass on the dresser. Her guest didn't take the proffered chair—or drink—instead coming to stand by the porthole, which was half-covered by a hideous paisley curtain. She reached up to tug it open, though there was nothing but night to be seen.

"I would ask you to keep an open mind to what I'm about to say," Rachel said, "but I know it's still clamped tight onto the idea that there is some mundane explanation behind everything we've seen. Nevertheless, you've been unable to find one that binds all of this together, yes?" There was a touch of French to her inflections; she must have spoken it exclusively with Charlotte, their shared tongue.

Avis slumped into the chair by the dresser, folding her arms across her chest. "I've yet to identify our saboteur, if that's what you mean. Our only concrete evidence of anything at all is the tampering that caused our navigation error. Everything else—these ghostly figures and visions—can all easily be put down to febrile imaginations and a hefty dose of suggestion. It's clearly been in somebody's interest to spread the idea that the ship is haunted, and sailors are a superstitious lot."

"What about Müller?"

"What about him? Until such time as he can be re-examined, I have to assume that he is most likely a very sad coincidence. We'll have that confirmed soon enough, once Usher's given him the once-over."

Rachel sighed, and Avis flared with irritation. How could this woman act like her adherence to rational belief was tiresome? She reached for the sherry, knocking a good third of it back in a single slug before setting it down between them.

"You're right," Rachel said then. "The séances are fabrications."

Avis inclined her head. "Of course."

Rachel blinked. Clearly she had been expecting a larger reaction. "But the spirits are not. They may not speak to us in words, but they are real and they do communicate—if one can hear them."

Avis rolled her eyes. "D'you think I haven't heard that one

before? Half the Spiritualists I expose come out with the same nonsense—oh, they had to put on a show to be taken seriously, but the *communion*, that's real. They really *do* channel the dead."

"Not the table, not the communion. They're… out there," Rachel said, gesturing widely. "Everywhere. In the world. They have no interest in us, but sometimes they intersect, they brush against us. They… echo, from another place, another time."

This was a new one, at least. Not an entirely new concept, but not one she had ever heard espoused by a medium. Avis pursed her lips, a frown creasing her forehead, and shook her head. "That might explain the visions, or even Henri on the deck there. But could your echoes kill a man?"

"No." It sat there between them, sharp-edged despite the sound. "Something's wrong. It shouldn't be happening like this."

"Forgive me but that sounds half-baked."

"If I had all the answers, my name would be Avis Lovelock," came the retort, and now Rachel did reach for the glass, one long finger worrying absently at its rim. "I don't know what's wrong, but I think I can find out. With your help."

"*Mine?* Why?"

Another sigh. "Because you're clever. Observant. You have a knack for getting into people's confidences somehow. And because you can sense them too. The echoes."

"Excuse me?"

Rachel looked down into the glass she held, swirling it not in circles but back and forth, side to side, the liquid sloshing closer and closer to the rim with every tip. "Are you going to continue to pretend you felt nothing in the engine room?" She lifted her eyes back to Avis's. "Are you going to pretend you aren't *haunted*, every day?" She set the glass down with a quiet clink. The surface of the liquid within continued to sway back and forth. "I don't know what it is that you see or hear in those moments of distraction, but I feel it. I feel it in the air around you, and I feel how much it hurts you." Rachel's eyes had taken on a liquid sheen in the lamplight and Avis had to look away for a moment.

"You forget," Avis said. "I know how this works. I know you're clever and observant too, Miss Rachel Duquesne. I know the difference between otherworldly divination and plain ordinary looking. I know that you are very good at the latter—you have to be to play-act at the former."

"Whatever the method, the facts are the same."

Avis gave a bark of a laugh. "That I'm insane."

"No," Rachel said quickly—almost angrily, in fact—and to Avis's shock she did just what she had done earlier that day in the sick-bay and surged forward to kneel in front of her, staring up at her, eyes a burning amber. She stopped short of reaching for Avis, her hands clenched together in her lap.

"You are not mad. Don't think that," Rachel said. "Whatever story you have told yourself, however you've reasoned it away, your gift is to be cherished. It is part of who you are. And..." She gave a ragged little sigh. Tears tracked down her face now, though her voice was its usual low and steady self when she spoke. "I think that, somehow, it saved my life last night. I felt it."

Avis swallowed the lump in her throat, mouth twisting as she fought the automatic, humiliating mirror response to seeing somebody else cry. "I don't know what you think you—"

"Don't. Enough." She did reach for Avis now, lifting her hands to rest on her knees. "I know what I felt. I felt it leave with you too, in the morning."

Now Avis felt her cheeks begin to flush, and she scowled. "This is nonsense, all of it. I've *proven* the sabotage. Once we get Müller re-examined, this will all be over."

Rachel's mouth flattened to a line of tamped exasperation. "Fine. Usher examines the body when?"

Avis shrugged. "At the captain's leisure, I suppose. Or King's. They've given their blessings but seem in no hurry."

Pushing down on Avis's knees in a motion that felt simultaneously presumptuous, perfunctory, and impossibly, intimately familiar, Rachel rose back to her feet. “It will be tomorrow. I’ll lend my voice to the call. But in return, if he died by impossible means… will you agree to at least give my way a chance?”

“What does Gideon think to this new phase of your spiritual investigation?” Avis asked then, cocking her head up at Rachel.

“Gideon has other things on his mind. Do we have a deal?”

Avis had become very good at ignoring movement in her periphery. Such it was that she did not look past Rachel but up at her face, more or less, as she gave a reluctant nod. “Very well,” she said. “*If* the man really did drown several decks down, or something similarly far-fetched, we’ll follow your path for a while and see where it goes.”

Only then, as Rachel turned to go, did Avis look towards the motion at the corner of her eye to confirm that the sherry in the glass had not stopped moving since Rachel had set it down some long moments before. In front of Avis’s eyes, minutes ticked by, and it continued to swing slowly back and forth in its vessel like a stormy sea.

Twenty-Five

Avis had never been at a post-mortem before, and if the captain had gotten his way, she wouldn't have been at this one either. She'd had to argue her way in, and to add insult to injury, Usher wouldn't allow her to bring her coffee with her—even though she *distinctly* saw him take a nip from his flask before picking up his instruments. She supposed it might actually help with the steadiness of his hand, though it didn't matter much when the patient was already dead.

The body had been brought back to the sick-bay; poor Herr Müller was being carted around more than a soup tureen during the crossing. Luckily Charlotte had been discharged the day before under Gideon's watchful eye, so it was just the two of them overseeing the re-dissection. The body lay on one of the sick-bay berths, which had been covered with waxed canvas, though Usher had assured her there would be "minimal leakage" this second time around.

"Are you expecting to catch something I don't?" he asked with a hint of amusement, bending down to examine the corpse's head and neck closely. "Or have you been hiding a medical degree from me this whole time?"

"Oh, you know me, I just like being around death," Avis breezed. "So let's say he drowned. What would the telltale signs be?"

"Well, if this was a fresh death there'd likely be foam in the airways, but we're several days late for that," he told her. "Klein noted it in his report, but it could be fabrication. Likewise diluted gastric contents—you swallow a lot of water when you drown, it turns out. Unless it's a dry drowning."

"A dry drowning?"

"That's when the throat spasms and closes up, and so the water never reaches the lungs. But it wouldn't fit here. It tends to set in later on, and mostly affects children."

Avis's hands curled into fists momentarily. "I see. So what evidence might remain at this stage?"

"Well, there's sometimes bruising in the neck or back, though that could be from having a fit..." He paused, rolling the body off one shoulder and peering closely at the skin of the back. Despite his relaxed drawl and general attitude, his movements were careful and respectful, and she wasn't surprised so much as relieved. "But I don't see that here. Not surprising, but it would've helped strengthen the case, I suppose. Really the biggest sign'll be the state of his lungs. And spleen, believe it or not."

"Oh, I believe it."

"Hah. Well, there's nothing else for it... Are you sure you want to stay?"

"How else am I going to horrify all the duchesses at dinner? Lay on, Macduff!"

Usher harrumphed and moved down the body, using snips to cut the dark thread that Dr Klein had used to close his incisions. Despite her protestations, Avis *did* find the sight of the slit peeling open somewhat gruesome, and she cast her eyes to the opposite bunk while Usher worked. She remembered Charlotte lying there, wrapped in blankets, with Rachel knelt at her feet, a saint and her penitent. Whatever was between them was real enough to bleed when it was severed.

"Aha, here we are..." Avis glanced back just in time to watch Usher lift an organ from the chest cavity, a slab of pink and mottled red that glistened slightly as he hefted it in his hands.

She wished she hadn't looked. "Now, in a drowning victim I'd expect it to be overextended from taking in water, and sometimes that can mean it crowds up against the ribs. So if I can find impressions made from one onto the other, that would support the theory."

Gently he lowered the lung to the surface of the makeshift table, leaning in to begin a closer examination. It just looked like one big mass of meat to her, something the French would call a delicacy, though she'd never been less tempted by a sweetmeat in her life. Usher muttered to himself, moustache twitching as he ran a finger across the surface of the organ. After a moment he straightened up, frowning. "Well, I'll be damned." He sounded genuinely surprised.

"I feel as though you're about to tell me something impossible, Usher."

The doctor sighed and tocked his tongue a couple of times. "Sorry to disappoint, Miss Lovelock. Let me put it like this… I'm neither infallible nor all-knowing—no man is. There may be some other explanation here. But Klein did not arrive at his conclusion without evidence. To all appearances, and the best of my personal understanding of the human body, Friedrich Müller died by drowning."

Avis grimaced and turned away from the makeshift table as he went back in, presumably for the spleen. Usher seemed entirely compos mentis, but he'd already admitted to seeing things at least once. Could she trust him?

There was the sound of flesh parting behind her, the wet squelch and moist rasp of skin on organ. Suddenly something occurred to her.

"Usher. That memory you spoke of, the one at the camp."

"Mm… hmm?" She supposed interrogating him during an autopsy might invite a certain level of distraction. Perhaps he'd be more candid this way.

"You said you saw the Indians. But you hadn't reached their camp yet."

"No, we wouldn't for another two days. Had to wait for the

storm to die down and for things to get passable. It's no easy feat moving an army."

"And what happened when you did?" Avis asked, risking a glance over her shoulder at him.

He paused, elbow-deep in the corpse's chest cavity. "They were celebrating. They'd just had an altercation with another tribe, and apparently won it. Mackenzie waited 'til dawn and then sent men in. He was just planning to round them up, I think, but one of their sentries saw the scouts and got a shot off. It went about as you'd expect from there." His expression sobered as it hadn't even when he'd been rummaging through Müller's insides. "Eventually he *did* manage to march them off, without any chance to get their clothes, cooking utensils, horses."

"So you'd seen… what? Something that hadn't happened yet?"

"I know. It doesn't make sense. But yes, what I saw in the storm, days before… It was that forced march, the one that took them from their homes. The one where women and children died. For a long time, I thought…" He trailed off, and Avis turned back around, prompting him with her body language, her expression, to continue. He did, with great reluctance. "I thought God had shown it to me so that I could have stopped it. And I didn't. If I ever had the chance to do it again… I'd make sure to act."

The guilt and shame in his voice was too much, too familiar. Avis knew what it was like to have a failed responsibility hanging over one's head, one that would never go away despite all the logical thought in the world. "That's not how it works," she mumbled, and turned away again so he couldn't see the hot flush in her cheeks. "You're not… It's not your fault. Anyway. I should go tell Rachel about your findings. She'll be thrilled, I'm sure."

And with that she edged out of the room, grateful for the distraction even if it came with a side of crow.

* * *

To her credit, Rachel did not gloat. Indeed, she did not even force Avis to verbalise the results of Usher's examination. When Avis entered the main saloon where they had agreed to assemble, Rachel, alone at her little table with a coffee pot and a book, simply looked up, met her gaze, and nodded. She rose and gestured for them to leave, falling into step beside Avis as they exited the saloon, heading for the stairs to the lower decks.

"Did you attend the examination personally?" was all she asked.

"I did."

"That must have been difficult."

Avis frowned. "Why?"

Rachel cast her a sidelong glance. "I'm not sure," she said. "But I feel that it must."

Perhaps it should have been. Having been haunted by the spectre of her drowned sister's death for over half her life, the experience of watching another victim of (evidently) the same fate be taken apart in front of her ought to have been a very special kind of torture. But while gruesome and more than a bit unsettling, it hadn't even crossed Avis's mind to compare the scenarios. Firstly, though Patience had presumably at some point been subjected to a similar examination, Avis had not been present for it. Secondly, it was hard to truly recall how she had felt in that moment, imagining Patience lifeless on a slab, when her sister had by that point already become a recurrent presence by her side.

"I appreciate the concern," was all she could think to say to Rachel. Then, "Where are we going?"

"I want to speak to everybody we can find who has seen or experienced something they can't explain on board the ship. We'll listen to their stories and visit the locations."

"Hm."

Rachel stopped, turned, and folded her arms. "You promised me an engagement in good faith, Miss Lovelock. I hope you're as good as your word."

"It's not that. It's just..." Avis shrugged. "A very mundane way to investigate, I suppose."

"I've never done this before, have you? I am merely trying to follow the leads we have. We start with this, and if I'm right, and *if* we stay open to it"—a warning look—"perhaps the places we are sent to will tell us their story."

"I suppose it can't hurt. C'mon, let's get chatting."

They started in first class, given its proximity. It took some investigation just to find the man from the first sighting on deck, one Mr Herbert Beckwith. They eventually tracked him to *Excambion*'s reading room, which Avis had been unaware of until that very moment. It was a high-ceilinged room with expansive windows that let in the sharp sunlight. Armchairs littered the carpeted expanse like the showroom of an extremely prolific upholsterer.

Beckwith sat in one of these chairs, a thick tome in hand: *The Coal Question; An Inquiry Concerning the Progress of the Nation, and the Probable Exhaustion of Our Coal Mines.* He was a portly man with a prominent chin and expectant eyebrows, who made a pointed attempt to ignore both women even as they stopped before him. Avis frowned and then turned away, noisily dragging over the nearest chair and depositing it inches away from his knees. She sat, one elbow smeared across the armrest. "Mr Beckwith. We have some questions for you."

"I'm occupied," he said, glancing up from his book long enough to give her a pointed look. "This is the *reading* room."

"I'm quite aware of that fact," Avis replied, "and if there was a speaking room I would have accosted you there instead. Alas, the Hamburg Line did not think to furnish this fine ship with such amenities."

Rachel cleared her throat. Avis tutted and tried again.

"Mr Beckwith, we just want to talk to you about the things you saw on deck the other night."

This was a far more successful approach. Beckwith lowered his book into his lap, eyeing the two women and puffing himself up with importance. "You're not here to accuse me of making things up, I hope. Because I don't take kindly to being called a liar."

"My days of making such accusations are far behind me," Avis told him, hand on heart. "Just tell us what you saw."

He recounted his stroll along the deck before dinner and the realisation that there was something odd strewn across the forecastle, his attempts to get a crewman's attention, the moment when it all dissolved and melted away. Rachel was particularly intrigued by this last detail, asking him to repeat himself and questioning his description until Avis could've repeated it back to her by heart. It was clear that he certainly *thought* he had seen several dead bodies on deck, and that he was not a man given to fanciful meanderings of the mind.

"That was supremely unedifying," Avis said as they left the reading room behind. "We can't know what he saw, only what he thought he saw. And what he thought he saw makes no sense. Unless you can pull some meaning from it?"

Rachel shook her head, tendrils of hair brushing the back of her neck. Avis blinked and pulled her gaze away. "Not as of yet. Let's talk to the crew and see what they say."

They descended below decks and began their interviews. Avis was known there by now and while not every crewman was forthcoming, they did manage to find several who had encountered inexplicable phenomena while carrying out their duties. Many reported unexpected figures, like Charlotte's sabre-carrying Henri, and more than once they described them as "melting away into nothing", much as Beckwith had. There was no trigger for these events, no obvious link between one and the next. Most of the witnesses had rationalised them away, too busy and exhausted by their gruelling shifts to spend much time trying to make sense of the strangeness stalking the corridors.

Avis was gratified to hear that a handful had also found themselves slogging through passageways seeping with water, driven to raise an alarm only to find it had vanished when their hand found the bell. *Excambion* was a well-kept ship; her crew would know if she were taking on ocean water.

"Well?" Rachel glanced back at Avis as they made their way along the narrow corridors towards third class once more.

"Well, what?"

"What do you think?"

"Oh." Avis shook her head. "I don't know. Under normal circumstances, I could tell you at least three or four different ways you could rig what they saw—pulleys, puppets, shadow-play, mirrors…"

"Have you truly seen all that? People go to all that trouble?"

Avis raised her eyebrows, although Rachel was no longer looking back at her. "Not everybody has the novelty of a twin to misdirect and divert," she said. "Many mediums mount really quite elaborate tricks as part of their work—particularly on stage, of course."

She was rewarded with a small flinch, though if she hadn't been watching for it, she might have missed it altogether. Alone on stage, without a twin to play against, would Rachel resort to even cheaper and more elaborate hoaxes? Avis imagined her waving paper "spirits" about, chiming bells with her feet, expectorating chewed-up wads of "ectoplasm". It didn't fit with her understanding of this serious, complicated woman, but then, what did she know? Desperation made people do terrible, stupid things.

They heard yet more stories in third class: strange noises like thunder in the night, ghostly sightings, and one old man who claimed to have seen lights dancing on the water, just as Charlotte had. The Frenchwoman had appeared subdued and embarrassed about her experience; Avis didn't think she would have shared that detail widely, so how could he have known?

"All right, so there's some commonality," Avis said as they sat down in one of the booths. Though it was late for lunch, Frieda had insisted that they stay for some leftover stew and a beer. "We have floating spectres, lights on the water… What else?"

"Corpses. Both real and unreal." Rachel tapped her fingers on the table, her gaze fixed on the middle distance. "There must have been an accident Baynes doesn't know about. Something that brought death here, pulled the spirits closer."

"I suppose we could go back to the records room and look at old logs. The purser might know something, or at least point us in the right direction."

Rachel gestured vaguely upwards. "Lead the way."

Avis lifted her eyebrows, glancing at Rachel's still-laden plate. "How are you so strong when you never eat?"

"I eat," Rachel said quickly. "I'm just very careful about it." She hesitated, then added, "Uncle Waylan was always very particular about our food. I suppose it's become a habit."

"He's not here to see you now."

"And yet sometimes it's as if I hear his voice just over my shoulder."

Avis repressed a shiver, put on a cheerful grin. "You'll forgive me if I finish *my* plate before we go?"

"I suppose—provided you tell me what's on your mind."

"Excuse me?"

"You're not satisfied," Rachel observed. Avis bristled. She hated that this woman had so quickly caught the measure of her, seemed to know before she did how she felt.

"Oh, yes? What 'tell' am I exhibiting that gave you that idea?"

Rachel's lips twitched. "You keep glancing at the door when you think I won't notice."

Avis sighed, flipping her fork and pressing it down on a soft piece of potato, watching it squelch mushily between the tines. "I wanted to speak to a particular passenger—well, crewman now. Slippery fellow named George. Well, he *says* his name is George, but I'm certain he's lying."

"Ah, Jorge." She pronounced it with soft 'g' sounds, suddenly sounding French again.

Avis's eyebrows winged upwards. "He's *Spanish*?" she asked, assuming that Rachel's strange pronunciation was an artefact of her second language.

Rachel shook her head. "Portuguese," she said. "Half. On his mother's side. But he's worried that Americans won't know the difference, and with things growing heated between America and Spain…"

"He thought it best to conceal it. Is that all? Damn," Avis muttered. "I thought perhaps there was something there." She frowned. "How did you find all this out?"

Rachel shot her a patient smile. "Most people find me very easy to talk to, Avis."

"That astounds me—I find you uniquely charmless."

"Mm." The smile widened, and Avis felt a worrying little flutter in her stomach. "Eat. We've work to do."

Twenty-Six

THE PURSER KNEW little of the history of the ship before he joined the crew, but he did have several large tomes of old ship's logs going back to *Excambion*'s maiden voyage in early 1890. He was well disposed towards Avis after the residual benefits from her previous day's work, and so it was simple enough to convince him to let her and Rachel pore over the logbooks—provided they did not remove them from the room.

Avis knew she should be petulant. There was a whole ship full of rich people to impress, wine to drink, and fun to be had, and here she was stuck in the records room again. She found she didn't much care, however, because the mystery of the haunting had her fully in its grasp. There would be more free wine and impressionable millionaires in her future, she was sure of it. But there was only one *Excambion* and her time aboard was limited.

And the company?

She looked up from her logbook, ignoring Patience's presence and focusing on Rachel, bent over her own books across the way. It had been a surprisingly tolerable day, despite the fact she'd been forced to act as if the "hauntings" were genuine. Rachel was thorough and thoughtful, and though she was not nearly as much fun to wind up as Brooksbank, she had a similar knack of connecting to people, getting them to open up about their experiences without embarrassment or fear.

Perhaps it's because she takes them at their word, rather than mocking them for it.

Avis scowled, watching as Rachel set one book aside and pulled another close. There was that, but there was also something more. Most of the mediums she had encountered were vain and selfish creatures, concerned only with their own reputations and coffers. While she knew Rachel had her plans, her interest in the events on the ship didn't seem motivated by self-aggrandisement. Her worry from the night before hadn't abated, and rather than hide in her room and lick her wounds she was here, right alongside Avis.

She actually cares. Perhaps your initial reading was wrong, for once.

The other woman lifted her head, and Avis was too slow; Rachel caught her looking, and returned that look with an implacable, unreadable gaze of her own. Her eyes were that clear blue-green in this light, and they pierced straight through her. After a moment, Rachel spoke. "Have you found something?"

"Mm, no, nothing except completely mundane maintenance reports. I'm beginning to think Baynes had the whole of it when he gave us her history. The man clearly needs to get out more."

The corner of Rachel's crooked mouth quirked up, just a bit, and Avis felt a thrill of triumph. "Any job worth doing is worth doing well."

"That's the refrain of overachievers the world over," Avis said, shaking her head. "Makes me sick."

Rachel's smile widened. "I'm afraid you're not fooling anyone, Miss Lovelock. This isn't your first time in the records room, after all."

"I didn't find anything useful then, either, although at least it wasn't a… What is it you call it in the colonies? A snipe hunt?"

"It does seem that way." That tiny smile melted away. "Anything traumatic enough to draw the spirits to this ship in these numbers ought to be *somewhere* in these records. Baynes should know about it. The captain should know about it."

Avis narrowed her eyes. Rachel blinked.

"Is there something wrong?"

"Yes. I can't make you out." Avis tapped her stubby little pencil on the logbook in front of her, then flipped it closed with puff of dust.

Rachel's lips twitched. "Perhaps you aren't supposed to."

"You move through the world with such certainty. The stories you spin, the lies you tell, nobody would doubt that those are strongly held convictions."

Rachel glanced about them, perhaps to check the purser was nowhere to be seen. "Nobody apart from you."

"Well, yes, but I'm remarkable," Avis said with a wave of her hand.

"Terminal, crushing adherence to suspicion and empirical fact in the face of a beautiful, mysterious world is only remarkable insofar as it's one of the saddest things I've ever witnessed, but go on."

Avis bundled that particular statement away for later examination. "But you do believe in *something*. And that something, you cannot fully grasp and do not fully understand, and you seem content to simply"—another vague hand gesture—"wonder. To not know. I confess I find that more difficult and more alien than those Spiritualists who believe in the Veil, the beyond, who think they know its workings."

Rachel pushed her own log aside and reclined back in her chair, crossing her legs at the ankle. She had an easy freedom with her body that Avis envied, and she wondered if it came from all the "channelling" she did, if playing at being other people somehow made her feel more embodied in turn.

"That story my brother told was mostly true," she said. "About seeing our parents at the end of our bed on the night of their death. But there are two missing details. One is a lie: he never saw them. Only I did, although he's been telling his version for so long I think he might now believe it. The other is an omission." Rachel sat up straight again, smoothed her hands across her thighs. "I didn't see them after they died. The vision came hours before the crash."

Avis frowned, straightened up also. "I'm sorry, so you're saying…"

"My parents' ghosts appeared to me while they were still alive."

"Of course they did," Avis said with a snort. Rachel's expression did not shift; she was neither offended nor driven to leap to her own defence. She merely nodded calmly, and there was something about her certainty that stopped Avis from remonstrating further. She told herself it was because it was useless to argue with someone so obviously delusional, but there was a small voice—not Patience's, but her own—that asked, what if?

THEY LEFT THE records room soon after, as it was nearly time for the second sitting of dinner and Avis had sworn to take at least *one* meal in first class today. Rachel was reluctant to attend but Avis chivvied her along, remembering how little she had eaten at midday. The dining room was nearly full when they arrived, and Avis paused for a moment to scan the room, ignoring the maître d's attempts to guide them towards the few remaining seats.

Brooksbank and King were seated at the captain's table, and the three men were deep in conversation, with King doing most of the talking (and gesticulating). It was almost surely about their inconvenient haunting situation, and yet without anything concrete to share—or even a reasonable guess, at this point—she was loath to join them. The captain was drinking deeply from his wine glass and Avis could not blame him. Third Officer Baynes hovered nearby. He looked worried, and kept trying to exchange glances with Brooksbank, who was studiously ignoring him.

Usher was ensconced with strangers, for the most part, though Mr and Mrs Armitage were there as well. She'd catch him later in the smoking lounge; not even the pleasure of his company could convince her to subject herself to more of the woman's hand-wringing. Clarissa and Sarah were nowhere to be seen, likely having eaten during the first sitting, and Charlotte and Gideon—

"I'm going to go."

Rachel had spotted the pair first. They were seated near one of the windows, and though there were others at their table they ignored them entirely. Gideon was turned towards the widow, his expression rapt and solicitous, and Charlotte glowed under his gaze. Their heads were tilted together, and whatever bon mots they were exchanging to earn such satisfied smiles were lost in the clatter and clamour of the room.

Avis turned to see Rachel's retreating figure, dark skirts flaring out behind her in her haste. She considered calling after her, but what would she say? There was no softening that blow.

Her immediate reflex was to let Rachel go, to eat her own dinner in peace. What business was this of hers, really? Any of it. But the insubstantial figure that stood in Rachel's wake, watching not her—for once—but the retreating woman, pricked at her conscience. And after glancing about for Baynes only to find that he had disappeared, she caught the arm of a passing waiter. "Could I request two meals on a tray, please?"

The waiter had tried to accompany her to carry the tray, and on the steep stairs down to the first-class cabin block Avis slightly regretted refusing, but she arrived at Rachel's stateroom in one piece. It occurred to her only belatedly that perhaps Rachel could have gone somewhere else—possibly down to third class—but on approach she could see that the room was not only occupied but its door was slightly ajar, swinging gently with the rocking of the ship. Through the gap, she had a view of a sliver of a scene: the vanity, and Rachel's hands resting upon its surface. In one, she held the handsome gold-and-emerald stick pin that she so often wore, twirling it around, back and forth.

Avis had her hands full, but she managed a muffled knock with her elbow on the door, which had the secondary effect of pushing it open.

"If you're going to skip dinner as usual, you ought to at least do it properly."

Rachel looked up, and to Avis's horror her eyes were gleaming with unshed tears. She seemed confused for a moment, her gaze darting between Avis's face and a spot over her shoulder, but then she came back to herself and sighed softly. "Miss Lovelock. I'm sorry I left so abruptly, but I assure you, I am fine. You should get back to your adoring fans." Her tone was weary, with only a tinge of the dryness Avis had come to expect.

Avis had done her duty; she could simply leave a plate she knew Rachel would not touch and go eat in her own room. There was no reason for her to have anything to do with this complex situation. She did not need to entangle herself any further with the Gordian knot of Rachel Duquesne's private life.

Avis put the tray down on the vanity and moved to sit on the bed behind the medium. She spoke to Rachel's back, though she could see her face in the mirror. "I don't have to tell you it was never real."

In the mirror, Patience flinched.

"And if that changed what she felt," Rachel said, "what any of us felt, that might mean something. But once again you have illustrated that for all your perceptiveness of their traits and habits, you have no understanding of people or their lives." Rachel's shoulders were rigid, her voice tight with carefully controlled anger. It was better than sorrow.

"Is it not better for it to be over, though? All the play-acting, the pretence of it. However much she believed or didn't, it was never about *you*."

Now Rachel turned, her face a mask, cheeks stained with heat. "And yet that was the most I could hope for, and now it is gone. For some it's all that's left to us, prising contentment out of the dregs of what life offers. I would have expected you of all people to understand."

Anger flared in Avis's stomach—not at Rachel, but on her behalf. In their first few days on board *Excambion*, it had been little more than a curiosity to observe the strange balance of the relationship between the twins and their sometime patron, the comfort Charlotte took in Rachel's "channelling" of her late husband, without acknowledging any of the attendant implications therein. But then came the events on deck during the storm and what followed: Rachel's remarkable feat of strength and tenacity in saving Charlotte at such personal risk, Charlotte's withdrawal in response, the apparent claim now staked by Gideon that shut Rachel out entirely. At first, this had struck Avis as a comeuppance—brutal, perhaps, but deserved, since had she not after all told the story that led to it, the lie of Henri's possession of her body?

But now... It was as though the past two days had revealed a new woman to Avis. Clever, thoughtful, determined, and, more than that, something she had never found before: an equal.

Except that was another lie, wasn't it? She'd known from the first moment she saw her that Rachel would prove to be more than a match for her, and not just professionally. Every time their eyes met there was something there: a challenge, but also a meeting of the minds.

In that moment Avis found that she didn't care whether Rachel had brought this on herself, only that she understood that whatever she shared with Charlotte Berthault was so much less than she deserved.

"Me, of all people?" Avis shook her head. "I, more than most, will never understand that kind of compromise. Don't you want to be wanted for *yourself*? For who you truly are, wholly and unconditionally?"

"And if I cannot have that? I suppose you think it is better to be alone." Rachel's laugh was a brittle thing.

"Yes! By God, yes. Better to be alone than live a lie, a thousand times."

"How dare you say that to me?" Rachel was on her feet in an instant, a tightly coiled spring, and Avis could not help but compare her to a jungle cat as her green eyes flashed in the lamplight. "*You* who dart at the periphery of every group like a moth to a flame, but more cowardly than any insect, for you're fearful of being burned. *You* who needle and prod, all to be seen and heard and remarked upon, so that you leave an impression when you withdraw. *You* who are so afraid to be alone that you have created your own spectre to hang about you so that you never have to acknowledge your own emotions. Your entire existence is a lie, Avis Lovelock, and the saddest part is that you won't even admit it to yourself."

Avis was already on her feet. She didn't remember standing. Her heart hammered; her barbed tongue sought purchase on a smart riposte and caught upon nothing. She opened her mouth and the words that emerged were the very last thing she wanted to utter. She heard them as though from someone else's mouth, that of a lost, helpless child. "Can you… see her?"

"I don't have to see her to know she's there. That you've anchored her to you." Rachel reached for her and Avis flinched, but she only rested a hand on her chest, above her heart, in a gesture that was both formal and intimate. "Better to live a lie than be alone."

Avis waited for Patience's rejoinder to this, be it castigation, or mockery, or a cutting insight. But there was nothing, and when she looked in the mirror, her sister was nowhere to be seen.

She lifted her own hand to cover Rachel's, as though between them they were holding her heart in place as it threatened to beat a hole through her ribcage.

"Do you love her?" Avis asked.

Rachel's brow knitted in bemusement at the apparent change of subject. "Charlotte? No. At least, not in the way you might think." Then, "Why?"

"Just… trying to ascertain how big a fool I am," Avis said, before she kissed her.

Twenty-Seven

It was a tentative sort of thing. Avis wasn't even sure *how* one kissed, when it came down to it, and this was more of a touch, really, her dry lips unparted, their pressure feather-light. She lingered barely a moment before drawing back, doubt wedging itself into the space between them, flushing her cheeks with sudden shame and uncertainty.

"My apologies," she muttered.

Rachel's hand slid out from under hers, up over her collarbone, and around to cup the back of her neck. She pulled Avis closer, and before that doubt could rear its head, she kissed her again, and again, and again.

The thrum of the engine and the wash of the waves was nothing against the racing beat of Avis's heart, her breath catching and her pulse thundering in her ears. Rachel's kisses were sure and hungry; this was no mistake, no accident to explain away.

Just as on the night they'd lain entwined in Rachel's bed, their heat flowed one into the other, shared and multiplied. That now familiar scent of cloves and sandalwood filled Avis's senses. She tasted metal and realised that her lower lip had cracked between Rachel's teeth, her blood mingling with saliva on their tongues. There was a barbaric thrill to this, and it emboldened her to reach for Rachel, to dare to touch her body in the way some small part of her had ached to these past long days—to map the contours of her narrow hips, the peaks of her shoulder blades. The layers of stiff boning that obscured the shape between was an unwanted barrier with which she soon grew impatient, though when she moved to the fastenings of Rachel's gown, Rachel reached for her hands.

"Wait," she said, and peeled away from their embrace and made for the door. For a jagged moment Avis thought she meant to leave, but she only pushed it shut and turned the key in the lock. When she turned back, she all but glowed in the lamplight, her cheeks and lips and even the tips of her ears flushed pink. Slowly she approached. "Are you sure? That you want this? Want me?"

She was braced for another rejection. The realisation hit Avis like a physical blow, and a fresh tide of shame flooded her body as she remembered every single occasion she had pitched her words to Rachel for the express purpose of causing hurt or anger.

"What I want…" Avis reached for Rachel, pulled her closer, began to tease at buttons and loops with fingers that trembled almost as much as they had the night they were both soaked through and freezing. "What I want, I don't even know how to put fully into words. But… you, yes. You."

Though she had lived a full and varied life, there were some things Avis had yet to encounter. The mechanics of two bodies together was one, yes, but what was stranger and newer still was this: the tenderness with which Rachel kissed her, touched her, laid her down, the hunger and the wanting. The first time they had been this close, this undressed, they had both been almost entirely numb with cold. This time Avis felt the opposite, suffused with heat, every nerve singing, every sensation sharpened to a point. Though deeply concerned at first that she did not know what to do in such moments, she was surprised to find that when it came to it she could do no wrong. Every touch, every exploration was met with approval and encouragement, whether verbal or unspoken, as though she had opened at the middle of a book only to find she had already read it.

In the aftermath, when they had untangled their limbs and retrieved blankets from beneath them to cover up before the chill in the air could catch them, remorse crept in once more.

"I've been so cruel to you," Avis said, their faces so close she needed only to whisper—which was fortunate, because she wasn't sure she could make such a confession in full voice without it breaking. "Without mercy or sympathy."

"Why does it make you so angry? The sittings, the channelling?" Rachel smoothed a hand down her side, fingers tracing along her back. "It's not the lying, for you lie often. What is it?"

Avis sucked in a breath, the pleasant sensation of Rachel's touch warring with the roiling in her stomach. "My mother," she said. "After Patience died, she went to a medium. To several. She sold my father's things, then the rest, just to pay their fees. She was so determined to reach the daughter she'd lost, and they gave her the illusion that she could. And… she lost herself in it."

"Ah." There was just that, one quiet syllable, and yet it said volumes. Rachel understood the determined grief her mother held, the descent into desperation, the way that candlesticks and platters would disappear in order to pay for another sitting, another message from the beyond. Then, "I'm sorry. Sometimes it does not close the wound; it only keeps it raw and weeping."

"The longer it went on, the more she changed. She became desperate, hungry for any word from the Other Side. She disappeared, became unrecognisable. And perhaps…" Avis felt her throat close around the words, and bent her head, pressing into Rachel's embrace. Rachel stroked her back, her shoulders, silent and reassuring. After a moment Avis mastered herself and spoke. "Perhaps she was right to pull away. I could have prevented my sister's death, and yet I did nothing. She is dead because of me."

"What happened?"

"We were on holiday in the Lake District. It was after my father had passed, and I think my mother was trying to convince us all that things were still normal—herself most of all. Patience had been an absolute pain the entire weekend: arguing, winding everybody up, taking my shoes, my hat. The day before we were meant to return home, we were picnicking on the shore of some lake or other. You have to understand that even then I was able to read people exceptionally well, and I picked a fight with Patience that day knowing it would get her goat. I was just so tired of her, of my mother always taking her side, so I provoked an argument and then splashed off into the lake so that she couldn't have the last word. Except as I did so, I *knew* she would follow, and that she wasn't the strongest swimmer. But I didn't turn back, even when she started calling my name."

The memory echoed between them, and Avis wondered if Rachel could hear it too. There had been no splashing, no fuss. Just a few pathetic repetitions of her name, increasingly few and far between. And then silence.

There were no tears left to cry for this particular memory, but Avis shut her eyes tightly, resting her forehead in the crook of Rachel's neck. "My mother rightfully knew my part in the tragedy. She barely spoke to me of it, except when she was in the worst of her moods. In the end, I lost them both."

"You were a child," Rachel said. "Observant as I'm sure you must have been, you could not have predicted what happened."

"I did though," Avis insisted. "I knew she would follow, that she could not stand to let me get away with the final say."

"That is a far cry from wanting her to drown. From *causing* her to drown. I'm sorry, Avis. Just as your mother's loss warped her, it has twisted you too. You must understand that."

Avis didn't, not really, having spent so many years with guilt riding her, but she was grateful for Rachel's compassion nonetheless. That she was able to accept the kindness for what it was rather than brush it off as sentimental treacle was progress, at least. Something tickled at her memory then, and she opened her eyes. "You said I created her. Created my own spectre."

Rachel reached to sweep a damp tendril back from Avis's forehead. "Didn't you?"

"I mean… yes. So I have always assumed. But I would have expected you to tell me she was a spirit; Patience's soul still tethered to me after death. Anchored, you said."

"I don't pretend to the certainty you do about anything, but I don't think that's how any of this works."

Avis slumped. "So I suppose we are in agreement on one matter, then. I *am* mad." She wasn't at all sure how she felt about that.

"Oh, no." Rachel shook her head. "I think the ghost you see is quite real. As I said, I sense her with you. I just don't think she's made of Patience's soul."

"Then what?"

"She comes from here." A kiss to the forehead. "And here." Another touch to the heart. "I think you split yourself into two and hid a part of yourself in this other place. She's not your sister's ghost. She's yours."

Avis sighed. "That just sounds like a very poetic way to describe madness," she said with a weary smile.

"I suppose on this matter, as so many others, we must be content to disagree after all." Rachel leaned to touch her lips to Avis's in a slow, sweet kiss, missing the urgency of before but containing no less promise, though it was interrupted by an audible complaint from Avis's stomach.

"We should eat."

Rachel made a face. "Cold French food. Thank you, but no."

"Actually, it's charcuterie and bread," Avis said. "I didn't trust myself to ferry hot food down the stairs." The hesitant expression didn't shift, and Avis reached for Rachel's hand beneath the covers. "You helped me banish Patience, at least for tonight. Let me help you banish your uncle. Eat with me?"

The repast was surprisingly intimate. They both re-donned their shifts and wrapped blankets around their shoulders, as the air in the cabin still held a bite. There was no table, and only one chair, and so they sat on the rug, tray between them. Avis was famished and dug in immediately, laying cheese and cured meats on generously buttered bread. Rachel was predictably reticent, selecting an olive from her plate and nibbling at it experimentally.

"So what was it?" Avis asked between bites, tasting salt and butter. "Was it about the money, your uncle keeping you from your food? Was he a skinflint?"

Rachel considered this, rolling the olive between her fingers. "No. Well, he was, but that wasn't his motivation. It was just part of the masquerade, you know. The mysterious Duquesnes, orphaned at thirteen, sylph-like and insubstantial, one foot in the grave themselves. It made what we do more believable."

"I've heard of suffering for one's art, but that takes the cake. Pun intended."

"Hm," Rachel hummed, giving a faint smile. "It wasn't really suffering, after a time. We got used to the constant gnaw of hunger, to always saying 'No' when we wanted to say 'More'." She set the olive down and picked up a slice of bread, reflexively beginning to shred it into smaller pieces. Avis reached over and placed a hand on her wrist, and she flinched. "It becomes a habit."

"I'm learning that even the habits of a lifetime can be broken," Avis said, running her thumb across the delicate skin of Rachel's inner wrist, white etched with blue like fine bone china. "And that some things must be eaten whole to be fully appreciated."

With her free hand Rachel picked up the olive again and, after a moment's hesitation, slipped it past her lips. Avis watched her roll it across her tongue, imagined the briny juices pricking her salivary glands, felt her own mouth begin to water. Rachel's jaw worked, the muscles flexing, and when she finally bit down, Avis felt a thrill cousin to the release she'd experienced in bed not half an hour before. Rachel's eyes fluttered closed for a moment, reverent, and when she opened them again she reached for another.

Even with this new-found enjoyment, Rachel did not or could not eat very much, and Avis didn't press the matter, happy to have watched her savour something, at least. After, they returned to bed, and Avis wilfully abandoned the charting of time passing, along with any other plans she had for that night. Here and now, in this moment, it was hard to remember why she had ever cared about such things as hauntings and saboteurs.

Rachel was similarly diverted—during one long, delicious silence, she did a quiet 'Hm' of recognition, and when Avis enquired as to its cause, she chuckled.

"I just remembered that Charlotte is to marry Gideon. They made it official this morning."

"Oh, Rachel…"

"No, no, what I mean is that I had forgotten. All day, all through our investigations, it was all I could think about. Was I angry, envious, bereaved? I couldn't decide. I cycled through them all. But now… I just forgot." That slightly lopsided smile turned almost shy.

Avis smiled in turn, but it morphed into a yawn. "I should sleep," she said, shifting to get up.

"I wish you'd stay."

Avis hesitated. Did she dare? "I am not a peaceful sleeper—you saw that."

"I know."

"If Charlotte or your brother—"

"What on earth could they possibly have to say under the circumstances?"

Still, a part of Avis wanted to refuse, to peel apart from Rachel and flee. It seemed impossible that she could have so many brand-new experiences in such a short space of time and something not… break. Implode. Malfunction. And yet in that moment, the path of least resistance, the simplest and easiest and by far the most attractive route, led her further down this selfsame unfamiliar road.

"All right," Avis said at last, and as she did a smile crept across her face of its own accord. "Then I'll stay."

Twenty-Eight

Avis woke to the sound of thunder. No, not thunder—something sharper, closer.

She slid from the bed, padding towards the porthole and brushing the curtain aside. There was no rain lashing the glass, no jagged streaks of lightning, but there *was* light, flickering far out on the water.

Squinting, she leaned in, pressing the edge of her hand to the glass to shield her eyes. It was cold against her palm and that cold seeped through her. The light danced on the waves, closer, now farther. It should have been impossible but she knew it was flames, like the reflection of candles on glass. Avis turned but the room was dark, the lamps unlit. Behind her, something crashed.

She knew she should wake Rachel, but even as the thought arose she was moving towards the door, bare feet scuffing the rug. Though she was a believer, far more so than Avis, she didn't think she could bear it if she were to shake Rachel awake only for it to all melt away—no thunderous noises, no dancing flames.

So I suppose we are in agreement on one matter, then. I am *mad*.

Grabbing a dressing gown from the back of the door, Avis fumbled the lock open and crept outside. The corridor was empty, the lamps low, and she wasn't entirely sure where she was going, but something pulled her onward.

Down, down, down she went, the plush carpet giving way to wood, and then cold metal. She was in the bowels of the ship now and the sound reverberated all around her, a shuddering, groaning noise like the rumination of a great animal. She was going towards the engine room, she realised, and she knew that was a good idea, because where better to find proof of what was wrong than the place that had seen death once already?

It was warm when she entered, and damp. The great machinery churned on in the nighttime, pushing them forward, and something compelled her just the same. It was gravity, it was time, it was *knowing* that the answers were close at hand, if she could only see them.

Something flickered overhead.

Avis looked up. Above her hung shadows, dark shapes floating formlessly, distorted in the dim light. As she watched, they began to resolve, like the shapes on deck—a leg here, the curve of a shoulder there. Were they shadows, or were they bodies? And were they suspended, or were they on the surface, and she below them?

As soon as the thought entered her mind, she began to feel it—the weight of the room pressing in around her, heavy and wet. She stumbled forward, her eyes drawn ever upwards to those dark figures. They did not struggle or even twitch; they were still save for the gentle drift that drew them from one side of the room to the other. She heard another rumbling crack, but it was different than before, the sound both muffled and echoing out in rings around her.

It was difficult to breathe. She sucked in a breath to prove she still could, but it was harder than she wanted it to be. The realisation did not panic her as much as she thought it would; it was hard to think of anything much except the bodies above her.

Peaceful. They looked peaceful, and Avis yearned for that feeling as well. She'd spent so long fighting and it had led nowhere. Better to be peaceful and still.

She coughed. Her lungs burned, and each breath was harder to draw than the last. The weight was almost too heavy to bear, and she dropped to her knees, shoulders bowing, back arching. Something filled her throat, her mouth, her nose, and she couldn't breathe, couldn't cough, couldn't do anything but curl her fingers against the floor. Perhaps she should have woken Rachel after all.

"Miss Lovelock? Dear God, what's the matter?" Somewhere in the periphery of her vision, Usher's face swam into view.

She opened her mouth to respond and seawater gushed out, acrid and briny. And then it all went black.

I know moonlight
I'm walking in the moonlight
Lay this body down

I go to judgement
In the evening of the day
Lay this body down

THE ONLY THING she recalled from the first time she woke was a pain in her chest that was at once deep and sharp, and the burning of bile rising in her throat. If there was more than that, it was lost to her subconscious by the time she cracked her eyes open again to find herself staring up at the dim-lit dark wooden ceiling of the sick-bay, identifiable mostly by the pervasive smell of astringent cleaning products and the hard berth. A large, warm hand rested over hers, though its owner was not within her present range of vision.

"They could at least see fit to make us comfortable when we're ailing," she said. Or, at least, that is what she would have said if she had any voice at all, but what emerged was instead a dry, monosyllabic croak.

“Don’t try to speak.” Brooksbank’s familiar drawl. That, then, explained the hand, both in size and presumptuousness.

“You’d… like that, wouldn’t you?” Avis managed, gratified that she could at least whisper. “Silencing me at last.”

“We were concerned it was going to be permanent for a while there,” Brooksbank said. He was doing his best to match her light-hearted tone in kind, but as his face came into focus, it reflected what she had heard in his voice: worry, even fear.

“What happened?” she croaked. “Did a water tank burst?”

“Not that we’ve seen.”

“And besides,” came another voice, “the ship doesn’t store salty water.” She twisted to see Dr Klein, his hair slightly less frantic, standing in the doorway. There was a moment of dissonance—hadn’t Usher found her? Where was he? Why was Klein there instead?—but it faded under the weight of her weariness. “You’ll be fine, but Mr Brooksbank is right. You should stay quiet, rest up.”

Never in her life had Avis taken well to being told to “stay quiet”, but for once she had no choice but to acquiesce. Her throat and chest ached, and besides, what would she say? *The haunting is real, and I was nearly its next victim?* It was preposterous enough just to think it; she couldn’t imagine uttering it aloud.

Even if it was true.

“I know that look,” Brooksbank said, giving her hand a squeeze before releasing it. “You’re puzzling something out. I look forward to hearing your theories, because I’m still stumped about all of this.”

She cleared her throat, about to disappoint him, when a clatter of footsteps in the hallway distracted them both. Rachel was fully dressed, but aside from that looked very much as Avis last saw her: tousled and rosy-cheeked. Though in this instance the exertion clearly came from a hurried trot to get here.

She ignored Brooksbank entirely at first, moving straight past him to crouch by Avis’s bedside, just as she had with

Charlotte the previous day. Though Brooksbank might not make the connection, Avis most certainly did, and her stomach fluttered as Rachel reached for her hand. "Where did you go?" she said, though it was clear from her tone that her overriding emotion was concern, not admonishment.

"I go where I please." Avis shot Rachel a warning look, and belatedly, Rachel registered that they were far from alone.

"And yet now you're here. And damp," she said, her fingers brushing Avis's wrist. "What happened?"

"She was found in the engine room," Brooksbank said, helpfully allowing her to rest her voice. "According to the good doctor here, she was very nearly in the same state in which we found Herr Müller."

Rachel gave a quick intake of breath, fingers tightening around Avis's hand. "What did you see?"

Avis just gave a tiny shake of her head. *Later*, she mouthed. Then, "May I go?" she asked the doctor, her voice slowly growing less hoarse and frail as she put it back into use.

"I'd really prefer to keep you for observation," he said as she sat up and swung her legs over the side of the bunk. "But"—he sighed—"I can't stop you from leaving."

Between them, Brooksbank and Rachel helped her to stand, and it was almost amusing how solicitous they were being—or it would've been, if she hadn't felt so utterly wretched.

"I see you're back in post," she said to Klein as he checked her pupils and pulse.

"Usher's doing," he said. "I don't know if he was keener to see me receive fair treatment or to be rid of the job himself, but regardless, I am grateful to him."

"I have cause for gratitude myself," Avis said, noting Rachel's curious expression. Another question she'd be answering later.

"Take care, Miss Lovelock. Don't let her sleep unattended," he directed at Brooksbank.

"I won't," both he and Rachel replied.

The sick-bay was one floor away from the first-class cabin block, and it was once they were safely up the stairs that

Rachel dismissed a bemused Brooksbank, who departed only with a promise that Avis would seek him out as soon as she felt well enough. Once he was gone, Rachel began to steer them back to her own cabin.

"It's already warm," she said. "And you have clothes there. And food." There was no sign of movement, or people coming or going, and only now did it occur to Avis to ask the time, shocked to discover it was not yet five in the morning.

"It felt like days."

"That's what losing consciousness will do for you," Rachel said darkly. "It is not a natural sleep. Come on."

Though she was clearly burning with curiosity, she did not insist that they speak as soon as they were safely ensconced back in her stateroom, instead bundling Avis to bed and slipping in beside her. She had a book in hand, so clearly had no plans for conversation at all for the rest of the night.

Avis was relieved. She wasn't sure at this point what she would say if she *was* asked what had happened.

There was one thing she had to say, though. "How did you know to come looking for me?" she asked, turning onto her side to face Rachel. "I could have just gone back to my cabin."

Rachel pursed her lips, setting her book down on her chest. "Your clothes were still on the floor," she pointed out, and Avis felt a bit silly, but then Rachel tipped her head to one side thoughtfully. "No. It wasn't that. I woke, out of nowhere, and had a sense that something was amiss. As though I was being told that you were in trouble and needed help. I couldn't ignore it, so I had to find you."

"Mm, well, thank you. It would have been a bit awkward if Brooksbank had insisted on watching me sleep instead." They shared a chuckle, and then Rachel picked up her book again, and Avis rested her head on the pillow as sleep began to overtake her. Across the room, Patience stood by the door and smiled.

* * *

Avis's incisors caught on a loose edge of her lower lip, stripping the little flap of skin from the surface. The air stung as it hit the newly opened wound, and she pulled it between her teeth, tongue searching the rough surface for another thread at which to pull.

At length, King looked up from the letter before him. "I'm not sure I fully understand what I'm looking at here," he said. "Are you telling us that *Excambion* is, in fact, haunted?"

Avis glanced at Brooksbank. He did not meet her eyes. "I am not," she said. "But I am saying that I cannot conclusively prove that it isn't. Too many of the events on board defy mundane explanation. There is a consistency across the various experiences and sightings that cannot be accounted for. And the nature and origin of Müller's… accident, and my own, remain obscure."

"But you *did* discover sabotage."

"I did. There is no question that somebody—quite probably still on board—was determined to delay *Excambion*'s voyage by tampering with the navigation system. Perhaps they had information suggesting your sale was time-sensitive. Or perhaps they thought the navigational errors would be put down to this haunting, and they sought to encourage further speculation. But, as things stand, I have been unable to connect the tampering with the compass directly to the other events on board."

"I thought you said she was the best you could find." This was directed at Brooksbank, who shifted uncomfortably where he stood.

"I've seen her work, Mr King, and if there was obvious trickery afoot I have faith she'd find it." Avis didn't like the way he hedged his words, or the way he angled himself away from her, as though he was trying to cut any connection they shared.

"Well, clearly our saboteur is cleverer than that. The payments involved in this sale are enormous—whoever it is that wants to stop it is clearly putting a similar amount of investment into it. I knew we should've gotten a man in," he added. "Women are too susceptible to this sort of hysteria."

“Er, I’m not sure—”

“No, Brooksbank, that’s quite all right,” Avis said, smiling sweetly at each man in turn. “I’d be happy—delighted, really—to step aside from my sleuthing duties for the remainder of the voyage. I’m sure you can find a man to locate your saboteur without my aid. Before they strike again, even.”

“I— You think they’re going to act again?” King frowned, looking like nothing so much as a wizened baby who’d just been confronted with the idea of naptime.

“Well, I can’t say for sure, being as I am *hysterical*. But yes, I’d wager the odds are good. We’ve got, what, two more days on this journey? They don’t know that I’ve just delivered that letter to you. They’re going to want to forestall this sale however they can, and if that means more delays, or worse, they’ll probably try and make it happen. But as you say, it’s none of my business, so… best of luck, gentlemen.”

“Miss Lovelock, wait!” But Avis didn’t heed the call, instead stalking out the door with her head held high. It was an act, of course; despite having gotten a few more hours’ sleep she was exhausted, and her body ached as if she had spent several rounds in a ring with a prize fighter. But she wasn’t going to give them the satisfaction of seeing her limp away, so she waited until she was safely out of sight on the garden verandah before slumping into a waiting deckchair.

As she had predicted, hurried footsteps dogged her path. “Miss Lovelock. You’re— Are you all right?” Brooksbank looked genuinely worried, but maybe he was just afraid she’d eviscerate him for his cowardly ways. “Can I help you get somewhere more comfortable?”

“I just need a moment,” Avis wheezed. “Nearly drowning takes it out of one somewhat. Don’t hover, man. Sit down if you must stay.”

Brooksbank pulled the next deckchair along closer and perched on it, his knees comically bent like he was a schoolboy on the bottom step of a staircase. “I’m very sorry about that,” he said. “Please rest assured that I still have every faith in your abilities, even if this has proven beyond you, and my original offer stands. I'll ensure you find work in New York."

"Work..." Avis laughed, though it turned into a slightly breathless cough. She shook her head. "I'm not even sure what my work is any more. What am I, a professional sceptic who can no longer say with certainty that the spirit realm doesn't exist? What is that?"

Brooksbank looked pained, but after a moment, he tried, "An entertainer? Isn't that what you've always been, after all, when it came to your stage shows? Why should that change?"

"Mm, perhaps you're right. I suppose I'm the only one who thought what I did was any more important than a coin trick."

"Even if you're not convinced there's not... something out there, what those Spiritualists were doing was still fraudulent. Debunking their efforts was worthy," he said earnestly. "Certainly more so than the coin tricks *they* were pulling."

Avis gave a weak smile. "Where was all this heartfelt defence in with King, eh?"

"I-I didn't realise he was such a regressive," Brooksbank stammered. "He's always been perfectly stand-up with me."

"Can't imagine why that would be."

"At any rate, I'm sorry—for what he said, and for what you've been through. The least I can do is make sure the rest of your passage is comfortable beyond reproach."

"I like the sound of that. I'll take three prawn cocktails to start, and a bottle of champagne to wash it down with. And if you could throw dear Mrs Armitage overboard that'd be grand." Brooksbank's expression was laughably bewildered, and Avis couldn't help but take pity on him. "I'm kidding. She'd probably just float anyway, with all that hot air. But I'm serious about the champagne."

"Of course. Anything at all."

"I shall have to nearly die more often." An old thought tickled at the back of Avis's mind. "While I have you, what's going on with Baynes?"

"What? Nothing! I mean... What d'you mean?"

This collection of responses was interesting indeed, and Avis fixed her eyes on her companion, who had gone an attractive shade of puce. "Well, it's certainly *not* nothing going by that reaction," she said. "He kept trying to catch your eye last night at dinner."

"Oh, that..." Brooksbank shook his head rather too vociferously. "That's nothing to worry about."

"You'll forgive me if I'm unconvinced."

"Just leave it, Avis, would you? It's none of your business. King says you're done, you're done."

Avis fell silent. Brooksbank had never spoken so sharply in her presence, either to her or to anyone else. Though she was far from satisfied with his response, she was too stunned to argue further, and seeing his window for escape, Brooksbank muttered something about her "damned champagne" and fled.

Twenty-Nine

AVIS HADN'T BEEN back to her own stateroom since the previous day, and although *Excambion* had now reoriented south and come away from the far northern reaches to which they had accidentally diverted, it was still rather chilly when she entered.

She opened up the valves that controlled the heating and set to washing and changing her clothes. It wasn't very long before the expected knock came at the door.

Rachel had changed also. With her usual dark skirts she had donned what looked very much like—

"Isn't that my cycling jersey?"

"You left it in my room," Rachel said.

"So you stole it."

"Well, I don't know what you expect. Am I not a swindler and a charlatan? Speaking of which, where did you get an unopened bottle of champagne?"

"Ah, now *that* was a gift. Brooksbank feels guilty. It's a guilt gift." That or a bribe—after their awkward exchange about Baynes, Avis was no longer sure.

Rachel put the bottle back on the vanity where Avis had set it and turned into the embrace that awaited her. Avis buried her face in the crook of Rachel's neck, Rachel's scent mingling with her own where it hung on the jersey fabric. For a long moment they stood, connected, but eventually Rachel pulled back.

"You need to tell me everything you saw and felt."

"King fired me. Called me hysterical. I *felt* like punching him."

"Avis..."

"I mean, I didn't ask for this job and I wasn't even technically being paid, but— *Ouch*, don't squeeze, my ribs hurt like they've been used as a xylophone."

"I know they do, that was on purpose. Come, sit down. You need to tell me what happened below decks."

As best she could, Avis recounted the dream—or not a dream, perhaps—that had led her to the engine room.

"I can't quite explain it," she said in the end. "It was as though the longer I looked at those figures just floating up there, the more I was sucked into *their* world, or *their* moment in time, I suppose. Until at last... well."

Rachel frowned. "It doesn't make sense."

"Well, of course it doesn't. None of this does."

But Rachel shook her head. She reached across the berth to trace idly across the back of Avis's hand where it rested on the bedspread. "More than that, though. These visions, the sounds, even the cold, these are all consistent with the echoes and memories that I've seen and sensed in other places—those lingering remnants I've spoken about. But they're not... *conscious*. They have no purpose at all, let alone a malign one. They can't cause harm. Only people can do that."

"People?"

Rachel's hand stilled, and she fixed Avis with a long look. "People who are sensitive. Like you. Like me. I've met others. Some... it's as though their will is a physical force. Generally not within their control. I sat with a woman once in Italy. The night before her daughter was to leave to take up holy orders, every single religious icon in the house was smashed, torn apart, wrested from the wall, scratched out, one after the other, by an unseen force. She believed there were demons within her daughter, wanted an exorcism, but the priest saw only an angry young woman. I saw her too, but I saw what he could not: her power. Her anger was like the prevailing wind."

Avis released a lungful of air in a rush. Even she was not immune to Rachel's ability to spin a story. "What happened?"

Rachel smiled. "I channelled the woman's late mother to give her some advice. She told her that she wanted to see her granddaughter free to love and to travel. There were no further desecrations."

"Just like that."

"Just like that. She was so relieved, she never even thought to question why her mother didn't speak Italian."

Avis chuckled, then the implications of this sank in. "Hang on though, you're not saying that a *person* is responsible for the deaths? Someone else on the ship? In addition to these... echoes?"

Rachel's expression grew sober once more and she shook her head. "Like you, I find that implausible. There has to be a connection. In truth it feels like *everything* must be connected: the sightings, the attacks, the sabotage... They're all acting towards one goal. But what could do that is beyond my ken. I would theorise that perhaps..." She flattened her lips to a line, narrowed her eyes. "Perhaps when the events in a place are *so* traumatic, *so* extreme, the combined suffering of those involved manifests some remnant of that same will, and perhaps that could then act upon others, but..." She sighed, shoulders slumping. "Perhaps, perhaps. The fact remains that we found evidence of no such event in *Excambion*'s history. And I'm no expert, but nor have I seen any signs of repair at that scale." Rachel paused. "Why are you staring at me?"

I could love you.

Avis shook her head to clear it. "You are extremely clever. I don't pretend to fully appreciate your thesis, but your insights, your clarity... Rachel, I know that you seek a future that doesn't rely on your brother. Why not do what I do?"

Rachel blinked. "Excuse me?"

"Become a mentalist." Avis grinned. She couldn't quite believe she hadn't thought of it before. "Rather than deceiving people about spirits and the Veil, you could be entertaining them on an honest footing, open that what you do is based in reason and observation."

Rachel's mouth was hanging open slightly, and Avis thought at first that she was simply lost for words.

"I could show you how I do it, the various tricks one can do using our skills. We could even do shows together while..." Avis trailed off as the future reared its head. What *did* lie next along their path? As individuals? Together...? It was a weighty question in the face of the events of the past day, and one she wasn't ready for.

She was shaken from her reverie by Rachel's hand detaching from hers as the other woman stood.

"An honest footing. Have you listened to nothing I've said? Have you learned *nothing*?"

"I don't—"

Rachel began to tug at the hem of the sweater she wore. "*You* are not honest, Avis Lovelock. These insights of yours do not spring from your giant, pure, rational brain. You have a *connection*, a conduit to knowledge beyond what can be seen with the naked eye, and you use it, every single day." She pulled Avis's jersey off over her head, tossing it onto the bed. Beneath it she wore a white button-down shirt that looked as though it could be Gideon's. Her cheeks held spots of high colour, her eyes flashing darkly, her hair framing her face in wild snarls. The perverse thought entered Avis's head that she had never looked so beautiful as she did in that moment.

Rachel stabbed an accusatory finger at Avis. "Every 'deduction', every 'observation' you make comes from a place that is *not* of this physical world. And you use it to predict card values! To tell people whose face is in their locket! You have this special, *precious* gift, and you use it to look clever. And you have the temerity to tell *me* that I could be using my gift better. If I was like you! My God, I would rather die in a gutter—no, I'd rather *marry*. I will marry some disgusting grey-whiskered banker and spawn a clutch of mewling offspring before I will get up on a stage and do what you do."

Avis felt very cold all of a sudden. Behind Rachel, a figure began to flicker into focus. She pushed to her feet, still unsteady. "Rachel, I didn't mean to..."

Rachel blew a lungful of air out through her mouth. "I know you didn't," she said, her eyes anywhere but Avis's. "I know you didn't. But there's still so much you won't understand. I don't know what the future holds for me. Or for..." She gestured between them. "For any of this. But I do know that here and now, you and I... we are living in different worlds, still." She stepped closer, leaned in to press a kiss to Avis's cheek. "Be safe," she murmured.

Avis blinked. Her eyes felt hot. "That's it?" she asked. "That's... all?"

"You were fired, remember?" Rachel said. "The investigation is over. Neither of us need do anything more. We should arrive in New York tomorrow, and we can get off this accursed ship and never look back." She turned to go.

"Don't you want to know what's going on?" Avis felt like her heart might arrest there and then, and yet when she opened her mouth to speak, *this* was what emerged? "Don't you want... a conclusion?"

Rachel paused in the doorway, face-to-face with Patience. She didn't turn. "Not everything ends with answers and explanations, Avis. Sometimes things just stop."

AVIS HAD TWO rules regarding the proper imbibing of champagne: one, that it should always be drunk in celebration; two, that it should never be drunk alone. She broke both those rules after Rachel left her cabin having smothered whatever nascent flame bloomed between them.

"Don't you say a word," she said to Patience, who stood like a sentinel by the door, her expression oddly melancholic.

"I don't need your help pointing out where I went wrong. I certainly don't need reminded what an *idiot* I am."

The cork was caught fast in the bottle, wedged in good and tight. Avis's palms were damp, allowing no purchase. She grimaced and wiped them roughly on her skirts before trying again, wedging the base of her thumb against the lip of the bottle and twisting hard enough to make her palms sting. Slowly it began to turn, working itself out millimetre by millimetre, and she focused on that, on the bite in her palms, anything except the emptiness that coiled in her stomach, the tears that pricked at her eyes.

She could feel the moment when the pressure inside the bottle took over from her efforts, the cork all but exploding from the neck and sending a froth of suds over the rug. She ignored it in favour of slopping champagne into the nearest receptacle: an enamel mug, white with a cheerful bouquet of flowers plastered on its side.

"I know. I *know* it was stupid. But she wants a future free of her family's influence, and opportunities to be independent are rare, even for women like us. Lord knows I haven't managed to get out of your shadow, no matter how far I've travelled," she added, shaking the bottle at her sister's shade. Patience didn't react save for a slow blink, a small and silent rebuke.

"And who's to say I was wrong, really? She's got some front, thinking she's better than me, claiming to *help* people. I help people! I help them not throw away their hard-earned money on frauds. I help them see the reality of the situation—we're alone. We're all alone."

She sank onto the bed, bottle clutched in one hand, mug in the other. She took a drink from the mug, barely tasting it, frowning at the dark patch on the rug. Across the room, Patience shifted, moved closer.

"Except we're not, are we? There's something out there, those goddamned echoes that won't leave us alone."

She drank again, and the champagne was sour on her tongue. Something flickered in front of her: Patience, the circle of her skirts covering the damp ring on the rug.

"I just want a day. *One* day when I'm not reminded of what happened. I'm sorry. I've said I'm sorry." Something inside her twisted, and she wasn't sure if it was grief or sadness or humiliation but it hurt all the same. She was sorry, but it didn't matter. Patience was still dead. Rachel had still left. The ship was still haunted, and she had no idea why.

She drank, and drank again, and refilled her mug for another draught. The champagne helped dull the throbbing in her back and chest but did nothing for the ache within. Another flicker and Patience was before her, giving off no heat, disturbing nothing underfoot. She reached out and Avis lurched back, head muddled, before shame washed over her. How dare she flinch away from her sister? She was ever-present, yes, a nuisance and a frustration, a reminder of the guilt she carried… but without her, Avis *would* be alone.

She forced herself to sit forward, and Patience's hand came to rest on her chest. She reached up to cover it and felt only the lonely thud of her own heart.

Thirty

PAIN LANCED ACROSS Avis's consciousness like a scalpel relieving an infected wound, a dull throb spilling from a sharp point at the front of her head. She welcomed it, a stark affirmation: proof of life.

On the nightstand by her berth sat the empty champagne bottle and ugly enamel mug, evidence of her folly. Beside them, her pocket watch reassured her that she had not overslept too egregiously; she could make the second sitting for breakfast if she could bring herself to eat.

Indeed, people were returning to their rooms now to prepare for the day. She could hear them tramping and chattering along the corridors. She groaned and pulled a pillow over her face. Usually she enjoyed listening to the world carry on around her but right now she craved blessed silence. Such it was that it was some time before she noticed the conversations happening outside were in a different tenor from normal: they were louder, went on longer, and had a strange edge to them that now that she forced herself to listen sounded akin to confusion, even panic. Something was wrong.

Avis roused herself into a tortured flurry of movement. Her brain swung back and forth like a clapper in a bell as she neatened her clothing, pulled on her boots. She was so distracted that as she was washing her face and hands it took a moment to notice the way the water stung her eyes, and the flavour that lingered on her lips.

Brine.

IT DIDN'T TAKE her long to decide on a course of action, even with a throbbing headache pulsing just behind her eyes. It was the same course of action she'd pursued with every new question that arose on this damned ship—find out as much as she could about what was going on. And for that, she needed Brooksbank. She found him near the gangway shelter by the bridge, which—as far as she could see—was strangely devoid of officers.

"I don't know." He held up a hand before Avis could even speak. He looked decidedly unkempt today, much as he had after his ill-advised drinking session with Usher on that first night. "I know barely any more than you."

"Has there been a mechanical failure?" Avis asked, undaunted, falling into step beside him. "I can't imagine anything else that'd cause the freshwater taps to suddenly start spewing salt water."

"I think yes," he said, "but apparently there's more to it? I couldn't make much sense of Baynes—the man talks like everybody's read the same books he has."

"Oh, Baynes happens to know all about this, does he? Just like everything else around here."

Brooksbank frowned. "No, Avis."

"'No' as in he doesn't know all about this?"

"'No' as in whatever you're thinking, Baynes is not your man." There was a funny edge to Brooksbank's voice that Avis could not quite put her finger on, and he was beginning to flush again.

"You seem very certain, but he's all over the ship's paperwork like a rash. Signing for crew, taking stock… and he looks more nervous the more digging I do. I really think—"

"Damn it all, Avis, it's me!"

This was enough to stop Avis in her tracks. "I'm sorry, what? What, exactly, is you? Is this a confession?"

Brooksbank spluttered, shook his head. "No, no, what I mean is... Baynes is nervous because he's protecting *me*. I have some little... items. In the hold."

"What on earth are you on about?"

"Just a few bottles of this and that. Quite a few. Some scotch, some port, some French brandy. I might have persuaded Baynes to... mislabel them. On their crate. And on the record."

Comprehension dawned. "As items with a lower import duty." Avis sighed in exasperation. "Why the hell didn't you just tell me as much? You must know I don't give a damn what you smuggle to the colonies."

"Well, I'm telling you now, so would you just... leave Baynes be, all right? The poor boy's nervous enough already." Avis didn't miss a fondness in Brooksbank's tone, but before she could probe any further, Brooksbank moved on. "Anyway. From what I could tell, it sounds like the machine that takes the salt out has broken. There are tanks with fresh drinking water filled at port, but those are running quite low by this point in the trip, so most of our remaining water is now seawater."

"You mean salty."

Brooksbank blinked. "What's the difference?"

"The addition of salt could be the work of our saboteur. Turning drinking water into *seawater* is a work of fantasy."

The man's mouth flattened to a line, and he gestured around them. The large grand foyer thronged with first-class passengers, wearing expressions ranging from irate to positively terrified. "I don't think our fellow passengers appreciate that distinction," he said.

"They're panicking about the haunting?"

"They're panicking about the haunting. But they don't know the half of it."

Avis lifted her eyebrows. "Oh?"

Brooksbank gestured. "We're less than a day's travel from

New York. Oh, they won't like eating cold meat and cheese for the rest of the trip, or the rationing of the fresh water reserves, but they'll get by on champagne and caviar. Meanwhile, as I understand it, the boilers will be running on salt water, which will quickly clog up all their… pipes and so forth."

"Will it, I don't know, "break" the ship? Are we in danger of a more serious failure?"

"Not for this short distance, but from what Baynes told me, everything will have to be completely dismantled, cleaned, and rebuilt. It sounds fairly catastrophic."

Avis pursed her lips. "A sale-ending sort of catastrophic?"

"By the look on King's face, he thinks it might be."

"Mm. Well. More fool him. He should have let me keep hunting for the saboteur." Avis smirked, though in truth the petty victory sparked precious little joy within her.

"I suspect he would be more receptive were you to approach him again now."

"I'm sure. But first, are you hiding any fresh water anywhere? I feel like I'm going to die."

KING'S LAST CHANCE was to locate the saboteur, and he knew it. Avis was the only person who had come close. Their conversation was a short one, and contrite on his part. Avis did not have the energy to rub it in particularly hard.

The same could not be said when she met up with Third Officer Baynes once more at the top of the main stairs leading below decks. Avis wasted no time in taking him to task.

"Why on earth didn't you just tell me about Brooksbank?"

The man looked stricken and began to stammer. "What? I… There's nothing… I don't…"

"Relax, man. Why you think I'd care about a few bottles of cognac I do not know. You should have just told me and saved a whole lot of wasted thinking time on my part."

"The… bottles." Baynes's expression cleared somewhat. "Right, yes. My apologies, Miss Lovelock."

Avis frowned. "Yes, the bottles. What else would I be on about?"

The officer shook his head vigorously. "Nothing, ma'am. It's as you say—I should have told you. I was keeping a confidence, but I can see now how that was in error. I'll, er, lead the way to the tanks, shall I?"

Examination of the marine evaporators showed, as expected, signs of tampering, although nothing that could point to a specific culprit beyond the fact they'd need the basic mechanical knowledge to interfere with the desalination process. Apparently they weren't even broken, but the "feedwater" was polluted and they would not be able to produce drinkable water—or water that did not line the boilers in a mineral crust—until everything had been descaled.

"So it actually *is* seawater we're getting, then? Without any purification?"

Baynes, still looking rather shaken, gave his usual stiff nod. "It seems likely, though we can't prove it. We have devices for measuring salt and other minerals," he added, "but unfortunately when the evaporators fail those are also put out of commission, until such times as we can get everything cleaned. They also took the copper sulphate we use to keep the tanks free of algae, though that's at least not a risk in the time it'll take to get to New York."

"Hm. I expect the doctor might know some other methods for analysing the water, though I'm not sure we have the time to be fussing around with that," Avis said. "One of the doctors, anyway," she corrected herself. Then she frowned. Something was scratching at the back of her mind, scrabbling for purchase.

"Baynes, aside from Brooksbank and myself, who else has been on one of King's tours of *Excambion*?"

He confirmed what she had suspected, and the pieces began to fall into place. It was time to find Usher.

* * *

First class was still in uproar when Avis returned to the foyer. She wasn't sure she'd ever heard so many affronted people speaking all at the same time. The captain, first mate, and various other members of the crew flitted from group to group trying to calm nerves and soothe tempers, with limited success. They were passing out bottles of water to all and sundry, and it was almost comical the way that grand dames and straight-backed gentlemen stuffed them greedily into every pocket and purse.

Also present, she noted, was Gideon Duquesne, Madame Berthault at his side, surrounded by the usual suspects hanging on to his every word. Avis did not try to get close enough to hear what he was saying; she wasn't sure she'd be able to resist a well-aimed punch. Of Rachel there was no sign, nor was there hide nor hair of the one passenger she was looking for.

It was a big ship. Almost too big, in fact. Trying to locate any given individual on it was like trying to find an ounce of restraint in the decoration of a Catholic church. Still, she would not be daunted, as something told her there was little time to waste. A few days prior, she would have put this down to having read the subtle signals of the various parties involved, extrapolating from what she knew of human nature and drawing a logical and rational conclusion. Now, however, all she knew was that there was a knot of dread in her stomach that couldn't be put down to her hangover and it drove her to stride from the foyer and begin a frantic search of the ship, from first class downwards.

She tried to work systematically—corridor by corridor, level by level—but this was prevented both by the slightly labyrinthine layout of the various utility and cabin blocks, and the occasional locked door that necessitated detouring, which worked together to create a pervasive sense of disorientation that was at first merely frustrating but quickly began to feel uncanny. With most passengers crowding into communal spaces to complain or just to seek more information, the other areas of the ship were unusually deserted, and yet Avis did not feel alone; rather she began to feel her steps dogged by the memories of the hundreds of others who had walked these hallways, and even the sense that they walked them still, now, alongside her. She was just mentally cursing Rachel for infecting her with her talk of remnants and mirrors and echoes when she turned a corner to find herself staring at, if far from the last person she wanted to encounter, certainly the one she was most afraid to.

In contrast to Avis's determined stride, Rachel drifted the corridors like a ghost unmoored, her dark skirts sweeping the floorboards. She was not peering into rooms but rather seemed to be listening for something, her head tipped to one side like she was savouring the final refrains of an aria. She didn't notice Avis at first, but when she did she gave her a nod. Polite, approving. "I take it you've had no luck?"

Avis shook her head, feet drawing her forward even as the rest of her froze in place. At length she cleared her throat. "It's—"

"Usher. Yes, I think so."

"He found me in the engine room. Once I thought to wonder what he was doing there…"

"He's in a great deal of pain," Rachel said. "Physical, spiritual."

"The way he's talked about war. If he found out about the sale or, more likely I suppose, somebody else enlisted him…"

"He's haunted by his past, what he's seen. It lives on within him."

It was as though they barely heard one another, reasoning from opposite sides in a pincer movement to one inevitable conclusion. Avis stopped walking when she realised they were now face-to-face.

"Rachel, about before—"

"Not now, Avis." The words were harsh, but there was nothing harsh about Rachel's expression or her tone. She reached out to clasp Avis's upper arm briefly, her grip both distracting and reassuring. "We have to find Usher; he needs our help. There will be time for us later."

She held on to those words—*There will be time for us later*—like a lifeline, nodding dumbly. Rachel squeezed her arm and then dropped her hand to her side, looking up and down the corridor. "Have you been to the engine room? He may try to disrupt even more essential systems."

"No." Avis shook her head, chewing her lower lip. "Everything he's done has been inconvenient, but not deadly. I don't think he wants to put anyone in actual danger. But…" Rachel tipped her head again, raised her eyebrows to prompt Avis to go on. "He may want to make a statement. Somewhere people might come across."

Rachel nodded slowly. "This latest trick is clearly an attempt to use the haunting… He can't be responsible for everything."

"No. I don't think…" Avis frowned. As hard as it was to admit, none of the strange things people had seen could be laid at a human saboteur's door. "The navigation, yes. This latest. But the hallucinations, and Müller…"

"Oh no, Avis. Müller…" That hand on her arm again as Rachel realised in the same moment as Avis what must come next, what would bring the story full circle, what would render *Excambion* untouchable.

Another body.

"I thought God had shown it to me so that I could have stopped it. And I didn't. If I ever had the chance to do it again… I'd make sure to act."

Avis nodded, heart leaping into her throat. "Somewhere that's quiet now. He'll need time to enact his plan."

They set out together, side by side, and neither of them spoke. There was nothing more to be said, save for the hope that they weren't too late.

Thirty-One

They had exhausted many of the indoor spaces between them, and so their path took them up the second-class staircase and then out onto the promenade deck, which was mostly deserted due to the still-bitter wind and overcast skies. Avis cleaved more closely to Rachel, who didn't rebuff her, and after a moment Rachel slipped a hand through Avis's arm to pull her nearer yet.

The promenade was lined with wrought-iron benches and deck chairs, and on a finer day it must have been a very pleasant place to spend an afternoon. It appeared completely empty, and Avis nearly suggested they turn around, but then she spotted the figure up ahead. Not Usher, but Patience, blurring in the spitting rain. "This way," she muttered, and Rachel followed without protest.

Soon enough, they spotted the stooped figure of Usher in what would usually be a prime sightseeing spot at the corner of the foredeck, just out of view of the bridge. Any other day, there would be crew up here, but the combination of the weather with the general mayhem below decks meant the space was broadly deserted. He had his back turned, and was fumbling with the contents of a small bag on the deck.

"What do we say?" Avis muttered as they crept closer. "I

don't know what we say." Avis was never lost for words when the aim was to look clever or to sting or even to amuse. She had never before felt the need she did now for words that would reach out, connect, calm.

"Just speak to him as a friend. Say what you need to hear when you are afraid and desperate." Avis wanted to retort that this was less than helpful, but then they were within earshot and she bit back the words.

Usher didn't notice them at first, intent on whatever task he had begun, but then he looked up to scan his surroundings and started to his feet, surprised. "Miss Lovelock, Miss Duquesne, what are you doing here?" he said, taking a step back towards the railing. He was holding a battered lighter in one hand, a paper bag in the other. What on earth was he planning? "I'd have thought you'd be inside, helping quell the panic over this latest spiritual manifestation."

"I… wanted to see you," Avis said. "To thank you. If you hadn't found me in the engine room, I might have shared Friedrich Müller's fate."

Usher's expression softened. "Oh, Miss Lovelock, it was my honour. I'm only glad to have found you when I did."

"How did you? Find me, that is."

"I was taking a constitutional," he said, and the answer was smooth, but she could see the lie in the creases of his forehead. "Got to keep the gammy leg limber and all that. I find the lower decks quieter, fewer people to dodge."

"The engine room isn't exactly a scenic route."

Usher smiled tightly. "One might just as easily ask why you were there, then."

She watched his grip tighten on the lighter and felt a drop in her stomach as the pieces began to slot into place. The lighter. The missing copper sulphate. Once lit, it would glow bright green. A figure doused in the powder would look otherworldly. He was going to give the ship one final haunting. "Samson. Please."

He shook his head, stuffing the bag into his pocket. "Just go back inside, Miss Lovelock. Avail yourself of champagne, since the water's gone off. Laugh at the civilians panicking. This is one mystery you'd be better off not chasing."

Avis dared to take a step forward. Rachel, still holding onto her arm, did the same. "We can't let you do this. Whatever you hope to achieve, it's not worth your life." She could smell it now, the fuel. Had he doused himself already? Or were his preparations as yet incomplete?

"I'm flattered you think so. But I'm not sure the great Avis Lovelock is right, for once." His breath was coming quicker now, and he shifted from foot to foot, wincing every time he put weight on his bad side. How desperate was he? How could she *help*?

Rachel spoke then, her voice low and calm. "She's already given a testimonial—the ship is haunted. I will as well. The sale will not go through."

"You have?" Usher looked at Avis, his expression perplexed. "But that's… You've spent the past week telling anyone who'd listen that all that was a crock of malarkey. That can't be right."

Avis's stomach twisted. Could she truly set her pride entirely aside? Her reputation? Thus far, she had only admitted that she could not disprove the haunting. This would be a step further. Rachel's hand tightened its grip on her arm. A man's life was on the line.

"I cannot explain away what has happened on board this ship," Avis said at last. "There is no mundane answer here that I can find. King won't get his proof. I have none."

"I see." Usher nodded, his shoulders lowering from where they had tensed around his ears, and she felt her own relax in turn. "Well, that's a surprise for sure, but it's as I said at that autopsy. Sometimes things just don't make sense. I'm sure no one'll judge you for admitting it."

"I don't know about that," Avis said. That was a worry for another day. "But can't you see? That means that whatever it is you have planned here… you needn't."

His hand sought his pocket again, reassuring himself his stolen stash was still there. "Quite right. How about you two head on inside, find us a table? I'll come join you for a drink in a moment, once I've got my head on straight."

"I think you know we won't do that," Rachel said gently.

The doctor's shoulders slumped, and he shot them a wry smile. He turned to look out across the water, and Avis watched his body tense. "Do… do you see that?"

Avis frowned, and she glanced at Rachel, who shook her head. "See what?"

"Lights… The lights on the water."

The women broke apart as they moved to join Usher at the railing to look out over the water. At the moment he had spoken there was nothing, but now, standing here beside him, Avis *did* see—dozens of flickering lights floating on the ocean's surface.

She gripped the railing. Her pulse once more leapt into her throat.

The lights were not uniform; they varied in size from mere pinpricks to lantern-sized to the vague dimensions of the lifeboats, flickering masses that bobbed and dipped according to the waves they rode on. She'd never observed them herself except through the glass of a porthole, but here in the open, staring down at them, it became very clear what she was seeing.

"It's debris on the water. It's on fire."

"Like the ship has broken up," Usher said, a strange note in his voice. "Funny, that. Feels like we're still afloat."

Avis heard it then. Shouting. Footsteps.

"Look." Rachel had turned and was pointing across the foredeck, and this time there was no mistaking what they saw.

The figures that ran back and forth flickered in and out like the flames, like Patience so often did, but Avis could still make out that some of them wore military uniforms. They heard a muffled booming sound and several men disappeared, dropping suddenly away from view, down into the solid deck as though it wasn't there anymore.

"What I saw in the storm, days before… It was that forced march, the one that took them from their homes. The one where women and children died."

"My parents' ghosts appeared to me while they were still alive."

"What the hell is that?" Usher asked. "Who are those people?"

"I know what people are seeing—what *we're* seeing. They're not echoes of the past." Avis reached out, Rachel's fingers immediately knitting through hers, gripping her hand tightly. "They're visions of the future."

Rachel frowned, and then slowly nodded as she saw what Avis had—the debris on the water, the panicked officers and soldiers, the flooded engine room bobbing with corpses. Somehow *Excambion* was showing them her fate.

"What the devil is that?" A pair of men had emerged onto deck some ten yards away, cigarettes in hand, and they stopped in their tracks as they took in the scene playing out in front of them. Avis watched their expressions go from nonchalance to disbelief to outright fear and felt a wave of dread herself. "That's not right—it's those spirits everyone's been seeing!" the first one said.

"They're coming for us," the second said, already backing away. "First the seawater in the taps, now this. We're never going to make it to New York."

As if in response to his words, the ship shuddered, a vibration that started low and reverberated up through the soles of their feet. The two passengers yelped and ran for the door. Avis looked to Rachel, who watched them go with a grim set to her lips.

"This could be bad," she murmured. "Belief is a powerful thing. People are already in a near panic. If they think something bad is coming, they may well conjure it into being."

"Hold on now, what are you saying?" Usher said. "This stuff isn't real, but it could hurt us anyway?"

"It's real," Avis found herself saying, "but it doesn't matter. Something doesn't have to be real to hurt, or worse. We need to get inside, try and calm people down. Convince them they're not in any danger."

Together they retreated to the safety of the interior, winding their way down the stairs until they found a quiet nook near the second-class lounge. Usher was pale, but when he met Avis's gaze the wild look in his eye had gone, leaving only regret and worry. "This is my fault," he said, shaking his head. "I primed people to believe in the haunting. If anyone gets hurt because I worked them into a frenzy, then I bear the blame. What can I do?"

"You're a doctor," Avis said. "People will trust you. Get up to first class, and try and talk some sense into anyone who'll listen. Either that this is some sort of harmless mass hallucination, if you think you can sell it, or the truth. Whatever works."

"All right. I'll do my best. And… I'm sorry. For what it's worth." He didn't wait for her to respond before departing, his hitched stride purposeful.

Usher was barely out of sight before Avis turned to her companion, gaze searching hers. *What now?* she wanted to say. And, *Forgive me*. Before she could choose either, another deep boom reverberated through the ship, and it even pitched slightly, both of them stumbling where they stood.

"What *is* that?" Avis muttered. "It doesn't feel like I imagine guns would. It's like the impact is beneath the water line… Is that a torpedo?"

"I'm afraid modern warfare is a little out of my area of expertise," Rachel confessed with a wry smile.

"Well, you can't be right all the time, I suppose," Avis said, daring to reach for her hand. Rachel took it, looking down at their clasped palms for a long moment before glancing up again at Avis. "How on earth is this possible? The ship isn't actually going to sink, is it?"

"I don't know," Rachel said. "I want to say no, but Müller drowned in the engine room. You nearly did as well. Clearly there's more crossing over than just echoes." The medium tugged her along. "We need to do something to help. Come."

Just what Rachel planned to do to avert this panic was unclear; indeed, people were already starting to fizz out of their rooms and lounges like bees from a shaken nest. "It's all right," Avis tried to assure them, "it's not real." But no one paid her any attention, especially after another *boom* shook the ship, causing men and women alike to scream and grab at the nearest handholds.

"We need to reach as many people as we can. We'll never make a difference going one by one," Rachel said. "Let's get to the lounge." Avis expected her to head up the stairs to first class, but instead she took the stairwell heading down.

As they rushed through the corridors further below decks it was as though *Excambion* felt their progress, for the ship began to pitch, and the air grew colder. Avis remembered this, and stopped. "This happened at the beginning of the trip," she said. "It began to flood."

"You experienced a ghostly flooding," Rachel said, "and you *still* refused to admit the spiritual world existed? You truly are the most hard-headed individual I've ever encountered."

"When you're haunted by your dead sister, it sets a fairly high bar for the phenomena you'll take seriously."

Rachel merely shook her head and muttered "Stubborn fool" under her breath, which warmed Avis to no end. They hurried down the corridor, ducking into the third-class lounge where semi-familiar faces peered out from booths and clusters of people. Avis soon spotted one particularly familiar face and pulled Rachel towards it, only letting go of her hand at the last moment.

"Frieda," she exclaimed, heart hammering. "How is everyone? Are they scared?"

"Of course they are scared, the spirits have come to sink the ship!" Frieda replied.

"It's going to be all right," Rachel said soothingly. "We can calm them, send them away. But we need your help."

"Mine?" Frieda looked confused, but she pulled the children in arm's reach towards her. "What do you need?"

"Can you gather everybody you can, and instruct them to go to the garden verandah?"

"The verandah? Won't we be asked to leave?"

"Not this time."

Avis glanced down. She could feel the water beginning to seep into her boots. "We should check on the engine room," she said.

As they traversed the narrow corridors that led to the utility areas of the ship, the world around them shifted. Not just physically, although the angle at which they had to walk grew ever steeper. It was as though they were beginning to exist in two states at once, the nightmarish reality where the ship was holed and fast flooding fighting for purchase over the physical realm they inhabited before.

"Is everybody feeling this?" Avis said. She raised her voice to be heard over the rushing water, and it echoed dry and empty.

Rachel shook her head. "I don't know. I think it's like an avalanche rolling down a hill. The more people are drawn in, the wider its field of effect becomes."

Another impact reverberated across the hull.

"And by your logic this must be caused by a person, correct?" Avis said, fighting the urge to yell over the groanings of the ship, trying to ignore them for the hallucinations they had to be. "This goes far beyond echoes."

"Everything I know tells me that it must."

"So that's Usher, then? Stands to reason, doesn't it?"

Rachel glanced Avis's way. "Perhaps. He's been through a great deal, seen a great deal."

"And this isn't the first time. The stories he told me, I dismissed them as the meanderings of a guilty mind. I never thought for a moment he was describing things he'd actually seen. If he did… then this isn't the first time he's been party to visions of things to come."

Rachel looked grim. "Perhaps he is sensitive himself, or perhaps this is the power of grief and regret. Or perhaps what is happening here goes beyond my understanding." The ship lurched, and she grabbed for the railing as they were forced to lean backwards for balance, then nearly fell as the gravity of the living world tried to reassert itself. The water rose up before them, getting deeper the further they went as one version of the ship succumbed to its damage. “I don’t think we’re going to make it to the engine room.”

“Rachel, we must, it’s where this started, it’s where we’ll see—”

“I know, but look.”

It was like the way one had to defocus one’s eyes to see an optical illusion. If Avis concentrated on the corridor before her, it was entirely empty and dry, not to mention on the flat. But if she allowed her focus to drift, let her eyes and mind wander, she could feel the water seeping into her skirts up to the waist, could feel the steep angle at which they walked, could see as well as hear the water pouring in ahead of them.

“It’s already flooded,” she muttered.

Rachel grabbed her arm with her free hand. “We must head up,” she said. “I need to find Gideon and Charlotte. I need to see them safe.”

Thirty-Two

THEIR PROGRESS WAS like treacle; a torturously slow climb through corridors where it was impossible to keep one's footing. They passed others facing similar troubles, though most were on the same climb they were, trying to escape floods they could only half see and did not at all understand. Avis's thighs and stomach ached from walking simultaneously up an incline and on the flat, her muscles screaming for a single reality to navigate. Rachel fared better with her strong body and balletic grace, but both were out of breath before they reached the upper decks.

Here, chaos reigned. Passengers cowered in corners, thrashed in the throes of who knew what, pointing and screaming as the ship appeared to fall to pieces around them. The braver among them ran back and forth either helping their fellow passengers or attempting to interact with the pressing issues facing the spectres of that Other *Excambion*, the ship in peril, though there was nothing they could do. The soldiers and crew on the ghost ship did their duties and suffered their consequences no matter what anybody here attempted, layered over and over as they repeated their ill-fated performance—crossing the deck only to be swallowed by it, being thrown by a sudden impact over the side into the water with its flickering debris.

As Avis watched one well-intentioned passenger try to come

to a hapless ghost-sailor's aid, she saw the latter fall through the deck as it collapsed beneath him and the former crumple where he stood and lie still. Was he dead? Was his body broken? Had he suffered the effect of a fall, just as Müller had drowned, in spite of the deck remaining solid beneath him?

Elsewhere, a crewman beat a canvas sheet against a licking flame that crawled down the wall of the first-class dining room, blistering the paint as it came. The sheet passed straight through the fire, which did not so much as flicker in the gust created by the blows. It was hungry for the gilt and fabric adorning the room and heedless of the attempts to stop it. It couldn't be a real fire, could it? As she watched, another crewman came to the first one's aid; his coat was devoid of the shiny buttons on his companion's, with a wide shawl collar. She could see the flame behind him, and through him. He wasn't real.

They passed Mr and Mrs Armitage. The former was lying splayed on the carpet, the latter kneeling over him in an opulent gown and sobbing. There was a gash on his leg and it was seeping blood into the fabric of her skirt. The blood was real.

It was as fascinating as it was horrifying, each small disaster its own microcosm of entropy; the power of death so great that it reached across space and time to invade them now like a flood overwhelming the breakwater. Avis was drawn to it, wanting nothing more than to poke and prod it until she understood it to her satisfaction—even if it meant burns, even if it meant blood.

Before she could give in to the urge to investigate, Rachel caught her arm once more. "I see them," she said, and tugged her along.

Gideon was in the garden verandah, exactly where Avis and Rachel had instructed people to assemble. A gaggle of crew and passengers had gathered around them. Gideon was holding the attention of all in his usual effortless fashion, and though they could not hear his words over the groans and cracks of the ship and the shouting of ghosts and passengers alike, it was clear to Avis from his expression that whatever he was intoning was absolute nonsense. Charlotte stood with the crowd, looking slightly calmer than some, though her brow was still knitted with worry.

Snatches of his words began to reach them as they approached—talk of calm, of attunement, of spirits, of course—and Avis consciously tamped down her crueller instincts so that when they arrived at their location her greeting was merely, "What on God's green earth are you telling these people, you fool?" and not something rather more unkind.

Gideon's reply came with a superior tilt of his chin that made her clench her fists in anticipation. "That you can remain closed to the ways of the spirits in the face of all this now positions you as the liar, I'm afraid, Miss Lovelock," he said, gesturing around them. "They are here. We walk among them, just as we always have."

"That's not—" Avis broke off to clench her jaw. A hand wrapped around her wrist. She stilled.

"Brother, these spirits are not with us in the way you think," Rachel said. Her voice was even hoarser than usual from the exertion of their climb and the bite of the wind outside. The verandah was barely warmer with every door open and flapping, the bangs adding to the ghostly sounds of the sinking ship. "They are a shade of things to come. They are not attached to souls. They do not think; they only act."

"They were certainly able to act when they killed that man!" Avis groaned to hear Sarah Fenwick's voice, thin with panic.

"These events that we're experiencing are so significant that they are manifesting in our world," Rachel said. How was she able to speak so calmly, so clearly, at a time like this? To spin a story that sounded so sensible in the face of all this chaos and uncertainty? Avis could not help but turn to gaze at Rachel as she continued, and many among the crowd suddenly did the same. Slowly but surely, she was wresting the stage from her brother. "Our own minds are allowing them to gain further purchase, to become real. We must fight that if we are to save the ship, and ourselves."

"But how?" This came from Charlotte Berthault, who stood

by Gideon's side but stepped forward now towards them, as though drawn by Rachel's voice. "How, when our own eyes are showing us these visions from hell?"

"We need to set ourselves against them, banish them, as one," Rachel said. "On this occasion, we need to close our minds to what lies beyond, and anchor ourselves back in the here and now before anyone else is hurt. If you will all follow my lead, I can help."

She raised her voice to be heard over the furore outside, the wind, the banging of the doors, but her eyes were fixed squarely on her brother. Avis watched him weigh up the situation. It was clear that he was out of his depth; unlike his sister, Gideon Duquesne's act was entirely façade. Rachel's visions, her insights, were hers alone, her brother only the face, the ringleader—and so in the here and now, with a ghost ship breaking to pieces around him, could he cede that control and let his sister take the lead? He broke eye contact with Rachel and glanced at his new fiancée, who was gazing at Rachel with an expression of nothing short of awe. Avis watched his blue eyes harden into ice.

"You have allowed yourself to be corrupted by the mentalist," he said, stepping forward as though on a stage, trying to draw the audience's attention back to him. For extra flourish, he swept up one black-clad arm to point a long, pale finger in Avis's direction. "Miss Lovelock, with her rational explanations and craven suspicions and empty, Godless heart, has convinced you to ignore the evidence of your own eyes. These are clearly souls crying out in need! The last thing we must do in this moment is close ourselves off to them. We must join hands together and invite them to speak to us, to share their pains and show us how to see them safely to their rest!" The young man sounded like nothing so much as a preacher, the musical cadence of his accent more pronounced than usual as he delivered his speech.

"That isn't going to help!" Rachel snapped. But the assembly—from first class to third, from passenger to crewman—had already begun to shuffle obediently to hold hands in a winding snake around the verandah at Gideon's urging. Rachel turned to Avis, her expression stricken. "This will be the end of us," she said. "I know it. My brother will doom us all."

Avis bit her lip and tasted blood. "Usher," she said. "If he's playing some part in all of this, perhaps he's better placed than most to help us end it."

"Where would he have gone?"

To this question Avis had no answer, but with no better plan the pair exited the verandah and began to weave their way towards the bow. Sure enough, the figure of the doctor stood precisely where he had what felt like a year before, rifling in his pockets distractedly. The scent of fuel stung at her nostrils as they approached.

"Usher, no," Avis said, picking up her pace. "We've been through this. This is not the way."

"I'll come join you for a drink in a moment, once I've got my head on straight," he said, then he paused and smiled sadly. He turned his head, and his body tensed. "Do… do you see that?"

"Oh no…" Rachel murmured.

"Lights… The lights on the water…" Usher flickered.

"It's not him," she said. "It's a shadow, from before." She turned to Avis, reaching for her hands. "The past, the present, the future, it's all coalescing."

There came an almighty groan from the ship and it pitched forward so hard that the pair lost their balance, stumbling against the railing. Usher was gone, the yells and screams around them rising in volume as seawater surged onto the deck. They were sinking. Avis could hear chanting floating on the wind from the garden verandah, though she couldn't make out the words.

"What do we do?" Avis asked, and Rachel smiled. She pulled Avis towards her, wrapping an arm around her waist, her other hand gripping the railing.

"I think," she said, "that at the right moment, we close our eyes, hold our breath, and let go."

Thirty-Three

Rachel?

It was dark. She was numb. Weightless and heavy both at once. Her hands were gripping something, but her mind could not quite determine what it was.

I'm here.

Are we in the water?

A pause for thought.

After a fashion, I think.

They were floating. They were floating, but she couldn't feel the surface they were floating upon.

Are we dying? Are we dead? Rachel, are we dead?

Amusement. Even mockery.

Wouldn't it be funny if we were? That would prove you wrong quite decisively, wouldn't it?

Avis twisted this way and that. Frictionless yet constrained. Where *was* this?

It's time to go, Avis.

Patience's voice was closer than Rachel's, louder. A whisper, but right up next to her ear, inside it.

Just like me. Lungs full of water. Cold. Heavy. You're over the worst of it now, sister. It's peaceful from here. From here you just let yourself sink.

You're drifting, Avis. Come closer. Follow my voice.

Avis tried to thrash, but she couldn't feel her limbs.

I don't know how! There are no directions here, you're just a voice!

I don't mean with your body. Focus, Avis. Anchor to me.

Patience covered her like a cloak.

Don't leave, Avis. Don't you dare leave me behind again.

You're slipping. Stay with me.

Stay with me.

Stay with me.

Avis tried to suck in a lungless, airless breath. When that didn't work, she tried to scream. The strange blanket of Patience grew heavier and she began to sink: darker, quieter, more numb. Patience was right. It was easy.

Avis!

Something scrabbled for purchase on her mind. A trickle of worry, but beneath that, something else. Frustration. Irritation. Impatience.

Rachel?

The frictionless suggestion of a sigh.

Still here.

I feel you.

I have you.

A flood of warmth. Hands clasp. Foreheads touch.

There are others. We need to find them, lead them back.

What, everybody?

No. Just enough, I think, and the rest will follow.

Avis could almost feel herself frown. She cast about around her, but other than Patience's grasping echo there was nothing.

I can't feel anybody else. I don't know how.

Help me find Charlotte.

I told you, I c—

Yes, you can, Avis Lovelock. You found Patience and she doesn't exist. You can find someone who does. Set your mind to it! Help me!

That irritation again, the sharp edge: that was Rachel. The hungry, empty well: that was Patience. Avis cast outward in search of purchase, trying to picture in her mind what Charlotte Berthault would feel like. Her character at once forceful and somehow removed. The deep, lingering sadness. At first, there was nothing. And then—

Henri?

Non, Charlotte, c'est moi.

Rachel! Où sommes-nous? Sommes-nous mortes?

Non, nous sommes perdues. Aidez-moi à trouver Gideon.

That should be simple enough; we just need to look for the largest, most fragile ego.

Another flicker of amusement, and Avis felt the hook that connected them dig deeper.

But we've already found you, Avis. Enough nonsense. Go, find Brooksbank.

I don't know how.

Then you'd best stop prevaricating.

Don't leave me.

There was no point in hiding her fear, her desperation. She could feel it spilling from her like water through a sieve.

Don't worry, I'll find you again.

Cast adrift once more by Rachel, who seemed to have found her feet—figuratively speaking—very quickly in this strange nothing place, Avis was once more alone in the dark.

Not alone, sister.

There it was again, that suffocating fog that wrapped around her senses, that threatened to consume her. Brooksbank. Who was Carlton Brooksbank? He was tall and lanky, well groomed but never overdressed. But that wasn't it. That wasn't right. *Here* he was none of those things. Here, he had no form, no long, loose limbs, no neatly trimmed moustache. What was there here? Who was Brooksbank without his physical form?

A little warmth trickled past Patience's dark cloak. Avis grasped at it, invited it to seep into her. Sunshine on skin. Bright-blue skies. Then the memory of a scent—coal smoke, grease. Of course. Brooksbank loved travel, loved engines. Ships, trains, the smell of a busy station or bustling port. Then an acrid smokiness, a sharp sting in the nostrils, a burn in the throat. Cigars, fine bourbons and port. Once the sensations began, they came thick and fast, and Avis drank of them deeply, greedy for those pleasures as experienced by another: rich food, fine wines, dancing pressed close to another firm body, the scratch of a shaven cheek against one's lips.

Brooksbank had already found Third Officer Baynes by the time Avis located him, the two unable to hide here what they had so carefully concealed on board *Excambion*. He was glad to have run across her; his open-hearted concern for others radiated around them in waves.

Avis did not have to explain what they needed to do. Brooksbank already knew, perhaps because it was so in his nature to reach out to others with warmth and friendship.

We'll find them.

Once one was open to them, there were other sensations to be found in this formless place, bobbing like buoys of experience tethered to the souls that held them dear. It was by allowing herself to float on the strains of a tuning orchestra that Avis found Clarissa and Sarah together. Quite sure they were dead, they had found one another in the nothing, each seeking out the other as they always had in life. The laughter of children led her to Frieda, who had already gathered her sons and daughters close, and was looking for their father. She seemed almost sorry when Avis found her instead.

Slowly but surely, souls pooled together, and as the assembly grew in number, it grew in strength. With each passenger or crew member who joined came their connections to others on board, and soon they had amassed people unfamiliar to Avis or Rachel, connected to somebody else in the root system spreading from those they had found.

No man is an island.

Usher was out there still, a small, dark spot of misery floating in the nothing. Avis could feel him, taste the sweet sting of whiskey, but she couldn't reach him. It was impossible to gain purchase on a soul in so much pain—at least, not without allowing herself to be drawn into her own. As she felt Patience's dark pull once more, Rachel's warmth crept around her like a shawl, like a hand slipped into hers. Joined now by Gideon's slightly cloying presence, she nevertheless provided immediate comfort.

Leave him be. He'll be swept along with the rest of us. I think there are enough of us now.

Enough for what?

Enough to remember where we belong. There is no sensation here, no physical form, no surfaces, no sounds, no smell or taste. We are floating souls in a nameless sea, cast overboard from our vessels. We need to climb back into them.

Comprehension began to dawn for Avis—and with it, dread.

I don't think I can. Rachel. These people, with their passions and sensations and memories, I've never had any of that. All I have is petty victories and recrimination. There's nothing to anchor me out there. And here.

Here you have me. I'll be your anchor, Avis. I always have.

Listen to me, Avis. There is no "here". Whether there's another world beyond our own or not, this place is not it. This is a place of nothing, of absence. Whatever pull you feel here, it comes from within you. There's nothing else. Whatever part of yourself you've broken off, it's still just you. Of all people, I should not have to tell you this.

I'll take your word for it. But I still don't know the way back.

Arms around her, tightly. A flicker of distaste that had to be Gideon, ignored.

Stay with me. I'll see you safely out. But you'll have to decide for yourself what to bring back with you, and what to leave behind.

Only later would Avis think back to that moment and see it for the point of transformation that it was. Oh, it wasn't the only aspect of her time on board *Excambion* that challenged her or forced her to question her choices. Rachel's dismantling of her whole psyche had been devastating enough in its own right, and seeing the extent to which Usher had been shaped by his experiences had been sobering as well.

But here in this nowhere space, surrounded with nothing but other souls, Avis had for the first time begun to understand what it was to move through the world, shaping your surroundings and letting yourself be shaped by them in turn, rather than skating across its surface—and throwing in the occasional rock.

It was not Avis's fierce rationality that brought the people of *Excambion* back to themselves, to their prone bodies lying on the cold wooden deck of a ship that was once again just a bit off course.

It was Clarissa's love of the glint of green Chartreuse in a tiny crystal glass, the smooth weight of pearls warming around her neck, the soft fur of her little dog between her fingers.

It was Lydia's craving for something new with every moment, the thrill of flirtation and the crush of heartbreak, the way she sought new sensations and experiences, good and bad, with every turn of the seasons.

It was Frieda's desperation to feel her children's hands in hers, to have solid ground beneath her feet again, to keep a house and quietly grieve her husband.

As Avis became aware of the wet boards soaking through the back of her dress, of the heavy rain stinging her face, of the aching of her body abused by the toil of these past few hours of wakeful panic, she knew that left to her own devices she would never have made it back.

Thirty-Four

DAWN BROKE ON *Excambion* to reveal a ship forever altered by its encounter with the unknown. Though it had not been subjected to enemy fire in truth, it still bore the scars of the Arctic storms that had battered it, not to mention the scrapes and ashes of a long night of panicking men and women tipping over lamps and fighting to escape seemingly locked staterooms. In the first-class saloon, everything that could be moved had been used to blockade the doors, leaving the upper-class passengers without a place to eat and forcing them to "slum it" in second class. There had been malfunctions in the engine room, though with the tireless work of the engineers they were once again heading towards New York and the end of their journey at last.

The crew and passengers were hardly less affected. The sick-bay saw a steady stream of concussions, broken limbs, burns, and lacerations from the panic they had been through. Klein was hard at work all through the night and Usher had volunteered his services as well. Avis wondered if the chance to help and heal would be a good thing for the obviously unsettled doctor, or if the wake of the ship's ordeal would be too like the conflicts that haunted him.

She had lost track of Rachel in the aftermath. She had been

swept off with her brother and Charlotte among a throng of needful passengers, and Avis hadn't felt minded to follow along. It was clear that most of the people had no concept of what had happened to them, though plenty had theories, each more preposterous and grasping than the last. She wanted to castigate them, but then, how could she even begin to explain what *had* happened? She could barely fathom it herself.

But with the hours that passed, the theorising began to subside, replaced with a sort of wilful lapse of memory: people who had woken up confused and afraid were increasingly unsure that anything at all had happened—beyond, perhaps, feeling faint. As usual, the human mind's ability to invent whatever fantasy most suited it in the moment never ceased to amaze… and irritate. Avis found it almost more annoying than the wild theories.

Still, the sun was warm and they were alive and afloat. For now, that was enough.

They had not been thrown too far off course by a few hours absent navigation, and less than a day after the events following the salt-water sabotage the horizon began to glow with the lights of the American coastline. Even at their current limp, Avis was told by a rather bedraggled Baynes, they would make land within a scant few hours.

The wind had dropped, but the air was still cold, and the merriment at their impending disembarkment kept most below decks even for this momentous view. When Avis emerged on deck, only a few people were leaning on the railing looking out from the bow of the ship at the twinkling lights on the coast. Among them, she spotted Usher's rangy form, still in his rumpled brown day suit. As she approached, she was suffused with a strange sensation of melancholy and regret. Was it the memory of what she'd felt in that other place, or had the experience left her with a strange new sense for the moods of those around her? She pushed the musing aside for now. Changed she might be, but there were limits.

She made sure to be heavy enough of foot that her presence

did not come as a surprise. "How long have you been away?" she asked by way of greeting.

"Hm? Oh, not very long," he said, turning. His face was haggard but calm. "Only went out a couple of months ago. I guess you could call me a bit of a homebody. In fact, this was the first time I'd ever left the country, believe it or not."

"I'm not one to judge. This is my maiden voyage, too," she replied.

"First, but not last, I'd wager. You've got plenty of adventures ahead of you, Miss Lovelock, I can tell." He pushed off the rail and gestured to her. "Come on, walk with me."

They made their way towards the stern of the ship, passing the others who had come out to get their first sighting of the city. She noted that the excitement wasn't limited to one class –women in fur muffs and tall hats mingled with men whose shoes were probably lined with paper.

"Hell of a first trip you've had," Usher commented then. "And I've heard from some folk that you're the reason we made it through in one piece. I hope the bigwigs have thanked you generously."

"Oh, no, that wasn't me," Avis said. "I think it's Rachel Duquesne we have to thank for that. Still, I doubt the 'bigwigs' are particularly pleased with either of us at the moment. I think it's safe to say I have not disproved their haunting."

Usher gave a hoarse chuckle. "No, I'd guess you haven't."

Excambion's wake spread out behind her, quickly shrouded by the darkness of the open water. At the bow of the ship the promenade deck did not reach all the way to the prow, with the lower deck jutting out in front of them, and during the day one could watch sailors running back and forth on various duties below. Here at the stern, the deck ran all the way to the edge, the ship dropping away sharply beneath them.

"Why did you do it?" The drop was dizzying. Avis wrapped her fingers around the railing, her knuckles leeching white.

Usher didn't flinch, didn't prevaricate. "I couldn't stomach the idea of the Spanish getting a hold of this ship, using it to run troops and guns across the ocean. I'm not a soldier any more, but stopping the sale… Maybe it'd weaken them a little, cut the war a little shorter. Maybe it'd keep a few more people alive."

Avis nodded, silent for once. Had he succeeded? The ship *was* haunted, or at least possessed of an otherworldly connection, but the memories of all aboard were already being overwritten by more plausible explanations. When they reached New York, *Excambion* might still be snapped up by the Spanish and added to the armada. The disaster it had tried to warn them of might still come to pass.

Usher began to recite then, as was his wont, though it went beyond the normal line or two that he often peppered into conversation.

> *"Sunset and evening star,*
> *And one clear call for me!*
> *And may there be no moaning of the bar,*
> *When I put out to sea,*
> *But such a tide as moving seems asleep,*
> *Too full for sound and foam,*
> *When that which drew from out the boundless deep*
> *Turns again home."*

"I'm not familiar with that one," Avis said, watching him as he watched the sea.

"Tennyson. He was your poet laureate, up until he died."

"Ah, well, that explains it. He's a bit morose for me. All those elegies and odes, and all that lotus-eating. To my knowledge, he didn't pen a single limerick."

Usher laughed, though it was a hollow sound. "Seems appropriate after what we've just been through. The fire, the boat sinking… How many people died the first time round, do you think?"

"I'm not sure they have yet," Avis said. Usher tipped his head to the side, inviting her to go on, and she did, despite not knowing how she was going to explain *any* of this, to him or anyone else. "I've been in the logs, read them all the way back to the beginning. *Excambion*'s never had a catastrophe of that size. But perhaps she's due one, and we happened to get a preview. I don't know." The words were less bitter in her mouth than on previous utterances. "I think it was a bit of a fluke. At least, I hope it was."

Usher nodded, though she could tell by the set of his mouth that he wasn't completely convinced. "Those things we saw. The… visions of the future, as you have it. Everything that happened, Müller's death. That's exactly what happened to me at Camp McKinney, isn't it? It was a warning. And just like then, I didn't do anything to stop it."

"I don't think you were in much of a position to do anything, even if you had wanted to," Avis said. "I don't really understand it myself but I think that these… echoes were always going to spill over."

It wasn't quite true. Rachel had posited several possibilities and only one involved no third party. Usher could very well have unconsciously conjured those ghosts, just as he had consciously tried to scupper them. But Avis was beginning to learn a lot about her ability to lie when the lie kept somebody safe.

"I still sent us off course," Usher said. "I still polluted the water supply…"

"Judging by the amount of champagne being drunk in second class this morning, I'm not sure anybody minds that any more," Avis said, and Usher snorted his amusement. As though she had reminded him of it, he withdrew his battered hip flask from his pocket and took a swig before offering it to Avis.

She took it, taking a tentative sip. The bourbon cut its usual burning path down her gullet, but she was learning to enjoy it. When she tried to return it, Usher gently pushed her hand away.

"Keep it," he said. "I've plenty others. I don't need that one."

Avis glanced down at the flask in her hand. Its top half was wrapped in a thick, stained leather, oily to the touch. The bottom half was a dark, pitted metal. She slid a thumb along it, feeling the history there, every bump and crevice. Usher smiled, his posture relaxing as he watched her heft it.

"I'm glad you came along when you did yesterday. Glad I was there to help out after everything went to hell."

"So am I," she said, and was surprised by how much she meant it. She remembered the look on his face the day before, standing at the railing with the lighter in hand. If they parted ways now, where would his path take him? The gut-churning uncertainty prompted her to speak. "I won't tell. About the sabotage. You could walk right off this ship, join me in New York, help me figure out these Yankee shores. I could use a familiar face that isn't Brooksbank and his terrible earnestness."

"Wish I could," Usher said. "New York's a hell of a town." He reached for his pocket reflexively, then gave a weak chuckle as he realised the flask was gone. "You know, we didn't know about germs, back in the war. Sure, Pasteur was over in France doing his research, but there wasn't much time for reading scholarly papers when you were up to your knees in blood on the battlefield. And that was the whole problem—you'd go straight from one soldier to the next, trying to patch up a musket wound to the shoulder when your hands were covered in the blood of a dozen other men, not to mention dirt and shit and who knows what else. I'd wager most of those men died because of us, the doctors trying to do some good. Sure, the bullet may have opened the wound, but it was us that packed it full of germs with our ministrations. And then we had to watch them die, sweating and shaking and leaking pus from under their bandages. It was a hell of a way to go and, in the end, most of it could've been prevented by just washing our hands." He chuckled, but it was the empty rattle of a final cough. "We learned from our mistakes, and now we save more people. But that doesn't erase the ones who died before, doesn't make their loved ones miss them any less. We've still got that blood on our hands."

"That doesn't mean you have to punish yourself," Avis protested.

"I know," he said, nodding over her shoulder. Avis twisted around to see two crewmen emerging from below decks and heading straight towards them. A pair of handcuffs dangled from the belt of the one in the lead. "So we'll see what the courts say. You've inspired me, Miss Lovelock: honesty above all else. I've things to answer for, both now and in the past. It's time."

He was culpable for the sabotage and the way it had contributed to the passengers' hysteria, she knew that. But it hadn't been malice that had driven his actions, but grief. Grief and a desire not to see the sins of the past repeated. He was responsible for what had happened, yes, but not guilty. Avis didn't have much faith in the courts coming to the same conclusion, however. "Oh, Samson. You honest idiot."

Usher flashed her a sad grin and stepped around her, holding up his hands. "No need for theatrics, boys. I'll come quietly." The crewmen exchanged glances; clearly they had been expecting a raving lunatic or criminal thug, not a doctor with a rumpled suit and an affable smile. He glanced back at Avis, who clenched his flask in crooked fingers like she was gripping his lapels, begging him not to go. "Goodbye, Miss Lovelock. I look forward to seeing your name in the papers."

She watched as they led him away, Usher's familiar limp somehow the proudest thing she had ever seen. As he disappeared through the doorway she unscrewed the cap of the flask once more and took another swig, the bourbon burning away the lump in her throat.

As the liquor and sadness both pooled in her stomach, Avis braced for a dark flicker in her periphery, but none came.

"You'll have to decide for yourself what to bring back with you, and what to leave behind."

Rachel's meaning wasn't lost on her; it was impossible to misunderstand or be misunderstood in that Other place. She could choose to come back as she was—fractured, a dark, bitter piece of herself remaining outside of her body, flitting in and out of her sight in the imagined shape of her sister, sniping and castigating her and never letting her forget what she had done, and perhaps one day driving her genuinely mad. Or she could choose to leave Patience behind—let the shadow of Patience go and absorb that broken-off piece back into herself, darkness and all, to finally reckon with the grief and hatred and, more than that, the uncomfortable fact that whatever the truth about ghosts from beyond the Veil, there were most certainly phenomena in this world (and within Avis herself) that defied scientific explanation.

But decisions weren't simple in a place with no speech, no artifice, no lying to yourself or to anybody else. They came from somewhere deeper than the conscious mind: they were felt, not thought. Whatever Avis had decided, that knowledge was hidden from her for the time being. She had regained consciousness on deck alone, and had been alone since, with no memory of the choice she had made. She felt different, certainly—at once more alive than she'd ever been and yet strangely unmoored—but then the events of these past few days were more than sufficient to rock her understanding of the universe and her place within it by themselves. Whether Patience was gone for good, only time would tell.

THEY ARRIVED AT New York Harbor a few hours later. Avis had been to her room to collect her things, pushing the empty bottle of champagne under her vanity and straightening up to stare into the mirror. No sisterly visage awaited her there, merely her own face, pale and smudge-eyed from lack of sleep and near-death experiences.

She did not weep for Usher, but only because she had no tears left to cry. It was ironic, when the taps were still running with salt water, that she should have none of her own to shed for a man she had grown to respect and care for.

Still she ached, for him and for herself, for the lives studded with loss and pain that had led them here. Perhaps it wasn't Usher alone that had called the spectres to *Excambion*, but her, and Rachel, and the no doubt dozens of others aboard the ship who carried their heartache close, drawing yet more despair from the aether until it fractured time itself.

She thought of her own guilt, the spectre-sister that had followed her from her broken home to the distraction of London, and all the way aboard a ship bound for the New World. The truth was a balm only for those able to hear it, and those with their heads clouded by grief were deaf to its entreaties.

Avis was certainly not so deaf with grief as to miss the ship's whistle when it announced their arrival into port, and she gathered her valise and stuck a poorly treated hat atop her head before heading above deck once more.

Other than her perfunctory debrief with a still rather haggard Baynes, nobody had sought her out since the confusing events of the previous day. Not the captain, nor King—even Brooksbank was nowhere to be found. Presumably they had heard all they wanted to. As the passengers gathered to disembark, however, she spotted a head poking up slightly above the milling crowd and elbowed her way towards it.

"Carrie! You've been avoiding me."

"Miss Lovelock. I'm afraid I've been kept busy by the company ever since we got within radio distance of the city," he said with an apologetic shrug, tugging on his rumpled suit jacket. "But you're quite right—I've been derelict in my duties as host. At the least, I've booked a room for you at the Waldorf Astoria and there'll be a cab waiting for you when you disembark. I do hope that's all right."

Avis started. She had barely thought about what she'd do when on dry land. It was frankly remarkable that Brooksbank had remembered under the circumstances, but then, that was exactly the sort of man he was. "That's very kind of you," she said. "But there's really no need. If you can point me to where I might find a ladies' boarding house..."

"Nonsense, I won't hear of it," he said. "I assure you, it's no trouble. But you might need to give me a few weeks before I'm able to introduce you around—I think this business is going to take a little longer to clean up than I originally thought."

"Of course." Avis hesitated. "They can't possibly sell *Excambion* now, can they? Not after what just happened."

Brooksbank's mouth flattened to a line. "King certainly plans to try," he said. "I suppose we'll have to wait and see."

Avis tried to tell herself it wasn't her problem any more, if it ever had been. It was only partially convincing. "They'll probably call it ergot poisoning. Or carbon monoxide."

"Probably," he agreed. "Ironic that the more people got swept up in it, the less it looked like a haunting. If they'd been there…" Brooksbank broke off, a shiver running over his shoulders. He'd been a beacon in the darkness to Avis, but clearly the experience weighed heavily on him. "Well. I think I'll be sticking to dry land for the foreseeable, let's just say that."

The last gangway was hooked up to the side of the ship, the gates opened, and passengers began to pour off onto the dock. A dark shadow caught the corner of Avis's eye, but she didn't turn to look. Brooksbank spotted some sort of reaction from her, though, because he cleared his throat.

"I can ensure you and the Duquesnes have one another's addresses," he offered.

"Mm? Oh." Avis shook her head abruptly. "I don't think that will be necessary. I see no reason why our paths should cross again."

Brooksbank's expression was laughably bewildered. "Indeed? I only thought that you and Miss Duquesne had become rather… close over the course of the voyage. And what about your vow to ensure they didn't dupe any new targets here in New York?"

"I think it unlikely," Avis said. "And all in all, on balance, I'd rather move on."

Looking decidedly bemused, Brooksbank made a vague sound of acknowledgement. "Please, don't let me keep you. I'll find you at the Waldorf Astoria in due course, and I'm sure you'll be taking the city by storm in no time." He extended his hand then, smiling warmly. "It's certainly been an experience, I'd say."

"That it has." Avis took him by surprise by covering their

clasped hands with her left, letting her grip linger a moment before releasing him. "Best of luck to you."

"I'd say the same to you, but I have a feeling luck will have nothing to do with whatever you get up to next."

She smiled, a brave echo of her usual wolfish grin. "Luck is for gamblers. I have no intention to wager on anything but a sure bet."

Avis had not felt particularly as though she had grown "sea legs" while on board *Excambion*—far from it, in fact: in almost every respect she felt as though she had become increasingly unsteady the longer she'd spent on board. Nevertheless, it was an odd sensation to be back on a surface that did not shift gently beneath her feet.

The crush of people around her would have once felt invigorating, but she was too aware that there were a hundred, a thousand, dreams and fears encapsulated in the crowd, all too fragile and uncertain. Still, she had to smile to see families reunited and newly arrived immigrants stepping foot onto their new homeland, and she tried to hold on to that feeling as she stepped back to look up at the great ship that had brought them there. *Excambion* was a marvel, there was no doubt of that, but her future was still uncertain.

But then, isn't it always? You can't let that stop you, Avis. You know what you need now. People. Connection. And sometimes, a little faith.

She turned, casting her gaze this way and that, but all around her were signs of life. There was no shadow-sister, no shade following her into this new land of opportunity to guide her and dog her steps. No, for once, Avis was alone.

But not for long.

Epilogue

A MUFFLED BANG. *A deep, long groan of tortured steel and timber. Figures floating, faces turned heavenward. Lights on the water.*

A sharp *knock-knock-knock* and the cheery call of "Paper!" broke the silence, and Rachel Duquesne blinked rapidly, returning abruptly to the present moment just in time to prevent her eggs from burning, but too late for the toast. Scraping off the black, she dumped the whole lot onto a plate anyway. There were advantages to living in a single room, but in her early days of learning to cook it had become annoying having her bed linen perpetually infused with the smell of burnt food. Still, she enjoyed living in a boarding house, cheek by jowl with other women. Though she had not made too many friends herself in the past few months, she found that she liked the background chatter of other students and young working women back-and-forthing in the hallway outside, going about their colourful, busy lives.

Retrieving the paper from her doormat and her plate from the counter, Rachel sat at the tiny little half-moon table that sat beneath the room's single window. It was screwed shut, but it barely mattered; at this time of year it was as impossibly hot outside as it was in, and one just had to get used to feeling sticky and unwell at all times. The view looked out across the courtyard to the other wing of the building, which suited her just fine. People had always interested her more than vistas.

The front page of the newspaper was unremarkable. With the war in something of a holding pattern there was little to report upon, and so it was mostly preoccupied with local political matters and society gossip dressed up as news. Rachel soon flipped to the internal pages in search of the more interesting stories that she generally found buried there. She was not to be disappointed. Her breath hitched as her gaze alit on a familiar name.

THEFT AND BATTERY SOLVED WITH UNCONVENTIONAL AID

> Police have charged Elbridge McGrath, a young man of West End, with assault and theft today after a longstanding case was solved with the help of a consulting investigator. The case, which originated on March 13, concerned Westervelt Lane, who was knocked down in the street and robbed of several valuable personal items while going about his business. The case was complicated by the different stories told by bystander witnesses, and it was long assumed nothing would come of the investigation. The intervention of a Miss Avis Lovelock, a self-styled "consulting investigator", soon tied up the discrepancies and allowed the items, including an heirloom watch, to be retrieved from Mr McGrath's lodgings. Though no connection between the two men was obvious, it became clear that Mr McGrath had once served as Mr Lane's bank clerk, which allowed him to gain knowledge of the items of value. He has been remanded into custody for trial.

Rachel couldn't help but laugh. She had of course thought of Avis often since that fateful journey, and was half surprised not to find her name in the music hall listings in the weeks that followed. That she had restyled herself now as a consulting investigator and was lending a no doubt trenchant helping hand to the police force was really too perfect.

Was this the reason she had woken with a strange, unsettled feeling in her gut that morning? The reason she had been more-than-usually plagued with reminders and musings on the events on board *Excambion* since? Was it only the anticipation of seeing this name in print? It was plausible, she supposed, but it didn't quite sit right.

A globule of egg fell from her toast onto the page and she wiped it off with a thumb, smearing the text. A pity. She was half minded to keep a clipping of the article. Perhaps she'd be able to convince one of the girls in her class to swap. Taking it as a sign that breakfast shouldn't be stalled any further, she dug into the meal, eating steadily and carefully, washing it down with lukewarm coffee. Even as her ribs disappeared and her cheeks unhollowed, she treated every meal like a ritual, a small but vital acknowledgement that the body was as important as the soul, that it was part of what made her whole. Rachel spent quite a bit of time trying to convince herself she was whole, here, alone, following her own path rather than one dictated by others. She was getting quite good at it, most days.

Gideon and Charlotte had gone back to France after only a few weeks in the States settling their uncle's affairs. As expected, there had been little in the way of cash, and what there was had been left to Gideon "to distribute as he saw fit". She suspected it was Charlotte's doing that she saw any of it at all, plus a generous gift that would cover her first year's rent and tuition at Barnard.

Their departure had been a bittersweet milestone, her longed-for independence delivered by the removal of her twin and the woman she cared for deeply. They had promised to write and asked her to visit, but as their ship pulled away from the dock its whistle had sounded more like a funeral bell. Of course, as Rachel well knew, funerals were rarely the cut-and-dried end of anything.

She began to flip through the paper in search of the letters page when another name caught her eye.

Espíritu Santo.

Buried in a little column of digests was reporting on the most recent losses for the Spanish navy—among them, an auxiliary cruiser en route between Spain and Cuba, carrying Spanish troops. It was scuppered off the coast of the Republic of San Domingo. All lives were lost.

Rachel set her coffee down before it spilled. Her hand was trembling. Somehow she knew that this was it. This was *Excambion.*

She read the whole column several times but there was nothing more there, nothing to confirm her hunch. She didn't need confirmation. She had seen it happen once, twice, a dozen times—the muffled explosion of a torpedo hitting home in the engine room, the low groan of the ship as it began to take on water, and then the panic of the crew, its officers rousing the sleeping soldiers who rushed onto deck only to fall into splintered pits as the ship began to collapse and sink.

And, after it all, the scattered debris on the water dancing with flames.

There was another knock on the door—only two raps, sharp and impatient. She ignored it, reaching up to rub a hand over her chest, feeling the thud of her heart. She was here, she was alive, but all those men were dead. Nothing had changed. No one had been saved.

The knock came again, and it was so demanding that she stood despite herself, walking woodenly to open the door and dismiss whoever it was that thought themselves so entitled to her time.

As she reached for the handle though, her pulse leapt into her throat. For a fraction of a second, it was as though there was a presence in the room with her. Her skin prickled.

She snatched the door open and found herself face-to-knuckles with a raised hand ready for a third assault.

"Knock twice if there's anybody there, eh? I assumed this was a studio, but based on how long that took I assume you have a grand foyer and three sitting rooms at least."

"Avis." As if the newspaper had summoned not one but two spectres from her past, Avis Lovelock stood at her door, a fashionable trilby hat perched on her head, a playful quirk to her lips. "Did you see it? The *Espíritu Santo* in the paper? Is that why you've come?" Finally, after far too long, when Rachel had missed her every single day.

"No! I mean, of course. I mean, not really." Avis frowned, eyes darting away and then back to Rachel's. "You're studying," she said, then.

She'd barely had time to glance into the room—and Rachel kept it tidy besides—so she wasn't inferring that from anything she had seen there. Which meant that Avis had been keeping tabs on her. Rachel felt a bloom of heat in her chest, her gut, and nearly forgot to nod. "I hope to, at any rate. At the moment I'm revising for entrance exams. Psychology. I thought perhaps it was time to stop wondering and start asking questions."

"I'm glad." Avis hesitated. Then, "I tried to stop them. When I found out the sale was going ahead, I tried to get Brooksbank to... Well, I'm not sure what I would have said, and at any rate he wouldn't let me anywhere near it. But I did try." She sniffed. "Is something burning?"

"Burnt," Rachel replied, the heat rising to her cheeks and the tips of her ears. "I saw your case in the paper."

"My case? Oh..." Avis scrunched up her face, shook her head. "I've been doing some favours for a— Well, not a friend. More a reluctant acquaintance. And they pay me." She tipped her head from side to side. "I suppose it's a job. I have a job now. It's... good."

"Yes, it's good. You're helping people."

Avis, I've missed you. I know why you didn't seek me out. I didn't seek you out either. But you're here now, and–

Rachel saw a shape in her periphery—perhaps one of the other girls, passing on her way to work, clad in a dark dress, with dark hair. She felt a rush of bravery. "Won't you come in?"

"Is there coffee to go with the burnt whatever-it-is?"

"There is. It's cold."

"I'm really very busy."

"I'll make some fresh."

"I suppose I can spare a moment."

Avis looked instantly at home in the little one-room apartment in a way she never had in the staterooms of *Excambion*. Immediately after she entered, Rachel watched her give the room a full and thorough once-over before making a beeline for the window.

Rachel had expected to be embarrassed by the tiny studio—this was the first time she'd had a guest—but as she watched Avis peer out the casement at the apartments opposite she felt only a deep sense of felicity. She smiled and took a step towards the window, coffee pot temporarily abandoned. "The view is my favourite part."

Avis turned and shot her a little smirk. "We'll see if you still like it after the couple across the way have their baby. I suspect the noise will carry *straight* across, and they keep their window open at all hours." Her expression softened, though her dark eyes didn't lose their twinkle. She stepped away from the window.

I've missed you too.

Acknowledgements

THE THING ABOUT this whole writing malarkey is that with every new project we undertake, the list of people to whom we owe our undying gratitude gets ever longer, and the inevitability that we miss somebody out gets ever more, well. Inevitable. With that said, here we go...

Thank you to our wonderful beta readers—Ben and Sam and Chelsea and Dave and, of course, Faith. Your insights were invaluable and your marginalia gave us life. Thank you to our agent John Baker and to his sometimes-co-agent Julie Gourinchas, who said the fateful words "why don't you set it on a ship?" that helped us bring everything together. Thank you to our amazing editor, Amy Borsuk, and the whole team at Solaris. Thank you to our families for cheering us on and dutifully coming in on the chorus with the obligatory "so are you famous yet?" and "wait wait it's HOW long until the book is out?" Thank you to the Edinburgh SFFH community and the Inklings and Team JJ and the Scream Club and the Snark Chums and all the other little gangs and group chats who keep us entertained and mostly sane on our continuing journey. Community is everything and we're lucky to have you all.

And thank you to you, if you picked this book up to read it and have stopped by these acknowledgements to see who helped make it happen. Cool kids stay for the credits. I hope you had as good a time voyaging with Avis as we had creating her.

About the Authors

MK Hardy is the pen name for Morag Hannah and Erin Hardee, two geeky women living and writing together in Scotland. They are both communications specialists working in higher education. With backgrounds ranging from museum interpretation to web design, and from science communication to ghost tours, they are devoted to storytelling in almost every aspect of their lives and work. When they are not telling stories they can be found singing in choirs, foraging for fungi, and working on their 1880s fixer-upper.

@mkhardywrites.com
@mkhardywrites
www.mkhardywrites.com

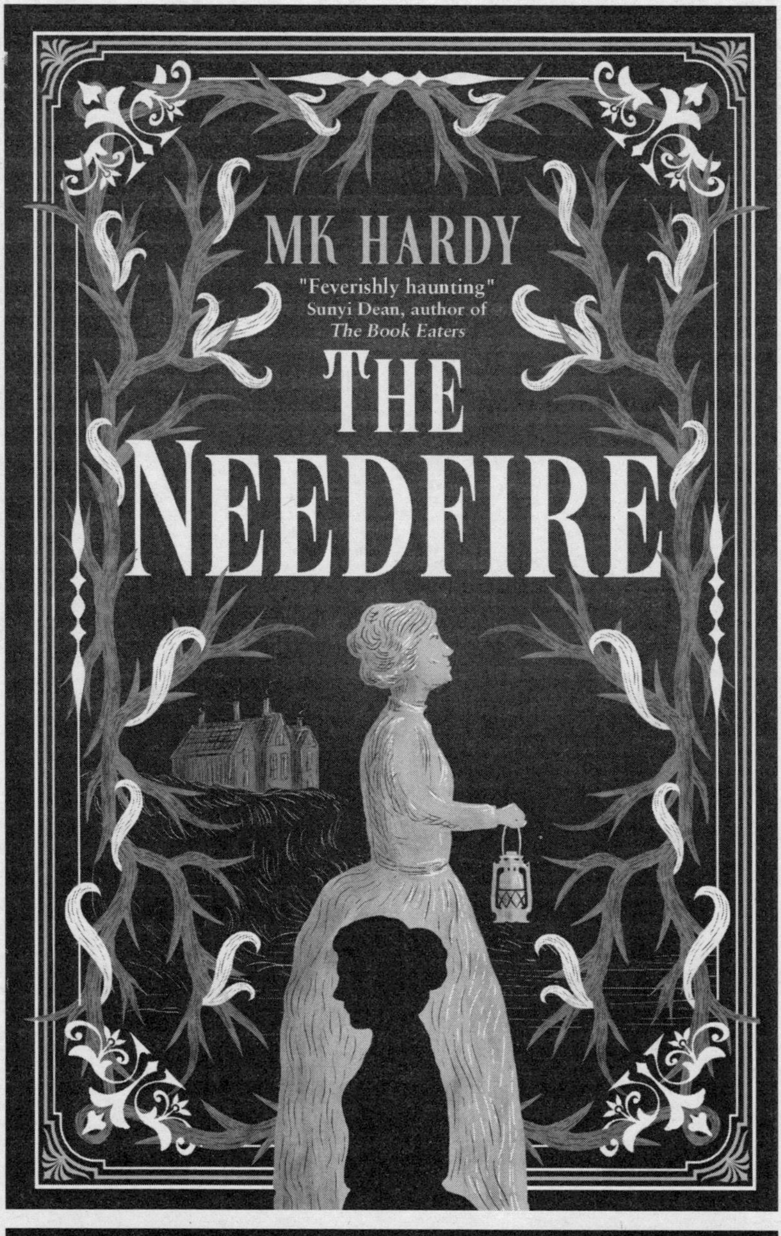
MK HARDY
"Feverishly haunting"
Sunyi Dean, author of
The Book Eaters
THE
NEEDFIRE
SOLARIS